THE ICON COLLECTOR
The Blood Legend

John Williams

__The Icon Collector__
The Blood Legend

Published by JWB Publishing
Gilbert, AZ
www.johnwilliamsbooks.com

ISBN: 978-1-7344476-0-6 (printed soft cover)
ISBN: 978-1-7344476-1-3 (ebook)

Cover Design: Marcus Williams
Editing: Christine Rabe
Media: thebrothersrabe.com

Printed in the United States of America
2020

THE ICON COLLECTOR
The Blood Legend

Introduction

The presenter introduced Manny Benson as the "man of God who brings the fire from heaven" to the fifty-thousand people crammed into the Ankara Stadium. As Manny approached the podium to address the people, a rifle shot rang out and hit Manny in the right side of his neck. As he fell to the platform, the second shot hit him squarely in the back of the head, spraying blood on the people standing in front of him.

Manny heard a loud ringing noise and felt his body violently surge upward in a blur of red and white light. It happened so quickly Manny had no time to think. The blurry white spots in front of his eyes quickly dissipated and he began to see more clearly.

Is that me down there? Manny thought to himself as he slowly drifted away from the scene and out of his body. The last thing Manny noticed before he disappeared through the rafters of the auditorium was a pool of blood draining away from his body.

This seems like a dream. Such a vivid dream.

Still floating upwards, Manny looked down at the gold dome roof and saw the shooter running with a rifle strapped to his back, heading for the maintenance stairs. He watched the man descend the stairs and disappear down the side of the building.

It was a beautiful day in the city of Ankara nonetheless; the sun glistening off various Turkish rooftops and glass buildings. From this height Manny could almost see the Black Sea to the north.

"Come up here!" a voice commanded and Manny's vision blurred. He was transported up through the sky with blinding speed. When the motion stopped Manny saw the mountain of God, haloed in a thick fiery cloud of glory. Thunder, lightning and voices were coming from the mountain. Everywhere he looked were houses, trees, roads and… people, flying in the sky, thousands of them, coming and going as far as the eye could see.

"It's beautiful," Manny said to himself. "It's simply beautiful."

Chapter One

Manny was bored out of his skull. It seems he had been sitting there most of his life. In fact he had been sitting there most of his life because it was his dad's church. Pastor Harold Benson took over this small congregation in 1964, two years before Manny was born. Manny grew up in this church and the seat he always sat in, Sunday after Sunday, seemed to have his butt prints in it.

The hangover Manny was experiencing didn't help either. His fortieth birthday was in a couple days and Manny had a few more beers in celebration than his wife would have liked. Joanne Benson constantly reminded Manny that he "had to be an example" since he is the preacher's kid. He'd heard her say this since the first day they met twenty-two years earlier in high school. But Manny was sick of faking it for his dad and the church. Ever since his older brother Harry died, Manny never quite cared what the church or his dad thought.

Pastor Benson was in the middle of his sermon, the same sermon Manny walked out on every time his dad preached it; the part where Christ said, "I am the resurrection and the life, whoever lives and believes in Me shall never die. Do you believe this?"

"No, I don't!" Manny mumbled as he made his way toward the double doors leading to the vestibule.

"Happy Birthday," Fred whispered as he opened the doors for Manny to exit.

"Thanks," was his reply. He reached into his pocket for the new pack of Camel filters he bought to celebrate his birthday. Fred smiled and patted Manny on the back as he passed through the doors.

The weather was always beautiful in Arizona and Manny expected the warm blast of air to hit him when the outer church doors opened. He put both palms against the doors and swung them open as if he was leaving a wild, wild west saloon, making a loud banging noise that shook the whole church. This was Manny's trademark exit for years and his mother gave up scolding him for it.

Peter "Rock" Reed, Manny's best friend, found Manny around the corner amongst the garbage cans halfway through his first cigarette.

"What's cookin' birthday boy? Dad's preachin' gettin' to ya again?" Rock asked.

"Thought I would come out here for some fresh air," Manny replied, taking a deep draw on his cigarette and coughing a little bit.

"Manny, you look worried. Everything O.K.?"

"Oh, it's just that it's my birthday on Tuesday and I can't help but think about Harry. If he was alive today, he'd be forty-two years old," Manny said.

"Yeah, I've been thinking about your brother too. You gotta wonder what he'd be doing today if he was around," Rock replied.

Manny looked down and stepped on the butt of his cigarette, snuffing it out. Reaching for the

Camels in his baggy slacks, Manny pulled out the pack and flicked another smoke to his lips.

"You know what irks me the most about Harry?" Manny blew a stream of smoke while slightly turning his head away from Rock. "Dad keeps preaching about how Jesus raised Lazarus from the dead year after year, you know, the resurrection and the life." Taking another long drag on the cigarette, Manny looked up in feigned religious reflection.

"Yeah, I know."

"Why didn't God heal Harry?" Manny said angrily. "Rock, he was only seventeen years old! His whole life was in front of him!"

Manny put the cigarette butt in his mouth, freeing up his right hand to put over his heart.

"I swear to God, Rock, if I had the gift of healing, I'd heal everyone. I'd heal everyone in the world for Harry's sake!"

Rock was Harry's best friend when he died. Matter of fact, Harry was the one back in grade school that began to call Peter Reed "Rock." It was in Sunday School that the story was told how Jesus changed Simon's name to Peter; which meant Petra or rock. So the next day at school, as a joke, Harry nicknamed his friend. The name took and before long everyone began to call him Rock. In high school no one really knew Rock's real name and when a new teacher would refer to him as Peter, Rock quickly made the correction: "I'm not Peter. I am The Rock! Like Peter in the Bible!" he would say.

As Rock matured in high school, the name "Rock" became who he was on the football field. At five foot eight and built like a cement truck, Rock was quarterback Harry's favorite player to hide behind when the wall of opposing players came crashing across the line. One minute there were ten angry players bearing down on Harry and then like magic, there would be none. A hole greater than the Grand Canyon opened up as Harry ran through the opposing players with the football. Rock held off the opposing players as if he were God holding back the Red Sea for Moses.

Harry Benson Jr., the eldest son of Harold Benson Sr., the senior pastor of East Valley Community Church, was Chandler High's star football quarterback since his sophomore year. Harry was tall and quick. He had a knack for dodging opposing tacklers by juking this way and that. Often the tackler became the tackled as Harry weaved his way down the field. In his junior year he grew two inches and gained ten pounds. It became even more difficult to bring him down. The weightlifting and running paid off because the opposing teams sent two and sometimes three players in on a play to stop the super star. But Harry was so strong that he laid out the opposing defenders by lowering his helmet and hitting them head on.

His junior year, the town came out for the Friday night games to see Harry destroy the defenses and put on a show. He added a new twist to his repertoire called the stiff arm. Before he discovered this new skill, Harry wrapped both arms around the ball and barreled straight ahead, leading with his helmet. Now armed with this new stiff arm weapon, instead of splattering his enemy tackler with the head on approach, Harry merely placed his hand on the enemy's helmet and shoved him to the ground. This was easier and less painful than the head-on suicide approach.

Harry never passed the ball. He was the running quarterback. The media called him "little Juice" because he resembled O.J. Simpson as he zig-zagged down the field. The coach for Chandler High wanted to open up the opposing defenses and take the pressure off his star quarterback in his senior year, so he implemented a passing game.

Chandler High lost only one game during Harry's junior year, the 1980-1981 season, and that one game loss was to Higley High at the State Championship. The coach (and the newspapers) said it was because Chandler did not have a passing game…their Achilles heel.

The Championship game was tied at twenty-one in the fourth quarter with 26 seconds on the clock. Harry Benson ran the ball for two touchdowns and sent two Higley defenders to the hospital for x-rays. Rock punched in the other touchdown late in the fourth quarter to tie the game and claimed he was the one who sent the two Higley boys to the hospital.

Higley High was on Chandler's twenty-yard line, threatening another touchdown when they fumbled the ball with a minute left to play. Chandler recovered the fumble. Harry ran three plays from the Chandler twenty and moved the ball to the twenty-nine yard line, just short of a first down. Twenty-six seconds were left in the game and seventy-one yards to go for the win. History says that if Chandler had any kind of passing game, they might have won the Championship. History will never know.

All of the Higley football players and the rest of metropolitan Phoenix watching by television knew WHO would get the ball and WHAT he would do with it. If they only had a passing play.

Harry took the snap from the center and sweeping left, he tucked the ball under his left arm and followed Rock laterally across the field waiting for a hole to open up. Instead, there were eleven defenders like a tsunami chasing Harry backwards towards the wrong goal line. Rock was flattened and fell down. Every Chandler receiver, end, and halfback were left entirely alone on the field as the whole Higley football team came crashing down upon Chandler's star quarterback.

If they only had a passing game Harry could have pooched the ball to an open receiver and easily run for a touchdown, winning the game.

Higley got the ball back with five seconds remaining and kicked the winning field goal. Score: Higley 24, Chandler 21.

Harry Benson spent the rest of the evening, indeed, the following week, in physical therapy in order to heal his defeated body. If only they had a passing game.

Hopes were high for Chandler's 1981-1982 season. Over the summer the coach wisely implemented a passing game and Harry proved to have quite an arm.

Pastor Benson rigged a Goodyear tire, tied by a rope and hung it from one of the large cactus branches in the back yard of their home. Harry, Manny, and Pastor Benson would take turns each night throwing footballs through the opening of the tire. Actually, Pastor Benson did most of the ball retrieving since his throws ended up far from the tire.

Pastor Benson marked off ten yards, twenty yards and thirty yards in white spray paint, then the boys threw at the tire from the respective marks. Harry would chide young Manny and challenge him with wagers in order to make a game out of the exercise.

The competition between the brothers that summer became stiff. It got to the point where Manny was more accurate at throwing the football at all the distances. The word got out that Harry's little brother was creaming him in the tire throw and crowds began to appear every night in the Benson's backyard to watch the rivalry; at least until practice started for the new school year.

When Harry died a few months later, Pastor Benson and Manny went into the backyard and took one last throw at the tire. Manny watched as his father untied the tire and threw it in the trash heap.

"I don't know, Manny," Rock replied. "God has a plan. We'll never know why He let Harry die."

Manny took a disgusted look at the burning cigarette that was building an ash between his fingers and then looked over at Rock and said, "That's bull and you know it. That's just an excuse for a church that doesn't have any power or any faith. Dad preaches and preaches about God's power and how great God is. But I just don't see it. Every once in a while, sister so and so will testify that her nephew got saved or healed from drugs or delivered from a car accident but where's the power to heal the sick like Jesus did? Where is the power to raise the dead like Jesus did? And where was the power to heal Harry Jr. when he was sick?"

"Manny, we can go over this again and again, but it won't bring your brother back. Can't you see how this is killing you? You're drinking more than ever before and now you're smoking those disgusting things. What's next for you? Everyone is concerned."

Manny didn't want to argue with his friend like this. He knew Rock was right, but he didn't know what to do. The sting of Harry's death twenty-five years ago still hurt. Harry was his big brother and his best friend.

"Do you ever think of that day when Harry collapsed on the field?" Manny asked.

"Yeah, every single day I live I think of it," Rock replied.

The football season started in September and Chandler High had won all of their games up through November — seven wins. Harry Benson was being hailed as the greatest quarterback to ever come out of Arizona. College scouts showed up for every game and rumors were flying about where Harry might play college ball. He would definitely be the number one choice for most major colleges. At six foot five and two hundred and twenty pounds, he was the biggest and the fastest quarterback ever to play high school ball in Arizona.

Friday, November 12, 1980 was Chandler's rematch game against Higley High, the state champs. Higley won all their games up to this point with no losses. The stage was set and the bleachers were crowded for the Chandler home game rematch. Everyone at school and in town wanted revenge. No one wanted it more than Harry.

Over the summer Harry grew two more inches and was busting out with muscles. On top of that, Harry had become a marksman passer. He could see over the other smaller players, which allowed him to have excellent vision on the field for passing.

At six foot five and muscle bound, he struck fear in the hearts of the opposing teams, like Goliath did to the Israelites. It took at least three players to bring him down and when he was toppled, he smashed everyone under him. Harry was ready for the rematch with Higley and he vowed to not only win but to crush them.

But earlier on game day, while eating lunch, Harry felt a sharp pain on the right side of his head. As he grabbed at his head Harry heard a sound like garbled water. It lasted only for a second, then it went away. When he stood up, Harry felt light headed and saw spots in front of his eyes; tiny lights that fanned outward, then faded away. Harry took a drink of water from his bottle and scurried around in his pack for the Tylenol the trainer had given him for the various pains he suffered. After downing three tablets,

Harry headed for the pep rally that was soon to start.

In the locker room, while the coach was giving his final game speech, Harry became dizzy and faint. He put his head down between his knees and the team thought Harry was praying. Manny knew different.

Over the past few weeks Manny had noticed a subtle change in his older brother. Sometimes he would slur his words and other times he would stumble over his shadow. Recently he confided in Manny that he had been having strange dreams of bright lights and fire. This recent admission was after Harry had his bell rung in game four. Coach Riker took Harry out and benched him for a couple of plays. Manny thought that Harry had a slight concussion that many quarterbacks experience when they are thrown violently to the turf.

It was at the end of the second quarter when Harry fell down and collapsed. He had thrown three touchdown passes and run for two more. Manny saw his brother take the snap from center and while moving backwards, faked a handoff to the halfback. As Harry began to raise his arm to throw the pass down field, he suddenly fell to the ground. The image it conveyed was of a large building collapsing in a heap of dust and smoke.

"Two smokes are enough for me right now," Manny said. "We better get out of here before my mom catches us and spanks us again. Remember that?"

"I'll never forget it. It's probably the main reason I don't smoke today. Boy, did she ever wail on poor ol' Harry, huh?" Rock recalled.

"Yeah, Harry had a heck of a time sitting down after that. Mom pretty much blamed Harry for having the cigarettes, but I'm the one who got them from a kid at school," Manny said.

"Did Harry ever smoke after that?"

"No, I think that cured Harry of putting anything but food in his mouth. I don't think Harry ever tried alcohol or pot either," Manny said.

"Right. All Harry had on his mind was football and girls. In that order," Rock said.

It was noon and the church was about to be let out. Rock had to get back to his ushering and Manny had to get to his car before the crowd wished him a "Happy Birthday."

Joanne, Manny, and their twenty year old daughter Sissy took separate cars to church. The girls loved to linger after church and help with the nursery. Manny never lingered. He went directly home, popped open a can of beer and wiggled into his swimsuit for an afternoon dip in the pool.

Chapter Two

The doorbell rang and Manny ran to the side window, eased open the shutters, and noticed Rock's Ford pickup idling in the driveway. Opening the door, Manny suddenly became self-conscious with only a towel wrapped around his neck. He once was a burly six foot four football player like his brother but now, at almost forty, he was Buddha-like, his daughter told him. After a shower, Manny would look in the mirror and rub his belly for good luck. Buddha was not to blame for the gut...it was the beer!

"Rock! What's up?" Manny said as he flung the door open.

"Hey buddy, I almost forgot your present. I put it in the truck and meant to give it to you at church," Rock said.

Rock stretched the little wrapped box across the threshold of the doorway and said, "Amy wrapped it for me."

"Well, come in. The girls aren't home yet. How about a beer and a swim in the pool?" Manny insisted, then accepted the gift and put it on the foyer table.

"I can't. We're all meeting for lunch down at the café in a bit. But we'll see you tonight for dinner, right?" Rock said, and backed away from the door.

"That's right. My birthday dinner. I almost forgot."

"Anyway, I got this gift for you when we were in Turkey last January. I know how fascinated you are with artifacts and icons and junk like that," Rock said scratching his head. Manny could tell he was worried about his truck idling in the driveway by the way he kept turning to look at it.

"Turn your truck off and join me at the pool," Manny said. "It's my birthday for crying out loud, or it will be on Tuesday. Amy is probably chatting up a storm with Joanne and won't be at the café for another hour…at least!"

It was true. When the girls got together, time stood still and Rock knew it. He ran to his truck, turned it off and put the smiley face visors in the front windshield to block the intense sunshine. Rock galloped back to the front door like a little kid who had found someone to play with.

Rock found the best shady place he could under the umbrella and sat down with a beer. Manny removed the towel from around his neck and placed it on a lounge chair. Hoisting the beer to his lips, Manny drained the sixteen ounce can in one long gulp and then slapped his tanned belly for good luck.

"Time to open my present," Manny announced. He carefully unwrapped the paper and tossed it into the wind. He opened the box to find a plain round clay pot about four inches in diameter. On top of the pot was a clay lid with a knob. Around the lid was a thick yellowish sealing wax. Obviously the wax was applied years ago by a dripping candle because it was wavy, yellow and uneven.

"Well, well, well," Manny exclaimed. "What do we have here?"

He pulled the container close to his eyes. He thought there was some sort of marking imprinted on the wax.

"Looks like the capital letter I. Do you see that Rock?" Rock removed his sunglasses and squinted at the container.

"And here, it looks like the letters *w, a, v, v, n* and *s*."

Manny slipped on his sandals and excused himself. He hustled up to the house to get his digital camera. Dusty, the family mutt, just appeared from behind the rocker on the porch to see what was going on. Manny stumbled over him, running back to the pool with his camera.

"Rock, put it there on the table and I'll take some pictures of it." Rock sat up slowly and wondered what all the fuss was about.

"Where did you get this beauty anyway?" asked Manny.

"Amy and I were visiting the city of Antalya after a day of sightseeing when we fell upon a flea market along the water front. You know Amy, she loves to wheel and deal for trinkets to bring home to the kids." Rock adjusted his position in the lounge chair and took a sip of beer. "Anyway, I was looking at some blankets when a man came up and offered me this little pot."

"He just came up to you and said, 'Hey, you want to buy this clay pot?' For no reason at all?" Manny put it down and stared at Rock in the glaring sun.

"Yeah, just like that. In broken English he insisted I have this precious pot. He said something about the blood of Christ, referring to the pot," Rock said, taking another swig from his beer. "I didn't take the guy seriously. Come on, the blood of Christ? Give me a break! He was just scamming me."

"How much did you pay for this clay pot? I mean, if he was scamming you, he would be asking hundreds, maybe thousands of dollars."

"That's the funny thing, now that I think of it. The guy looked me straight in the eye and said, 'What would you pay for the blood of Christ?' I told him five dollars."

"Five dollars?" Manny was waving his arms now. "If this was Christ's real blood it would simply be priceless. That's a hoot!"

"When I told him I would pay five dollars for the pot, he had the same reaction you had. He busted out laughing too," Rock said with a smirk. "He asked if I had a friend who might like it; a birthday present or something. What a coincidence, I told him, I had just the friend who would love the little clay pot for his birthday. So he gave me the clay pot and said, 'Well, here you go. Tell him Happy Birthday for me. This will be our little gift to him, OK?' Amy wanted to show me some earrings and when I turned back, he was gone."

"Did you catch his name, Rock?"

"I think he introduced himself as an icon collector."

Ever since he was a child, Manny was fascinated with ancient Biblical artifacts, archaeology, and mythology. He would bend the ear of anyone unlucky enough to be within range to expound upon his newest idea on what happened to Noah's Ark, the Ark of the Covenant and whose image it was on the Shroud of Turin. But more than anything else, Manny loved to talk about his theories concerning the blood of Christ.

"Imagine Rock, just imagine. If the blood of Christ was actually in this clay pot, scientists around the world would go crazy wanting to analyze it." He was wild eyed. Manny lost all interest in his second beer and was pacing back and forth poolside.

"Think about it. If Christ was actually born of a virgin, then God was His actual birth father, not Joseph. At conception there are forty-six chromosomes necessary to create a human being. Twenty-three from the biological mother and twenty-three from the biological father. If God was the biological father of Christ, then twenty-three chromosomes imparted to Christ at conception are divine. Do you realize what I'm saying Rock? Anyone discovering even the tiniest drop of the blood of Christ would be discovering the DNA of God!" Manny was sweating now, excited about the possibilities.

"Scientists looking through their microscopes at the DNA of God might be looking at the beginning of the universe, for all the created universe had to have started with God's DNA," Manny said.

Rock finished his beer and stood, looking for a graceful way to leave.

"Sit Rock, let me finish," Manny insisted.

"If this little bottle," Manny picked up the little pot and was tossing it back and forth between his sweaty palms like a football. "If this little clay pot contains the blood of Christ, then imagine what it could do in healing the sick; or raising of the dead; or even...time travel! The possibilities are endless!"

Before he could go any further the little clay pot slipped out of Manny's oily hand. He quickly turned and reached for it with his other hand, stretching over the pool's pavement like a football player catching a pass in the end zone. But Manny's feet gave way and he fell like a ton of bricks, all two hundred and seventy pounds, upon the edge of the pool. The little pot smashed into a thousand pieces upon the pavement, while Manny's head came down, smack dab in the middle of the broken shards. Rock watched Manny's forehead bounce off the pavement in horrified amazement and, as if in slow motion, he watched Manny's body roll over the side of the pool and crumple into the water.

When Manny came to, he was under the water with his arms folded across his chest.

Oh my God, I'm dead, Manny thought. *I've drowned myself!*

Before Manny could clear his head, a strong arm came from under the water and lifted him to his feet.

Ouch, why are there rocks and mud on the bottom of my pool?

When Manny opened his eyes, the water must have skewed his vision because he saw a man dressed in animal skins helping him out of the water.

Off in the distance, as if seeing through a mosquito net, Manny saw Rock waving his arms wildly. Manny glanced down and noticed he was wearing a cloth around his waist, standing in a muddy river; not his swimming pool at home.

Manny involuntarily raised both arms to the sky and felt his face begin to burn with fire.

Oh, my goodness, Manny thought. *It just can't be!*

"You are My Son, the beloved; in you I am delighted," the voice crackled from the sky.

Manny looked up where the voice was speaking and saw the most awesome and fearsome cloud of fire he'd ever seen. The sound from the cloud resembled thunder as it rolled across the sky, crackling, booming, and whooshing. It was so overwhelming that Manny wanted to faint.

A flash of light shot out from an opening in the cloud. Manny watched as the light turned into a fire and hovered directly over him until, like a waterfall, it poured down upon him.

"It is true cousin," said the rugged man next to Manny, "you are the Messiah!"

Turning toward those on the riverbank the Baptist yelled, "I have baptized you in water, for that's what I was sent to do; but here, see this Man before you, He will baptize you with the Holy Spirit and fire!"

In the distance Manny could see the palm trees and the umbrella swaying in the wind around his swimming pool. On the concrete near where Manny fell into the pool, he noticed the soles of Rock's shoes. Rock was lying down on his back as if he were dead.

He must have slipped and fallen too, Manny thought.

Deep sorrow swept over Manny because the Man he was inexplicably inside of and possessing, the Man he was somehow feeling and experiencing, shifted his weight and began to take steps away from him. Manny stood dumbfounded in the river, watching the back of the bronzed Man walk further and further away towards the shore.

A couple of friends at the riverbank helped the man put on His robe. Manny watched Him tie the rope around His waist. After the Man strapped the sandals on His feet, He walked up the riverbank toward a distant road. He turned toward Manny in the water and stared at him for a long minute.

What is He looking at? Manny wondered. *Can He see me?*

He got his answer when the Man waved at him. Manny waved back and that's when the Man smiled.

Chapter Three

The fresh coastal breeze poured in from the gulf of Antalya. It was hot and humid even at seven in the morning. Overlooking the Turkish harbor, Mr. Boergenes, also known as The Icon Collector, was always amused by the early risers who took to the sails and drifted off toward the Mediterranean Sea.

He was served orange juice and kabak boregi, a sweet pastry, by one of his attendants, an heir of the Knights of the Beloved, on the veranda as he sat down in his favorite two hundred year old wooden chair. The chair had to be at least two hundred years old because underneath the cracked leather seat ran a wooden support piece with a brass name plate affixed to it that said, "Geo. Washington. Continental Congress." The chair was a gift from a well-to-do American admirer whose great grandfather was once the President of the United States and owned the chair.

To an outsider, Mr. Boergenes (Bo-er-jen-ness) seemed to be quite wealthy, with many Knights at his beck and call; two hundred in all. He refused to think of them strictly as attendants or servants, although that's what they were. Mr. Boergenes thought of them as friends. Most of Mr. Boergenes' "friends" not only grew up on his estate, but they were born there. For hundreds of years these select "friends" and their heirs made a vow to eternally serve the

Boergenes family; to maintain and defend the vast Boergenes estate with their lives, if necessary.

The Boergenes estate encompassed over one hundred acres, extending from the two-lane highway that winds around the eastern part of the Gulf of Antalya, straight down the hillside, ending at the beach. The highway veered northward away from the estate, causing the property to virtually be on a dead end street.

Nestled in the trees and hidden down the hillside sat an ancient array of buildings. None of the servants' houses nor the Boergenes mansion could be seen from the road. They were completely hidden by the thick trees.

There was a twelve foot high electronic gate at the entrance of the estate. A long cobbled road led down the hill to the property. Two Knights of the Beloved dressed in military attire stood armed with walkie-talkies and rifles, guarding the entrance. A large wooden sign hung on the fence above the gate with the words, *WHOM JESUS LOVED*, in ancient Greek lettering.

The only place on the estate where Mr. Boergenes could get away and be alone was in his chapel. The three thousand square foot room was added to the main building in the early thirteen hundreds, directly after the Ottoman Turks conquered the land. The chapel had a fifteen foot high wooden ceiling with brick outer walls and beautifully polished mahogany floors. At the far end of the room was a simple wooden table with candles on it. A well worn leather chair and an oriental rug faced the table. On the wall was a floor to ceiling blue tapestry that said

UNDER THE BLOOD written in white Greek letters. This was the only room on the estate that the Knights were not allowed to enter, except of course when it needed to be dusted and cleaned.

The mansion itself was built in a huge square over a period of several hundred years. In the fifth century when the mansion was first constructed, from a docked ship at the base of the property, a person could look up the hill and see a big box-like structure embedded into the side of the hill.

As the centuries passed, remodeling and updates ensued and multiple military turrets were added to the roof for protection. Six story high lookouts were assembled out of brick and stationed strategically throughout the property. Tunnels linked the towers together with an underground armory. Huge marble pillars were added around the structure, to not only protect the mansion from potential enemy attacks, but to support elaborate reinforced rooms that were added to the mansion over the years.

Various empires conquered the land through the centuries which caused new threats to the mansion. With each new challenge, the caretakers would go to work and build more secret underground vaults, rooms and tunnels to protect the priceless artifacts housed there.

Today, if one looked up from the base of the hill, they would see a forest of trees. Trees were planted everywhere on the property in the sixth century and now they completely surrounded the mansion.

Up the middle of the hill, in amongst the trees, ran a beautifully manicured lawn. The lawn ended at an elaborate fountain that sat in front of the second story veranda that overlooked the ocean and the Olympic sized swimming pool. The early morning sailboats would never know that there was a twenty-five thousand square foot mansion sprawled across the hillside if it weren't for the trees.

With high powered binoculars though, one could witness seven Knights of the Beloved dressed like Turkish soldiers lined across the front of the veranda at ten yard intervals with rifles slung over their shoulders. If you watched very carefully, in increments of ten minutes, every other guard on the veranda would put binoculars up to his eyes and begin to scan the ocean. The other Knights immediately unslung their weapons and held them at the ready. Most days an eighth man could be seen standing on the veranda early in the morning, dressed in a long monk's robe, looking out over the horizon.

Mr. Boergenes finished taking in the fresh morning breeze and headed for his chapel but sudden and shocking images flashed into his mind. Vivid pictures streaked across Mr. Boergenes' consciousness with such force that it practically knocked him to the marble foyer floor. A cloud, a light, the thundering voice from heaven echoing down the river's canyon cascaded into Mr. Boergenes' mind.

"Sir, are you alright?" asked the alarmed Knight guarding the chapel's entrance. The other guards within range sprang to and came running as if Mr. Boergenes was under attack. This, after all, was their mission in life, their divine calling, to protect and to serve this one man.

"I am quite O.K.," Mr. Boergenes said, stretching out his arms to hold them back. "I simply need to sit down and be alone for awhile. You know I do this from time to time. Thank you for your concern."

The guard unlocked the chapel door and Mr. Boergenes slipped inside. As the door closed, he reassured the group of concerned men that everything was fine.

A flash, a voice, thundered "This is the Son of Mine, the Son of the Beloved!" The words crackled. The light was blinding.

Was this a vision, something deep from the past, or was it occurring right now?

Young Boergenes saw Jesus moving through the water towards him. *Is my cousin really the Messiah?* he thought to himself.

Jesus climbed out of the water and young Boergenes offered his hand and pulled Him up.

"Lord, let me help you with your sandals." Bending over, young Boergenes retrieved the Master's sandals while the other bystander unfolded and dusted off Jesus' cloak.

Before the three reached the top of the bank, Jesus turned around and stared in the direction of the Baptist, who now was lumbering towards the other side of the river. Glancing over, young Boergenes looked upon the Master's face and noticed His gaze was not upon the Baptist at all but fixed on something else in the water. He quickly traced Jesus' stare to a point in the water and there it was, a man, like a ghost, standing in the water staring back at them. Jesus looked over at young Boergenes and with a twinkle in His eye lifted His right arm and waved.

The Master quickly trudged over the riverbank and headed for the dusty road that lay to the east. But young Boergenes remained on the riverbank transfixed on the image in the water until it faded away.

What does this mean? Young Boergenes wondered to himself.

"Come, cousin and hurry. I have much to tell you," Jesus said, beckoning for young Boergenes to join them on the road.

Mr. Boergenes came back to himself and staggered his way to the front of the chapel where the leather chair sat and before he could feel his knees sink into the thick oriental carpet, Jesus was speaking to him from the past again.

"My dear brother, are you listening to me? You drifted away for a moment," Jesus said.

"No Lord. I mean, yes Lord, I ...mean I am perplexed by that ghost of a man in the water," young Boergenes replied. "And not only that, there were clouds of thunder and voices from above that came from the river. What am I to think of these things?"

Jesus laughed and put His arm around young Boergenes' shoulder and drew him to Himself.

"Cousin, there are many things I want to share with you but at the moment I overflow with unspeakable joy."

Jesus suddenly stopped and raised both arms to the sky and shouted, "Oh Father, I sing to You a new song! I shout the good news of Your salvation today. For You are great and greatly to be praised."

After a brief pause, Jesus took in a deep breath and continued, "Let the heavens rejoice and let the earth be glad. For I have come to judge the earth. I shall judge the world with righteousness and the peoples with Your truth." With that, Jesus lowered His head and arms and resumed walking, as if He were in a great hurry to get someplace.

Young Boergenes was having a difficult time keeping up with the Master as he walked quickly along the path. The Lord's mood changed when He began to speak.

"Dear cousin, in me you have life and life more abundantly. Life that exceeds those in the world, even to the end of the age. You are a lampstand, an olive tree, pouring forth oil at the appointed time. Do your ears hear my words?"

Mr. Boergenes opened his eyes and saw Jesus standing above him in the chapel. The words from the blue tapestry hanging on the wall, *UNDER THE BLOOD*, were superimposed upon the vision of Jesus" face. Mr. Boergenes bowed his head and said, "Yes Lord, I hear and understand that now is the time to usher in the end of the age. I have given Manny's friend the clay pot as you have instructed."

There was once an early church legend called The Blood Legend. It was the story of Joseph of Arimathea, a wealthy man, who brought his servants to the place where Jesus was slain for the purpose of removing Jesus from the cross before the Jewish Sabbath was to commence. Legend had it that Mary, the mother of Jesus, Mary of Magdal, Apostle John, John's mother and a few others were at the scene when Joseph showed up with his cleanup crew. It is said that they were in shock over Jesus' brutal death and just stared at the bloody body that was still hanging on the cross.

It was the weekend of the Passover celebrations and millions of people milled about the area. The drunken Roman soldiers who supervised the crucifixion left Joseph and the others alone at the crucifixion site while they hurried to dispose of the two crucified criminals' bodies in the local dump. Joseph immediately instructed his men to take Jesus' body down from the cross and hustle the body to his own personal tomb not far from Golgotha, but not before allowing Jesus' mother to cradle her son one last time on her lap.

Joseph of Arimathea gave instructions to the remaining men to gather up any items left lying around on the ground, which included the bloody wooden crosses, before night fall. With sack cloth bags, they picked up items such as wasted wineskins, bowls used for the sour wine, torn pieces of clothing, and the crown of thorns that Jesus wore on His head. Well-worn whips, clubs, and other garbage were hastily retrieved and thrown into bags.

As the men loaded up the cart, Joseph brought out several clay cooking pots and laid them on the ground next to a flat wooden shovel. Nicodemus the Pharisee showed up with a cart full of precious burial ointments and saw Joseph fall to his knees, scooping up the blood that had pooled at the foot of the cross. Apostle John joined Joseph on his hands and knees, scooping up the blood. They placed the bloody clumps of mud into the pots with their bare hands. Nicodemus followed suit by picking up the shovel and filling several containers himself. Finally, the pots were loaded into Joseph's cart and hauled off to the barn behind his home just as the sun was setting.

After the resurrection, Jesus appeared to five hundred men and women and laid His hands on each one. This was confirmed by the Apostle Paul's letter to the Corinthians. Included in this number was Joseph of Arimathea and Nicodemus the Pharisee, for they both became believers after the resurrection. Jesus took these men aside and personally instructed them, as He did the eleven Apostles.

Weeks later Joseph and Nicodemus presented each Apostle with several small clay pots sealed in wax with the Apostle's initials embossed in the lid. Tied around the rim of the pot was a scroll that dangled from a scarlet string. The writing on the scroll said, "Whoever eats my flesh and drinks my blood has eternal life." At the presentation, which occurred in the home of Joseph of Arimathea, Joseph and Nicodemus explained to the Apostles that they were simply following Christ's explicit instructions in giving them the pots.

Gifts to the Apostles were not unusual occurrences during this time. In fact, the Apostles were forced to store many of the special items given as gifts at Apostle John's large home in Jerusalem. Most of the small clay pots that

Joseph gave to the Apostles ended up in storage there also.

The Legend continued that Jesus instructed Apostle John privately concerning the blood that was collected and the fact that he would live to be a very old man. History testified that John was the only Apostle who had not experienced martyrdom, and relics of his life, ministry and burial have yet to be found. They said he disappeared into obscurity and died of old age somewhere in Asia Minor. Legend had it that the clay pots were out there somewhere, hidden, waiting for discovery.

Chapter Four

"Tell us what happened, Manny. Rock said you had some kind of epiphany at your pool today," Amy Reed asked, pleading, waiting for another juicy Manny Benson story. Amy, Rock's wife, loved Manny's stories. She always fell for his punch lines, hook, line and sinker.

Manny was known for telling great stories and stretching it out for the desired effect. Rock just sat there with his hands in his lap staring off into space. Amazingly, Manny had not ordered a pitcher of beer as was his custom. He would normally say it helped in digesting red meat and white meat and dark meat and any kind of meat. But not tonight.

They were all there at the Steak House for Manny's fortieth birthday dinner—born June 6, 1966. Pastor Benson had reserved the Wrangler Room for the occasion.

Betty Benson, Manny's mom, brought a room full of balloons and flitted around seating everyone. Mr. and Mrs. Kingston, Manny's in-laws, were there to pay for the dinner. As wealthy Chandler residents, the city named the road they lived on after them, Kingston Road. Rock and Amy's two sons were there, Archie and Billy, both in their twenties. They lived at home and ran the family farm with their dad.

All in attendance at The Steak House were members of Pastor Benson's church. Mr. Kingston was on the search committee that voted to have Harold Benson installed as pastor in 1964. Pastor Harold was twenty-two years old when he became head pastor of the booming Chandler congregation of thirty-two members. They could hardly pay his salary. But over the forty years he had been pastor, the attendance had swelled to three hundred faithful church members. Sometimes the church ballooned to three hundred twenty-five when the Pastor rallied the troops to go out and knock on doors. He used to say, "Why let the Mormons have all the fun," knocking on doors that is.

Finally, Sissy Benson was there, Manny and Joanne's only daughter. She ran her father's insurance agency without much help from him.

"Well Amy," Manny said, "I don't know what to tell you. I had an experience today that was difficult to understand. Joanne had an experience too. Something you read about in books. Kind of fantastic, you know? All I can say right now is that I think I saw Jesus in a vision!" Manny looked over at Rock who slumped further in his seat.

"Hey Rock, why don't you tell us what happened today?" Manny offered. "Rock was there and had an experience too, if you call falling down and sleeping by the pool an experience!" The birthday party turned to Rock, waiting for him to say something.

"All I remember is Manny slipping on the pool pavement and falling into the water." Rock sat up in his chair and leaned forward. "I stood by the edge of the pool not knowing what to do. I swore he had killed himself. His big ol' head just bounced off the pavement. I thought it killed him!”

Mrs. Benson interrupted and pointed a finger at Manny. “How many times have I told you that it’s dangerous to run around the pool. It’s slippery and dangerous!” The women nodded in agreement.

Rock continued, “Anyway, I stood there in a panic going for my cell phone when Manny came lunging out of the water mumbling words like he was a crazy man. You know Pastor, like in one of your meetings,” Rock said, referring to the Holy Spirit nights at the church. Rock turned toward Pastor Benson and the Pastor’s face flushed red.

“Exactly,” Manny said, “Exactly like that!”

“The next thing I know, I see Manny raising both his arms like he just scored a touchdown and he’s mumbling more gibberish. I look up and the sky is as clear as a bell and the next thing I know, I’m laid out cold on the ground with Manny standing over me with a big stupid smile on his face like he’s seen God or something.” Rock said. “I was still groggy from the fall, I guess. So Manny drove me home.”

“I went back home after dropping Rock off,” Manny began, “and Joanne drove into the driveway from church and when she saw me, she wanted to know if I had an accident because there was blood streaming down my forehead with little gashes here and here.” Manny ran his fingers across his forehead trying to feel where the cuts were. Everyone leaned in to get a good look.

“I got worse cuts on my head from a football game. This was nothing,” Manny said.

"So Joanne got me a wash cloth and held it to my forehead. Then I realized that there were broken pieces of clay pot all over my pool and I was afraid that Dusty would cut himself. So I rushed to the pool and started picking up the pieces when I noticed that where the pot had landed and broken on the cement, there was a little puddle of goop that didn't dry up from the heat." Manny brought both of his hands together in front of him and formed a circle with his fingertips of the amount of goop he had found.

"I reached down and pinched the goop and it felt like oily grainy dirt. Then for no reason at all I took the goop and rubbed it on my forehead and immediately the bleeding stopped, and the gashes disappeared." He flung his arms open as if to release a dove from his grasp.

"Poof. Gone!" he said, glancing over at his dad.

Then Manny's daughter Sissy spoke up and said, "Yeah, when I got home I saw dad showing mom his forehead and going on about some miracle, visions and stuff. In one hand he had a bloody washcloth and in the other he had a clump of oily dirt. Mom was just standing there with her mouth wide open. Dad turned to me with a look I've never seen before. Wild and crazy-like. Then he turned back to mom, touched her on the forehead and said, "Be healed of your arthritis." Mom fell down and passed out like they do in grandpa's meetings." No one turned toward Pastor Benson this time, even though he was beet red, because they were transfixed on what Sissy was saying.

"Yeah just like that," Manny repeated, "just like that!"

"I couldn't believe it," Sissy continued. "I didn't know what to think. Here's dad with blood all over him and mom ends up on the kitchen floor, not moving a muscle," Sissy said, acting out her exasperation.

"Then mom wakes up with the same wild look in her eye and says that Jesus touched her." Sissy then looks over at her mom.

Joanne kept the story going. It was her turn to speak.

"Manny touched my forehead and I fell backwards. When Manny pulled his hand back I saw it wasn't Manny's hand at all but the hand of a man with a beard and a tan colored robe. I was falling one way and the man, I assumed it was Jesus, was walking by me the other way." Joanne made a forward motion with her arm.

"He just walked by and touched me on the forehead at the same time Manny touched me, saying, 'Pnuema Adonay, Pnuema Adonay.' I watched Him walk by me while I floated to the ground. He was touching others the same way He touched me and there was a huge crowd of people pressing in on Him; but I saw His legs and the sandals wrapped around His ankles. I saw the garment He was wearing and it hung just below His knees. The hem of the robe had a design like diamonds on it." She retrieved a pen from her purse and drew a diamond pattern on a napkin.

"I saw the purple rope tied around His waist. It had a real tight weave. The ends of the rope were tied in a knot and moved slightly as He walked. But He walked quickly through the crowd saying, 'Pnuema Adonay,' over and over again. The crowd finally enveloped Him from my view but I could still hear Him saying, 'Pnuema Adonay,' over the noise of the crowd in the distance. Someone's shadow came over me, so I looked up to see who it was and there was Manny and Sissy standing above me in the kitchen."

"After Joanne told us about her brief experience with Jesus, I ran to my study and found this glass tube," Manny said, reaching into his shirt pocket, pulling out a glass test tube with a cork in it. He gently rocked it back and forth between his thumb and pointer finger. The substance in the tube looked gray in color and slid like mercury in the glass vial. The glass tube sat on Manny's dusty bookshelf filled with tiny seashells from Hawaii before he emptied the shells onto his desk and used it to put the goop into.

"I ran to the pool with a spoon and scooped as much of the substance into the vial as I could. Then," Manny hesitated because he suddenly realized how crazy the next thing he was about to say would sound. "Then I scraped and scooped as much of the goop I could into my hands and rubbed it all over my body!"

"You didn't!" Joanne admonished.

"Yes I did. I figure if this stuff is good enough to heal the cuts on my forehead and your arthritis, then it's good enough for my whole body!" Manny said glaring back at Joanne.

At that moment Pastor Benson busted out laughing. He just couldn't hold it in any longer. Pastor slammed his hand down on the table and grabbed his stomach. The idea of Manny rubbing gritty goop all over his 270 pound body like a mad man was just too much to handle.

Then everyone at the table began to laugh spontaneously, Manny included. They were howling so loud that the Wrangler Room door opened and a waitress peeked in to see what the fuss was about. She started laughing too.

Manny was close to the door and could see out into the main restaurant where people eating their dinners were also laughing hilariously. The whole restaurant had been turned upside down with laughter.

After fifteen minutes the restaurant quieted down and dinner was served. Pastor Benson was still holding his gut and made the comment that his stomach was going to be sore in the morning.

After dessert, Amy leaned over and quietly asked Joanne if she was *really* healed of arthritis. Everyone knew how horrible and painful her arthritis was.

"You tell me. Watch this!" Pushing back her chair and walking to an open area of the banquet room, Joanne began to do windmills and jumping jacks. She held up her hands like a magician and wiggled her fingers back and forth, bending them this way and that. Then she bent over, hoisted herself to a handstand position and let her legs dangle in the air. "I haven't been able to do this since High School," Joanne said upside down.

"You tell me if I'm healed!" Joanne came down from her hand stand, straightened her blouse and sat back in her chair. The birthday group broke out into applause. It was great to see Joanne moving her body again.

If rubbing gunk all over my body was weird, Manny thought, *watching Joanne walk on her hands was weirder!*

Joanne began to have arthritis after Sissy was born. It had gotten worse and worse as the years wore on. And the medicine did not help. The side effects ranged from dry mouth to outright vomiting. One year her hair started to fall out. It came back in when she stopped taking the medicine. A couple of years ago Joanne's hands and feet began to look knobby from the calcium build up in her joints. From that point onward, Joanne rarely wanted to be seen in public, unless of course it had to do with a church function. But thanks to the Lord, today she was healed!

Manny felt different also. It was as if he had been washed from the inside out. Maybe cleansed was the word. Manny reached into his baggy slacks and located the cigarettes that had been his habit for several years and crumpled them in his fist. "Man, these are nasty things," he mused, "I can't believe I smoked these things!"

"Hey everyone," Manny called out, "I know what I want for my birthday!" Once he got their attention, he said, "Let's end this wonderful evening in prayer!"

Manny closed his eyes and bowed his head, clasping his hands together the way Mom taught him to do as a child. The rest of the party sat there in shock, looking at each other.

"Go ahead Dad, you start," Manny said, not moving a muscle. All bowed in prayer as Pastor Benson cleared his throat.

"Dear Heavenly Father" barely came out of the Pastor's mouth when Manny heard a loud crashing noise all around him. Startled, he opened his eyes to see a man dressed in a dazzling white robe floating down towards him from a cloud that opened and closed behind him. The room became bright white. Manny could see nothing in the room except the glowing man who landed directly in front of him.

"My name is Michael," the angel said. "Do not be alarmed."

Manny sat paralyzed, his hands still clasped in prayer, scared to death. The angel stood nine feet tall and was as big as a pro football linebacker. His shoulder length hair was bright gold and his flowing white robe seemed to shine outward, as if light was coming from it. The angel's face shone so bright that Manny could not make out the facial features, but he didn't think he looked human.

"I have been sent here to tell you that the gospel of the kingdom will be preached in all the world as a witness to all the nations and then the end will come. That time is now! You are to preach the gospel of the kingdom and usher in the end of this age. You are to prepare the way of the Lord. You are to make straight in the desert, a highway for our God." The angel's words burned into Manny's mind. "The glory of the Lord shall be revealed through you and all flesh shall see it together, for the mouth of the Lord has spoken."

Michael paused for a moment and said, "Search the Scriptures, Manny, for your destiny and the destiny of the world lies therein. Find the sacred vessel and listen to him." Then as suddenly as the angel appeared, he disappeared. But the cloud remained and clung to the ceiling.

Those sitting at the banquet table had fallen asleep and slumped over in their chairs. Manny noticed a startling silence in the restaurant, except for a firetruck's fast approaching siren and honk. Manny opened the banquet doors and saw that everyone in the restaurant was asleep, including waiters, waitresses and cooks. There were several people laid out on the floor near the cash register, who were either waiting to be seated or in line to pay their bill.

Manny stepped over the patrons sleeping at the entrance and looked outside. Pedestrians across the street were staring and pointing at the roof of the restaurant. Manny went into the parking lot and looked up. A cloud of smoke and fire was resting on the restaurant roof. Someone must have called the fire department and the SWAT team because they screeched to a halt in front of the Steak House.

Chapter Five

It was late before the Bensons got home that night. A HAZMAT team was called to the restaurant because of the curious fire and cloud that continued to burn on the roof all night. The late night news reported that hundreds of people had passed out due to a gas leak in the building, even though the restaurant was not hooked up to a gas line.

The morning papers featured the freak occurrence on their front pages: "Dozens of Blind People Healed at Local Restaurant" read the Arizona Republic headline. Apparently there was another banquet at the restaurant where dozens of blind and disabled people had gathered for a seminar to discuss the issues of the disabled in the community. Everyone in the banquet was healed of their disabilities. People got out of their wheelchairs and started running all over the room. Blind people were screaming that they could see. A man was arrested for yelling hysterically at a police officer that his leg had miraculously grown back. Many of these folks ended up in jail the paper said, for causing a public disturbance.

Manny could not sleep all night. He laid in bed with startling images of a massive angel and six lane highways in his head. The voice of the angel burned in his heart: "Make straight in the desert a highway for our God."

The Arizona Tribune took a different angle and on their front page feature wrote: Fire Heals The Blind. "A local restaurant was set ablaze by the power of Christ, says Queen Creek resident Manny Benson, who witnessed the event. How do you explain such things? One minute we were praying and the next there was a fire on the roof. Can this have something to do with the blood of Christ?"

❧

"Sir, we may have a potential problem," said the young man on the other line.

"What kind of a problem?" Carlos asked. To his left he could see St. Paul's Cathedral from his bullet proof limousine window. He chuckled at the thought of the medieval structure burning to the ground in 1666 in the Great Fire of London. One day, Carlos thought to himself, he might want to be married in St. Paul's Cathedral. All the important kings of Europe were married there. Carlos wondered if he would be the first homosexual king married in the holy Cathedral.

Wouldn't that cause St. Paul to turn in his grave?

"We have a Polycarp Directive, sir, per your orders," the voice said.

Juan Carlos lived in a global empire with access to instant information. He dreamed of ruling the world with a single touch of his finger, like many enlightened young men who ran in his circle of influence. London was Carlos' playground and he was only there to finish his collegiate studies. Once he graduated, he said he wanted to rule the world from Jerusalem; an ambitious young man.

Recognized as a genius, Carlos was sent to London at the age of fifteen to attend college and was a semester away from completing his graduate degree. Soon he would be called Doctor Juan Carlos and would be on top of the world.

Carlos was dark skinned with short cropped brown hair. He stood about five foot seven inches in his black Spanish made high heeled boots. He swore he was a little taller than what Napoleon was when he conquered the world. If Napoleon didn't have an issue with his height, neither would he.

Carlos' father was the aging king of Spain, Juan Carlos I, Third Bourbon restored ruler of the realm. Carlos was a short version of his famous father but swore he would never make the same mistakes his father made. To rule Spain under a declared democracy had been a sign of great weakness and a grave mistake for his father. The history books have proved that the ignorant and petty populace cannot rule themselves. Progress can only be gained through one kingly bloodline and the centralization of power in one man, the king!

In the midst of his enlightened mentors, The Brethren, Juan Carlos II had sworn an oath to restore his rightful place as dictator king over all of Spain; to rule with an iron fist as his ancestors had for hundreds of years. At age nineteen, Carlos needed only to wait upon his father's passing, then he would fulfill his destiny to Spain and to the world.

"Are you certain this concern falls under the directive?" Carlos asked the voice on the phone. "For if it does, there will be hell to pay. We can't let the complacent church out of her cage on my watch!"

Twice in history, the Christian church had turned the world upside down with miracles, power, and fire. The first show of power was directly following the resurrection of Christ. Unprecedented signs, wonders and miracles were displayed in such a fashion that the world turned away from idols and began to follow the teachings of Christ. If the Christians had not been brutally massacred before the fall of Jerusalem in AD 70, who knows what the world's religious, political and economic systems would look like today.

The second show of worldwide church power had to do with Saint Polycarp in AD 156, one hundred years after the Apostles died. Polycarp was converting the world to Christ, in the same manner the world was converted by the first Apostles, except Polycarp did it through the blood of Christ! At least that's what his writings said. Following Christ's resurrection, the Apostles spoke of the power of the Holy Spirit as their means of mighty power without reference to the blood of Christ. Signs and wonders were performed in large numbers by the Apostles but there was no mention of fire as a manifestation of their power either. But in St. Polycarp's movement, the specific mention of the blood of Christ and the accompanying sign of fire, as the contact point for power, became evident.

World economies suffered under Polycarp's revival, so say the secular historians, as the economies had suffered in the first century when the Apostles turned the world upside down. The known world in the second century was nearly converted to Christianity if it had not been for Polycarp's mysterious death.

The Brethren placed the Polycarp Directive in the charge of their brightest young protege Juan Carlos II. He studied the history that pertained to The Directive which was passed down from generation to generation to each newly appointed 'Guardian.' Carlos was surprised to find that the Prince of Wales was the previous Guardian of the Polycarp Directive.

The Directive monitored two very specific events world wide: miracle healings that claimed to be performed by Christ's blood and supernatural fires accompanied by a cloud. The assumption was that one did not appear without the other. The two together spell potential disaster for the world.

The theory was that once Christ's blood begins to work miracles and the fire appears, international revival would break out like a brush fire. If billions of people throughout the world were converted to Christ, they would no longer participate in the underground economy of drugs, pornography and alcohol. A world revival involving billions of converts could cripple the tobacco, pharmaceutical and the lucrative medical industries. Hospitals could shut down, governments might become paralyzed, and the world economies would screech to a halt. Not to mention the effect a world revival would have upon organized religions. An empty mosque or synagogue would not be good for business.

The phenomenon of mass Christian revivals by blood and fire remained to be the number one threat for those in control of the world's system, The Brethren. The Directive was in place for a good reason: to identify the revival phenomenon and snuff it out before it became an international problem.

Since Polycarp's death in the second century, the Directive had rarely been activated. After all, the idea of Christian revival through the blood of Christ is merely a theory. The only real revival threats in history had been the spiritual fires in the upper room with the Apostles on the day of Pentecost and with Polycarp's revival; but nothing further in history regarding blood and fire that caused any concern.

Carlos and his Brethren were keenly aware of the Blood Legend but did not believe that Christ's blood was ever collected in the first place. If by chance the legend was true, the likelihood of blood from the first century surviving into the twenty-first century was very remote. The molecular structure of blood simply breaks down and deteriorates within a few years. The first century technology provided no means by which to preserve blood, let alone to have it survive two thousand years. The blood threat had been minimal until now.

"Not on my watch!" Carlos yelled into his cell phone. "Eighteen hundred years have gone by without as much as a flicker and you're telling me the building was on fire all night without burning the place down?" he said, hissing at the tourists walking toward St. Paul's Cathedral.

"Maybe it's a fluke," he said.   "I want you guys to investigate and get back with me as soon as you have something." Carlos snapped the cell phone shut and threw it on the black leather seat of the limo.

"Not on my watch," Carlos said over and over.

Carlos' black diplomatic limousine stopped in front of the British Museum. A helicopter hovered overhead. Four bodyguards jumped out of a black SUV that was following and fanned out. Carlos waited for his door to open and then proceeded up the stairs into the museum. Heading west, Carlos wound around the halls leading to the Western Asian collections and before proceeding down the stairs to the basement he looked over at the two large human-headed bulls from the 7th century BC, Khorsabad.

Beautiful creatures, he thought.

Once in the basement, Carlos made his way through several corridors before he came to a door that was labeled Holy Land Exhibits. Unlocking the door and turning on the light, he was always shocked at how dusty and dirty the room was. Boxes and debris were strewn about.

Much like Jerusalem itself, he thought. *A place of global irritation. A place that needed a good cleaning.*

On the floor in the middle of the room were two replicas of the ancient temples that once sat near the temple mount in Jerusalem. Just behind the two replicas sat a spectacular model of a third temple, the one Carlos designed and affectionately called *his* third temple.

The first model was Moses' wilderness tabernacle adorned with small animal skins. A linen fence went around the display. The tabernacle was crude and simple. Moses had it made that way so that the Israelites could pack it around the wilderness with them.

The second model was Solomon's temple and it was three times the size of the first model. It looked like a tall square building with brick walls around it.

Israel rebuilt the second temple many years after it was destroyed, called Zerrubabel's Temple. Then King Herod refurbished Zerrubabel's temple, which had fallen into disrepair, when he ruled from Jerusalem.

Carlos' third temple model stood four feet high and ten feet long and dwarfed Solomon's temple. The wall around the building was so wide that the builders put miniature cars on the wall, showing that vehicles could drive in two lanes on it. This model was overlaid with gold, along with its colonnades and pillars. Lights were placed around the display to make it stand out from the other two models.

Carlos spent a year having these models built to his exact specifications. This was his final project in support of his doctoral thesis.

Carlos dedicated four years to studying the history of Israel in relation to their beloved temples. With an undergraduate degree in Psychology, a minor in Humanities, and a doctorate in Religious Studies, Carlos felt like his college studies were complete. He arrogantly felt qualified to take on the world.

These three models were his crowning college achievement and were to be proudly displayed as the centerpiece in the newly built Holy Land Exhibit Hall; the exhibit hall that was generously donated to the museum by the Carlos Family of Spain.

Compelled to study the history of his Spanish forefathers, Carlos became curious about other types of governments that were ruled by dictatorships over the history of the world. This led to a study of the major world religions in relation to their views on dictatorship. Carlos formed a geopolitical theology he called the divine right of dictatorship. Carlos wrote his final dissertation on the results of his findings: The Mandate for Divine Dictatorships and The Temples They Loved.

Carlos stood with his arms crossed, admiring his beautiful temple. His thoughts drifted to the Polycarp Directive and his face blushed red with anger.

A world Christian revival could ruin everything, Carlos said to himself.

Carlos knelt down next to his beloved temple and put his hand on the roof. Lifting the heavy dome off its base, Carlos set it on the floor beside him. Hunching over the walls and looking inside the temple, Carlos reached into his coat pocket and pulled out a tiny intricately designed throne. He lovingly held the throne in the palm of his hands, staring at it for several minutes. Then he carefully placed the throne in the middle of the room called the holy of holies.

Chapter Six

There are three seasons in the Phoenix east valley: Sunny and cold; sunny and warm; and sunny and hot. On Manny's birthday, it was sunny and blazing outside. So hot that Manny decided not to put down the top on his 1958 Porsche 911 on the way to the office.

Manny could not concentrate on his work. There were insurance contracts to sign and clients to follow up with.

Sissy Benson, Manny's daughter, ran the Benson Insurance Agency pretty much by herself. She was licensed to sell all the products: life, health and auto. She laughingly told clients that her dad came in to "supervise" and shuffle papers, and then he was off to play golf all day; which wasn't half wrong.

At nine o'clock Sissy came shuffling through the front door fumbling a wad of papers that she plopped on her desk in the front lobby.

"Dad I'm here! Happy Birthday," she shouted, expecting a reply from her dad.

"I'm here too but I'm leaving," Manny said with a raised voice. "It's all yours. I'm going over to Grandpa's church to hang out for awhile."

"OK dad," Sissy said, putting her lunch in the fridge. "I'll call if I need you." She never did.

There were a million questions in Manny's mind and he had to find some answers. On Sunday he had seen the Lord and an enormous angel. His wife, of all people, was doing handstands. People were mysteriously healed at the restaurant. Why was all this happening?

Michael told him to search the Scriptures and Manny was determined to do just that. But what or who was the "sacred vessel" he was to find?

Pastor Benson's church had a small, rarely used library equipped with Bibles, dictionaries and lexicons. It was a Tuesday morning and Manny knew that nobody would be at the church, especially in the library.

Once in the library, Manny went right to work. He pulled down an interlinear Greek-English New Testament, where the Scripture was laid out in the original Greek, with the English translation written next to it. Next he found a Strong's concordance that listed all the words found in the Bible. Then Manny looked around for a Bible dictionary and found several grouped together on the upper shelf.

He sat down at the study desk and spread the books out on the table. He closed his eyes and instantly saw the angel's words in his mind: "I have been sent here to tell you that the gospel of the kingdom will be preached in all the world as a witness to all the nations and then the end will come."

Manny found this verse in the New Testament book of Matthew. The first thing that struck him about the verse was the phrase "gospel of the kingdom." Is the gospel *of the kingdom* different than what churches are preaching today? Manny wondered. Why would Jesus use these words?

Manny noticed that this *kingdom* gospel was to be preached *in all the world. This thing must be worldwide!* Manny said to himself, trying to comprehend the meaning.

As a witness to all nations. A witness of what, their sin? Their rebelliousness against God?

And then the end will come. Well, that's pretty clear, Manny said shaking his head. Clear as mud.

The angel told Manny that he was to usher in the end. What does "usher" mean? Manny went to his Webster's dictionary and found the definition of the word. It means "to be a forerunner!"

The light began to go on in Manny's mind as he grappled with what was being said.

I am to go into all the world and be the forerunner for Christ's return? No way! That's impossible! Manny thought to himself. Who was he but an insurance agent in Chandler, Arizona?

Manny closed his eyes again and saw the words: "You are to prepare the way of the Lord. You are to make straight in *THE DESERT,* a highway for our God.*"* Now Manny was beside himself. He could still see the six lane highway leading up to a stadium lingering in his mind.

Manny went to the Strong's concordance and looked up the word "desert" and found the reference he was looking for in Isaiah 40:3. As Manny read the passage he came to verse 5: "The glory of the Lord shall be revealed and all flesh shall see it together." Manny noticed that Michael didn't quote the passages exactly as written in Isaiah but added the "you are" to preach, "you are" to prepare and "you are" to make straight in the desert.

Manny stood up and stretched, putting his reading glasses on the top of his head. He picked up the Bible and read the verse from Isaiah again.

Something is very familiar about this passage, he thought.

Manny went to the margin of the Bible to see if there were any other Bible references connected with this verse. To Manny's amazement, there was a specific reference to Isaiah 40 in all four of the New Testament Gospels. Every one of the gospel references referred to John the Baptist preparing the way of the Lord's first coming. That was obvious. But none of the verses said anything about preparing the way of the Lord *in the desert.*

Manny went back over the verses again and in Matthew, Mark and Luke it says, "Make His paths straight," omitting the words "in the desert." The gospel of John's version simply states, "Make straight the way of the Lord," also with no reference to the desert.

Could the desert be a reference to the Arizona valley where I live? Manny pondered.

He found the same to be true of the reference in Isaiah concerning a "highway for our God." None of the gospels mentioned that John the Baptist was to build a highway in the desert. The Baptist's ministry was in the wilderness, not the desert. Could it be that Manny was to build a highway for God in the Arizona desert? The idea was mind boggling.

Manny put the Bible down on the desk and paced around the room.

This is impossible, Manny said to himself. *How could I possibly be the one to prepare the way of the Lord's second coming?*

It was almost eleven and Manny had been at the church for nearly two hours. Normally he would have stepped outside for a cigarette by now but the thought never occurred to him. Other things occupied his mind.

What if what the angel said was true? If this is true, then we are living in the last days right now. If this is true, then according to Scripture there will be a worldwide revival. If this is true, then the Rapture is about to happen. If this is true, the antichrist is alive and about to enter the world stage. If this is true, then the temple in Jerusalem is about to be rebuilt. If this is true, then the Great Tribulation is at the doorstep.

"If this is true," Manny said out loud, with a sense of dread, "I am the one God is calling to usher in the end!" He shuddered at the thought.

Pastor Benson knocked on the library door and slowly walked in. He looked white as a ghost. Hunched over and acting like he was going to have a heart attack. Pastor did have a flair for the dramatic.

He motioned for Manny to give him a minute before he could speak. After clearing his throat and taking a deep breath, Pastor Benson said, "Manny, I came to the church about an hour ago and saw your car outside. I had some calls to make so I went to my office. When I unlocked and opened my door, there was a long haired man sitting in one of the leather chairs facing my desk." Pastor cleared his throat again and nervously scratched the side of his face.

"Well, I was surprised of course and demanded that He leave my office at once! The man in the chair stood up, turned around and held out His hands for me to see." Pastor Benson jumped out of the chair and grabbed Manny by the shoulders and started shaking him.

"It was Jesus, Manny! It was Jesus!"

When the Pastor got a hold of himself, they both sat down. Manny put his hands up to his head because it felt like it was about to explode.

"Manny, I sat across from Jesus at my desk and He leaned forward and talked with me for a long time!" Pastor Benson said. "I couldn't believe it. And guess what we talked about, Manny?" Pastor was about to jump out of his chair again. "Take a guess Manny!"

"You talked about me and the last days!" Manny said from behind his hands. "You talked about me ushering in the end of the age. You talked about me building a highway in the desert leading up to a stadium. You talked about me starting a worldwide revival." Manny said. "Did I leave anything out?"

"Yes, you left out that you won't be alone in this. Rock and I are to help accomplish your task. You left out that we will be ferociously persecuted and in grave danger all the time. You left out the fact that the Lord said we are in the generation that will go up in the Rapture!" Pastor Benson said. "Imagine, we're not going to die but be caught up in the clouds!"

Pastor jumped out of his chair and grabbed Manny from the back by his shoulders and began shaking him again. Manny just sat there with his head buried in his hands.

"The Lord told me that we will work signs and wonders the world has never seen." Pastor Benson exclaimed. "And like the children of Israel in the wilderness, a cloud of His glory and fire will accompany us wherever we go!"

Pastor pulled Manny up by his armpits and dragged him down the hall into the sanctuary. Manny fell to his knees as soon as they walked through the doors.

"Look at that Manny!" Pastor screamed, obviously out of his mind. Over the podium and above the platform was a cloud as thick as smoke. Inside the cloud was a burning fire, breathing in and out as if it were alive. The room rumbled with the vibration from the cloud and Manny, now on all fours, tried to keep his head up. Failing miserably, Manny plopped to the floor. He frantically reached into his pants pocket to make sure the vial of oily blood wasn't broken. With a hand around the unbroken vial, Manny protected it with his life as he succumbed to the floor. This vial, Manny believed, had something to do with all this!

Pastor Benson ran up to the podium and opened his Bible to Ezekiel 1:4 and began reading out loud: "Then I looked and behold, a whirlwind was coming out of the north, a great cloud with raging fire engulfing itself; and brightness was all around it and radiating out of its midst like the color of amber, out of the midst of the fire."

He read the next verses about the four living creatures, their wheels and wings. Pastor then read the verses describing the vision of the Lord in the fiery firmament and when he read through most of verse twenty-eight, he stopped and looked up at the cloud hovering above him and read the last sentence: "This was the appearance of the likeness of the glory of the Lord."

Manny was flat on the floor. It felt like someone had poured cement into him and as hard as he tried, he couldn't get up. Manny could hear his father reading from the pulpit but was helpless to respond. He opened his eyes and looked at the carpet. All he could think about was that he hoped the janitors cleaned the carpets on Monday, when they cleaned the rest of the church.

"Do you know what else the Lord told me today, Manny?" Pastor Benson now was feeling it. His arms were outstretched at his podium like Charlton Heston in The Ten Commandments.

"He told me that He wants to use this old church building for His glory; to get things rolling for your ministry." The Pastor said answering his own question.

"And do you want to know what else, Manny?"

Manny just laid there listening, watching as an ant walked across the floor in front of him.

"The Lord told me that He wants you to start preaching here at the church starting tomorrow night!" the Pastor said, closing his Bible. "I thought I'd never see the day, Manny. I thought I'd never see the day! Happy Birthday, son," the Pastor said, shaking his head.

Pastor Benson stepped down from the pulpit and took a seat on the front row, contemplating the burning cloud. Manny just laid there on the floor, thankful that the ants were not eating him alive.

Pastor closed his eyes and tried to remember anything he had learned from the past about God's glory. *The Hebrew word for glory is kavod,* he thought, and it means "heavy in weight" and "shining majesty." When the glory of God crosses paths with the soul of a man, the experience overwhelms the recipient and causes him to succumb under its weight; just like we see in the Old Testament. This is why people *fall under the power*, said a guest evangelist once, who slayed the Pastor's congregation years ago. The evangelist told Pastor Benson that God's glory is the manifestation of His presence when it touches a man and individuals buckle from its weight. Pastor admitted to himself that it didn't make much sense at the time.

Pastor Benson sat and gazed into the glorious cloud. The glory seemed to be God's presence manifest on the physical plane; for God was not a physical man, Pastor noticed, but something else, something glorious, something not comprehensible to his mind. God appeared to be hidden in a cloud; the burning fire inside the cloud is the actual person of God in His original state of being.

If it weren't for the cloud hiding the fire, Pastor Benson thought, *the glory of His true nature would certainly consume him.*

At least this was his impression of it.

When God first revealed Himself to Moses, He "appeared to him in a flame from the midst of a bush." God revealed His true spiritual nature to Moses as a burning fire, not that God's person is an actual fire, but resembles a fire. For if God's nature is an actual fire, it would have consumed the bush. When this phenomenon is seen or experienced by man it is called the glory of God, for lack of a better way to describe the fire that He is and the cloud that hides Him.

When God revealed Himself to Israel, "they looked toward the wilderness, and behold, the glory of the Lord appeared *in* the cloud." Later, "Moses went up into the mountain, and a cloud covered the mountain. The glory of the Lord rested on Mount Sinai, and the cloud covered it for six days. And on the seventh day He called to Moses *out of the midst* of the cloud. The sight of the glory of the Lord was *like a consuming fire* on the top of the mountain in the eyes of the children of Israel. So Moses went *into the midst* of the cloud and went up into the mountain." God was not the cloud itself but hidden in the midst of the cloud, protecting anyone coming in contact with His true nature: an awesome burning fire.

Scattered throughout Scripture God's glory is revealed within its pages. But the most startling revelation of God's glory is in the nature of the Messiah, the true fire of God come in the flesh. The proof that Jesus came directly from God is clearly seen when Jesus was transfigured before His three disciples Peter, James and John. "His face shone like the sun and His clothes became as white as the light." Jesus' true nature is the glory of God, a burning fire, the same fire that burned on top of Mt. Sinai, and the same fire that was burning in Pastor Benson's church that very moment.

Manny's experience on the sanctuary floor was not unlike the experience that Peter had when he saw Jesus transfigured: "But Peter and those with him were heavy with sleep; and when they were fully awake, they saw His glory." They fell asleep under the weight of Christ's glory and when they woke up, Jesus was seen for who He really was: a glorious burning fire!

Pastor came to the sudden realization that he really didn't know much about the Lord. From this point forward, he knew it was not going to be business as usual in his little church.

Chapter Seven

Rumors in a small church spread faster than a nasty rash and Pastor Benson's church of three hundred members was no exception. All the church seats were packed on Wednesday night because the faithful had heard the stories surrounding Manny, Joanne and Pastor Benson. There hadn't been this much excitement in the church since the Benson brothers started winning football games for them some twenty odd years earlier.

He sat in his dad's office wringing his hands and biting his fingernails. Manny stood up and looked out the office window. He couldn't believe his eyes; the parking lot was full of cars and trucks, something he hadn't seen since his football days.

It was almost seven o'clock and cars were still streaming in. Pastor Benson was out in the parking lot directing traffic which is something Manny had never seen. Now he was really nervous.

Manny reached for the pack of cigarettes that was usually in his pocket but found only the pack of gum that Joanne gave him. She said more than once that his breath stank like a dirty ashtray if he didn't have gum to chew on.

The other thing he felt in his pocket was the mysterious glass vial. Manny found comfort knowing it was there.

"Seven straight up!" Pastor Benson said, barging through the door, more excited than a coffee addict standing in line at Starbucks.

"Manny, you ready?" Pastor asked, motioning for Manny to hurry up and follow him.

Pastor was wet with sweat but managed to quickly comb his hair back and head for the sanctuary door leading to the platform. Pastor could have said to Manny, "Dead Man Walking!" because it felt like he was walking down the hall to his execution.

Pastor whisked through the sanctuary door first and took his normal position behind the pulpit. Manny came in behind his dad and shyly took a seat on the platform. He was terrified. Not only were all the seats filled with people he had known all his life but there were people he did not know lined up in the back and overflowing down the side aisle; and people were still out in the vestibule trying to get in.

While Pastor Benson opened with a word of prayer, Manny took the opportunity to look for his wife in the crowd. He thought if he could just see her smiling face, it would help calm his nerves. It didn't! She looked more frightened than he; her knuckles turning white in front of her as she attempted to pray.

Where is Rock?

Manny could depend on a dumb but encouraging smile from his ol' friend. He scanned the crowd but Rock was nowhere to be found.

"Hey Buddy!" Rock whispered as he snuck up to Manny on the platform. Rock reached out his big arms and gave Manny a bear hug.

"Pastor wanted me to sit here with you tonight," Rock said. "Let me tell ya, I'm good to go!" Rock said this like they were in a high school football huddle, ready to attack the opposing team.

"Good to see you, Rock. I'm glad you're here," Manny said, leaning into Rock without being too obvious. "Looks like we're in the big game together again, huh?" Manny said, patting Rock on the knee just before he stood up to speak to the church.

Standing at the back of the church were two men who looked like they didn't belong. With sunglasses and greased back hair, the two just stood against the wall staring straight ahead. If the crowd got too close to them, the men would sharply elbow them out of the way.

A cloud of fire slowly materialized and hovered at the ceiling above where Manny stood. A gasp went through the crowd just as Manny opened the new Bible his dad had given him today. Many in the crowd were pointing at the phenomenon and Manny felt like he needed to address it before he read his text.

"This is what you came here to see tonight," Manny said, turning slightly and putting his palms upward toward the cloud. "Certainly you did not come to listen to me. You all know me and you know I do not deserve to be up here tonight. This cloud is why I am here." Manny pointed toward the manifestation near the ceiling.

"This cloud is the glory of God; the same glory cloud that was with Moses in the wilderness; the same glory cloud that hovered over the temple in Jerusalem; the same cloud that appeared when Jesus was baptized and transfigured on the mount. This cloud is the same cloud that received Jesus into heaven and this same cloud," Manny reached into his pocket and slowly removed the vial and put it on the podium. "This same cloud will bring Jesus back from heaven very soon!"

The two men at the back wall removed their sunglasses and pushed their way through the crowd toward the side aisle. They wanted to get a closer look at the cloud and take pictures of it, if possible. The miniature cameras snapped dozens of pictures from chest high as the men inched closer and closer down the side aisle toward the platform. The shorter of the two suddenly began to tremble and looked over at his cohort in terror. He felt nauseous and trapped in the small hot room. The taller man gave him a "get a grip" look and continued clicking off pictures.

"Let's turn to Luke 4:17," Manny told the congregation, letting his reading glasses plop down on the bridge of his nose. "I want to read something that Jesus said and *didn't say* that pertains to us tonight." Manny squinted at the fuzzy text. He removed the glasses and could see the text perfectly.

"Jesus was in his hometown of Nazareth when He spoke these words, like I am in my hometown standing before you tonight. Jesus read a passage out of the book of Isaiah 61, which says: 'The Spirit of the Lord is upon Me because He has anointed Me to preach the gospel to the poor; He has sent Me to heal the brokenhearted; to proclaim liberty to the captives and recovery of sight to the blind; to set at liberty those who are oppressed; to proclaim the acceptable year of the Lord.'"

Manny picked up his Bible off the pulpit and began to pace to his left. He felt uncomfortable behind dad's oak podium. It was like a barrier between him and the people.

"First of all, I want to say, the Spirit of the Lord has been placed upon me this week to do all these things that Jesus did; to preach the gospel; to heal the sick; to free people possessed by demons." Manny was taken aback when he said "possessed by demons." He wasn't even sure if he believed in real demons.

Manny realized that a greater force was speaking through him. Manny turned around and looked up. He swore he saw a man on fire in the cloud. He rubbed his eyes and looked again. The cloud was slowly moving toward him and another gasp came from the crowd as the cloud hovered directly above Manny's head.

"Let's turn quickly to Isaiah 61 and read what Jesus *didn't* say on that Sabbath day in Nazareth." Manny was in a hurry now. He felt a warm vibration emanating from the cloud just above his head and his knees weakened. He didn't want a repeat of yesterday and to be stuck to the floor in front of four hundred people.

Gripping the podium with both hands, Manny read Isaiah 61 all the way down to verse 2 and looked at the crowd. "Jesus proclaimed the acceptable year of the Lord in the first part of verse 2 because he was the Messiah and fulfilled this prophesy to that point," Manny said. "What the Lord did *not* proclaim was the second part of verse 2 because it was not yet time to fulfill that part of the prophecy," Manny said.

"I am here tonight to tell you that now is the time to fulfill the rest of Isaiah's prophecy. Let me read it aloud: 'And the day of vengeance of our God!'"

Manny stepped to his left again and the cloud followed. Some of the people were looking at Manny but most were transfixed on the cloud above his head.

"An angel appeared to me Sunday night and told me that I was to usher in the end of the age; the age before 'the day of vengeance of our God,' and we all know what day that is: the Great Tribulation!"

Manny went back to the podium and flipped the pages of his Bible.

"Finally, let's go back to Luke 4 and look at verse 21." Manny said, waiting for the sound of the pages to stop turning.

"As Jesus said in the synagogue that day, I say here tonight, 'Today this Scripture is fulfilled in your hearing.'"

When Manny was finished the cloud began to move throughout the crowd. People stood and came forward, weeping. Dozens began kneeling on the steps of the platform, wailing as if they had lost a child. Many more had been slain in their seats, not given the opportunity to come forward.

Manny finally buckled to his knees on the platform. Rock was right beside him crying like a baby on his hands and knees. But Pastor Benson had rallied his ushers, or tried to, in an attempt to minister to the fallen members. What Pastor didn't realize was that God had things well in hand. Jesus was very experienced with large crowds.

The cloud found the two spies who were desperately trying to escape. They were pinned between slain bodies and the side wall. The shorter one was doubled over in pain, snarling like a dog. The other had a panicked look on his face and was reaching for the revolver strapped to his leg.

Manny looked over just as the cloud passed by the two men and watched them drop to the floor. *"The day of vengeance of our God" has begun,* Manny thought. A weird ghostlike creature came out of the shorter man and vanished.

Manny reached up to the podium and grabbed his Bible. Finding the book of Acts, he turned to Chapter five and read the story about Ananias and Sapphira. *Don't mess with God is the message here,* Manny said to himself, slowly closing the Bible.

Meanwhile, Joanne missed everything that happened after the point where Manny said, "Let's turn to Luke 4:17" because she passed out in her chair. Joanne saw a red and blue light flashing when she woke up. There were still dozens of people sleeping throughout the sanctuary, oblivious to the paramedics and the police trying to figure out how the two men died. The shorter man had a contorted grotesque look on his face that resembled a gargoyle. His hands were drawn in and twisted like claws. Not a pretty sight to see.

The next day, the news media converged on Pastor Benson's little Chandler church to get interviews and set up for Sunday's service. The Chandler police were called to direct traffic and to make sure the news trucks parked where they were supposed to. CNN, NBC, ABC, CBS and even ESPN had correspondents on sight.

Umbrellas, folding tables, and miles of cable cluttered up the empty lots next to the church. Dust clouds from the semi-trucks hung in the air and the neighbors complained. But the restaurants were full, the grocery stores were running out of bottled water, and the gas stations were lined up with cars from out of the area. Contrary to the complaints and inconvenience, the glory of God was good for the city of Chandler.

Business at church was good too. Dozens of Pastor Benson's parishioners were calling, weeping, repenting, and giving money. Reports of miraculous healings were coming in to the church office. Couples wanted to set up appointments for marriage counseling. Some had even come to the church to sit in the sanctuary and others came to watch the media circus take over the neighborhood. Pastor could not keep up with it all. He was in heaven.

Unfortunately, the media found out where Manny worked and lived. Sissy was bombarded at the office first thing in the morning with reporters asking about her dad. She finally had to lock the doors and go home.

Manny and Joanne had reporters pounding on their Queen Creek home waking them up early in the morning, demanding that he talk with them. The home phone began to ring at seven and didn't quit all day long.

Manny called Rock from his cell phone and Joanne called Amy from hers. They needed help!

Rock and Amy hurried right over, driving past the church on the way. Manny opened the gate at the side of the house and let Rock drive through to park in the gravel.

"This is crazy!" Rock said, scooting out and running around the truck to open the door for Amy. As Amy gathered her purse from the front seat and fluffed her hair, she said, "Manny, have you seen the trucks and the mess at the church?"

"Only what I've seen on the news," Manny replied.

"We saw your dad out there directing traffic with a grin on his face. He's in hog heaven. Best thing that's happened to him in years," Rock said.

After everyone was safely in the house, Manny asked Rock if he would go with him to run some errands; to be his bodyguard so to speak, if need be. They jumped in the Porsche, hit the garage door opener and honked at the reporters as they backed out of the driveway. Manny noticed that a few of the reporters were sprinting toward their vehicles with the intention of following them. Manny sped off, taking a few clever side streets and ended up at his office in Chandler. Driving to the rear of the building, he parked in a handicapped space and covered his car with a tarp.

Manny ran into his office, picked up his laptop computer and the mail and ran out. He noticed a couple of characters pacing back and forth at the front of his office but they didn't see Manny enter the office from the rear.

Manny tossed Rock the keys to the Suburban that he kept in the parking lot and asked him to drive.

"Not enough room in my driveway for all the vehicles," he told Rock, ducking down in the passenger's seat to avoid detection.

Once safely on the road again, Manny sat up and shuffled through his mail.

"Let's go by and see how dad is, Rock," Manny said.

The pile of mail was three inches thick and half of it was advertisements. Manny was looking for a commission check from an insurance carrier and started ripping open the mail. The glory of God or not, the bills had to be paid. He pulled each envelope apart, glancing in to see what it was. Then Manny came to an envelope that looked and felt different from the rest. Instead of tearing it open, he held it in his hand and looked at it for a long time.

"Hey Rock, where was that place you and Amy went to in Turkey? You know, the place where you found that little clay pot?" Manny asked.

"Antalya? On the Mediterranean Sea?" Rock answered.

"Well, I have an envelope here that is postmarked from Antalya, Turkey a week ago!" Manny said, carefully tearing open the envelope.

Inside, there was a handwritten letter and a cashier's check. Manny put the check on the dashboard without looking at it and unfolded the letter. He read the letter out loud to Rock: *"My Dearest Mr. Benson, I pray this letter finds you full of love and the Spirit. This check is a small donation towards your new ministry. More will be forthcoming. We must not arouse suspicion. Please deposit this money into an account for your new ministry. The End of the Age Ministries. Use the funds for the glory of God. In the name of Jesus Christ. Amen. The Icon Collector."*

Manny retrieved the check from the dash and looked at it. "Holy Cow, Rock!" he said. "You won't believe this!"

He handed the check to Rock and when Rock saw the amount, he pulled the Suburban over to the side of the road and screeched to a halt.

"It says one million seven hundred and fifty two thousand dollars, Manny!"

"And sixty-three cents, Rock. And sixty-three cents!" Manny added.

Rock turned the Suburban around and headed for the bank. Checking on Pastor Benson could wait!

Chapter Eight

The two men looked nervous waiting at the display case. At the front gate they were interrogated and their vehicle was searched. Told that no one was allowed to drive inside the estate, they were transferred to a military Jeep and driven to the compound under armed guard. At the front door the men had to submit to a security wand search by spreading their arms and legs and removing their shoes.

While they were searched, a guard held a weapon on them. Not allowed to take any electrical device inside the mansion, the men emptied their pockets of cell phones, hand held computers, battery operated remote controlled car keys and hearing aides, if they had any. The men felt naked without their shoes, belts and cell phones. Intimidation would describe their feelings, surrounded by fierce soldiers.

"We could die in this place and no one would ever find us," the doctor from New York said, once inside the mammoth mansion. The other man, dressed in a cheap wrinkled suit, was the doctor's accountant and present to make sure the deal went smoothly.

Before them was a bullet proof glass display case sitting on a marble pillar in the middle of the foyer. Inside the case was an ancient manuscript about two inches thick, opened at the middle and propped up so the writing could be seen. The yellowish manuscript was bound by three leather strings. The writing on the document was crudely scribed and the pages showed rust colored ink runs.

"I wonder what this is?" the doctor asked.

"I haven't seen a photo of it in any of the history books or journals either. Looks valuable is all I can say," replied the accountant.

Mr. Boergenes entered the room wearing a long tan robe with a hood on the back. He was wearing a white shirt and a tie underneath and a black velvet sash was tied around his middle.

"Pardon my delay gentleman. There's always the Lord's work to be done."

"Pleased to meet you Mr. Boergenes," the doctor said with a slight nod, shaking his hand. "My name is Dr. Brent Scovall and this is my associate Alan Dirskovsky."

"Pleased to meet both of you. Shall we join in my office and do some business?" Mr. Boergenes said, moving toward the open door.

"Wait!" the accountant said. "Please tell us about this manuscript displayed here in this case."

Mr. Boergenes smiled and placed his right hand on the glass. "This, my friends, is the original Book of Revelations, penned by the Apostle John on the Isle of Patmos. It is sealed here in this hermetically secure environment so that it will not deteriorate."

"This is the original Revelation manuscript?" the accountant asked, looking closer at the pages.

"The manuscript was written in candle light in a small cabin that Apostle John shared with other roommates for several years. Very little of the manuscript is done in ink. Most of the lettering is done in the Apostle's own blood," Mr. Boergenes said. He took his hand off the glass and put it up to his frowned forehead.

"That explains the running of the ink on the pages, right?" the buyer said, pointing to the document.

"Yes, dripping blood from one's arm has a tendency to run a little bit."

The accountant thought for a second and said, "I do a lot of reading and on a lot of subjects but I have never heard this about the Apostle John. How do you know these things?"

Mr. Boergenes wheeled around and headed for his office. "I have other manuscripts written by companions of John who confirm these things," he said.

After seating the two guests in his office, Mr. Boergenes sat on a leather couch across from them. Mounted on the wall above Mr. Boergenes' head was a glass box the size of a large picture frame. Inside were twisted wooden vines, resembling barbed wire, in the shape of a crude circle.

"My God," said the buyer. "Is that what I think it is?"

"Yes it is!" Mr. Boergenes replied. "I am not worthy to have it on my wall."

"That is priceless!" the accountant said.

"More priceless than you know," Mr. Boergenes said bowing his head.

Dr. Brent Scovall was a wealthy eccentric who fancied himself solving ancient mysteries of antiquity. The mystery of how the pyramids were built was one of his projects. Scovall spent millions hiring engineers, sending them to pyramid locations in Egypt and having them compete to come up with the best theory of how the great pyramids were constructed.

Doctor Scovall was the philanthropist who discovered the ruins of Sodom and Gomorrah, complete with detailed analysis of the soil that contained radioactive material. He also produced a two part Discovery Channel series on tracing the path of Christ's cross and the crown of thorns entitled "Chasing the Cross and The Crown." Neither the cross nor the crown of thorns were discovered by Dr. Scovall's team, but Scovall traversed the Middle East with movie cameras spinning an exciting tale of what could have happened to the relics.

The crown of thorns mystery was solved this day, however, hanging on the wall, resting peacefully behind the head of Mr. Boergenes.

Dr. Scovall and his accountant were in Turkey because of an unsolved mystery concerning Mary Magdalene's presumed marriage to Christ. Dr. Scovall wanted to solve the mystery and televise the discovery on worldwide television. A small number of intellectuals at the Vatican who knew of Mr. Boergenes' ancient relics told the doctor that he might be able to provide proof that Mary Magdalene did not, in fact, marry Christ.

"The world seems to have gone after this notion that Christ was married to Mary and had children with her," Scovall said, staring at the display on the wall.

"And they are saying that Christ's heirs survive to this day and are in hiding from their enemies, the Catholic church! The Catholics are pretty bent out of shape about it," the accountant said.

Mr. Boergenes agreed to meet with Doctor Scovall in order to put to rest this age old myth. Sure, the Roman Catholic church had gone astray many times over the past sixteen centuries but who hadn't? The history of the Bible is a story of a chosen Jewish people who rarely walked the straight and narrow. Yet, God fathered his only Son through the bloodline of imperfect Jewish people. And in the same way God loves His wayward Israel, He loves his beloved Catholic children. For we have Israel to thank for bringing forth the Messiah to the world and we have the Catholics to thank for keeping and preserving Christ's words for the world.

"Gentlemen, Christ was never married to anyone," Mr. Boergenes began. "Yes, the Priory of Sion was established in 1099, this is true. But the Priory was never involved in commissioning the Knights Templar in order to retrieve and protect documents that supposedly proved Christ and Mary were married and had children. This was never a secret that needed to be protected. The Catholics were not concerned about an heir of Christ being seated as head of the church, removing them from power. This is pure fiction!"

Mr. Boergenes scooted back and sunk into the overstuffed couch. A faraway look came over his face.

"It is true, there was a king; a French king named Godefroi de Bouillon who did conquer Jerusalem in 1099, but he did not found the Priory of Sion in Jerusalem as many think. On his journey back home to France through the ancient city of Ephesus, the king discovered the true secret of the Holy Grail and appointed his Priory to operate from there. His discovery remains a secret to this day. It is sad that so many men have wasted their lives over the centuries chasing the Holy Grail," Mr. Boergenes said while moving behind his desk and sitting down.

"I assure you gentlemen, there are no heirs of Christ, none whatsoever! And the Holy Grail? Well, it exists but it is not the heirs of Christ living somewhere in obscurity as the Da Vinci Code people suggest!"

"As you know, we are here for proof, any kind of proof," Dr. Scovall said.

"Yes, I know and I have proof but first we must come to an arrangement," Mr. Boergenes said while opening a drawer at his desk.

"Of course. Of course," Dr. Scovall said, elbowing the accountant to speak up. The men came prepared with millions of dollars to invest.

"An arrangement that would be satisfactory for all parties, I'm sure," the accountant said. "We have money already wired into your bank here in Antalya. All you have to do is pick up the phone and..."

Putting up his hand, Mr. Boergenes motioned that he was not finished talking. He pulled a leather folder out of the drawer and laid it on the table. Untying the leather strap, Mr. Boergenes pulled out several documents, turned them around and placed them in front of Dr. Scovall on the table.

"Before we go any further, I need for the both of you to sign a confidentiality waiver saying that you never met me, never came to my house and that I am not the source of your discovery. Is that agreed?" Mr. Boergenes said with a stern look on his face.

"Next, any remuneration exchanged in this transaction is to be sent to this man at this address as a donation," he said while pointing at the man's name on the sheet of paper. "It will be tax deductible in your country, I presume?" he added. "Gentleman, do you agree?"

After the men signed the forms, Mr. Boergenes placed them back in the folder, lifted himself out of his leather chair and opened the office door. An attendant handed Mr. Boergenes a three foot long bronze box the width of a small briefcase. The attendant leaned over and whispered into his ear, "They have arrived." Mr. Boergenes nodded his acknowledgement.

He placed the box on the table and carefully opened it. Inside were three ancient scrolls perfectly preserved. Mr. Boergenes lifted out the smallest of the scrolls and began to unravel it in front of them on his desk.

"This, my friends, is your proof. This is a writ of marriage for Mary of Magdal; to indicate they were signed, dated and witnessed by the apostles," Mr. Boergenes said with a gleam in his eye. "Guess who the rabbi was who presided over the ceremony?" Mr. Boergenes turned the document toward the men who jumped out of their seats to see.

Suddenly there was a sharp knock on the door and Mr. Boergenes handed the scroll to the doctor and promptly exited the room.

"My God. I can't believe this! Is that Jesus' signature?" Scovall said.

"And look! Are those the signatures of the Apostles? Unbelievable!"

"I count eleven signatures. Weren't there twelve? Hmm…and Judas killed himself after the crucifixion! If Jesus signed the writ, then Mary Magdalene was married before the crucifixion."

"What is the date scribbled there?" Scovall asked.

The door opened and Mr. Boergenes entered apologizing.

"Business, business. I'm going to have to cut this short, gentlemen," he said, standing at the door.

"Mr. Boergenes, this is unbelievable! I don't know what to say. I'm holding in my hand a marriage certificate for Mary Magdalene signed by Jesus and the Apostles? This certainly disproves the Da Vinci Code myth," Scovall said.

"Alan, can you read who the groom is? And the date?" Dr. Scovall asked his accountant.

The accountant leaned in, lifted his glasses and squinted. He could read the Greek letters pretty well and just when he was about to identify the signature, Dr. Scovall excitedly spoke up.

"We haven't discussed a price yet, sir. If this is what you say it is, well, I can't afford it. I can tell you that right now! I'd have to say it is priceless!"

"I suggest then, doctor, you let my men wrap the document in a secure package and take it with you. Have it tested, examined and let me know what it is worth to you. All I ask is that you abide by our agreement. Understood?" Mr. Boergenes said.

After closing the lid, Mr. Boergenes picked up the box and quickly left the room.

The accountant went to the door after Mr. Boergenes exited and said, "Sir?"

Mr. Boergenes kept walking but turned his head back. "Yes?"

"Do you have the manuscript of the Revelation open on that page for a reason?" The accountant asked, pointing over at the display case in the middle of the foyer.

Six men in Turkish turbans came to an abrupt halt when Mr. Boergenes stopped and walked back to where the accountant was standing at the door. He looked the accountant up and down, then put his hands on his hips.

"You remind me of Cephas, one of Christ's apostles; always curious, always asking questions. Yes! In answer to your question, the manuscript is open to the next event in history; Revelation Chapter Six. The Lamb is about to open the first six seals; the beginning of sorrows that Christ spoke about," Mr. Boergenes said, looking up at the ceiling. "He's about to open the seals."

He put his hand on the accountant's shoulder to get his full attention. "I sense the Father calling you, so I will say this: seek Him before it is too late, before the Lamb opens the seventh seal and the seventh trumpet sounds; for at the last trump, the words of our brother Paul to the Thessalonians will find its fulfillment." Mr. Boergenes closed his eyes and cited Apostle Paul's words from memory. "For the Lord

Himself will descend from heaven with a shout, with the voice of an archangel, and with the trumpet of God. And the dead in Christ will rise first. Then we who are alive and remain shall be caught up together with them in the clouds, to meet the Lord in the air. And thus, we shall always be with the Lord."

"Mr. Dirskovsky, you do not want to miss that day, the day of redemption; the day of the last trumpet; the day of your Rapture. For immediately following the Rapture, in the time of the seventh seal, God's wrath will be poured out upon the earth. You do not want to be there for that! Are you following me, Mr. Dirskovsky?"

"But my church teaches that the Rapture will occur before the Great Tribulation and the Christians won't have to go through it," the accountant replied.

"This is true. The church will not be in the Great Tribulation after the Rapture. But before the Rapture there are six seals that the church must endure. These first six seals are considered birth pangs, contractions, of smaller tribulations that build up until the seventh seal is opened and the Believer is taken away into heaven. The church, contrary to what they are taught, will have to endure these smaller, but significant upheavals. Jesus called the first six seals the birth pangs, the beginning of the end. The end comes upon the world when the seventh seal is opened and the angels start blowing their trumpets. The church will not be here for that!" Mr. Boergenes said, patiently.

"I've been taught that the birth pangs of wars and rumors of wars; famines and earthquakes have been building up for a hundred years. All we as a church have to do is wait for the Rapture," the accountant replied, trying to argue. "My pastor says the Rapture is the next event in history."

"I know what the church teaches; you must not be deceived. All you need to know about the end times, the time we are entering, is in the Scriptures. Read it as it is written, not as it is interpreted.

"Let me say this though, Mr. Dirskovsky, the disciples understood Jesus' teaching on this matter because Jesus was very specific in every detail. He spoke of a time before the Great Tribulation where unmistakable signs would occur. Not random wars here and there or random earthquakes once in awhile. Jesus said that the world would begin to experience major earth shaking upheavals and massive brutal world wars. The scope of which are unmistakable signs. These events would bring on world wide famine and pestilences, caused by the types of weapons used in global warfare. These beginning events will cause false prophets to appear and worldwide lawlessness will become rampant, more rampant than it is now. Again, when this happens, it will be an unmistakable sign of the end. I assure you, these events have not occurred yet, but they will and soon!

"Jesus did not say He would rescue us from tribulation. Matter of fact, He said just the opposite. He told His disciples that they would experience tribulation. And they did; so will we. We should expect to go through the initial birth pangs of tribulation. Yet, it is brother Paul who clarified the issue by saying that the Believer was not appointed to wrath. Thus, the day of wrath will commence after the church goes through the beginning of sorrows and is taken away! This is quite clear in Scripture."

Mr. Boergenes patted the accountant on the shoulder and looked over at Dr. Scovall, who was glancing back and forth between the crown of thorns and the scroll in his hand, dumbfounded and bewildered.

Mr. Boergenes left for his next appointment.

On the second floor was Mr. Boergenes' private office complete with a conference table and chairs. Floor to ceiling windows gave a beautiful view of the city to the north. At the foot of the city was the Bay of Antalya, glistening in the noonday sun. Cruise ships were docked in the bay with tourists milling about. Beyond the bay was the Mediterranean Sea as far as the eye could see. On the horizon were barges and tankers, coming and going to their destinations.

"The view is wonderful here isn't it? Far away from our duties!" the Vatican priest said, staring out of the window.

"And far away from our problems and concerns!" the other Roman Catholic priest replied.

"And far away from the global catastrophe, if war breaks out on the temple mount," the High Priest from Jerusalem said in a gloomy tone.

"And we're here to prevent that from happening, gentlemen," Mr. Boergenes said, bursting through the door and setting the bronze box on the conference table.

"Sit, sit. We have business to attend to."

On the top of Mount Moriah in the old city of Jerusalem sits one of Islam's holiest sites; the Dome of the Rock. The Muslims believe that Muhammad ascended into heaven from a rock that the dome covers. They purposely built their dome in 691 AD over the presumed ruins of Herod's Jewish temple, at the exact spot of the holy of holies; Israel's holiest site, or so everyone thinks!

To reconstruct another Jewish temple on Mt. Moriah was not an issue for the Jews until 1967 when Israel captured the temple mount. Then it became possible to build a temple there. For forty years Israel has been waiting for an opportunity to remove the Muslim dome from the temple mount so that a Jewish temple could be built on that site. The problem is, any act of aggression to remove the Muslim holy site would be a cause for an international war, since three major religions lay claim to the temple mount and dozens of nations desire to worship there. Israel is not prepared to wage a war against the world so that it can have its temple built; at least not yet.

Practicing Jews believe that when the Messiah comes, he will deal with the profane Dome of the Rock and that's when the temple will be built. They believe that the man who builds the next temple will be their Messiah. That will be their sign, proving he is the One.

"Gentlemen, I believe we are living in the moment of Christ's appearing," Mr. Boergenes began to say.

"All of us here have a vested interest in this event. For you Rabbi, your people look for the Messiah. And you Catholics, your people look for His glorious return. For both of you, before the Lord appears, a temple has to be built to house Him, do you not agree?"

He looked at them, waiting for them to nod their heads. Once he received their affirmation, he went on.

"As long as there is not a rebuilt Jewish temple, the Lord will not come! Everything God does is according to Scripture and the Scripture says, for the Jew, the Messiah will come to His temple. For the Catholic, Evangelical, and Protestant, the temple has to already exist before their Messiah appears.

"According to Scripture the Catholics believe the man of sin has to desecrate the temple during the Great Tribulation before their Christ will come. Either way, the temple has to be built, regardless of your religious view of the situation. I believe the time is now!"

"Thank you, Mr. Boergenes, I appreciate you inviting me here," the high priest said in his best Aramaic, clearing his throat. "But we have a slight problem on the temple mount that prevents our beloved temple being re-established there; the hated Muslim Dome! It has been there so long, the world would turn against us if we took care of the situation ourselves. I do not see a way possible to build our temple without the miracle of the Messiah's assistance in removing that profanity."

"Rabbi, I fully understand your concern and that is why I invited you here today. According to Ezekiel's prophecy the Messiah will deal with the Dome of the Rock in His own way and in His own time. I will share that with you in a minute. But for now I have a solution to the problem that will, I think, be satisfactory to all religious groups and nations involved," Mr. Boergenes said, reaching down, opening the bronze box and pulling out a long scroll.

"Gentlemen, as you well know, Solomon built the first temple in Jerusalem on that mountain. Where on the mountain may be the question. That first temple existed for four hundred years until it was completely destroyed and left in a heap of rubble. In 520 BC, Zerubbabel, the governor of Jerusalem, began his project to rebuild the temple with the same dimensions and on the same exact location as Solomon's temple. But Zerubbabel's temple was neglected for hundreds of years and became nothing more than a place of storage until Herod came along.

"In 37 BC Herod tore down Zerubbabel's temple, enlarged its foundation and repositioned the structure to accommodate its size. It was a temple for King Herod's majesty more than a temple of God's glory.

"Herod's temple was destroyed in 70 AD and sat as an ancient ruin all these years. In 691 AD the Muslims built that dome of the rock on the temple mount believing that they built it over

Herod's temple and the holy of holies. Herod had no regard for the sacredness of where Solomon built the temple on the mountain. The placement of the temple on the mountain was divinely inspired by God and God expected Israel to keep it that way throughout history.

"King David, in 850 BC, desired to build the first permanent temple for the Lord in Jerusalem but God would not allow David to construct it. So, King David instructed his young son, Solomon, to build the temple when he became king instead. Second Chronicles says that David gave his son Solomon the plans for the vestibule, its houses, its treasuries, its upper chambers, its inner chambers, and the place of the mercy seat, which is in the holy of holies; including where to place the temple upon the mountain of God. The Scripture says that David received the detailed plans of the temple directly from God."

"Let me get this straight. Are you saying that when Herod reconstructed the temple, he moved the holy of holies?" the high priest asked.

"No. I'm saying that the holy of holies is not exactly where the Muslims in the fifth century nor the Jews today think it is. If you recall wasn't it Constantine's mother who divined to the world that the wailing wall is where the ancient temple originally was built?" Mr. Boergenes sat back to see where the conversation would lead.

"So you are saying that the Dome of the Rock is *not* sitting on Solomon's original holy of holies?" The High Priest was animated now.

"Rabbi, what I am saying as clearly as I can is that the Dome of the Rock *may not* be over the original holy of Holies."

"How do you know this to be true? What proof do you assert?" the High Priest asked.

"Because of this scroll here in my hand." Mr. Boergenes carefully placed the scroll on the table and unrolled it.

"This is one of king David's rough drafts showing the placement of the temple on the Mount. This is a rough draft because David had several other drafts and locations on the mountain where Solomon might build the temple."

Six more hands reached out to hold the parchment flat on the table. The parchment was remarkably preserved and the placement of Solomon's temple was clearly seen on the draft.

"You notice where Solomon's temple is on this plan?" Mr. Boergenes said, pointing at the center of the drawing. Using his finger he traced across the parchment from right to left, from east to west, and tapped.

"The empty space you see here gentlemen, is where the Dome sits today! About fifty yards from the original temple on this draft. Remember, this is only a draft."

"I'll be," sighed the high priest as he sat back in his chair. To think all these years Israel could have built her temple without too much of a problem."

"And to validate that, this is one of David's certified drafts for the temple on the Mount, see here in the left hand corner? That is David's signature." Mr. Boergenes tapped on the spot. "Furthermore, as you will notice, this is not a copy, but one of David's original inked plans for his son, Solomon."

The Jews have struggled for centuries with the idea of building a Jewish temple in the same location on the mount where the Muslims have a sacred shrine. Even if a temple could be built beside the Dome of the Rock or somewhere else on the mountain, would it be kosher to do so? It had been inconceivable that a Jewish temple could be built on the temple mount, sharing the 35 acres with the Muslims. The only remedy was for the destruction of the sacred Dome and Mosque before a temple could even be considered.

According to prophecy, Mr. Boergenes made a convincing argument that the temple could be built near or next to the Muslim shrine. In the book of Ezekiel, God was speaking to the prophet in a vision about the new temple standing at the east gate. It was as if God was looking over from the temple at the Muslim Dome and said, "When they set their threshold by My threshold, and their doorpost by My doorpost, with a wall between them and Me, they defiled My holy name by the abominations which they committed; therefore I have consumed them in my anger." This showed prophetically that the temple was to be built near the shrine on the east side. It also showed that God would deal with the Dome in His own time, "consuming them in my anger." This was the prevailing thought on the matter by Jewish and Christian scholars since Constantine's mother declared where the holy sites were originally located.

The fact of Ezekiel's passage remains; God expects the temple to be built near or next to the Muslim shrine as "the place of My throne and the place of the soles of My feet, where I will dwell in the midst of the children of Israel forever."

Excited and rejuvenated by the prospect of building a holy temple in his lifetime, the high priest took a detour through Spain before flying back to Jerusalem. An important meeting was called by the King of Spain and the High Priest was expected to attend. The two Catholic priests remained at the Boergenes estate and enjoyed a wonderful dinner with their host. It was a Monday evening in Turkey and the priests were not expected back at the Vatican until Thursday. Mr. Boergenes requested that they stay with him for a few days and take in the sun. The weather in Antalya was exquisite this time of year and by staying at the estate, one could avoid the tourists.

Chapter Nine

"Make straight in the desert. Make straight in the desert," Manny heard ringing in his head all night. Dreams of coliseums, highways and multitudes of people invaded his sleep.

Manny slipped out of bed and went to his office at the front of the house. He opened the blinds and looked out. Security guards had roped off the property; every inch of his one and a half acres.

Twenty cops were working around the clock, in shifts, to protect their newest celebrity. He was under siege by the media and felt safer that the cops were there.

Closing the blinds, Manny fell to his knees at the couch. Such incredible things had occurred in only five days; his mind was reeling. It was early Friday morning and Manny just wanted to sleep. The voices, visions and dreams made sleep impossible.

Manny closed his eyes and tried to get a grip on himself.

What is happening? he asked. *What do I do now?*

All he saw in his mind was a huge stadium filled with people in vivid living color. He opened his Bible and began to read in the gospels.

Astonishing, he thought to himself. *I don't remember reading this before!*

Manny read through Matthew and was amazed by two things: Jesus spoke of the kingdom of heaven and then He healed the people; *all the people*. The preaching of the kingdom had something to do with the healing but he didn't know what. He also noticed that Jesus' healing power included those with "torments and those who were demon possessed." Whatever that meant.

When Manny started the first chapter of Mark, he noticed that when Jesus taught in the synagogue, "they were astonished at His teaching, for He taught them as one having authority, and not as the scribes." For forty years Manny was never astonished by any preaching he had heard, let alone anyone who had authority. Especially not the poofy haired evangelists that Dad invited to the church, who tried to push people over and beg for money.

But what really caught Manny's attention in this passage was the outburst of the man in the synagogue who apparently had an "unclean spirit." Manny had no idea what an unclean spirit was. Up until now, he didn't really believe in this type of hocus-pocus. The contorted gargoyle of a man in the church began to change his mind.

He read the verse over and over again. "Now there was a man in the synagogue with an unclean spirit. And he cried out saying, 'Let us alone! What have we to do with You, Jesus of Nazareth? Did You come to destroy us? I know who You are the Holy One of God!'"

Why did these demons cry out like this? What was Jesus preaching that caused this reaction?

Manny went back to the previous verse and pondered it. They were astonished at His teaching. What *was* He teaching? He taught them as one having authority. *What authority?*

"Could it be that Jesus' teaching was about the kingdom of God coming down in power to deliver mankind, not only from sickness and disease, but from demonic strongholds? Were demons real?" Manny said out loud.

Could it be that Jesus was telling the men in the synagogue the story about how the Serpent rebelled, how he seduced Eve into sinning and how the devil had possessed mankind for thousands of years? Could it be that Jesus had arrived to deliver Israel from the bondage of the devil, much like Moses delivered Israel from Pharaoh's bondage? Could this type of teaching have caused the demons inside of the man to cry out, "Let us alone?" Is this the message that Jesus preached?

Manny leaned back and thought for a moment. *The church today teaches the Bible, Genesis to Revelation, but does it teach the gospel of the kingdom? The gospel of power and deliverance? The gospel that includes healing and demons?*

Manny had never seen a person healed in his church, nor a demon cry out. Pastor Benson would have such a disturbance dealt with swiftly. Anyone crying out would be physically removed by the ushers and told to leave. The church service was meant for "decency and order" and for the studying of Scripture; not for healing and certainly not for any kind of demonic deliverance. *Those things were not meant for today, were they?*

Manny had a strange feeling that all his questions would be answered real soon!

The cell phone rang and jolted Manny upright.

"Dad, it's six o'clock in the morning. What's up?" Manny said, rubbing his eyes.

"Son, are you awake yet?"

"I haven't slept all night, Dad. I'm in my study."

"Good, well, I think we might have a problem. I mean, it's a good problem, but it's a problem."

"Dad, spit it out. What's going on?"

"I'm here at the church and there's got to be at least a thousand people standing out here! With sleeping bags, camper trailers, you name it, we got it!" Pastor Benson said excitedly.

"But Dad, it's Friday morning! What are so many people doing out there?"

Manny got off his knees and sat down on the couch, peeking through the blinds at the cops outside.

"They're here to get healed, to witness the cloud, and to see if any more people die in your service!"

Manny knew that's why the media was there, too; fiery clouds killing people make great news.

What a nightmare, he thought. *What are we going to do?*

Then Manny had an idea.

"Dad, remember that healing guy that held huge tent meetings?"

"You mean Oral Roberts?"

"Yeah, that guy. How many people could his tents hold? Five, ten thousand?" Manny asked. "Could you call his organization and see how fast we can get some tents out here? Also, call Mr. Kingston and get permission to use the property behind the church for services. We'll need water, port-a-potties and concessions. And I'll talk to the cops out front about getting some security and traffic help for you at the church. We'll probably need permits, etc. Can you handle that, Dad?" Manny said, knowing that his dad was having the time of his life.

"I'm on it son. Oh, by the way, where are we getting the money for all this?"

"Like you always said dad, 'Where God guides, He provides!' Just email me the church's bank account info and I'll have a hundred thousand dollars wired into the account. Will that be enough?" Manny said, tongue in cheek. Manny didn't think that his dad had ever seen that kind of money at one time; especially not in the church's account.

By the time Sunday rolled around, there were five thousand people standing in long lines up and down Arizona Avenue. Red and blue police car lights were flashing while the officers attempted to direct traffic within a five mile radius.

Port-a-potties were strategically placed near the two huge circus tents that Pastor bought from a local car dealership. Oral Roberts' ministry didn't use tents anymore.

Concession stands had been set up to provide free water and food to the crowds. Chandler and Mesa ambulance services were on hand in case anyone fainted from the heat or a heart attack. No one knew exactly what would happen but the community was ready.

Mr. Kingston, Manny's father-in-law, graciously allowed Pastor Benson to use the twenty acres on each side of the church for parking. He also allowed the massive red and white tents to sit impressively on his property behind the church. Ten thousand chairs were rented along with a mega watt sound system that rivaled any rock concert.

The media trucks lined both sides of the street in front of the church for a city block. The commentators had their own sleeping trailers in which to retreat from the hot sun when not on camera. The grounds around the church looked like someone spilled long multi-colored cables of wet spaghetti; the mass of cords were stuck to the ground with yellow duct tape.

The only place that had air conditioning for protection from the hundred degree weather, other than the television trucks, was the small church. And that's where Manny was hiding out.

Manny arrived at the circus early in the morning by police escort. When he saw the red and white tents behind the church he wondered where the rides were. No ferris wheels and no roller coasters. He marveled at how the tents overshadowed the small church and the long lines of people sitting in lawn chairs waiting for the show to begin.

Simply amazing, Manny thought.

Traffic helicopters from local news stations arrived around eight in the morning and circled, keeping their cameras glued on the event. When the cloud appeared over the church, the cameras zoomed in on the ball of fire as it disappeared downward through the roof of the church. They swore the swirling fire was in the shape of a man but the replays couldn't confirm it. Then the white cloud, imploding with bursts of lightning and rumblings, completely engulfed the church building.

A voice was calling Manny from the church sanctuary. Thinking it was his dad, Manny went to investigate and saw the fiery cloud appear over the podium.

"Come up here!" commanded the voice.

Manny went and stood at the podium. He put both hands out to steady himself. That's when he noticed the vial; still sitting on the podium where he had left it Wednesday night.

"Ah, the cloud appears over the blood," Manny thought to himself. *"Very interesting."*

A wind was blowing in the sanctuary similar to the micro bursts that frequently occurred in the desert valley, stirring up dust and debris. Church bulletins and Kleenex tissues swirled around in the midst of the pews.

"Lord, does this have something to do with Your blood?" Manny asked.

Next to the vial was Pastor's Bible open to Joel 2. The portion from verse twenty-eight to the end of the page drew Manny's eyes because it was marked in yellow. When he got to verse 30, Manny read the verses out loud: "And I will show wonders in the heavens and in the earth: Blood and fire and pillars of smoke. The sun shall be turned into darkness, and the moon into blood, before the coming of the great and awesome day of the Lord."

We certainly have blood, fire and smoke, Manny thought. *But what does it all mean?*

The very last line on the page said: "And it shall come to pass..." When Manny turned the page, the wind was blowing so hard, he had to hold the pages down with his hands. "...That whoever calls on the name of the Lord shall be saved."

"That's what this is all about?" Manny said out loud. "The Lord wants to save people before He comes back? That makes sense."

A picture of an oblong globe appeared in Manny's mind. The globe opened at the middle and spread out to reveal a world map. The map began to ignite into flames in various countries. Australia, Japan, England, Greece, Sicily, Argentina, New Zealand. The map ignited with fire and was completely consumed. Manny noticed that a tidal wave of fire came up out of the Pacific Ocean and crashed down upon the West Coast of America. After it fell to the shore, the waves gathered as a river and flowed into Arizona, suddenly pooling at the freeway near Pastor Benson's church. The river's torrent continued to well up and build until it exploded into a fire that covered the entire earth.

Standing at the imaginary freeway, Manny looked over and saw that fire was pouring out of a football stadium, like lava; the same stadium He had seen in his dreams.

Leading up to the stadium was a six lane road packed bumper to bumper with cars. The people in the vehicles seemed to glow as if they were on fire also.

"Manny, make straight in the desert! As the Baptist did in the wilderness, you are to do in the desert. What the Baptist did with water, you are to do with the Spirit. As the Baptist stood in the river, you stand in the fire; the fire of My glory!"

Manny sank to his knees and cried, "Why me Lord? Why me?"

Of all the people in the world that were more worthy, righteous and deserving, Manny thought, *why choose me?*

His miserable life flashed before his eyes and Manny felt humiliated and ashamed; a worm in his own eyes.

Then as Manny wept, slumped over on the platform, gentle hands touched his shoulders and lifted him to his feet. He opened his eyes and was standing face to face with a glowing Man. Manny had not noticed that the cloud came down from the ceiling and covered him like a blanket. Inside the cloud, he saw a Man who appeared to have fire burning from the midst of His being, as if He were a molten furnace. As hard as Manny tried, he wasn't able to focus upon the Man's face. It was veiled for some reason. So Manny looked down, scanning his whole body, fixing his eyes on the Man's feet. His feet had five toes each that looked very old, ancient even, and resembled brass burning in a furnace.

Manny assumed he was face-to-face with Jesus or God, at least an angel, but he didn't know which. Manny slowly scanned the body once again, ending up at the veiled face. The body was the same as the feet; molten lava in a burning furnace. It was difficult to see details because the whole body fluctuated in constant motion as if it generated, as it were, atomic energy. There was an awareness that life itself began from this spot, from this Person, from this

Presence. In fact, Manny realized he was standing at the center of the universe, at the beginning of creation.

The cloud was so thick that the helicopters could not get a glimpse of Manny when he exited the church. As he walked, Manny looked at the watch his daughter gave him last year. He could never quite tell where Mickey was placing his left hand, above the number on the watch, or below it? But he could certainly see that Mickey was holding up his long right arm high above his head, covering up the number twelve with his little black gloved hand.

He walked the fifty yards to the circus tents, while dozens of men held the flaps of the red and white striped tent open for him. On the way to the platform at the front of the massive tent, Manny turned his head and looked out into the crowd. People were crammed in along the edges and groups stood in the back waiting for the show to begin. The noisy crowd hushed when Manny walked up the few steps to the platform. Everyone was gawking at the cloud that followed Manny, then it suddenly began to spread out over the entire crowd.

When Manny walked up the steps to the wooden podium set at the front of the large stage, the realization hit him that he hadn't changed his clothes all night.

What do I look like, he thought?

His mom was going to kill him and if she didn't, his wife would because Manny remembered what he had on all night and it wasn't his Sunday best. Manny began to smile and grabbed the podium with both hands to prevent himself from falling over if he began laughing. The morning papers the next day, around the world, showed Manny gripping the podium, bowing his glowing head, eyes wide open, and grinning from ear to ear. Manny wasn't smiling about the wrinkled khaki cargo shorts and the well worn flip flops he was wearing, but about the old brown t-shirt, torn under the right armpit, he had been wearing all night. On the front was a faded image of Jason Whitehead in his round wire glasses with a wispy cloud touching his forehead. On the back in black faded letters it screamed *Imagine There's No Heaven.*

With seven thousand people seated before him, he had no fear, even though it looked like he had just woken up. It made little difference that possibly millions of people worldwide were watching by television. The fear came when he located his wife Joanne sitting in the front row, bent completely over, shaking her head.

"Zoom in on his face. It's on fire, it's glowing!" the producer yelled into his headset.

Manny had no idea that his face was glowing until he noticed that people were pointing and gasping. Pastor Benson and Rock ran to the platform and handed Manny a mirror. He practically blinded himself when he saw his own face. It was glowing like the sun, radiating outward.

No wonder I feel so good, he thought.

Pastor Benson went to the microphone, stood next to Manny, and thanked everyone for coming. He apologized for any inconveniences, gave some announcements about the location of port-a-potties, and then turned it over to his son.

Rock remained on the platform but Pastor Benson took a seat on the front row with his wife and Joanne, who was still bent over from embarrassment. No one knew what was going to happen next. They watched Manny, like everyone else, as the fiery cloud hovered over his head.

Manny backed up and stood in the middle of the platform and looked out into the crowd of people. He stood there for several minutes before turning and motioning for Rock to remove the podium. The podium was whisked away.

Manny found all of the television cameras and looked directly at each of them, surprised he was not experiencing stage fright. Then he looked up and stared at the cloud that was vibrating just above his head.

"I know the Man who is in that cloud," he said, pointing upwards and leaning into the microphones. The sound of his voice was shockingly loud. It took a moment to adjust to the echoing effect, hearing his own voice roll down the valley.

"This morning I went into that cloud and met Him! I don't think I knew God until today, really. I mean, I accepted Him like many of you have, but I never really knew Him.

"I'm not going to stand here and tell you about God. You already know about God. You read about Him, you're taught about Him, you know about God. No, you will meet Him for yourself today, right where you sit."

The cloud began to move and spread out over the people.

"Here's the deal, you may have come here out of curiosity to see fires, clouds and miracles but in a minute you will encounter the living God for yourself. For these things are happening so that you will believe, believe in the God that's up there in the fire." Manny pointed at the cloud again. "He is able to help you and save you from bad things that are coming!"

He stepped to the edge of the platform and raised both arms like Moses, rip in the armpit and all.

"I am here to proclaim that the end of the age is upon us and that it is time to meet your God; the God of fire!"

Suddenly the cloud dropped like a net on all the people, including the television commentators and crews. Fire appeared on their heads and there was dead silence.

T.V. monitors were fixed on Manny because the camera crews were overcome and could not move. Producers were yelling into their headsets, "pan to the crowd, pan to the crowd," but for a long second, no one moved.

People watching around the world were also caught in the glory, sitting in front of their televisions, with fire on their heads. Countless millions, in a dozen time zones, watched as Manny spread forth his arms.

Then it began; the screaming, shrieking and the loud wailing. Hundreds of people started shaking like they were having seizures. Their faces were contorting and grunting like wild hogs. In a flash, hideous ghostlike creatures flew out of the tops of people's heads and vaporized. One in particular flew in Manny's direction and looked around, seemingly confused. When it saw Manny, it screamed in terror and disappeared.

Rock and Manny stood on the platform and watched the amazing deliverances. It only lasted a minute or two, when suddenly more people began to scream and shout. People out in the aisles were jumping up and down, leaping and dancing for joy. The two of them watched as hundreds of people leapt out of their wheelchairs and cast away their walkers; young and old alike.

Wave after wave of people were being healed and delivered. The blind could see; spinal injury victims were sprinting in front of the platform; arms and legs were growing back in front of their eyes; ugly tumors dropped to the floor; the deaf could hear.

Even miracles such as minor dentistry and orthodontics were performed. Cavities were filled with gold crosses and teeth were straightened without braces. Others wept, repenting and speaking in tongues; just like on the day of Pentecost!

Not having his Bible handy, Manny asked his dad seated in the front row if he could borrow his. Mr. Benson jumped up, walked to the front of the stage and handed it to Manny. "Oh, by the way, I think the passage you want is in the second chapter of Acts," Mr. Benson suggested. Then before Mr. Benson sat down he whispered, "It's right after the book of John, son." Manny stood there with a blank stare on his face, looking at his dad with the Bible in his hand. "Son, remember your Bible lessons. Matthew, Mark, Luke and John and then comes the book of

Acts." Still staring, Mr. Benson got angry and said, "In the New Testament, son. The *New Testament!*" Manny fumbled through the pages until he found the second chapter of Acts and briefly read the passage to himself.

"Isn't God truly great?" Manny began. "I want everyone to remain where they are right now and listen to what the Bible says. These things have been done to show us that God is alive and real.

"What has occurred here this morning was recorded in the second chapter of Acts. 'When the day of Pentecost had fully come, they were all with one accord in one place. And suddenly there came a sound from heaven, as a rushing mighty wind, and it filled the whole house where they were sitting. Then there appeared to them divided tongues of fire, and sat upon each of them. And they were all filled with the Holy Spirit and began to speak with other tongues, as the Spirit gave them utterance.'

"It says here that people in Jerusalem were amazed and marveled at these things. They were perplexed and asked, 'What ever could this mean?'

"Here we are, amazed and perplexed. I am sure millions watching by television are also. But let me make it clear that I had nothing to do with these miracles. I can assure you that Manny Benson cannot work one miracle or perform one healing."

He was pacing now, getting up steam.

"Peter tells us right here in the book of Acts who is doing these miracles. 'Jesus of Nazareth, a man approved by God to you by miracles, wonders and signs which God did through Him in your midst.' It says right here that God did these miracles." Manny pointed up toward the ceiling.

"You may be asking,'What do we do now?' After all, none of us have ever seen this type of thing before. It has to mean something! Well, the proper response is…" Manny moved the Bible closer to his eyes. "'Repent and let every one of you be baptized in the name of Jesus Christ for the remission of sins; and you shall receive the gift of the Holy Spirit.'"

Manny put the Bible under his left arm and grabbed the microphone. Thousands were cramming in the aisles and jammed in the space up front.

"First of all, let's repent, then we'll figure out where to get baptized later, OK?"

And he led everyone in a prayer that made Manny's mother weep. She couldn't believe that this was her beer drinking, chain smoking boy up there, leading thousands to Christ. She wasn't even sure Manny was saved until today!

While weeping, Mrs. Benson reached down to scratch her leg. She rubbed her calf up and down like she normally did in church and noticed that the bumps on her right leg were gone. She reached for her left leg and felt the same thing: smooth! Mrs. Benson bent over to see that her varicose veins and cellulite were completely gone. When she raised her hands in praise and shouts to the Lord, she noticed that the liver spots on her hands and arms had disappeared. That's when she lost it and began dancing like the crazy Pentecostal ladies that she criticized so often.

"I'm healed! I'm healed!" Mrs. Benson screamed more than once.

Maybe the Pentecostals aren't so crazy after all, she yelled to herself.

Chapter Ten

The High Priest flew from Antalya to Madrid on a private jet and arrived before night fall. An emergency meeting in Spain had been called at the last minute.

At the Madrid Barajas airport he was hustled to a side exit, while others found his bags and transferred them to a small jet; but the Priest himself clung desperately to the plans he received earlier that day from Mr. Boergenes.

The air was cool and crisp when his feet hit the tarmac. Dressed as a civilian, the Priest looked like a normal businessman except for his long white beard. When traveling outside of Jerusalem, American children on vacation would point and yell, "There's Santa Claus! There's Santa Claus!" This confirmed his belief that all Americans were ignorant buffoons.

Poking his head through the small Leer jet's door, the Priest looked around and noticed there were only five seats. It was a short, 90 minute flight to Mallorca, but claustrophobia gripped him and he stepped back. Sweat poured over him in waves as he became nauseous. But he had to remind himself that this small sacrifice was for the sake of the holy temple.

Lights from Castello De La Plana could be seen as the jet passed over Spain's western coast. He craned his neck to see the lights of El Planetario before the view was obscured by the darkness of the Mediterranean sea.

Thoughts of the glorious appearance of the Messiah filled the High Priest's mind. He wondered if the stars in the night's sky gave a clue to this wonderful event. He imagined that the planetarium's powerful telescope knew the secret of the future.

Oh, to see beyond the stars and to gaze into the thoughts of heaven; to know the day of Israel's Redeemer!

The Balearic Islands were wonderful this time of year, except for the hordes of tourists. The constant breeze blowing off the ocean allowed the island to remain warm year round but never blistering hot.

The jet landed at the Palma International Airport on Spain's largest island, Mallorca. The Gothic Palma Cathedral overlooking Palma de Mallorca's harbor was a thirty minute drive from the airport, where the meeting was to be held.

The Priest's mouth watered as he thought of biting into one of Mallorca's specialties, an ensaimada, a spiral pastry dusted with powdered sugar. He had lost two hours traveling from Turkey to Spain and was famished. The Priest's driver looked at his watch and agreed that swinging by The Forn des Teatre, an old pastry shop, couldn't hurt.

But it did.

The evening meeting was to begin at nine and the High Priest was late. However, before he could be seen by the others, he had to change into his robes and headdress. The Brethren expected him to look the part and he wasn't about to disappoint them.

He entered by The Capella Reial, the royal chapel at the back of the cathedral, and quickly changed. The High Priest swished through the side door that opened to the Bishop's Throne, a marble chair embedded in a Gothic vaulted niche behind the altar.

"You're late!" the man said, sitting on the throne.

The Gothic church was dimly lit except for the lamps high above in the alcove.

Surprised by the voice, the Priest stopped, adjusted the purple sash around his waist and said, "You are quite right. I am painfully late."

When the Priest approached the throne he saw clearly that it was the young son of King Juan Carlos of Spain, his arms resting firmly on the marble chair. The lamps were repositioned to provide a halo effect above his head. A light flashed brilliantly around Carlos and when the Priest approached the three steps leading up to the throne, he could see a gold crown, studded with diamonds reflecting upon his head.

The Priest resisted the urge to bow before this majestic sight. There was such a strong invisible urge to do so.

"Did you know that our family is Jewish?" Carlos said. "Father doesn't want the world to know. But it's true!" Carlos crossed his legs, leaned forward and looked at his fingernails in a feminine way.

"When Isabel, the Queen of Castile, and Fernando, King of Aragon, were married in 1469, together they formed the Christian nation of Spain. Although they were called the Catholic Monarchs, in actuality they were Jews, Jewish

Christians," Carlos said. "If you study the history and especially if you look at the paintings, you will see the Jewish resemblance."

Carlos slipped off the throne and retrieved a large library book that was lying on the floor. Flipping the pages, he came to a side profile drawing of Carlos I of Spain, 1479-1516.

"Look at that nose!" Carlos laughed. "If that's not Jewish I don't know what is!"

Flipping the pages again, he came to the Felipe kings of the Hapsburg Dynasty, 1556-1746. The pictures were full color paintings and revealing.

"Carlos I married a Jewish girl and from that union came Felipe II. Look at him; he's a full blooded Jew!"

Carlos was self absorbed and indulgent; not aware of anything around him. But the Priest grew restless, knowing that the others were waiting. He wasn't quite sure why young Carlos was going on like this but the history lesson on the Jewishness of the Spanish Monarchs was certainly intriguing.

"Sir, don't be concerned about the Brethren. The meeting will start when we arrive and not a second before!" Carlos said, as if he could read the High Priest's thoughts.

"Move closer. I want you to see this," Carlos said, pulling at the Priest's arm.

"Look at Felipe II. See, he looks fully Jewish. Now look at his son, Felipe III and now his son, Felipe IV. A transformation is taking place. Do you see it?"

The Priest leaned in and squinted. Yes, he could see the change.

"Felipe II, III and IV married Gentile girls," Carlos said, turning the page. "And look what you get when you mate a Jew with a Gentile." Carlos turned the page to proudly show a full color portrait of Carlos II.

"A superior human being!"

The High Priest drew back and took in the portrait. It looked exactly like young Juan Carlos. The full length painting portrayed a gay man dressed in men's clothes. The slight feminine features, the coy girlish facial expression, and the obvious red lipstick, gave it away.

Even though he knew Carlos' logic of ethnicity was strangely askew, the homosexual implications were startling. But it wasn't for him to judge Carlos' sexual preferences. After all, he was a modern Jew, in a modern world; tolerant of all ethnic groups and preferences.

"This is the perfect expression of mankind today. Isn't it?" Carlos said. "Look at this beautiful painting! The uniting of the Jew and Gentile in one glorious gender."

Carlos was speaking as if he were possessed.

"And not only that, the divine union of the male and the female in one body; forming the perfect universal man!" Carlos said as if pleading with the High Priest to understand him.

"Jew, Gentile, man, woman! All in one person, ME!"

The High Priest did understand the young Juan Carlos perfectly. The revelation was overwhelming, and it made perfect sense. A Prophet would come and appeal to all mankind, not just Israel. And to all different kinds of people, including homosexuals.

Moses spoke of a man who would come from amongst his brethren Israel; a dynamic man, powerful and brilliant; able to appeal to the masses. A young man like young Juan Carlos. The High Priest was almost converted.

Is Juan Carlos that man? The one Moses predicted would come? Was young Carlos able to unite and lead his people, indeed the world, into the new age?

"I perceive you see my divine vision," Carlos said. "Let me put the cornerstone in place, so that you will have no doubt who I am.

"King Fernando and Queen Isabel, the first monarchs of Spain, were both from the tribe of Judah. Although my father is also from this holy lineage, his blood line has been watered down from four hundred years of Gentile intermarriages. This explains his weakness as a ruler.

"My mother, on the other hand, is a pure blooded Jew. No Gentile has polluted her," Carlos said.

"And guess what tribe she is from."

The Priest was nodding his head now realizing fully who Carlos was.

She is from the tribe of Judah, the Priest thought to himself.

"That's right, sir," Carlos said, reading his mind. "She is a pure blooded Jew from the divine line of David. And according to Scripture who am I?"

Carlos left the library book in the Priest's hands, sat back down on the Bishop's Throne, and crossed his legs. Carlos dangled his penny loafer on the end of his right foot, reassuming his kingly posture.

The High Priest stared at the girlish portrait of Carlos II in silence, then turned toward the throne and knelt in obeisance.

"You are *the* Prophet of Israel and of God," the Priest said with head bowed. He removed his headdress and laid it at Juan Carlos' feet. Beside the headdress he placed David's scroll and softly scooted it toward the Prophet without looking up.

"Master, this is a gift for your new temple," the High Priest offered.

Juan Carlos bent over, picked up the scroll, and unrolled it. He knew instantly what it was. All the pieces to Carlos' puzzle were magically falling into place. His Muslim friends would surely assent to his building a temple next to theirs. It was his divine right. They would never dare to deny Juan Carlos, their Prophet also, a tabernacle on the holy hill. They knew he would destroy them if they did.

"When my father dies," Carlos said, "I will be King Juan Carlos II, in the same manner as my forefather in that beautiful portrait. I will rule Spain from Madrid; then I will rule as king over the Western European Union from Brussels and then finally, I will declare myself the Divine One's holy prophet from the newly built temple in Jerusalem."

The Most Holy Brethren, as they like to call themselves, were waiting patiently in the Old Chapterhouse library which was the largest private room in the church. They were carefully studying Carlos' model of the temple that he proudly displayed on the conference table, lights and all.

Carlos had called the emergency meeting of the Brethren to discuss a solution to the Temple Mount problem and the Polycarp Directive. The conversion of the Jewish High Priest, at some point, was necessary for their plan to succeed. For it to happen tonight was a surprise to everyone, except for Carlos, who was their prophet. Carlos knew that he could convince the High Priest who he really was.

The Most Holy Brethren date back before Christ and were formed in order to preserve the identity of the twelve tribes of Israel. Scattered throughout history, they feared that Israel's twelve tribes would be lost. Secretly the individual tribes chose worthy volunteers who would represent them. From generation to generation, the representatives raised sons to carry on the tradition. Twice a year the Brethren would meet in different countries to discuss issues and swear in new members.

Eventually the families of Israel were dispersed throughout the world but the Brethren made an effort to settle in Europe. The myth of their secret existence fueled the families of Israel worldwide to contribute funds for their support. As a result, the Brethren became rich.

Over the centuries the Brethren collected billions of dollars. With the need for secrecy and a place to hide their money, the Brethren joined forces with the banking geniuses of the Knights Templar in the fourteenth century to form the Swiss Bank, the most secretive and mysterious banking system in the world. Today the Brethren own the elite Swiss banking system and manage their vast fortunes from there.

The Brethren represent the twelve tribes of Israel and their purpose has evolved from simply protecting their family heritage to global domination. For two thousand years, the Brethren were wandering Jews until five hundred years ago they came up with a plan to strategically plant themselves in select European countries. They grew in size and strength and rose through the ranks of European power. From Europe they would acquire the resources to one day reconquer the holy lands, kick out the Arab Muslims and bring the displaced Jews back to their homeland. Once Israel was secure in its own land, it would be a small step from Europe to conquer the world.

The Brethren's plot was suspected by the European fascists in the 1930s. The fascists knew that the Jews controlled every major industry in Europe and were burrowed in like ticks in the European political machine, poising themselves for rebellion and takeover. The only way to put an end to this rising threat was by persecution and extermination.

Adolf Hitler led the charge against murdering all the Jews he could. He found it impossible to uncover who the Brethren actually were. So Hitler reasoned that if he uncovered one or more of the twelve Brethren, he could subsequently track down all the Jewish heirs throughout the world, making sure none survived. Even then how could he be sure he got them all? In Hitler's mind it was easier to eliminate *all* the Jews, hopefully killing the Brethren in the process. His plan was to eliminate the Jews in Germany and then, once the art of killing was perfected, he would expand the genocide worldwide as his empire expanded.

Hitler reigned for 13 years and disappeared to South America, faking his own death, never to be seen publicly again. But The Brethren survived Hitler's onslaught of the Jews and live on today. They not only survived but are in full control of Europe, including Germany. Hitler has to be rolling over in his fiery grave.

Although millions of Jews were killed in Hitler's Final Solution, the final joke was on him! After the Second World War, the Brethren seized the opportunity, exploited Hitler's onslaught of the Jews, and negotiated a homeland for Israel in 1948. The Brethren conquered the Holy Land ahead of their schedule, thanks to Hitler.

The Brethren controlled the ten nations of the Western European Union: Belgium, France, Germany, Greece, Italy, Luxembourg, Netherlands, Portugal, United Kingdom, and Carlos' Spain.

Members retained power over England through the Prince of Wales. The Prince was another in a long line of Brethren representatives. The eleventh Brethren member settled in Poland. To round out the twelve, the United States government was under the

Brethren's control and had been for two hundred years.

The Holy Brethren are the most powerful and ruthless political group in the western world. As if that isn't enough, their roots are deeply religious, especially since Israel regained her homeland. It is believed that they possess the original writings of Moses and have secreted the scrolls away until they can bring them back into their beloved temple one day.

The Brethren's mission has broadened over the years to include fulfilling Moses' prophecies about the Messiah. The Scripture that drives them is the prophecy found in Moses' Deuteronomy 17: "When you come to the land which the Lord your God is giving you, and possess it and dwell in it, and say, 'I will set a king over me like all the nations that are around me,' you shall surely set a king over you whom the Lord your God chooses; *one from among your brethren you shall set as king over you*; you may not set a foreigner over you, who is not your brother."

This prophecy was fulfilled when David was anointed king over Israel. But the Brethren see it as a signpost for the crowning of their future king, the young prophet Juan Carlos.

The second prophecy is equally as important because the Brethren see how perfectly it pertains to their Carlos. It is found in Second Samuel 7 where God is speaking prophetically through King David about Israel's future, before David's death: "When your days are fulfilled and you rest with your fathers, I will *set up a seed after you*, who will come from your body, and I will establish his kingdom. *He shall build an house* for

My name, and I will establish the throne of his kingdom forever." The Brethren do not believe this prophecy has been fulfilled yet, even though some argue it pertains to Solomon. The basic problem with the Solomon theory is that Solomon did not "establish the throne of his kingdom forever." Solomon failed according to the Jews. A throne for a Jewish king has not existed for thousands of years! Let alone a national temple in Jerusalem from which to worship. The coming Jewish Messiah will build a temple in Jerusalem and establish his throne forever.

The Muslims have their shrine, the Catholics have their holy sites, but the Jews, who claim divine right to the land, do not have a holy temple. The Brethren and their Prophet are committed to changing all that in one fell swoop.

Carlos' conversion of the High Priest at the Bishop's Throne was key in implementing his plan to build a temple in Jerusalem. Without the main religious figure in Israel on board, it would be impossible to garner Jewish support for the task. The High Priest's job now was to be Juan Carlos' spokesperson and convince Israel that Carlos was their coming Prophet and king, the fulfillment of Scripture.

When the wooden doors to the library opened, the Brethren rose from their chairs and bowed their heads as Carlos entered the room. He couldn't remember a time when they did not bow to him. The High Priest followed behind carrying David's temple scroll. He placed it on the table where Carlos would be sitting.

Carlos embraced each delegate and whispered, "Peace to Jerusalem." The Brethren whispered in return, "From Jerusalem to the world." Then each delegate kissed the Star of David on the front of Carlos' golden crown.

Before he was seated, Carlos held out his arms and praised the temple on the table. The Brethren broke out in applause, nodding their heads, smiling at one another. With Israel established and Jerusalem back under their control, all that was left was building the temple. They knew only the coming Messiah could accomplish that. From the temple he and his prophet would conquer the world, end world hunger, and bring peace to the world. The Brethren also knew that they were in a favored position to rule and reign with Carlos and the coming Messiah over the world. They weren't in this for nothing.

Carlos introduced the High Priest from Jerusalem and together they explained in detail how they would build the temple within ten years. Carlos planned to celebrate his thirtieth birthday in Jerusalem and dedicate the holy temple at the same time. With great procession and the Brethren at his side, he envisioned marching gallantly into the Jerusalem Temple with the coming glorious Messiah, not on a lowly donkey like the phony Christ did two thousand years ago, but upon a beautifully majestic white steed. The Brethren envisioned Carlos with the Messiah taking the throne, all gloriously televised to the world of course.

"And speaking of world wide television," Carlos said, "Who is this Manny Bernstein character, is he a Jew?"

"It's Benson, sir," the representative from the United States said, "Manny Benson. And he's not a Jew as far as we can tell. Our genealogical people have traced him back pretty far and see no connection to Israel."

"Of course he's not a Jew. Look at him," Carlos said, holding up a London newspaper with Manny's color picture on the front page. "He's obviously a flat nosed Gentile!"

"Yes, we have intel on him. He was born in Arizona to a Christian minister. A wife and daughter. Brother died in High School. Owns an insurance agency. Is forty years old and can barely read and write. There is nothing distinguished about him and, in my estimation, pretty easy to deal with," the U.S. representative said.

"Oh, I can see that," Carlos said sarcastically, "Didn't he get away with killing two of our operatives a few days ago? Pretty clever fellow I would say!"

"Not exactly, sir. Reports say the cloud killed them. We have some extraordinary pictures the two men took before they died." The U.S rep passed the digital copies over to Carlos.

"What is this?" Carlos yelled. "Are you kidding me? This is nothing more than an old parlor trick, done with smoke and mirrors." He passed them around for the others to see.

"Yes, that may be true but we have to explain to our people what happened tonight in Benson's meeting. Some of us saw it first hand on television. Aerial views of a burning cloud, Benson's face on fire, and the miracles. Pretty impressive stuff, don't you think?"

"First of all, doesn't Scripture speak of a son of perdition, in Daniel I believe, who will come to deceive with lying wonders; to steer the world after him?" Carlos said.

"Excuse me sir," the representative from France said, "I believe it is the Christians and the Catholics that speak of an anti-Christ that will come and do as you say."

"Well, gentlemen, if the world needs an anti-Christ then Manny Benson is your man! Born on June 6, 1966," Carlos said, reading from an open file.

"Isn't 666 the number of the Christian's anti-Christ?" Carlos asked, not wanting an answer.

Carlos reached for a Bible that was sitting on the shelf and flipped it open to Revelation 13. He didn't want the Brethren to know he had most of the Christian Bible memorized.

"Right here it says, 'Let him who has understanding calculate the number of the beast, for it is a number of a man: his number is 666.'" Carlos said and flipped the pages back to another passage.

"Even an imbecile can see that Bernstein's birthdate is 666 and his fortieth birthday was June 6, 2006, for crying out loud! Didn't all this cloud stuff start occurring around his birthday?

Soon he'll claim he's Moses because Moses was forty years old when he left Egypt and then forty years after that he delivered Israel; and then Israel wandered with Moses for forty years," Carlos laughed. "Did you see the way he held his arms out when the cloud came down tonight? That was classic Moses."

Carlos put his head down, silently speed reading the book of Matthew. When he found the passage in Chapter 24, he held his finger on the page, looked up at the Brethren and recited the verses aloud from memory. "Then if anyone says to you, 'Look, here is the Christ!' or 'There!', do not believe it. For false Christs and false prophets will rise and show great signs and wonders to deceive, if possible, even God's people. Therefore if they say to you, 'Look, He is in the desert!' do not go out."

"This is the Christian Christ who makes these statements. They believe whatever is written here, the fools!" Carlos said. "I don't believe this rubbish but they do! So use their own Scriptures against this Manny imposter. They are like sheep. They will believe anything we tell them!"

"Yes, indeed," the representative from Germany said, "He's a false Christ! That explains his signs and miracles. My constituency is all too familiar with false Christs and charismatic men that lead the masses astray," he said, referring to Hitler.

"And for our religious populous," the rep from Belgium said, "all we have to do is lead them to this Scripture, spoken by their Christ, to confirm that they are not to go out to the desert in Arizona to see this deceiver! This is perfect. My people will buy it, hook, line and sinker!"

"Of course they will buy it because it is the truth," Carlos said. "We have nothing to worry about, gentlemen, in regards to this imposter. Let me tell you why. These Christians basically give up once their leaders die. John the Baptist was beheaded and what became of his disciples? Jesus deceived the people for only three years and was easily killed by our people. What became of Him? His disciples began a Catholic church that did nothing but persecute our people with the Crusades. What is the Catholic Church today? Nothing but a bunch of weak Gentiles."

"What about Polycarp?" asked the Prince from England.

The atmosphere in the room went chilly. The Prince is not the brightest of the Brethren but he is the most educated. It is said he knows a little about everything, but to run a country?

"What about Polycarp, Prince?" Carlos said, looking away from him with a disgusted look on his face.

Ever since the Princess was murdered, Carlos and the Brethren had lost respect for him. For a thousand years murder had served its purpose in furthering the Brethren's cause. But when a member jeopardized the safety of the others, with a personal agenda, it was not tolerated. The Prince was suffering the consequences of his continual foolishness by not being allowed to rule as King of England. The Brethren wouldn't allow it.

"Polycarp was a disciple of the Apostle John and if the legend of the blood can be believed,

Polycarp must have received the blood from the Apostle," Carlos said.

"It is remotely possible that the phony Christ's blood could have survived to Polycarp and that the blood had some special powers that caused fires and clouds to appear to deceive the people. But again, what happened after Polycarp was killed?"

"Nothing happened," the Prince said. "The blood legend died with Polycarp."

"That is correct, the legend died but before it did, Polycarp turned our world upside down!" Carlos pounded the table in sudden anger.

"How long was Polycarp allowed to operate before our Brethren got to him? Ten, twelve years?"

"It may have been as much as twenty years," the delegate from the United States said, "No one really knows, sir."

"Well, I purpose that we let this character alone for a while and see what he does. He may burn out on his own. If he is perceived as a threat, then we'll put an end to him and swiftly. Once he is gone, the fire and the smoke will vanish into thin air!"

Chapter Eleven

It was true what Manny's father always said, "where God guides, He provides," because at the end of the week Manny received three donations totaling fifty-nine million dollars. The Scovall Foundation donated twenty-two million; a university in Jerusalem twelve million; and the Roman Catholics at the Vatican gave twenty-five million dollars. The total did not include the hundred thousand dollars that trickled in from individual donors; people evidently appreciative of Manny's new ministry. With the Icon Collector's donation the total went well over sixty million dollars. Not bad for one week.

Three Christian television networks wanted to do an interview with Manny and talk about a regular daily program. The cloud, the fire, and the glowing face on Sunday made quite an impression; everyone wanted a piece of it. Not to mention the ratings that went through the roof. This was a money maker.

The newspapers were having a field day too. The color picture of Manny's glowing face and outstretched arms was on the front page of every publication. The rip in Manny's t-shirt and the Jason Whitehead image was airbrushed out. The saying on the back of his t-shirt was changed to *Imagine There Is A Heaven* in jest. The newspaper headlines read, "Holy Manny or Holy Moses!" A Middle Eastern paper said, "Watch Out Egypt, Here Comes Manny Moses."

The World Inquirer showed a front page picture of Manny's face pasted on the body of Moses holding the Ten Commandments. The headline read: "Manny Says He Is Moses Risen From The Dead!" The following article was three pages long with pictures of Manny standing on the platform like Moses. There was an aerial photo of Moses walking toward the tent with his face aglow. The World Inquirer put a robe on Manny and a wooden staff in his hand. The grocery store magazine scribbled a beard on Manny and he looked just like Moses. There was even a funny picture of Manny talking with Jason Whitehead saying, *Manny secretly meets with Jason Whitehead in the Vatican for inspiration.*

Not surprisingly, many of the major Christian denominations were split over Manny's new ministry. The Conservative Baptists and some evangelical groups were warning their congregations to stay clear of this heretical nonsense. After all, miracles, signs and wonders were not for today, but of the devil.

Other Bible believing churches said that Manny's ministry was not Scriptural, citing Biblical passages pertaining to the 'decency and order' rule. The Sunday meeting was certainly not orderly, at least when it comes to today's church standards. But Manny's meetings were certainly Biblical and Scriptural according to Manny. "Just read your Bible," he would say. "Jesus did these things every day!"

Amazingly, every single person who attended the Sunday morning service was healed. Among the healed was Mrs. Kingston, Manny's mother-in-law. She suffered from heart disease the last few years and if it weren't for medications, she would be bedridden today, or worse, dead. It was very difficult for her to get around, laboring daily under a weak heart. For years Joanne tried to prepare herself for the inevitable; a phone call that her mother had died from a heart attack. But instead Joanne received a call that her mother was instantly healed. On Monday, Mrs. Kingston got a clean bill of health from her doctor and had been calling everyone to testify about it.

And Manny was overwhelmed with the thousands of reports on the incredible healings and miracles performed on Sunday. His home, office and church phone were constantly ringing. Something had to be done. So Manny met at his home with Pastor Benson, Rock, and Mr. Kingston to discuss the situation.

Mr. Kingston became involved in helping Manny the minute he was healed on Sunday. It was not a physical healing like his wife's heart problem; he was emotionally healed and ready for action!

All his life Mr. Kingston had issues with money. His father was a poor farmer in Arizona who survived the depression and Mr. Kingston grew up vowing to secure himself financially so that poverty would not destroy him, like it did his father. He wanted to have more for his wife and children than what he had growing up.

Mr. Kingston's emotional problems and bitterness stemmed from his father's suicide when he was in high school. The harsh Arizona summers and the terrible droughts contributed to the suicide, Mr. Kingston reasoned. The worst part of the ordeal was watching his mother deteriorate both mentally and physically after the death. Mr. Kingston had to quit school in order to work the farm and care for the family.

For many years Mr. Kingston farmed the harsh land he inherited from his father in bitterness. The thousands of acres were worthless except for growing cotton and milking cows. It was too hot otherwise. No one wanted to live in the hot valley for any reason other than farming. The Mormons settled in the valley, by necessity, to get away from the persecution they experienced in Missouri. If it weren't for religious persecution, the Mormons would not have settled here either.

The dry desert land was good for nothing but eeking out a meager living for the brave soul who could endure the conditions. But all that changed after World War II with the invention of the air conditioner. Investors from the mid-western states and California wanted a piece of Arizona after that.

The twenty-five mile wide Phoenix east valley exploded in population from the 1950s to the 1990s as a result of the air conditioner. Struggling farmers quickly sold their land to ambitious home developers, becoming wealthy in the process. Land that was once harsh and worthless became priceless as hoards of people moved to the valley to get away from the big polluted cities, and to golf in the sun.

Mr. Kingston struggled to successfully farm the land until several large land developers from California began to make him offers. Instead of giving the developers the land they initially wanted in Scottsdale, Mr. Kingston made a counter offer for the land he considered worthless in Gilbert. In the process he became wealthy overnight. For the next forty years, Mr. Kingston sold property at a premium in Scottsdale, Mesa, Chandler, and Gilbert, becoming a multimillionaire in the process. But even with all the wealth, Mr. Kingston remained crippled with bitterness until Sunday morning when he was set free.

The cloud entered Manny's living room where the meeting was held when Pastor Benson opened in prayer. It clung to the ceiling and Manny was the first to see it.

"Look, we have company!" Manny said.

"That cloud is the reason we're here," Pastor Benson replied.

"It's a good thing too because I haven't a clue what we're doing."

"Well, I know what I'm doing," Mr. Kingston said, inspired by the cloud. "The Lord wants me to give you the one hundred and twenty acres I've been trying to sell by the freeway!"

"And I'm going to quit farming and follow Manny around the world!" Rock said, wild eyed.

"I'm supposed to help you build a stadium," Pastor said, rubbing his hands together, looking over at his son.

"On top of the property donation, I'm going to donate thirty million," Mr. Kingston said to Pastor Benson, pulling out his checkbook.

"Rock and I are to go around the world and preach the gospel until the stadium is finished," Manny said at the end, shaking his head.

Manny went to the window and looked out at the swimming pool where this all began over a week ago. He could still see the oily smudge on the pool deck where the clay pot was broken. The area around Manny's house was covered in shade and a light was flickering off the pool. Manny ran to the front of the house and looked through the shutters. The security force that guarded the property was all lying on the ground. Camera crews were aiming at the roof and the neighbors stood in their doorways craning to see.

"Quick, turn on the T.V.," Manny said.

Rock clicked it on from the remote. The local station interrupted regular programming to show Manny's house on fire and the security officers dressed in black lying on the ground. Sirens blared in the back ground and the news helicopter caught the whole scene from the air, following the fire truck to the house.

"With that cloud out there, no one is going to interrupt us. So let's finish the meeting and figure out what we're supposed to do next," Manny said, clicking off the television and sitting back down.

The three men were certainly not alone. The presence of God hovered in the room. The Lord told them exactly what to do and how to do it. They were reminded of Moses and how God spoke to him from the cloud on the mountain. They looked over at Manny to see if his face would start glowing again and when it didn't, they shrugged their shoulders and continued on with the meeting.

It was decided that Pastor Benson supervise the planning and the building of the stadium. Pastor knew best about parking, seating, and the location of restrooms. He was to continue pastoring the thousands who were being saved under the big tents. Pastor was to hire a staff to liaison between the thousands of ministers around the world who were calling for Manny to minister in their churches.

Mr. Kingston became the ministry's administrator, handling all the financial affairs. He would hire assistants and accountants to help sort out the finances. He set up the non-profit organization, hiring accountants and attorneys for the End of the Age Ministries. He hired a travel agency to manage Manny's worldwide itinerary. After a month, the travel agency worked full time for Manny.

Mr. Kingston evicted a telemarketer group and a computer repair business from the office complex he owned near the church to house the new ministry staff. He organized and hired security teams to provide Manny and his wife twenty-four hour protection.

With eighty-nine million dollars in the bank (after Kingston's donation), Mr. Kingston decided to buy a long range jet for the ministry.

The Challenger was an eight passenger jet that Mr. Kingston was planning to purchase for himself. Instead, he bought it for Manny. It flew anywhere in the world and had plenty of room to stretch out. As a non profit organization, most of the twenty thousand dollar a month jet expense could be written off.

"But we don't need an expensive private jet," Manny said raising his voice. "Jesus didn't have a private jet," he argued, trying to make a point.

"It was Mr. Kingston who bought the jet with his own money," Ryan pushed back, "and donated it to your new ministry. It's already paid for."

"But don't you think twenty thousand a month is a lot of money to spend on maintaining a jet when it could go for other needed expenses?"

Sitting in the Phoenix International airport Manny and Ryan were having a heated conversation. Ryan was just a kid and Manny's newly assigned business manager. Mr. Kingston was friends with Ryan's famous father and hired him to take care of Manny's finances while on this first world crusade. Everyone in Manny's ministry world was trying to convince him of the practicality of having a private jet even though he couldn't believe how expensive they were to maintain. After all, Manny was still a small town insurance broker in his head. He just couldn't fathom the kind of money that was pouring in to cover all of the expenses.

Ryan looked frazzled. His three piece suit was rumpled from flying all night to meet Manny in the private lounge at the airport. Ryan was in his late twenties and had graduated from a popular Christian College with a business degree and a minor in church finance. He was brilliant with the numbers but a little short on vision for Manny's miracle ministry, at least that's what Manny thought.

"Yes, but Jesus didn't have to travel to every continent on the globe," Ryan replied. "My father has a jet and doesn't travel a third of what you are beginning to do!" Ryan's father was the pastor of the fourth largest church in America and a jet was simply part of the deal of being a big time pastor. When you raised as much money as he did, you got a jet!

"Look Ryan, what I mean to say is, the ministry of the kingdom is not about jets and houses and T.V. ministry programs. It's not about raising money, living comfortably, and selling books and tapes."

Ryan looked uncomfortable, shifting back and forth on one foot then the other, stuffed into his business suit. A briefcase was bursting at the seams in his right hand and a hi-tech global phone was in the other.

"Sit down Ryan and relax. Please." Manny patted the plush chair next to him and made him sit down. "Indulge me as I explain to you the concept of *this* ministry."

Manny called over the lounge attendant and asked Ryan what his favorite drink was: specialty water with a twist of lemon.

"What is ministry all about, Ryan?" Manny asked, reaching for his glass of tea.

"Well, I've heard you in interviews say it's about the Holy Spirit ministering to the people." Then Ryan leaned over and whispered very quietly into Manny's ear, "But my father says…"

Manny knew exactly what his father believed and all the other church leaders in the world. That, in his opinion, had been the problem ever since the first century of the church. Over the two thousand year history of the church, the power ministry of the Holy Spirit had been replaced by the powerless teaching from the Bible. The modern day church was so indoctrinated with Bible teaching and Bible teachers that there was no room for the manifestation of the power of the Spirit in the church. This had always been Manny's pet peeve and another reason he hadn't been a part of his dad's church.

"I love your father, Ryan. He is a great man. But to God greatness is not a matter of numbers or how much money we can raise for the church. That may be his calling, I don't know. All I know is what I have been called to do and that's to walk as closely in His footsteps as possible. Those footsteps, at this point, do not include me flying around in my own private jet."

Ryan shifted in his seat, looked down at Manny's shoes and shook his head. Manny always wore tennis shoes, always. Unless of course he was wearing flip flops. Even when Manny was wearing a business suit for his insurance business, he sported tennis shoes.

"Ryan, as you know, my ministry involves a unique manifestation of fire. I'm not much of a Bible teacher like your father is. An angel told me to bring His fire to the world and how can I bring His presence to the world if I'm whisked away in limousines, hiding behind armed guards and traveling in private jets?" Manny motioned toward the bustling crowds that were hurrying back and forth to catch their planes. "That, Ryan, *is* the ministry that God has called me to! If I am not with *them* all the time, then how am I to do this ministry?" Manny based this on the fact that Jesus was always with the people.

Ryan got a twinkle in his eye and said, "Traveling to all these countries is going to make you extremely tired. If you get so tired and get sick, how will you be able to minister to the people?" Ryan saw his father get burned out and knew what he was talking about. There were times when Ryan saw his father sign documents or read some financial form while in bed, too exhausted to move.

"I only have a few years to do this thing before the Lord returns," Manny said, standing up and stretching. "And I'm not going to be hiding out in mansions behind barbed wire fences and isolating myself because I am inconvenienced and get tired!" Ryan winced at Manny's harsh comments because his father, indeed, lived in a huge mansion with a razor fence around it. Manny, on the other hand, still lived in a little house in Arizona; but that was about to end.

"Look Manny," Ryan said, " I respect your integrity and all but how are you going to properly do this ministry for God if you die from exhaustion? And concerning a barbed wire fence? You're going to have to move from your little house in Arizona soon or your little town is going to run you out on a rail. Mr. Kingston informed me that he has received calls about the streets around your house being clogged with cars and people, day and night. The police department had to hire five more officers just to block off your street!" Ryan was animated now and wagging his finger at Manny. "*Your* ministry," Ryan said sternly, "donated $50,000 to *your* local police department, just to keep them from kicking you out of *their* town! But how long will that last?" Ryan was making perfect sense but Manny wasn't going to get caught up in another argument about his earthly affairs. He realized that Ryan was thinking of Manny's best interest and was most likely put up to this by his father and many of the leaders in the church who supported Manny's ministry. Everyone wanted to make sure that Manny took care of himself and didn't burn out. But what they didn't realize was that when Jesus called you and anointed you to do a job for Him, He gave you an abundance of the Spirit to carry you through any situation. "If I die, I die!" Manny would say. The thing is, there was plenty of money in reserve to buy two or three jets; Manny was just having a hard time comprehending it all.

A commotion of people was forming on the other side of the glass where Manny was sitting. There was a hazard of being recognized everywhere he went now. Manny heard Ryan say under his breath, "Here he goes again!" Rock was over in the corner of the lounge, laid out on a couch, sleeping. He rose from his slumber and sprang into action, leading Manny into battle. His job was to fend off the crazies who wanted to strangle Manny for one reason or another.

"You can't go in there," the security guard said to the people gathering and pounding on the door to the private lounge. "It is restricted!"

Manny put down his drink and told Ryan to stay right there. He would be right back. Ryan winked at Manny and said, "Go and see what God will do!"

"Exactly," Manny replied.

And God worked wonderful signs and wonders in that airport lobby as Rock and Manny simply stood there at the door of the lounge. Blind eyes were opened. Cancers were healed. Crutches were thrown to the carpet as crippled people walked. It was noisy and there were people rejoicing loudly. That whole section of the airport gathered around to see what was happening.

It was interesting that whenever God worked in this way, Manny's attention was not drawn to the crowds around him, but to someone else off to the side. This time there was a man standing in the entrance of a novelty shop to his right with a white bandage over one eye. There was white tape extending across the patch in an X pattern and a yellowish blotch could be seen in the middle of the bandage. It was obvious that he had recently come from the hospital and was probably flying back home. Manny motioned to him to come near and the man touched his chest to say, "Who me?" The man looked around to see if Manny was motioning for somebody else. When he realized that Manny wanted him, he started to walk toward him. When the man approached, Manny said, "For anyone still not believing, I want you to see an amazing miracle before your very eyes. Watch and believe!" Manny turned to the man and said, "Would you take off your patch?" He suddenly looked frightened and said, "But I have no eye. It's gone! It's ugly!" Manny said to him, "If you remove the bandage and let everyone see that you do not have an eye, maybe God will do a wonderful thing for you! See what God will do!" With that the man fumbled with the tape on his forehead and began to rip it off. A gasp came over the crowd as they witnessed the empty orange eye socket. Then something amazing happened. The man doubled over and screamed, cupping his eye socket with both hands. "It burns! It burns!" Then the man straightened up, took his hands away from his face and there it was, for everyone to see; a brand new eye ball! "I can see! I can see! I can see!" hollered the man. Dozens of onlookers were crying and raising their hands along with the airport security guards.

Manny dismissed the crowd and told them not to miss their flights. He asked the man with the new eye if he would like to join them in the private lounge. Manny wanted to show him off to Ryan, who was still sitting in his chair sobbing profusely. Ryan seemed to always weep when the Holy Spirit showed up to work signs and wonders. Often when he and Manny worked together on a financial project, he would burst out crying. Sometimes they had to stop working because the salty tears would gush down from his face and ruin the paperwork. Rock on the other hand seemed to not mind any of it and always found the best place to take a nap.

"Ryan, I want to introduce you to...," Manny waited for the man to give his name but he was reluctant to do so. *He must still be in shock from receiving his new eyeball,* Manny thought. *It's not every day you get a new one of those!*

"My name is Eric Von Baederhoff," he finally said, "Very nice to meet you."

Ryan was still sobbing like a baby when they both shook hands. Ryan sat up with a start and said, "I know that name." Wiping the tears from his eyes with his wrinkled sleeve, he looked carefully at Mr. Von Baederhoff and said, "And I know that face! You were on the cover of Time Magazine last month!" Ryan vigorously stood up and took Von Baederhoff's hand and said, "You look better without that patch over your eye, don't ya think?"

Ryan quickly retrieved his bulky briefcase and rifled through it to find last month's Time Magazine. Sure enough, there he was, Mr. Eric Von Baederhoff, Time magazine's Man of the Year, in living color, black eye patch and all. Ryan handed Manny the magazine and he thumbed through the pages until the article was found.

Eric Von Baederhoff was in his late 30s and quite handsome without the eye patch. His grandfather was one of the early pioneers of the airplane industry and started his own airplane manufacturing company in the 1930s. After the Second World War, Eric's father Johansson Von Baederhoff, took over the company and retooled the manufacturing plant to include jet engine parts. By the late 1960s, Von Baederhoff Aerodynamics had become the premier jet manufacturer in the world. Today, under Eric Von Baederhoff's leadership, the company had risen head and shoulders above the competition. Von Baederhoff Aerodynamics designed and built planes for every country in the world and had become a multibillion dollar company.

"Does this type of thing happen often?" Von Baederhoff asked Ryan, nodding towards the crowd outside.

"Yep, all the time. It's been going on like this for a couple of months now. Haven't you heard of him in the news?" Ryan replied.

Von Baederhoff was handed a small compact mirror from his assistant. "Yes, I've heard of him from the news reports, but I thought he was a crackpot. I never thought anything like this was really possible. But now I know it is possible!" Von Baederhoff put the mirror up against his nose and stared directly into his own blue eyes. "Man, that's amazing, isn't it?"

The lounge was nearly empty, except for Von Baederhoff's four bodyguards, the two airport security personnel at the door, and Rock looking for another place to curl up like a cat to snooze.

After handing the magazine back to Ryan, Manny said to Von Baederhoff, "Aren't you going to be late for your flight?"

Von Baederhoff broke out into a wide smile that revealed his perfect teeth. "You're kidding right?" Von Baederhoff looked over at Ryan and asked, "He's kidding right? Don't tell me he doesn't know who I am!"

Ryan broke out into a smile also and looked down at Manny's shoes again. "With Manny here, what you see is what you get! He's getting to know the Father, Son and Holy Spirit but hasn't a clue who Forbes' richest man on earth is. You know the saying, 'Too heavenly minded...?'"

"I know who Bill Gates is." Manny protested. "And the guys over at Titan come to my meetings. Where do you think I get my shoes?"

Every week since the fire appeared, Manny had received about five boxes of brand new Titan shoes in size eleven. FedEx dropped them off at the house like clockwork and Manny's wife piled the boxes of shoes up in the garage. She couldn't give them away fast enough. Manny called Titan Shoes a couple of weeks ago and told them he didn't need any more shoes, but the next day he received another five boxes with a note attached saying, "It's the least we can do!" Not only that, but his wife got shoes and his daughter got shoes. They had Titan hats, Titan sweatshirts, Titan gloves. It was like Titan Christmas every week. There was a picture of Manny in the Los Angeles Times wearing a Titan ball cap and his ministry received a million dollar donation from

Titan Shoes. When Manny called the headquarters in Portland, Oregon to tell them that they must have made a mistake, they told him that the day after his picture was in the Times their sales in southern California went up one hundred percent. There was a merchandising opportunity in the Christian market and the world's businesses were suddenly jumping on the bandwagon. The one million dollars was a small percentage of the gross sales for the day.

"You mean to say he didn't know who I was when he picked me out of the crowd?" Eric Von Baederhoff asked. Ryan shook his head in the negative.

Eric Von Baederhoff was now considered the richest man in the world according to most estimates, surpassing William Door at MajorShift. This had made him quite a favorite of the tabloids. His handsome face and the trademark black patch were constantly splashed across the newspapers worldwide. He was called "The Pirate of the Skies" because of his shrewd business dealings and with the eye patch, he looked a little like a pirate.

"I had no idea who you were when I saw you standing outside of the crowd." Manny said. "I never have read the newspapers or watched the news on T.V. I used to prefer watching the sports channels! I love football." Von Baederhoff handed the mirror back to his assistant.

"God told me he was healing you the second I saw you with that bandage over your eye. It makes no difference to me who you are! God's love is for everyone. No matter what!" Ryan nodded in the affirmative. "Anyway, it's time for us to go," Manny said, holding out his hand. "God bless you Mr. Von Baederhoff. My guys are telling us our plane is ready."

"Wait a minute. Wait just one darn minute," Von Baederhoff said as he grabbed Manny's arm and wouldn't let go. "You say you don't know me, which I don't believe, and then you say God has given me a new eyeball, which I do believe and now you say you are going to get on an airplane and leave?" Von Baederhoff moved to within inches of Manny's face and said, "Do you know how many preachers like yourself ask me for money everyday? I'm sick of them! Bunch of phonies! And you are telling me that you are *not* interested in my money? Come on!" Manny could feel the heat from his breath when he spoke but Manny did not back down, even though the burly bodyguards made a move in his direction. Manny knew God would strike them before they could strike him! At least Manny was hoping so.

"Look," Manny said, "I really do not want or need your money. Really!" He backed away slightly. "Obviously you are a very important man, with bodyguards, personal assistants and with your face on Time Magazine. But I am not an important man. The only real and important thing I have in my life is this fire and that is very precious to me. He will never leave me. My wife might leave me, my daughter might leave me, and I could lose all my best friends, but God will never leave me."

Manny looked at the clock on the wall and realized he needed to stay here with Mr. Von Baederhoff, so he backed up and sat down. "Mr. Von Baederhoff, please sit here with me and let's talk." Von Baederhoff motioned off the bodyguards and sat down beside Manny. Rock found an executive leather bench and was lightly snoring off in the distance.

"Mr. Von Baederhoff, I do not have one thin dime to my name, yet there are millions of dollars in a bank account somewhere that Ryan here is taking care of for the ministry. The money keeps pouring in and I don't know where it is coming from. I don't ask anyone for a nickel." Manny put His arm around Von Baederhoff's shoulder as he began to weep. "I assure you, Mr. Von Baederhoff, I don't want your money!"

Von Baederhoff and Manny huddled in the lounge for over an hour. There seemed to be an umbrella of God's presence that lingered as they sat in the airport lounge and talked. Ryan moved to a round table in the corner pretending to be analyzing insurance documents. They could hear him over there rustling papers and crying like a baby. The fire of God at work again.

Chapter Twelve

Manny, Rock and Ryan flew out from Phoenix International in July for their first worldwide On Fire Tour. Two meaty bodyguards trained in martial arts and international protection accompanied the group. Before the plane left the airport the guards were on laptops and speaking into global phones, setting up security in the different countries.

The newspapers reported they witnessed a fire on top of the jet when it lifted off. The main tower watched anxiously to see if the plane would explode and come hurtling to the ground. Airport emergency teams were alerted but the jet made a turn and disappeared beyond the horizon.

The first churches that wanted Manny to visit were in the same countries he saw in his world vision map: Australia, New Zealand, Japan, the Philippines, Thailand, and China. Japan and China tried to block Manny's visit, but there were enough supporters to not only allow Manny access into the country, but access to their largest stadiums.

The crowds quickly became so large that Pastor Benson had to limit the rest of Manny's visits to coliseums, soccer stadiums, or open air meetings seating fifty thousand or more. The churches in each country had to work together in order for Manny to visit successfully. This brought the different factions together as a team.

They rented the facilities, paid for Manny's security detail and provided usher and parking support.

Advertising expense never was an issue because the world began to know who Manny Benson was. Many of the mass meetings were broadcast around the globe, as were the dates, locations, and the times of his meetings.

Manny became an international celebrity overnight.

What was unique about Manny's meetings was the fact that everyone attending was healed, regardless of their malady, affliction, or sickness. Blind eyes opened, the crippled walked, cancers were cured, deaf ears heard, new arms and legs grew from scarred stumps. You name it, they were healed. This was the reason for the large turnout. People were not required to stir up their faith or to suffer through long sermons by windy preachers. All they had to do was get to one of the meetings and they would be healed automatically. Manny never laid a hand on anyone for healing.

Another distinguishing factor of Manny's international ministry was the fiery cloud that hovered above his head. He simply raised his hands like Moses and the cloud would do the rest.

There was no music or entertainment, yet the meetings lasted over three hours! Manny simply walked out on stage, leaned on the podium, and people were saved, healed, and delivered. Dancing, shouting, and singing ensued, but there were no choirs, no rock bands, no special songs.

Some churches were offended that Manny didn't take offerings or beg for money. They thought he was missing a huge opportunity and didn't hesitate to tell him so. Manny suggested the organizers place garbage cans throughout the event and see what happens. The healed masses were so appreciative, the rubber trash cans overflowed with cash.

In the first three months Manny and his crew visited sixteen countries and conducted over sixty meetings. Ushers in the stadiums said the number of people healed could not be calculated because the crowds were so large.

Manny made it clear that he had nothing to do with the healings. He couldn't even say these things were happening because he was faithful or obedient or a good person. It was by God's grace and God's grace alone.

"Don't believe me," Manny would tell the interviewers, "you guys have taped practically every meeting. Go and watch the reruns for yourselves. You'll see that Manny Benson has nothing to do with these miracles!"

Secretly though Manny knew it had something to do with the vial of blood he kept in his pocket, but he didn't know what it was.

Before Manny and his crew took on the continent of Africa, they returned home to rest and regroup. Manny missed his dog and wondered how the circus tents were holding up. Joanne and Amy missed their families and church friends. They were excited about returning home and seeing everyone.

Rock on the other hand was so full of enthusiasm, he wanted to keep going and conquer Africa before going home, which would have taken another four months to accomplish. He was outvoted.

The body guards were exhausted and had outdone themselves under the extreme conditions. One guard named Sam said he was healed of a venereal disease in the New Zealand meetings and became a believer in the following meeting in the Philippines. He immediately became part of the family.

The pilot they called Skipper had the same thing happen to him. He never attended a single meeting but was healed of a severe allergy in the Melbourne airport. Skipper was inspecting one of the wings when he fell asleep on the wing and dreamed of a cat sitting on his chest. When he awoke, the paramedics were bundling him into the emergency vehicle with an oxygen mask on his face. Skipper got a glance at the jet before they slid him into the ambulance and swore he saw the plane on fire. They took him to an airport infirmary for observation. A fat hairy tabby cat wandered into the infirmary, jumped up on the bed and sat down next to his face. When he removed the mask and breathed in deeply, he found the allergy was completely gone.

"To tell you the truth, I have nothing to do with the miracles!"

Manny sat nervously, sweating under the hot lights as the reporter grilled him for details.

"You say this, Mr. Benson, but the fact is, these strange things do not occur any place else in the world, as far as I know! How can you say you have nothing to do with them? The miracles always occur where you are! How do you explain that?"

Manny reached over and touched the man's arm. The reporter was sweating and his makeup was beginning to smear on his forehead where he kept wiping it with his sleeve. Manny could see that the reporter was agitated and having a difficult time comprehending the miracles that had just manifested in his meeting that night. Three hours earlier at the First Assembly Church that seated 30,000 people, God worked signs and wonders for all to see.

Probably what had this reporter especially disturbed was what he witnessed with his own eyes near the beginning of the meeting. A large man in the second row had a convulsion, grabbed his chest and collapsed onto the people seated next to him. When they cried out for help, a doctor a few rows back came forward to offer assistance. The ushers also rushed to the man. The doctor took hold of the heart attack victim and cradled him in his arms. Manny was told later that the doctor's head moved back and forth as if to say, "There is nothing I can do. He's dead!"

Noise and outbursts were quite common in Manny's meetings because God was moving among the people working signs and wonders. All of Manny's life he'd heard preachers say that things in the church should be done in decency and order, but when he sees God moving in his meetings, who was he to tell God what to do? And that was the case with this man in the second row. He figured if God wanted to have a man fall over onto the floor in church, then have at it. It was not an unusual thing to see people in Manny's meetings, in the thousands, laying on a church's floor or a stadium's aisle, dead to the world.

An usher had to climb the ten steps up the platform to whisper in Manny's ear that the man in the second row had died. Manny had no idea! He opened his eyes and squinted to see what was going on. Twenty people were standing around the doctor, who was holding the dead man in his arms, all looking in Manny's direction. A couple of ushers ran toward the exit doors but no one else in the church had any idea what was going on. Manny shouted to the ushers to "Stop" and *not* call an ambulance. "The man is not dead," he said, "He's only asleep!"

Before the usher came forward to tell Manny of the heart attack, Manny was caught up in one of his visions. "Anything after the cloud arrives," Manny would say, "is His concern, not mine! God made it clear many times that He is the leader of my meetings, not me! If He is capable of creating the universe, then He is more than capable of running my meetings."

Sometimes Manny saw visions of the Lord during his meetings and sometimes he heard God's voice. Most times he just sat and worshipped along with everyone else. But this time Manny saw Jesus being taken down from the cross and thrown to the ground in a heap. In the vision he was looking at Jesus' broken body when a voice said, "Don't worry. He's asleep. He will rise up again!" It was at this moment the usher whispered into Manny's ear that the man was dead.

The ushers in the back of the church stood still as Manny got up from his chair.

"If there is anyone here tonight that does not believe, you will after you see this! For this man right here," Manny pointed toward the second row, "died just a moment ago from a heart attack." The whole congregation craned their necks at once to see the dead man. "And this has happened tonight so that you will believe!"

You could tell that the man was deader than a doornail because the color in his face had turned a bleached white. There was a purple color deepening around his eyes. He could not have been more dead than a sack of potatoes for that's what the man reminded Manny of, draped across the doctor's lap: a big ol' sack of potatoes!

"Rise up!" Manny yelled, shocking the crowd as they jolted in their seats. About a hundred people in the congregation suddenly stood to their feet. And the man with the heart attack sucked in air and jerked his head upward as if coming out of a pool of water. The doctor, in his shock, moved quickly away from the dead man and let him drop to the floor. The crowd gasped when they heard the "thump" of the man hit the red carpeted floor. A voice inside Manny's head said, *Don't worry. He's not dead. He will rise up again!* He would have laughed out loud if it weren't so serious. Fortunately, the man survived the fall, shaking his head while others helped him to his feet. Manny went back onto the platform, sat down, and closed his eyes.

"Are you OK?" Manny asked the reporter. The reporter stopped mid-sentence and "plop," down went his head on the interviewer's desk. The reporter's forehead hit squarely upon the yellow pad of paper that was before him. Manny heard the pen that was once in his hand falling off the desk and rolling across the floor away from them.

"Continue rolling," Manny said to the cameramen, "you are witnessing God in action!"

One of the things Manny noticed about the reporter when he first met him was the large lump protruding from his lower neck, about the size of a small tomato. The collar of his shirt partially covered it up. He watched as the lump shrank in size and disappeared. All that remained was a tiny slit where the lump once was, as if a doctor cut the skin with a scalpel on live television.

Manny heard another loud thump and he turned in his chair to see the program director fall to the ground, losing the contents of her clipboard as it clattered to the floor. Out of instinct Manny jumped up out of his chair in order to offer a hand but was pulled back by the short microphone cord that went under his shirt and attached to his shirt collar. Then he realized he was on live national television with no one to report the "news." So Manny turned towards the camera with the red flashing light and said, "Ladies and gentlemen, God is working a miracle before your very eyes tonight. You see it for yourself. And, I might add, I have nothing to do with these miracles."

Manny was constantly being accused of working witchcraft or magic to perform these amazing signs and wonders. The harsh accusations came from prominent leaders in the Christian church. They said he mesmerized the people and put them under a spell. Some had claimed that Manny was the anti-Christ. But all he really did in his meetings was simply sit or stand at the podium and let God do the rest.

"It is God who is performing what you are seeing here tonight. It is by His hand that this man has been healed. You have seen that for yourselves."

Manny heard screaming behind him. He turned to see the program director sitting on the black painted studio floor waving her right hand back and forth saying, "Oh, my God! Oh my God! I can't believe it! I can't believe it!" All the cameras in the studio whirled around and out of the corner of Manny's eye he saw the television monitor focus in on the director's fingers. One of the cameramen gasped and said, "No way! No way!" The man on Camera-Two yelled, "Are we getting this? Are we getting this?" So Manny glanced over to the men in the sound booth and they were giving a thumbs up. Another amazing miracle had just taken place.

Since Manny could not move because of his microphone, he motioned for a man off to the side in a bright yellow shirt to help the director get up.

"Help her up and bring her over here, please. We want to know what happened."

The director got on her feet and wobbled over to Manny, who was standing under the bright lights. America was watching.

"What happened to you? What's going on?" Manny asked.

He looked over and saw the reporter attempting to lift his head off the table. The reporter gave a mighty try, then surrendered helplessly. His head plopped back down on the yellow pad with a thud.

The program director could hardly stand up. She was trembling all over and kept shaking her right hand as if it were on fire. Her face had a look of terror. She glanced at her hand and then back at Manny. He shrugged his shoulders as if to say, "Don't look at me!"

"I can't believe it," she kept saying.

Manny interrupted her and asked again, "What has happened to your hand?"

She held it up and said, "My finger. My finger. I got my finger back. I got my finger back!"

When Evelyn was twelve years old, her father bought a beautiful ring for her birthday. It was her first ring. That night as she was playing in the attic at home, she got her ring finger caught on a nail as she was coming down the ladder. The attic ladder slipped and her finger tore away from her hand. She hung by her finger with her full weight upon it. She was rushed to the hospital but the doctors could not reattach the finger. This night in Studio B, God instantly grew her finger back on her hand!

"Do you want to know what is amazing about this?"she asked, displaying her new finger to

Manny. "Not only is there red polish on the new nail, exactly the same color as my other nails, but look here, God has put the ring on my finger as well!"

The man in the back booth was waving his index finger in a circular motion and mouthing something behind the smoked glass that Manny could not understand. The director wasn't any help. She just stood there staring at her new finger. So Manny turned toward the red light and someone yelled, "Ten seconds. Ten seconds." He looked into the camera lens and said, "It is by the power of God that these miracles have happened. Let Him touch you now."

"Two, one. Off the air!"

Out of the shadows at least fifteen crew members descended upon the listless reporter and the stunned program director. Manny stood off to the side trying desperately to untangle himself from the microphone wires. The reporter who had plopped upon the desk was helped to his feet and Manny watched as he drunkenly walked off to his dressing room.

It only makes sense, Manny told himself, *after an operation like that, a person has to have rest!*

"That was amazing," a man in thick glasses said, untangling Manny with the skill of a surgeon.

"Do you think God would heal me?" he asked. Manny told him that God could do anything, for anyone, at anytime. When the man freed him from the microphone wires, Manny pulled the man away from the crowd. The studio seemed to be filling up with people very quickly. Cast members taping a popular television show in the studio next door heard about the miracles and wanted to come see for themselves. Many of the actors knew the program director and couldn't believe their eyes. Then they started looking around for Manny.

"What's your name?" Manny asked.

"Herman. My name is Herman," he replied with a smile on his face.

"Well Herman, let's duck into the sound booth and see what God will do for you. OK?"

There were men and women sitting at dozens of monitors, some with headphones on their heads and some had them slung around their necks. Manny and Herman found a space in the corner of the booth and Manny told Herman that he did not do the miracles. It is God who does the miracles.

"Do you understand what I'm saying, Herman?" Herman looked like he was going to cry.

"You mean you aren't going to pray for my eyes?"

Manny told him that he didn't need to pray because God had already healed his eyes. Herman blinked several times. "That's weird. I can't see a thing. Everything is blurry."

"Herman," Manny said, "Take off your glasses!"

Herman removed his glasses and began to shout, "Holy Cow. I can see. I can see!" Herman bolted for the exit and began running all over the studio, yelling and shouting.

Manny bent over to pick up Herman's glasses off the floor and noticed little chunks of shaved skin lying on the inside of his glasses. Herman had been nearly blind because of severe cataracts in both eyes.

The local pastors who accompanied Manny to the television studio gathered around and ushered him to the lobby downstairs. Manny could still hear Herman shouting in the background.

"You don't want to go out there, Mr. Benson. The lobby is filled with a mob of people," the elevator guard said. "Let our security take you out the back way!"

Manny thought to himself, *What am I, a rock star? These people are the reason I am here. It's not an inconvenience. Let's go out there and see what God will do!*

So when the security guard opened the door, a crowd of people crushed in on them so much, Manny couldn't get out of the elevator.

"Hold the doors open and see what God will do!" Manny said.

When they stepped out of the elevator, the crowd of people parted in front of them. The ten pastors and the wary security guards followed as Manny calmly walked through the crowd toward the lobby doors leading to their vehicles outside.

Manny stopped in his tracks when he heard someone shout, "I'm healed. I'm healed. Praise the Lord, I'm healed." Then someone else shouted and then another.

In a matter of seconds the massive lobby of a thousand people erupted in praise to the Lord. Manny just stood there in the midst of the crowd of people holding onto the vial of Christ's blood in his pocket.

The security guards were the only ones without upraised arms. Their hands were positioned over their firearms, ready for a riot.

Manny finally said goodbye to the crowd and quietly left the building.

Manny's room at the Downtown Marriott was on the fifteenth floor. It had a wonderful view overlooking the city. He pulled up a chair and gazed out into the blackness beyond the city lights.

There was a time not too distant in the past when my life looked as dark as that horizon, he thought.

Manny was sad to think that while his life was turning around so wonderfully, the world's future didn't look so bright. It would be plunging into its own deep darkness.

The light on the room phone started blinking and then it rang. It was 12:33 am by Manny's watch.

"Sorry to bother you Mr. Benson," said the voice on the other end of the hotel phone, "but there are a few people here in wheelchairs that won't leave our lobby until you see them. Could you please help us out?"

Manny looked out the window and down toward the lobby. There were hundreds of people lining up across the parking lot and along the sidewalks.

"Don't call the police," Manny said. "I'll be right down."

He took a bite of the sandwich that was on the bedside table and looked at himself in the mirror.

"Ok Manny boy, let's go down there and see what God will do!"

Chapter Thirteen

It was September and, as was the custom this time of year, Manny and Rock went to their alma mater and from the back of the bleachers watched the football team workout. This season was different than any other season because four bodyguards trailed Manny to the high school. He was an international celebrity now and like it or not, crazy people wanted to do him harm.

Manny had only been home a week and people were yelling for autographs and wanting pictures. Since he was not promoting a movie or selling a record album, Manny didn't feel obligated to sign autographs. The idea of being a rock star bothered him. It was comforting to have the bodyguards close by, keeping the crowds away.

In amongst the growing number of gawkers were sick and wheelchair bound people hoping that Manny would heal them. If they could just touch the miracle man, they thought, healing would be theirs.

Manny and Rock sat in the sun drinking iced tea. Joanne made up the jug of tea, filled it with ice and sent it along with the boys. She said it was nice being home and normal for awhile, even if normal meant staying home with the shutters closed and making tea.

Manny watched the players run through their drills while condensation dripped off the plastic jug, falling into the blackness beneath the aluminum bleachers. The sound of helmets cracking and pads crunching brought back the memory of Harry's collapse on the high school football field. Rock's silence was evidence that he was thinking the same thing.

"Every year we come here," Rock said, breaking the silence, "trying to rid ourselves of Harry's demons. When we're all liquored up, we drive over to Harry's resting place and pour beer all over the mausoleum; thinking we're having a drink with him! Pretty stupid I think."

"But this year will be different, huh Rock?" Manny stood and picked up the plastic jug.

"Do you think Harry will be offended if we bring him some iced tea instead of beer?" Manny asked.

"As I recall," Rock said, "Harry never liked beer anyway!"

"I bet he'll love Joanne's tea," Manny said, jumping down two bleachers at a time.

"Let's go see how he's doing."

The back gate to the Valley of the Sun Memorial Park opened just as Manny's two SUVs drove into the driveway. The media were held back from entering but this did not stop the cameramen from fanning out and running along the fence. Trees, shrubbery, and assorted buildings made it difficult, but not impossible, to take long range photographs deep into the park.

Harry's mausoleum was an eight by twelve foot brown marble building sitting in the middle of the park by itself. Set back about a stone's throw from the road, the square mausoleum always looked strange and unnatural in this setting, Manny thought. If the crypt were not made of marble with an odd glass door in the front, it would simply look like another garden shed. He often imagined Harry opening his casket and looking out through the glass door at the sky and trees.

Great sadness came over Manny as he stood in front of his brother's tomb. He reached into his pocket and felt the long key that opened the mausoleum door. He always expected a smell of some kind when he opened the door but it never came.

Inside, Manny flipped on the lights. The recessed lighting focused its beams directly over the casket. The sealed casket was sitting about chest high upon a platform to the right of the door. There was room for two, maybe three people to stand shoulder to shoulder facing the casket.

"Rock, give me that tire iron, would ya?" Manny said.

Manny informed Rock what he was planning to do on their way over to the mausoleum, but wondered how he was going to open the sealed casket. The bodyguard suggested using the tire iron, so Rock climbed over the back seat, found the tire iron and hid it under his shirt.

"Now stand right there and block the window so no one will see what I'm doing," Manny instructed. "There's probably a law against opening caskets without a court order."

Rock smiled at the thought of the National Inquirer featuring Manny on the front page dressed as a body snatching vampire, fangs and all; confirming their claim that he might be the anti-Christ after all, or even funnier, the devil himself.

The two bodyguards stationed outside the mausoleum, grinned at each other when they heard loud creaking and banging noises coming from within. It didn't bother them in the least; they've seen it all.

Manny went all the way around the lid of the coffin with the tire iron, prying it open with a loud squeak. Sweating profusely, Manny wiped his forehead with the tail of his shirt. It was warm outside but it was extremely hot inside.

Finally he placed the tire iron in the crease at the front of the lid and heaved upward. It created just enough of an opening so Manny could squat down, place his hands firmly underneath the lid, and push it all the way open.

When the lid creaked to a stop, light flooded in and lit up Harry's corpse. Sweat was pouring from Manny's forehead as he bent over to see Harry's sunken and mummy-like face. Rock bent over and noticed poor ol' Harry's shriveled hands. Then he looked at his face which was wet from Manny's sweat.

Suddenly there was a loud explosion and the mausoleum shook violently. The tremor rocked them backwards and they fell to the floor. With a dull THUD the lid of the casket slammed shut. As the dust settled, the recessed lights flickered on and off creating a haunted house effect.

"What did you say, Rock?"

"I didn't say anything. I thought you said something, Manny."

There it was again, a muffled voice coming from inside the casket. Manny and Rock jumped to their feet and hoisted the coffin lid open. Light flooded into the casket again.

"Get me out of here! What are you trying to do, kill me? This isn't funny!" the man in the coffin said, trying to sit up.

"Is that you Harry?" Manny screamed, helping him out of the casket.

"No one's trying to kill you Harry. You've been dead for twenty-five years!" Rock said.

"Twenty-five years! I was just on the football field with a screaming headache and then I was in heaven for a few minutes." Harry said. "One of the Apostles was teaching me down by the river, then he said it was time to go and here I am."

"No, Harry, you died that day on the football field and you've been buried here in this little mausoleum ever since," Manny said, patting him on the back.

"I tell you," Harry said emphatically, "I was down by the river for only a couple of minutes and then the next thing I realize is, I'm in a dark scary box. I don't know what is worse, being in that dark box or seeing you guys; you guys look really, really old!"

"We are old, Harry. Twenty-five years older than when you last saw us at the game," Manny told him. "And talk about old, Harry. Look at you!"

Manny turned Harry so he could see himself in the reflection of the mausoleum glass door. Harry looked every bit the forty-two years he was. His hair was starting to gray and there were laugh lines at his eyes. The old black burial suit was starting to fade.

"Look at me Harry! Try and pay attention!" Manny said, firmly holding him by his biceps. Harry was as bewildered and disoriented as a person could ever be. It was akin to coming out of a coma after twenty-five years of sleep.

"This is really strange, I know, but believe me, we'll catch you up on all the details later," Manny said directly into Harry's eyes. "Things are a bit different from how you left them twenty-five years ago, so you'll have to be patient with us, OK?"

Rock gave his sunglasses to Harry and he put them on. After all those years in the dark, Rock reasoned, the Arizona sun had to be a little bright. But the Arizona sun doesn't hold a candle to bright lights of heaven!

"Hey Manny, you got something to drink? I'm parched," Harry asked, as Rock opened the glass door.

"Yep. I got just the thing: Joanne's iced tea. You'll love it!"

"Who's Joanne?" Harry asked. "You don't mean the skinny little Kingston kid who follows you around the church?"

"Yep. That's the one. The little skinny thing and I got married. Remember Harry, a lot of things have changed in the twenty-five years you've been gone. Try not to act too shocked, OK?"

Manny and Rock took a deep breath and grabbed Harry under the arms and brought him out into the open. Manny looked around but didn't see a cloud of fire above the mausoleum like he expected.

The bodyguards rushed over and put Harry into Manny's SUV and drove off. Now they could say for certain that they'd seen it all. Two men went into a sealed mausoleum, where a man had been dead for twenty-five years, and three men came out. They could see through the glass door that the coffin was still open. "You don't see that every day," the bodyguards whispered to themselves.

"Manny, what's the deal with all these bodyguards? Did you become president while I was away?" Harry asked.

"No, better than that," Manny replied, "I became an ambassador for Christ!"

Chapter Fourteen

"He did what?" Carlos screamed.

"NBC news just reported that he raised his brother from the dead," the lieutenant said while slipping the DVD into the recorder and pushing play.

The video showed footage of three indistinguishable men coming out of a mausoleum and getting into black SUVs. Pictures of the mausoleum and the words *HARRY BENSON* etched in marble were followed by photos of an empty casket, seen through the glass door. The photographer must have jumped the fence and run to the crypt to get his close up pictures.

"This nonsense has to stop. Why haven't we been able to get to him?"

"We caught up to Benson in Thailand where we have operatives, but they couldn't get close to him because of the cloud."

"Yes, I heard that the cloud made the agents terribly sick," Carlos said.

"What about sharpshooters. Can't they pick him off long range?"

"They tried in India but they weren't able to get a clean shot."

"What has happened to our explosives? Why hasn't that worked?"

"The bombs seem to go off after Benson leaves the area. Two men were killed in China trying to dismantle an unexploded bomb."

"We've got to eliminate this threat before he invades Europe with his deception," Carlos said.

The European nations were swamped with requests to allow Manny to visit and hold meetings. The Brethren worked overtime to keep Manny out. They were trying to establish a new law that would prohibit Manny from practicing medicine without a license. Since Manny did not actually touch anyone to perform the "medical procedure" of healing, the law was useless. So they dug deep and resorted to passing a law that prohibited him from practicing voodoo and witchcraft in public. The Brethren could not keep Manny out of their countries, short of killing him, but they sure could arrest him if he broke the law.

"He's already turned Asia upside down," Carlos said. "Those ignoramuses actually believe this guy is for real. He's got to be killed before he gets to our turf and ruins all our plans. Do you understand me?"

"What do you expect me to do?" the Lieutenant asked.

"I went back and studied everything I could about Polycarp. It appears this phenomenon has something to do with Christ's blood. Even though Christ was a phony too, there were reports that His blood held magical powers for those who possessed it. It looks like Mr. Benson may have gotten his hands on some of this blood."

In 160 AD the Brethren figured out Polycarp's secret, so they ransacked his quarters, retrieved the blood, and then were able to eliminate him. Up to that time it was impossible to kill him because of the cloud. The Brethren did not know if others had access to this magical blood so they set up the Directive as a future precaution.

"Lieutenant, find this blood and take it away from Benson. Then kill him! Understood?"

"Yes sir!"

"When you find the blood, I want you to bring it directly to me. I want to get to the bottom of this Blood Legend!"

"He did what?" Mr. Boergenes asked.

"Benson raised his brother who has been dead twenty-five years!" the assistant said.

"I'll be," Mr. Boergenes sighed. "I haven't seen anything like that since Jesus raised Lazarus from the dead. But after twenty-five years?"

Mr. Boergenes sat back in his chair on the veranda and stared out over the sea. He closed his eyes and tried to remember all the instances he knew where someone had been raised from the dead. Jesus raised a couple of people according to the gospel accounts, but they were not dead more than a few days. Paul raised up a boy who fell from a second story window and he recovered. The lad had not been dead more than a few minutes. Peter raised many people from the dead during his ministry. But he could not recall anyone being raised from the dead after such a long period of time. Then he remembered what happened when Jesus rose from the dead. He reached for his well worn Bible and opened it to

Matthew chapter 27 and read: "Then behold, the veil of the temple was torn from top to bottom; and the earth quaked, and the rocks were split, and the graves were opened; and many bodies of the saints who had fallen asleep were raised; and coming out of the graves after His resurrection, they went into the holy city and appeared to many."

One particular risen saint went into Jerusalem and coming upon Peter and John, told them how Jesus appeared to them. When the saint died he went to a place like a large prison with individual cells. The place was divided into two areas with an impassable gulf between the two. Souls could stand on the precipice and see other imprisoned souls across the divide. Most of the souls in the good side of prison were the children of Abraham like himself, he was told, and lived in relative peace. With no conception of time and nothing to do but languish, they existed as if one day was a thousand years and a thousand years was one day. The bad side of the prison was filled with cells as far as the eye could see. Shouts, wailing, and cursing could be heard continuously from across the chasm. No rest or peace existed there. A sense of evil emanated from those dungeons.

Angels from heaven have the unfortunate duty of guarding these prisons and were seen standing at the gates, pacing back and forth. They weren't the happiest looking creatures, endlessly standing like gloomy soldiers with swords in their hands.

"But one glorious day," the risen saint said, "the gray sky broke open and Messiah appeared with thousands of His angels. The gates swung wide open and Jesus marched in a glorious King. He gathered all of us together and declared His victory over death, releasing us from prison. Many of the saints were resurrected and found their way into Jerusalem, telling everyone how the Messiah set them free from death."

Mr. Boergenes pondered his recollection of the saint's story. He imagined the good side of prison still empty to this day; while the bad side remained full of evil souls.

The reason Abraham's side of the prison contained no inmates today was because the Believer was freed from the prison of sin and death. Mr. Boergenes closed his eyes again and tried to remember the millions of times he preached this very subject. When the Believer died today, according to brother Paul, he was instantly transported into the presence of the Lord. "To be absent from the body," the Apostle Paul wrote, "is to be present with the Lord."

Ah, such good news, Mr. Boergenes said to himself, *always good news indeed!*

Harry Benson's resurrection this day was a refreshing reminder of God's miracle power.

"I want our best men dispatched immediately," Mr. Boergenes said, calling his assistant. "Instruct them to stay in the background and help guard Mr. Benson and his brother wherever they go. This unusual resurrection will undoubtedly draw attention to the fact that he has the blood and Mr. Benson must be protected at all costs."

Mr. Boergenes rose up and the security guards on the veranda immediately closed ranks around him so that he could not be seen from the ocean. Once safely in the chapel, Mr. Boergenes stared at the words on the tapestry and sighed.

"Oh Lord, You are the Resurrection and the Life." Mr. Boergenes said out loud. "How I desire to stand before You once again, as in the days of old; to see my friends, to see my family and to finally dwell in Your house forever. I yearn for that day, Oh Lord! It has been such a long, long journey for me."

"You did what?" Pastor Benson said.

Pastor Benson nearly passed out with the news; but he was not surprised. That was secretly the reason he had Harry housed in a mausoleum, rather than cremated or buried in the ground. Pastor irrationally believed that Harry may one day be raised from the dead, even though he never told a soul why he insisted on a mausoleum for his son.

"Yes, dad, I've got him right here. Do you want to talk with him?" Manny asked.

"Well of course I do, put him on!"

Harry fumbled with the tiny cell phone, looking at it like it was from outer space. He had the same reaction when he saw the new cars on the road; "something out of a science fiction magazine," he said.

"Hi dad, how are you?" Harry said, holding the phone away from his ear.

"I'm fine son but the question is, how are you?"

"Well, dad, to tell the truth, I'm a little out of sorts. All I remember is falling down on the football field and the next thing is I'm climbing out of a casket."

"Yes, that would be disconcerting, son. How are you feeling?"

"I feel great really but I look forty years old. In my mind I'm still seventeen years old. This is so strange, it's hard to believe."

"For you and me both!" Pastor said. "When are you coming home?"

"I don't know but soon. Manny's taking me by the high school to show me some stuff. I need to change out of this old suit. It's driving me crazy. I feel like an old man."

"OK, well, it will be great to see you, son. We kept your room just the way you left it. I'll call your mom and tell her the good news. Put Manny back on, OK?"

"Yes, dad? Isn't this amazing?" Manny said, switching the phone to his other ear.

"To say the least, son. You're going to have to give me some time to prepare your mother for this. I don't want her having a heart attack when she sees him. So call before you bring him home."

"OK. We're going to the mall right now to get him some new clothes and then over to the high school to show him the display case and the memorial. I'll call before we bring him over."

At the Chandler Fashion Mall Harry couldn't believe his eyes. So many shops full of so many things Harry has never seen before. He was especially shocked by the way the little teenage girls dressed. They look like prostitutes he said. What has the world come to?

Manny didn't have the heart to tell him about what was on television these days. Demons manifesting through rock stars in music videos and soft pornography on daytime soap operas.

Harry went in to a dressing room at a popular men's store with a pile of clothes over his arm. After a few minutes, Harry called Manny in behind the curtain and asked him to look at the scars on his body. On the right side of his body near the collarbone were two puncture wounds and above his belly button was the head of a white plastic screw the size of a half dollar.

Manny learned about the process of embalming in high school and wrote a term paper about it. He explained that the upper scar near Harry's collar bone was where the mortician put in the embalming fluid and the lower scar was where he drained out the blood. The large plastic screw near his belly button is called the Trocar Button and fluids were removed from his organs through a tube inserted inside his abdomen. Instead of sewing up the hole, the mortician simply plugged it with a Trocar Button. Manny suggested that Harry go to a doctor and have the plug removed, if it caused any discomfort.

Instead of going to Harry's high school right away, Manny called a friend from the old football team who was a doctor at Banner Hospital. After explaining the situation and Harry's Trocar Button, the doctor agreed to meet with them at the emergency entrance. Manny was concerned that other objects might be stuck in Harry's body so an x-ray and a thorough physical was in order.

Manny was surprised when a team of medical experts met them at the curb. The MASH unit was led by his friend Doctor Jeremy Anderson, who was dressed in blue flowered scrubs. Harry thought that was strange too.

"Harry, is that you?" Doctor Jeremy asked, as Harry stepped out of the SUV. "Do you remember me Harry, from the football team?"

"As if it were yesterday," Harry replied, glancing at Manny with a smile. "You are the first string right end on offense and the tail back on defense. Your sister, Julie, the long-haired blond, is the cutest thing on two legs."

"Yes, she is still blond," Doctor Jeremy replied. "And a doctor here with me at Banner."

"Doc," Manny interrupted, "Harry has been dead for twenty-five years and remembers everything right up to the day he died, as if it were yesterday! He remembers what he had for breakfast, that last game, the last huddle, and the split second before he collapsed on the field. After that, he remembers zilch!"

"Unbelievable!" Doctor Jeremy said.

"Harry, tell Jeremy what he was wearing the day of the game, who his girlfriend was and what color shoe laces he wore for that game against Higley," Manny said.

"Well Jeremy, you were a lot younger yesterday, I can tell you that. You had your lucky Rolling Stones shirt on; the one you always wore on game day. Judy is your girlfriend and she wears too much lipstick. And you put on purple shoe laces, Higley's hated colors, as a reminder that you were going to pound Higley into the ground."

"Amazing," the Doc said.

"By the way, Jerry," Harry asked, "Manny hasn't told me how the Higley game ended up. Did we win or lose?"

"Let me put it this way, Harry," Doctor Jeremy said, "you would have been proud of your little brother. After you left the game, he threw for four more touchdowns and we finally creamed Higley sixty-three to nothing!"

"Wow. No kidding. Good job Manny. All our hard work paid off, huh!"

"On top of that," Doctor Jeremy put his arm around Harry's shoulder and walked him through the sliding glass doors, "Your fifteen-year-old brother, not only took us to State that year, but we won by a wide margin!"

"And guess what else," the Doc quickly added, motioning for the medical team to place Harry in a wheelchair.

"What, Jerry, what?" Harry asked anxiously, craning his head backward, sitting down in the wheelchair.

"Your little brother took us to State the following three years and we won those games too!" Doctor Jeremy said, motioning for the team to whisk Harry away.

"Manny became just as famous as you, Harry! Maybe more so. Can you believe that?"

They carted Harry off to a private operating room upstairs with two bodyguards in tow. Manny, Doctor Jeremy and the entourage followed right behind.

Doctor Jeremy and his sister Julie prodded Harry top to bottom and found him in perfect health except for the plastic screw in his stomach. The x-rays showed nothing unusual, but the CAT scan revealed an area in the brain where a tumor may have been.

Since Pastor Benson would not allow an autopsy after Harry died, it was inconclusive that a brain tumor was what killed him.

The medical team fingerprinted Harry and took blood samples to test his DNA. Dozens of photographs were taken and medical files filled out. If this was dead Harry Benson come alive, Doctor Jeremy was going to have it written up in the medical journals. How many documented resurrection cases does one stumble across in a lifetime? None?

It didn't take long before the staff at Banner Hospital confirmed who Harry was. A medical miracle? A spiritual phenomenon? A freak anomaly? They just did not know how to categorize it medically.

Doctor Jeremy had the medical staff line up and pose for pictures with Harry. Others wanted Manny's autograph, having seen him on national TV, but he successfully dodged their requests by heading down the hall toward the restrooms. Finding the stairs, he took off to the first floor where the chapel was. Manny quickly went in to the chapel and plopped down on the front pew, resting his arms over the back of the bench; stretching out his legs in front of him.

Rock followed Manny and quietly entered the chapel behind him. He took a seat in the back and closed his eyes. It's been a while since Rock talked with God. *Now*, he thought, *would be a good time to pray.*

Sam, the bodyguard, opened the door, poked his head in and looked all around. He decided to stay in the hall, knowing the room was safe, occasionally peeking through the chapel door window, keeping an eye on Manny.

"My God, Lord," Manny said out loud, looking up at the cross on the wall, "What have we got ourselves into?" Manny reached into his pocket and gently touched the vial, turning it with his fingers.

"I've got to admit, Lord, I'm a little overwhelmed," Manny said, slipping the vial out and looking at it.

"What could be greater than having my brother back from the dead? Nothing could be greater than that! What could be done to top that?"

Rock felt a tingling sensation rush over his body when the door opened and a breeze blew into the chapel. Opening his eyes he saw dozens of tall men in flowing white robes walk down the aisle and position themselves around the room. Each man had long blonde hair with gold bands around their heads. Their faces looked bronzed and tan, with huge protruding square jaws, perfectly shaven or hairless. He couldn't tell.

Six angels stepped in front of Rock and sat down in his row, three on one side and three on the other. Looking all around, Rock saw them fill the room. He could not identify the fragrance but it was coming from the angel sitting next to him; a hint of musk, a glorious smell.

Rock sat very still, afraid to move. But he did muster the courage to slowly turn his head and catch a close-up of the man's face next to him. His blond hair shone like it was bleached by a swimming pool's chlorine and the sun. The huge jutting jaw and the bronzed chiseled forehead were perfectly shaped. His head was three times the size of a normal man. He looked like the Neanderthal Man on the evolution chart in science class but much bigger.

The eyes of the Neanderthal, Rock observed, were beautiful and strange; they didn't look human. He squinted at his pupils and the follicles around the eyelid and concluded that the closest thing it resembled were the eyes of a lion. Matter of fact, if he had facial hair, the angel would look more like a lion than a human.

Manny was still praying out loud, oblivious to the room filling with angels.

"Oh, Lord," Manny was saying, "You have done a wonderful thing in raising up Harry from the grave. And now, Oh Lord, what can I do for you? You name it, I will do it!"

The cloud suddenly appeared at the front of the chapel and Rock noticed all the angels bow in reverence. Curiously, most of the angels had wings with feathers tucked tightly down the strait of their backs. The cartilage of the wings protruded from between the shoulder blades and stuck out of an embroidered opening in the garment. Rock imagined the angel trying to poke his large wings through the small hole while putting on the robe.

The fiery cloud slowly descended to the chapel floor and Manny fell forward from the

weight of it, landing on his knees. The Man on
fire stepped to the edge of the cloud in front of
Manny.

"Do you remember the promise you made to
Me, Manny?"

"Yes, Lord, I do. I swore that if I had the gift
of healing, I would heal everyone for Harry's
sake."

"It is time to keep your promise."

"What would you have me do, Lord?"

"Manny, you have My blood. Nothing is
impossible for you."

"But Lord, why? What does Your blood have
to do with healing and miracles?"

"Manny, My power emanates from the blood
and operates through it."

"I don't understand."

"When I was on earth," the Man on fire told
Manny, "My veins were full of My Father's
blood. When the Holy Spirit fell upon Me at
baptism, the blood My Father gave Me was
infused with divine power, the same blood and
power you have in your hand."

From the back of the room Rock could see a
figure in the cloud moving as if electrically
charged. Molten lava, without the bubbling, was
the image that came to his mind.

An arm appeared through the front of the
cloud and touched Manny's head. The fingers,
hand and forearm had a reddish glow. If it
weren't for the outer skin that seemed to contain
the fiery volcano, the intense energy would have
consumed Manny. "As I gave power to My
Apostles, I give you power. Nothing will be
impossible for you."

When Manny opened his eyes, the cloud was at the ceiling spreading over the chapel. Manny felt different; strong and aggressive. A fire surged through him from the top of his head to the bottom of his feet. An intense anger against sickness welled up within Manny and the expression on his face changed. He felt indestructible, like a warrior in a holy war, ready to eradicate all sickness, disease and death on planet earth.

Watch out devil, here I come.

Dozens of angels bowed their heads when Manny turned and faced them. He didn't see Rock fast asleep because the angels were standing, hoisting their long swords into the air. The only sound he heard was snoring from the back of the room. Finally, an angel leaned to his right so Manny could see; there was Rock, head cocked back and mouth wide open.

"Let's go!" Manny said to the angels, walking down the aisle toward the chapel door. Rock sprang to his feet when Manny touched him on the way out. The angels fell in line and followed Manny and Rock down the hall.

"The fire department's on their way," Harry said, running down the hall with a half dozen doctors and nurses trailing him. "There's a fire on the roof and they are evacuating the hospital."

"Harry, don't worry. The Lord has it under control," Manny told him.

"What's with the guys in the white sheets?" Harry asked jokingly, "Is it Halloween?"

The wings of the angels suddenly fluttered, like a squadron of fighter jets revving their engines, ready for takeoff. Harry became terrified when he saw that the heavenly trick or treaters were intense angels. At close range the angels looked like fierce soldiers, chiseled and ready for a fight. Harry didn't open his mouth after that.

"Here are our instructions: everyone in this hospital gets healed and cured from every sickness and disease. Is that clear?"

The angels nodded in unison.

"The world mocks healing evangelists who are trying to do God's work by saying, 'If you have the gift of healing, why don't you go through the hospitals and heal everybody?' Well, after today they will not mock us anymore, but rather they will be ashamed." Manny said. "Everyone here, I mean every living soul, gets healed today. Understood?"

The angels took off running and flying in every direction. They disappeared through the ceiling and fell through the floor, healing the two hundred and forty one patients on the seven floors of the Banner Medical Center. It only took them seven minutes to heal everyone.

Manny turned toward the shocked medical staff that accompanied Harry and asked where the morgue was. The basement.

Of course, Manny thought, *where else would a morgue be?*

Since Manny couldn't drop through the floor like the angels, he took the elevator. Once in the morgue, he found three black body bags lying in a cooler waiting for transport to the funeral home.

"Unzip those bags right now!" Manny said.

No one but Rock and Harry moved toward the body bags. The medical staff completely froze as their pagers began beeping. They had no idea what was going on. The beeping increased in number and got louder but no one dared look at their pagers.

Zip! The body bag was opened from bottom to top. Rock peeled back the plastic and the head of the first body was exposed. It was a woman.

Zip! Harry peeled back the second plastic bag. It was a young man with a gash in his head, a teenager.

Zip! The third was of an elderly man, white as a snowman.

Manny touched the forehead of the woman and said, "The blood of Jesus!" Immediately she sucked in air and sat up. He did the same with the teenager and the head wound disappeared. The boy took in a deep breath, shook his head and mumbled something about beer and driving his parent's car. Then the elderly man opened his eyes and said, "Mother? Where's mother?" The old man was looking for his wife.

The staff realized what was happening and helped the risen out of their plastic graves, fetching robes and bottles of water. Several doctors ran and phoned their departments, thumbing their pagers like a remote control.

"What? Every patient in our ward got out of bed and is healed? Impossible!" said one physician who wobbled her way to the door.

"Say what? Say it again?" said the young doctor who had patients on the stroke floor. "They all took out their tubes and did what? They found their clothes and walked out?"

Each doctor and nurse answering their pagers had the same reaction. The whole hospital was turned upside down with miracles. Even those in surgery were instantly healed, their wounds supernaturally closed and healed.

The same was true of the whole Banner medical staff. Diabetes, inner ear infections, ingrown toenails, high blood pressure, toothaches were healed. Over a thousand in all.

Four fire departments responded to the call. The media, of course, was broadcasting the fire. The police showed up and blocked off the area, no one was allowed to come or go, especially the patients.

The media set up positions in the parking lot to interview the few patients who had escaped through the police lines. They were saying crazy things like "angels, with bronze faces and golden hair, swooped down from above and touched them." One man reported that gargoyles were sliced to pieces after they had left his body. "Two angels," he said, "chased the hideous creatures around the room, killing them with swords." He was suffering from cancer before the angels appeared; now he was cured. The reporters thought he was delusional.

The bodyguards retrieved the vehicles and met Manny, Rock, and Harry in the underground parking garage, adjacent to the morgue. They sped away, honking at the crowds of reporters, medical staff and patients milling about everywhere. It was chaos and God once again broke the church's "decency and order" rule. Manny chuckled to himself from behind the tinted bullet proof windows, watching hundreds of people rejoicing outside the hospital.

"Now, this is what I'm talking about," Manny said, pointing to a man leaping in the air like a gazelle, unwrapping the bloody bandage from around his head, exclaiming that he was healed!

Chapter Fifteen

By five o'clock Arizona time every person in the world with a television heard that Manny raised his brother from the dead, along with three confirmed dead people from the hospital morgue. Manny managed to also heal over a thousand people at the hospital in less than ten minutes but nobody knew how. The Catholics called him a saint and many of the so-called Christians called him an imposter, the antichrist, unscriptural; and all the others in the world didn't know what to believe and didn't care. As long as people were getting healed, "God bless you Manny Benson!"

Sam, the bodyguard, called ahead and Manny, Harry, and Rock met with the principal of Chandler High. This was the site of the original school but it had been remodeled and rebuilt to the point Harry didn't recognize his old stomping grounds. Instead of being a school of a few hundred students like in 1980, Chandler High was over fifteen hundred strong and still growing. The place was huge to Harry, since it was only yesterday he was playing football here.

"Now look Brett," Manny said to the principal, "if for some reason you see a fire on the roof, for God's sake don't call the fire department. They're having enough trouble at the hospital and don't have time to come here."

Manny wasn't joking. He told the principal if there was a real fire for some reason, just let it burn. He would pay the damages later. They wanted some privacy.

"On one condition," Brett said, shoving a football at them. "Harry has to sign my football!"

"OK, but if he does, will you make sure nobody bothers us for awhile?"

"Yes, absolutely. Anything you want," he said, turning to Harry.

"Make sure you date it. It's going to go into the display case with the others!"

After he got Harry's signature, Brett trotted off to his office down the hall.

The two display cases were built a few years ago through generous donations from the alumni; one on either side of the double gym doors. The one on the left featured a full length color picture of Harry Benson running down the field. Trophies were displayed around the picture and each trophy had a plaque explaining the occasion, giving Harry credit for his athleticism. In the lower middle of the display was a smaller picture of Harry and Manny together, holding their helmets, cheesing for the camera, on that fatal game day against Higley. Underneath the picture was a plaque that read: Harry Benson. 1964-1981.

On the floor in front of Harry's memorial display was a brass rostrum, similar to a music stand, affixed to the floor. On top of the stand was a laminated book of Harry's football pictures.

The display case to the right of the gym doors was dedicated to Manny Benson and his four championships. This is where Harry spent most of his time, taking in every detail. There was a huge color picture of Manny, as a senior, dominating the display. He looked a lot like his older brother when he was a senior.

Harry noticed the number on Manny's uniform and especially the words on his red arm band: *m Harry's br*. The rest of the word on the arm band went around Manny's arm and could not be read.

"What's your arm band say, Manny?" Harry asked, staring at it for a long time.

"Look at the plaque down at the bottom," Manny replied.

"I'm Harry's brother?" Harry said out loud.

When Harry died, Manny wore his brother's football jersey number. He made sure all his football shirts had the red arm band sewn on. Half as a joke and half in anger, whenever anyone asked his name, his reply was, "I'm Harry's brother." As a player he would slam into the opposition on the field and say, "What's my name, what's my name?"

The local papers picked up on his idea and called him "Harry's brother" throughout his career. When the reporters interviewed him, they referred to him as Harry's Brother. Even the teachers called him that, except when he was in trouble. Then they called him plain ol' Manny.

Harry couldn't believe it. Each trophy, award, and accolade of Manny's display said the same thing.

"Manny, none of these trophies or plaques have your name on them. Matter of fact, I don't see your name anywhere here," Harry said. "All I see is 'This championship is dedicated to my brother Harry Benson' and 'This passing record is dedicated to my brother Harry.' I'm in your display more than you are."

"Wait till you see this, Harry!" Manny said.

Out in the courtyard was a life size bronze statue of Harry and Manny holding their helmets, cheesing for the camera, on Harry's final day. A bronze rendition from their picture in the display case. The words at the base of the statue read: "Harry and Manny Benson. 1964-1981." Tears welled up in Harry's eyes. He couldn't believe it.

"See Harry, there's my name, with yours. I died when you died."

The sun was lowering on the horizon and the statue cast a long shadow onto the courtyard. Manny and Harry spent another hour of walking around the school reminiscing over girls and glory, remembering the teachers and their friends as if it were yesterday. Some had died and others were married with children. Lately, most of the old school chums were attending Pastor Benson's church.

"Manny, how are mom and dad?"

"They took your death really hard, Harry, but because of their faith, they both survived it pretty well."

"And how's dad's church. Has it grown?"

"In the last four months, the church has added fifteen thousand members," Manny said. "Can you believe it? Dad has a mega church!"

"What? How is that possible? Dad could hardly handle his three hundred members; what's he doing with fifteen thousand? They can't be meeting at our little church, can they?"

"Before we go home, let's swing by the church and take a look," Manny said. "It's become quite a circus, you know."

When they drove into the church's parking lot, Manny thought Harry's eyes were going to bug out of his head. Manny wasn't kidding about the circus; the two huge tents proved it! Several media trucks were permanently parked in the lot across the street. Local television stations pooled their money and rented the cotton field from the disgruntled farmer, establishing a presence in what they called "The War Zone" across Arizona Avenue.

Reporters with television cameras ran up to the vehicles, turning the lights on, ready for action. Paparazzi with their ball caps on backwards were also in attendance, running down the streets waving their arms and shouting. They wanted pictures of dead Harry and the miracle worker. The magazines and papers were paying top dollar for their pictures. Famous celebrities took a back seat in the tabloids as the world chased after the Benson Brothers.

"Dad, we're about ten minutes away. Is mom ready?" Manny said into the cell phone.

"Oh, she's more than ready, son, but there may be a problem."

"What's that dad?"

"There's probably a hundred people here to greet Harry!"

"What about security?"

"At the last minute Mr. Kingston pulled most of the guys from your house and brought them over here. There's security everywhere but it's kinda crowded."

"Is Joanne there? Is she OK? I haven't been able to reach her."

"She's OK Manny. It's so loud in here, we can't hear our cell phones. She can't wait to see Harry!"

In the field behind Manny's house in Queen Creek, three men casually walked along the horse trail that wound for a couple of miles through the neighborhood. The back half acre was surrounded by a rusting metal fence and around the house was a gray cinder block fence. After dark, two men hopped the metal fence and approached the back gate. It was unlocked. The remaining intruder, a sniper, waited in the field for a clear shot.

"There are only two; one in front and one in back," whispered the intruder into his microphone, peeking through the gate. The gate squeaked and the security guard reached for his holstered weapon. Before he could fully turn, a silent bullet zipped through the air and hit him in the heart. The two intruders heard him fall to the ground and quickly ran to the front gate and looked over. The second security guard was standing in the driveway with his back to them. Instead of taking a chance on another squeaky gate, the intruder screwed on his silencer, steadied his aim and took a head shot, while the other ran to the body and pulled it into the front bushes.

They entered Manny's house, disabling the alarm, closing the shutters and began looking for anything resembling the blood of Christ. Finding a laptop computer and a digital camera, they stuffed them into a backpack. By the time the intruders finished their search, Manny's office and bedroom were completely torn apart. They found no blood except for the pool of blood they stepped over escaping out the back.

The two SUVs pulled up to Pastor Benson's home in the midst of flashing police car lights, yellow tape, and a crowd of people lined up in the street to catch a glimpse of their boys. Bodyguards jumped out and conversed with the security detail. Manny was learning that he did nothing until the bodyguards told him to. He was not allowed to open his own door or go into a room, including his bathroom at home, without it first being cleared by security.

They are taking too much time, Manny thought. *There must be trouble.*

He learned about trouble and the security procedures to prevent it in the various countries he visited. At least the SUV he was currently sitting in was bomb and bullet proof, supposedly. But in Japan and China, he would have been safer in a rickshaw, the way they drove on the freeways.

The bodyguard reentered the vehicle and told Manny that the security guards at his house were not responding to calls, so they dispatched a team to investigate. It was safer to stay in the protected SUV, if there was a threat, than to be exposed to hundreds of people, any one of which may do him harm.

A few minutes later the call came that two men were dead at Manny's house and that security was breached. The threat was imminent and Manny had to be transported someplace safe.

"We're not leaving without our families," Manny insisted.

"You must understand, Manny, the threat is imminent!" Sam yelled.

"I don't care. Get them out here and stuff 'em into the Suburbans. Then you can take us wherever you want, but we're not leaving without them."

Sam huddled with the security detail and the police, pointing this way and that. Immediately the men ran into the house and a minute later Pastor Benson and Betty were running out, ducking down like there was wind from a helicopter, being shoved into Manny's nine passenger SUV. Next, came Joanne and Sissy.

With Sam and the other bodyguard, this made eight and off they went, leaving the other SUV in the dust. Rock stayed behind, dismissing the crowd and stuffing his family and the Kingstons into the waiting vehicle, waving it off. Then he closed and locked Pastor's house, jumped into a Chandler police cruiser and sped into the night.

Manny's Suburban experienced the happiest reunion that ever was. Pastor and Mrs. Benson crawled into the back seat and into the arms of their resurrected son. Joanne and Sissy fell into the arms of Manny, on the bench seat in the middle. There were hugs and kisses all around; it was the happiest they'd been in years.

"Sam, can we stop the SUV somewhere safe?" Manny asked. "Mom and Dad haven't seen Harry in years and need to hug him properly."

It was like a rugby scrum in the back of the Suburban, with legs and arms, kisses and tears, all jumbled together.

"Sir, I will check to see if we were followed and then find a safe place for you."

Sam stretched his neck to see out the back window and barked into his headset that they were stopping for a minute. Sam instructed the driver to find a quiet gravel road and keep the engine running. Everyone piled out of the vehicle and gang tackled Harry like he just won the Super Bowl. Sam couldn't believe what he was seeing; the whole family on the ground, in the dirt and Manny standing silently beside him, crying like a baby.

This is what a loving family looks like, Sam said to himself.

Manny noticed his mother's beautiful face drenched with tears. All these years she quietly mourned for her son, grief stricken, creating deep lines in her face, but tonight the grief was completely gone, replaced by "joy unspeakable and full of glory." He suddenly realized what true joy really was. It was a loving mother receiving her beloved son alive from the grave. Truly joy unspeakable. Manny drifted off and imagined how Mary felt when she saw her precious Son risen from the dead.

"Son, come join us," Betty Benson said, after everyone got up and dusted themselves off. "This is the most incredible night of my life, son, next to giving birth to you two. This is right up there with that!"

"Yessir, Manny! This is the greatest thing," Pastor Benson said. "Your mom and I couldn't be happier. I just knew something like this was going to happen. I just knew it!"

Pastor Benson grabbed Betty's and Harry's hands and began to dance in a circle, kicking up dust and rocks. Manny stood there watching his dad with admiration and awe.

He believed. All this time, he believed and I was the one who didn't.

Manny began to cry again. Sam came over and asked Manny if he was alright.

"I'm fine Sam. What happened at my house tonight? Can you tell me?" Manny asked.

"It looks like the two guarding your house didn't know what hit them. The agent on the back porch got one in the heart and the agent in the front caught one in the back of the head. Professionals definitely."

"Where are they now?"

"Do you mean the bodies? I suppose they are in the ambulance waiting to be transferred to the morgue. Do you want to see them, Manny?"

Manny reached for the vial in his pocket and squeezed tightly. He knew it was Christ's anointing in the vial that was working the miracles. There wasn't a genie in the bottle after all. Just faith.

"Could you find out where they are? I've got an idea."

Sam made a couple of calls and found the ambulance still at Manny's house. He called the other SUV and told them to proceed to the safe house; they would catch up later.

"You've got men at the ambulance, right?" Manny asked.

"Yes we do."

"Get one of them on the phone. I want to talk with him, OK?"

Sam dialed the number and stared Manny in the eyes. After months of guarding Manny, Sam came to trust him, sort of. The things he did were unconventional, but inspired. While this guard duty was strange, there was never a dull moment.

"What are you up to now, Manny?" Sam said with the cell phone up to his ear.

"I'm not sure, but it's worth a try."

"We're on, here he is," Sam said, handing the phone to Manny.

"Hi, this is Manny. What's your name?"

"Frank, sir."

"OK Frank, are you ready for the thrill of your life. Something to tell your grandchildren?"

"I sure am, Sir!" Sam could hear the agent's eager answer from the front seat.

If he only knew what was coming, Sam thought.

"Frank, are you near the dead bodies?" Manny asked. "You've been next to them all night? Good. Are they in body bags?"

"No, sir."

"Now Frank, whatever happens, don't freak out. Can I count on you?"

"Yes, sir. You can count on me, sir."

"Frank, now hold the phone up to the ear of the body nearest you, OK?" Frank did as he was told.

"*WAKE UP!*" Manny yelled into the phone, "Wake up right now!"

Frank did freak out and screamed so loud everybody in the Suburban heard him through the cell phone. Sam grabbed the phone and shouted, "What happened Frank, what happened?"

"Oh my God, Sir. You won't believe this!" Frank said. "You won't freaking believe this!"

"Try me Frank."

"Agent Tuttle just sat up and opened his eyes! My God, Sir!"

Manny snatched the phone back from Sam.

"Frank, Frank, put the phone by the ear of the other body right now! Are you ready?"

"I am, sir!"

"*WAKE UP! RIGHT NOW!*" Manny shouted.

This time Frank dropped the phone and they could hear him scream all the way down the road because the body suddenly jolted upright and looked him square in the eyes. That's when Frank completely lost it.

Sam grabbed the phone and shouted into the phone for Frank.

"Frank's not here, Sir. He ran out screaming."

"Who is this?" Sam insisted.

"This is agent Rick Southland, Sir. I'm sitting in an ambulance with blood all over me, Sir. And Agent Tuttle is here with me. We're both soaked in blood, Sir."

Rick Southland was the head wound and Jimmy Tuttle was the heart shot. When the paramedics arrived, they were immediately placed in the same ambulance, obviously DOA. Unfortunately for Frank, he was the first FBI agent on the scene and was securing the bodies until they were taken to the hospital. It will definitely be something to tell his grandchildren.

The safe house was owned by Jansen Berry, the famous lead singer and guitarist for the J. Berry Band, who bought it in the late sixties. For the past twenty years he rented it out to celebrities needing peace and quiet. It was perched on top of a small hill in Scottsdale, a half mile away from the main road. The refrigerator and the cupboards were stocked with food, so Amy cooked spaghetti dinner for twenty people.

After the Bensons finally arrived, Sam gave them a tour of the ranch style home, placing

Manny and Joanne in one of the master bedrooms with bullet proof windows. Berry installed bullet proof windows in all his homes after Jason Whitehead was shot to death in 1979. It was just a precaution.

The bodyguards ate in the guest house while the celebrities feasted on home cooked spaghetti in the enormous dining room overlooking the valley. Manny sat back and counted his blessings, looking up at the vaulted beamed ceiling that reminded him of a ski lodge in the mountains. The conversation around the table was lively and it couldn't have been less so in Jesus' time after witnessing the miracles he performed. Manny knew what it must have been like for Mary and Martha to sit at the table with their brother Lazarus, whom Jesus amazingly raised from the dead. Here he was with his risen brother and it was joy unspeakable.

This is the way Christianity should be, Manny thought, *full of joy and life*.

"Manny," Pastor Benson said, opening his Bible. "What happened today reminded me of John the Baptist. Do you remember when he was in prison? He began to have doubts about Jesus, so he sent disciples and asked Jesus, 'Are you the coming One, or do we look for another?' Do you remember what Jesus did and said?" Flipping to the book of Luke, Pastor read out loud, "And that very hour He cured many infirmities, afflictions and evil spirits; and many blind He gave sight. Jesus answered and said to them, 'Go and tell John the things you have seen and heard; that the blind see, the lame walk, the lepers are cleansed, the deaf hear, the dead are raised, the poor have the gospel preached to them.'" Pastor put his arm around Manny's shoulder. "What Jesus did to alleviate John the Baptist's doubts was to work miracles to prove that he indeed was the One to come." Pastor turned in his chair and pointed at Harry. "If you have any doubts, just look over at the miracle of Harry and know that God has indeed called you to this; without a shadow of a doubt!"

There hadn't been time for doubts. Manny was running on instinct and he believed that the blood in the vial was the key to his success. He wondered what would happen if he lost the vial of blood. Would he lose the cloud and the miracle working power? There is no question that the men who were at his house tonight were looking for something valuable; so valuable they did not hesitate to kill for it. Could they know about the blood? Could they know of its power? If so, Manny and his family would be in constant danger. Just a short few months ago he was enjoying a cavalier lifestyle, with smokes in his pocket, beers by the pool, and living a lazy American life. Few in the world cared less about him. Today, though, he was the talk of the nations, with his own bodyguards, crowds of people pressing in from all sides, and mysterious men trying to kill him. This was serious business and there was no turning back now.

"Dad, what do I do now? I'm not prepared for this. Where do I go from here?"

"Well, son," Pastor Benson began, "let's evaluate the situation so we can make the right decisions here. First, these things are obviously happening because the world has entered into the last days. Isn't that what the angel, the Lord, and the Scriptures have told us?" Manny was nodding, beginning to appreciate the wisdom of his father. For many years Manny thought his dad was an ignorant small town preacher, believing in a powerless God and a Bible that was simply words on paper.

Why didn't God call dad to this worldwide ministry, Manny was thinking, *instead of me? He is certainly better prepared for it.*

He sat, listening to his wise Pastor, feeling like he was the ignorant one, not his dad. Funny how things come full circle.

"Since we are entering into the last days, we only have a few days, months, or even short years left before God takes us out of here. We're not talking decades, Manny. We're talking very soon!" Pastor said, speaking louder and louder, so that everyone at the table became quiet and listened. "Manny, this means that the possibility you will turn fifty is very remote, let alone enter retirement."

Pastor opened his Bible again. He felt more comfortable with the Scriptures in hand when talking about spiritual things. The Bible gave him strength just in holding it.

"Before you know it, you'll be in heaven and out of this world. You don't have time to be concerned about yourself or your family. All you have time for is doing the Lord's will before He comes. The days of pizza and parties are gone.

"Let's consider what has to happen next in the world, to give us an indication of how close we are to the end. I believe this will help you focus on the job at hand and not be distracted by the chaos around you. There will be a beginning of sorrows, the birth pangs Jesus referred to in Matthew 24. Wars, famines, pestilences, earthquakes. I believe these things are coming very soon and will be unmistakable signs of the end. Wars using nuclear missiles would scare everyone to death and be an unmistakable sign. Horrible famines and pestilences could come from these wars. Earthquakes could occur also or possibly Jesus was referring to the bombs themselves as earthquakes. Regardless, something involving wars that affect the whole world is about to begin."

"So if these are the last days," Manny said, "then the Antichrist must be alive and operating somewhere, right?" He had already been wondering about this.

"That is correct, Manny. And he most likely knows all about you!"

Manny hadn't thought about that. What a sobering idea.

"Could he be behind the shootings tonight?" Manny asked, knowing full well he could be. Who would want a magic blood potion to work miracles more than the Antichrist? Everyone knows that Hitler chased after a holy grail and the Ark of the Covenant in his quest for world dominance. Why wouldn't the Antichrist do the same?

"He could be behind it but what does it matter? The devil or the Antichrist is not your concern. You have a job to do and then the end will come," Pastor Benson said. "Then we can go be with the Lord and our families!"

"OK, where exactly are we right now," Manny asked, "I mean, in regards to history?"

"As you know, Manny, you are the one in Isaiah 40, to make straight in the desert, to prepare the way of the Lord's second coming. That's why we are building a stadium that seats sixty thousand people. People from all around the world will come to you there. Until the stadium is built your mission is to fulfill Matthew 24:14 and be the catalyst for a global revival, then the end will come."

"I always thought you said the church will fall away before the end?"

"Yes, the established church will most likely fall away, but at the same time, the Lord will bring in the largest harvest of souls the world has ever seen." Pastor Benson put his head down and thought for a second. "I can only imagine that the new believers in this great revival will be persecuted by the church that is falling away. After all, we are proclaiming Jesus as God but the antichrist's followers will be saying the antichrist Beast is God. The followers of the antichrist will brutally persecute the true believers. It only makes sense."

"You're right, dad, that makes perfect sense."

Manny and Joanne walked arm in arm down the path to the swimming pool, since they were not allowed to stand near the house, exposed to sniper fire. Twenty yards down the hill, though, the guitar shaped pool was secured by a ten foot cinder block fence that went all the way around the house. The only way a sniper could get to them was from the air and what was the likelihood of that? Bordering the lower twenty acres was a razor wired chain link fence. Security guards constantly paroled the perimeter with dogs and three wheelers. For the time being they were safe, nestled together in a hammock near the pool.

"Manny?" Joanne said, "What would you think if I didn't go to Africa with you guys?"

"What would you do if you stayed home?" Manny asked.

"Sam says we won't be able to go back to our Queen Creek home. It's just not secure. Amy and I thought it might be a good idea to get settled here at Jansen's ranch while you are away."

The place was nice, he had to admit. With ten large bedrooms, all fitted with their own bathrooms and refrigerators and two master bedrooms overlooking the valley. The whole clan could stay there if they wanted. The outside walls to the indoor pool had doors that rolled up in order to let the breeze flow through, giving the impression that the pool was under a cover, not enclosed indoors. There was a spa and a weight room that didn't seem so bad either. The outdoor pool down the path had a one bedroom house connected to it with autographed pictures of Mick Jagger, Ringo Starr, Peter Sellers, Ravi Shankar (George's sitar teacher from India, Manny explained to Joanne), and other extremely famous hippies from the sixties lining the hall to the bathroom.

"Does Rock know that Amy is going to stay here with you?" Manny asked.

"I imagine she's telling him right now," Joanne said, pointing to the winding path leading to the pool.

Rock and Amy were arm in arm, like love birds on retreat. Instead of coming through the gate to the pool, they split off on the trail that wound down the hill to the one hole golf course. Two bodyguards followed at a distance.

"Well, if you think you can live without me for four months," Manny said, feeling sorry for himself, knowing she could.

"The question is, can you live without my cooking?" Joanne replied, patting his belly, expecting it to bounce like it usually did; but it didn't. "Have you lost weight big boy? Or are you sucking it in?"

"I've lost twenty three pounds and four ounces, but who's counting. I'm surprised you haven't noticed before this?"

"I have noticed but you've become such a celebrity nowadays I can't get near you," Joanne said, nodding her head toward the body guards. Joanne wrapped her arms around Manny and squeezed real hard.

"You're near me now," he said, squeezing her right back.

The Bensons finally closed their eyes and fell asleep in the swaying hammock. Manny dreamed of fires, clouds and stadiums, while Joanne dreamed of Jansen Berry dropping by for a cup of tea.

Chapter Sixteen

After five months and twenty countries, their travels had gone nearly perfectly until a rebel group attacked their caravan. It happened outside Casablanca.

Manny and his entourage were on their way to visit the Strait of Gibraltar at the northern tip of Morocco for a little sightseeing before the long flight home. The coast road leading to Tangier, the tourist town on the Strait, was blocked by an aging military jeep. The caravan's lead driver saw the danger and knew what to do: he sped up and smashed into the jeep full on, moving it out of the way, spraying glass, gasoline and smoke everywhere. The lead van fishtailed as it was riddled with bullets and finally stopped dead in its tracks in the middle of the road. A fire ignited the gasoline near the stalled van and licked its way down the street until it met up with the gasoline pouring out of the tank of the overturned jeep. KABOOM. The Jeep exploded, sending shards of metal into the air. Pieces of metal and glass hit the bandits who were firing at close range. Three of them went down. One had his head sheared off, with blood pouring out of the neck; the head rolled into the ditch.

Men with black bandanas popped out of the bushes and fired semi-automatic weapons at the two remaining vans carrying Manny, Rock, and Harry. The three bodyguards had already dropped out of the vans before it came to a stop and were lying on the ground shooting at the dozen or so bandits. Several bandits got hit early and fell to the pavement.

"Stay on the floor," Rock yelled, "and we'll be OK."

It sounded like rocks were pelting the van except for the occasional bullet that penetrated the van and whizzed above their heads. The explosion of the jeep up ahead rocked the van and the heat could be felt from the back seats. PLUNK, PLUNK, PLUNK. It was raining metal and debris from the fallout.

Two cars quietly drove up from the rear and stopped about twenty-five yards from the action. The bandits didn't see them because of the smoke. Ten men in black turbans slipped out and quickly ran to the side of the road, disappearing into the field.

Bandits with three wheelers watched the action from the side of the road, revving their engines, waiting for their comrades to return. They didn't know what hit them. The two black turbaned men slit their throats so swiftly, there was no warning the others. From behind the three wheelers, the two black turbans steadied their pistols and waited for their brothers, who swiftly and quietly exited the second car to move forward and lay down in the tall grass. The turbans opened fire on the bandits, killing all but two who hid themselves in the seeming safety of the tall grass. Muffled screams were heard and then a gurgling sound as the bandits tried to breathe one last time through the gash in their necks. All the bandits were suddenly dead.

Manny's guards advanced over the ditch and into the grass once the shooting stopped. Eleven nicely slit bandits, draining blood onto the ground, were found sitting on their three wheelers without anyone around to show for it. Off in the distance two cars were speeding down the dusty road in the opposite direction.

"God works in mysterious ways," Sam said, turning back to the lifeless bodies. "I'm sure glad too. Or we'd be dead right now like these jokers."

The Benson Boys were still hunkered down in the van not knowing what to think. It was eerily quiet outside. The crackling fire and voices off in the distance were the only things they heard. *Did we win or lose?*

Rock finally poked his head up and saw the bodyguards walking back from the field. No one was around but a scattering of dead bodies on the ground.

"Stay down until we have an all clear, OK?" Sam said, looking off in the distance, his pistol still pointed upwards. He wanted to make sure no snipers were burrowed in some place, positioned to take a shot.

"What do we have, Sam?" Manny asked, scrunched down on the floor, his legs falling asleep.

"We have approximately twenty of the enemy dead and your driver here," Sam said. "That's why the van stopped. He got nailed in the chest. Otherwise we would have followed the lead van through the barrier. That's what the lead is for. It's harder to hit a moving target, you know."

"What about the ministers in the front van," Manny asked. "What about them?"

"Miraculously, they all survived; minor scratches and bruises. The same for the van behind you. Bullets galore but only this one casualty here."

Manny reached into his pocket and pulled out the vial and handed it to Sam. "Just put a little of this on his forehead and he'll wake up. He'll be fine." Sam popped open the cork and dripped the grit onto his pointer and touched the driver's forehead. The anointing from the blood touched the driver and he came alive just like the thousands of others in Manny's African meetings. It was strange but raising the dead had almost become common place the last few months.

The group decided to limp their vans to Tangier where Moroccan military helicopters were ready to fly them back to Casablanca and to safety. But Manny was hungry and decided they would stay for lunch. He wanted to see the Rock of Gibraltar.

From the restaurant that looked out onto the Strait, Manny was nearly finished with lunch when he noticed huge white clouds covering the southern coastline of Spain, where Gibraltar sat. The white fluffy clouds were normal this time of year and completely shrouded their view of the Rock.

"Hey guys, do you see that?" Manny said, pointing out at the faraway cloud that was fast approaching across the water.

"The cloud looks like the face of the devil," Rock replied, "and here it comes!"

Manny jumped out of his chair and ran down to the beach holding the vial tightly in his hand. As he often did in his crusades, Manny raised his arms like Moses and closed his eyes.

"You will not enter here," the cloud rumbled from over the water. "Not now, not ever! Europe is mine!"

Manny opened his eyes and saw the cloud transform into a dark tornado, ripping up the water underneath, rapidly moving toward them.

"I command you to cease, right now, by the blood of Christ!" Manny yelled.

The tornado was stopped in its tracks about a mile out, churning the water and causing waves to hit the beach.

"Because you have threatened me," Manny said pointing at the tornado, "I will indeed conquer Europe, starting with Spain, and all the nations after you will fall at the feet of Jesus!"

"I will destroy you before you arrive here. I will kill you." the voice said from the cloud.

"I command you devil to return to where you came from and leave us alone," Manny said, walking away from the tornado. "I want to finish my lunch!"

The wind was fierce, blowing driftwood and sand into the air, but Manny made it back to the restaurant and ordered a slice of blueberry pie. Blueberries were in season. They watched as the tornado ripped a path in the ocean back toward the Spanish mainland and disappeared in the distance. On the news that night it was reported that a tornado hit the southern coast of Spain and cut a destructive path northward, killing hundreds of Spaniards, before it hovered over the king's palace in Madrid and vanished.

The fire of Manny's first campaign burned fervently westward from New Zealand, Indonesia, Malaysia and India. Now, from the second campaign, the whole continent of Africa was ablaze with salvations, resurrections, and healings. The raising of the dead in the thousands in Manny's meetings competed in the media with the remarkable healings of the AIDS virus, since more than half of the African population was infected with the disease.

For obvious reasons, Manny set his heart on conquering Europe, but several European Union countries were strongly opposed to his *Sweeping the World with Fire Crusade*, as promoters called it. Spain led the charge against Manny's crusades by declaring his use of witchcraft to heal the multitudes and voodoo to create the fiery cloud. Germany, France and the Netherlands claimed that Manny practiced medicine without a license and were not going to allow this antichrist to upset their countries. But the Pope invited Manny to hold a crusade in the open square at the Vatican and promised to be in attendance. The Pope's endorsement opened the door for Roman Catholics globally to accept Manny with open arms. After that, it was difficult for the predominantly Catholic countries to keep Manny out.

Pastor Benson switched the itinerary from entering Europe next and scheduled the team to go into Saudi Arabia instead. The door suddenly swung wide open. The Saudis wanted to be the first Muslim nation to jump on the popular Manny band wagon. It didn't matter if it was a Christian crusade or not, the fact that it would make a great public relations statement was what mattered. Since the world was watching, Saudi Arabia wanted to appear cooperative to the nations who purchased her oil, showing that their country was a modern and progressive one. Of course the Muslims violently opposed the crusade, not realizing it was about the promotion of oil and nothing else; especially not Christianity.

Once Saudi Arabia was on board, Jordan and Turkey scheduled the Manny Show in their countries. Like dominoes they fell, one after the other. It didn't matter if the countries were Muslim, Islamic, Catholic or secular in their beliefs. It was a popular political move to have Manny and his risen brother visit their countries. Europe would just have to wait its turn.

By late March Pastor Benson had most of the walls to the ninety-thousand seat stadium almost finished. At the last minute Pastor Benson was inspired to add thirty-thousand more seats. Manny took his first tour of the grounds a day after he returned from Africa. The contractors promised that the project would take no longer than eighteen months to complete and would not cost a cent over seventy million dollars.

Five months to go, Manny thought. *Just five months to go.*

He was tired of the grueling schedule and the time away from his family. He wondered how business executives traveled year after year like this; such a grind.

Manny's personal priorities were dramatically changing from all the travel, especially after his near death experiences. He became very appreciative of his wife, family and friends. Instead of attending ball games or watching TV, Manny, Rock, and Harry were having parties and barbecues at Jansen Berry's safe house. Manny hadn't had a beer in months; and the cigarettes, well, they went up in smoke as well. Joanne's iced tea was Manny's drink of choice now.

Manny had lost another twenty pounds on his African crusade and was showing it off poolside for Joanne's fortieth birthday party when a black Hummer limousine and four SUVs appeared in the driveway. The garage door opened and the Hummer went all the way in. Manny's bodyguards were on alert, moving their heads like chickens in a barnyard, until the garage door closed. Manny noticed at least a dozen bodyguards come out of the house and walk down the path toward the pool.

"What's going on Manny? Who are these guys?" Joanne asked.

"Oh, it's nothing, honey. It's just your birthday present."

"But I thought your handsome torso was my present," Joanne winked, pulling the hair above his belly button.

"You'll forget all about my tummy when you see this, Joanne, believe me!"

The gate to the pool opened and ten bodyguards filed in, nodding to Manny's guards as if they knew each other. There were at least seventeen bodyguards in sunglasses standing around the pool waiting for Joanne's birthday present.

He came out of the house wearing a baseball cap and sunglasses, waving his left hand back and forth, talking on a cell phone.

"I don't want that bloody thing," he said. "Get me a new one or I'll have your hide for it."

When he got to the pool gate Joanne noticed who it was and about fainted.

"We met at the crusade in Johannesburg," Manny said. "I didn't tell you because I wanted it to be a surprise." It was definitely a surprise!

He walked across the deck and gave Joanne a kiss on both cheeks and said, "Happy Birthday darlin'." After embracing Manny like they were long lost friends, he sat down in the lawn chair next to Joanne and took her hand.

"Oh my gosh, it's Jansen Berry," she exclaimed, as if no one knew who he was. She was in shock, maybe even a little giddy, and definitely feeling faint.

He was dressed in a black t-shirt, cargo shorts and sandals. Jansen had the biggest smile on his face and kept looking over at Manny, winking.

Someone handed Jansen an iced tea and he sat back in the chair and sighed, still holding Joanne's hand. After a big sip, he said, "You're right Manny, she does make the best tea in Arizona." Joanne blushed.

"Jansen," Manny said, "Joanne here is your biggest fan. We are absolutely thrilled you dropped by today. Thank you very much."

"No, thank YOU, Manny. After what happened in Johannesburg, well, I owe you everything. If it weren't for you, I probably wouldn't even be here today," Jansen said, winking at him again.

"I appreciate your sentiment but it wasn't me who did it."

Jansen looked away and up at his old house, taking another sip of tea. It had been years since he visited the old place. He was an expert at changing the subject after years of practicing on reporters. Jansen was a Roman Catholic and would remain one till the day he died. That's just the way it was. Talking about the Lord was not something he was comfortable with, with Manny or anyone else. So he just kept looking up, remembering when he built this home on the hill.

"You know, I wrote the song 'The Fool' in this house," Jansen said. "Actually from here at the pool. I put the words down on a notepad and then went and finished the song at the piano." The black Steinway was still in the living room underneath a famous Andy Warhol painting of a can of tomato soup. "It took me about fifteen minutes to write."

"By the way," Joanne asked, "Who was the fool you sang about?"

"I am," Jansen said, almost happy she asked.

The J. Berry Band was one of the most famous musical groups in modern history.   In

1979 Jason Whitehead, lead guitarist, was shot to death at the age of forty and Jimmy Dancer the drummer died of cancer in 2001. All that was left of the Berry Band was Jansen himself at sixty-four and Davy the bass player, who was ageless. Jansen owned a ranch near Tucson and spent most of his time there. It took him less than two hours to drive from his ranch to Joanne's birthday celebration. He said he wanted to see the "old gal" again anyway, referring to his house in Scottsdale, not Joanne.

"Jansen, tell Joanne why you were in South Africa and how we met," Manny said.

"Well, we almost cancelled my concert at the Johannesburg Stadium, which seats about thirty-seven thousand, because Manny's crusade was in town at the same time and nobody was buying my tickets. The whole city was talking about the Miracle Man. Since the FNB Stadium, where Manny's crusade was held, filled to capacity twice in one day, I thought I should check it out," Jansen said, putting his drink down so he could talk with both hands.

"Two hundred thousand people were reported to have filled the stadium in one day!" he said. "I have never done that. The most I've ever gotten was maybe sixty thousand people in one night, maybe!"

"It might have something to do with the fact that we don't charge two hundred dollars a ticket, Jansen," Manny said, trying to be funny.

"And the fact that you have clouds of fire, healings and you raise people from the dead could have *something* to do with your popularity, don't you think Manny?" Jansen said.

Yeah, that might have something to do with it, Manny thought. He was reminded of something Jason Whitehead said in 1967, that caused an uproar around the world: "Christianity will go. It will vanish and shrink. I needn't argue about that; I'm right and I will be proved right. We're more popular than Jesus now." But Jason was dead wrong; the J. Berry Band was never as popular as Jesus. It only seemed that way for the moment. As far as Whitehead's prophesy that Christianity would vanish and shrink, just look at Manny's miracles sweeping the world and you could see that Christianity was alive and well. Jansen Berry just attested to that himself.

"Anyway, I snuck in to Manny's meeting and got a box seat in the VIP section. I couldn't believe all the people. It was the rainy season in Johannesburg and after the place filled up with people, I noticed there were thousands still, out in the rain, waiting to get in. It was crazy. The only time I've seen anything like it was when the Pope went to Poland a few years back. He rode around in a bulletproof Pope Mobile and spoke to millions of people at a time. But even for the Pope, it wasn't crazy and out of control like it was during my Berrymania days. Now the world is crazy for Mannymania and can't get enough." Jansen sat up and turned his back to Joanne so she could see the writing on his shirt.

"Look at this! I bought this shirt from a vendor at the stadium." The t-shirt had white lettering on it and said, *SWEEPING THE WORLD WITH FIRE CRUSADE*. A white world in red flames was centered on the back of the shirt and underneath were the words, *THE*

BENSON BROTHERS TOUR, 2006-2007. **Manny just shook his head, grinning. His ministry had nothing to do with the shirts, or any of the other items people were producing to sell at his meetings. Shirts, pictures of Manny (especially ones with the cloud over his head) and bumper stickers were the best sellers.**

"I'm sitting there in pain," Jansen continued, "because I discovered I had prostate cancer and was to have an operation immediately upon my return home. I could hardly piss and when I did, it was very painful. Evidently the cancer had spread throughout my body and the doc said I only had a few months to live. Can you believe that? I wouldn't have made it to my sixty-fifth birthday if it weren't for your husband here coming to Johannesburg!"

"It wasn't me, Jansen," Manny said, "It wasn't me!"

"OK, OK it was the Lord," Jansen said, "I'll give you that. Anyway, I was sitting there about to light up a joint and Manny came out onto the stage with a fiery cloud hanging over his head. I was thinking, that's pretty cool, a little special effects doesn't hurt the Miracle Man's mystique; you know I've seen it all. I went to a Marilyn Manson concert once and he had a similar smoky demonic thing going on, hanging over his head; scared the crap out of me, and I thought that was pretty cool. But like I said, I've seen it all, and Manny's little cloud was pretty cool.

"The atmosphere in the stadium suddenly changed, like all the air had been sucked out of the place and people started gasping for air; I started gasping for air; my body guards started

gasping for air. Then I saw all these weird ghosts popping out of people, screaming, swirling, shrieking. I began to shake and something came out of me, shrieking. I mean, I felt it come right out of the back of my neck, clawing at my brain as it left. My bodyguards fell down in a heap. People were collapsing everywhere and I looked at my watch. "My God," I thought, "we've only been here fifteen minutes. This Manny guy doesn't mess around.

"Fascinated and dismayed, I saw Manny just standing there with his arms up in the air. He barely said two words and the whole place erupted into chaos. Never seen anything like it, ever.

"Then I felt a sharp pain in my crotch and it was as if someone was fiddling with my, you know, my giblets. And then the pain was gone. I felt great after that and I feel great today; a new lease on life.

"I went to the doc and he said the cancer has completely disappeared." Jansen snapped his fingers, "Poof, gone, just like that!"

"Wow. Unbelievable," Joanne said, squeaking a bit when she said it. Manny wasn't *sure* if she was referring to Paul's story or the fact that the legend himself was sitting next to her talking about his giblets. In any event, it was a once in a lifetime birthday present; one she would never forget.

"When the crusade was over," Manny said, "Rock handed me a note that Jansen Berry wanted to meet with me in his sky box. Of course, I thought it was a joke. But Rock swore it was not. What would Jansen Berry be doing here,

I thought? When we got to his sky box, there were men lying all over the floor and Jansen here, staring out the window, in a daze. We talked till midnight and have become good chums ever since."

"What did you *chums* talk about," Joanne asked, mimicking Manny's tone of voice.

"We talked about how similar our lives were," Manny said, holding back a laugh. "You know me being an insurance salesman and him being an international rock star. We hit it off immediately!" Everyone roared with laughter, even the bodyguards snickered a little.

"Yeah, we're mates now," Jansen said. "From Berrymania to Mannymania. We're in the same league and all." Then Jansen stopped and reflected upon what he just said and realized they were not in the same league at all; not even in the same universe. Jansen was a genius songwriter and the world was his oyster for forty years. But Manny worked mighty miracles, the kind the world had never seen; in only nine months. How could you compare the two? Manny had done more for the world in nine short months than Jansen ever did in a lifetime of writing songs. If Manny and Jansen sat on a metaphorical teeter totter, the weight would shift in Manny's favor, leaving Sir Jansen hanging up in the air and Jansen knew it.

"Joanne, I want to give you a little birthday gift," Jansen said, motioning up at the house. Out stepped a man in black glasses and a business suit carrying a briefcase. While the attorney walked down the path, Jansen explained.

"I understand you love my old house and you know, I don't need it anymore. So I want you to have it, you know, for your birthday. What do you think?"

"I, I, I..." Joanne stammered.

"She'll take it!" Manny said.

"I had my attorney draw it up and all you've got to do is sign the papers, and it's yours." Jansen held the briefcase flat while the attorney took out the documents. He had her sign and notarize the documents on top of the briefcase. No fooling around. The bodyguards standing around made convenient witnesses.

"Now," Jansen said, "I guess *you're* the fool on this hill!"

Jansen stood to his feet and asked Manny to join him in the master bedroom; the one that overlooked the swimming pool. Once the bodyguards cleared the bedroom and closed the window curtains, Jansen told everyone to leave. He went to the mirror fastened on the wall next to the Van Gogh painting and removed it. Feeling the wallpaper, he pushed some invisible buttons beneath the paper and CLICK, it was the sound of tumblers on a lock.

"All very secret, huh?" Jansen said. "I saw it in a Peter Sellers movie and thought it was a grand idea!"

The seams of the closet door matched perfectly with the vertical stripes of the wall paper. You would never know it was there. Jansen pushed on the left side of the wall and the door opened on the right. He felt for the light switch and clicked it on. Inside the closet was a shiny black safe six feet high and four feet wide.

"Come on in and close the door. It's air conditioned!" Jansen said.

There was just enough room to open the safe all the way, but no more. The safe was built flush into the wall and once the door was fully open, Manny could see that it was ten feet deep. They both stepped in to the safe.

"In 1968 me and the boys went to visit the Maharishi in India," Jansen said, picking up a pair of purple wire rim sunglasses sitting on a shelf and put them on.

"We were having a fun time until we heard that our manager, Dirks, had died. We cut our Indian visit short and everyone went home except me. I took a detour through Turkey, Greece, and Italy with my road manager. We rented automobiles and rode on trains," Jansen removed a Nehru jacket from a hanger and dusted it off, holding it up to see if it still fit him. It did.

"We even hitchhiked some of the way and I've got to say, it was one of the best times I've had in a long time. I was free; free from the crowds and from those bloody bodyguards that were hanging around all the time.

"Not many people know this but I collect things, being a Catholic and all. I mean, I'm not a fanatic about it or anything. I just get a kick out of collecting stuff. In 1968 I was on a Mother Mary icon search; looking for things that Mary purportedly owned." Jansen picked through several things on the shelf, looked them over, blew the dust off, and placed them carefully back on the shelf without explaining what they were.

"Then in an Istanbul antique store, a fellow came in wearing a gelaba (a traditional long dress worn by Arab men) with about twenty bodyguards. He happened to be the store owner and I asked to speak with him. He recognized me immediately even though I had a fake mustache, my hair was slicked back, and I had thick glasses on to disguise myself. I told him what I was looking for and he said he had something of Mary's that was very precious to him, quite rare and extremely expensive. Well, that piqued my attention, of course, and I waited for him to pull it out and show me but he said it was so valuable he kept it at his house under lock and key. So James and I rented a car and drove to his house, or should I say, his huge mansion.

"You wouldn't believe it, Manny, the house was so huge and mysterious. It had a spooky mystique about it. Just the way I like 'em. The house was full of amazing artifacts stuffed in vaults and lying around on shelves. The things he had on the walls and in display cases were priceless. Extremely priceless, I kid you not! He made me sign a document that said I was never to talk about him publicly or reveal where he lived.

"Manny, do you remember reading about my death?" Jansen asked, with a quirky smile on his face. "Well, I had a car accident and the newspapers reported that I had died, so the Berry Band played upon that theme in our songs. Matter of fact, Jason and I competed to see how many songs we could write that had the 'Jansen Is Dead' theme in them. The Collector and I were standing in a vault much bigger than this one underneath his house and he asked me if I really died. Can you believe that? I was standing right there in front of him and he asked me if I croaked and had come back alive! Well, I told him it was a joke, a tongue in cheek thing and the J.Berry Band were having fun with it. And he told me that if we kept pretending that I was dead and playing with death so to speak, I would surely die, within a year! The power of death was not something to be toyed with, he said.

"Well, that scared me to death, pardon the pun. I didn't know what to think. Then he opened a drawer and took out a picture frame, this frame!" Jansen held it affectionately in his arms. The back was sealed with thick rust colored paper, almost card board. Framed in polished mahogany, approximately three foot by four foot in dimension.

Jansen hugged the frame to his body and closed his eyes. Suddenly the room went dark and something pulled Manny rapidly through the ceiling. He saw flashes of light passing by at a rapid pace; like a window seat on a very fast train.

When he stopped moving, the scenery blurred temporarily. Manny waited for his vision to clear when he heard thunder claps and lightning. He heard sounds of weeping, the kind that occurs after hours of crying; the kind of weeping only a mother can do after losing a child.

Manny's vision cleared and it looked like he was in a garbage dump. To his left were a group of people, primarily women, bent over. He moved forward to see what the fuss was about and there was a Man, at least he thought it was a Man, lying across the lap of a woman. *Is that Jesus?* Manny said to himself. *It sure doesn't look like Him!* A closer look revealed a crown of thorns upon His head and a face swollen beyond recognition. Blood was splattered everywhere. The woman, who must have been Jesus' mother, cradled Jesus' body in her arms, rocking back and forth, while the others stood around them, weeping.

Manny sidled up to a man who was with the group. A woman clung to the man in deep despair. When Manny was right next to him, he noticed it was the same fellow he saw when he fell into his pool at the baptism.

"Look what they did to my Master," the man said, weeping profusely.

"Yes, it is very sad but it is for the best," Manny said. "And in a few days He will come back alive."

The man turned and saw Manny's image next to him. His tears made streaks down his dusty face.

"You are the ghost from the baptism!" he said out loud. The woman looked in Manny's direction but couldn't see him.

"Who are you talking to dear?" she said, looking into her husband's face.

"It's a ghost!"

"I am not a ghost," Manny said, "but I am from a time in the future, many years in the future!"

"From the future? Why are you here?" the man asked.

"I do not know why."

"So you say that Jesus will come back alive? How do you know this?"

"He told you that He would rise from the dead in three days, didn't He? And He will! Where I come from it's all been written in a book."

"But it seems so impossible. He was so broken and battered."

"I agree. It does seem impossible, but it's true nonetheless. You will see Him in three days and He won't look like this, all beaten and bloody."

"You say you come from the future and this is written in a book?"

"Yes," Manny said, "it is written that Mary Magdalene sees Jesus alive first. Then she goes and tells the disciples. Jesus will appear to His disciples and then to many others, three days from now!"

The man turned and looked at the woman straight in the eyes. "Can you hear any of this?" She shook her head in the negative. "The ghost is talking about you, Mary. He says you will be the first person to see Jesus alive in three days. How does he know about you?"

"It's written in the book," Manny said as loud as he could. "It's written in the Bible!"

Manny felt a wind behind him and turned to see the back of Jesus, with a host of angels, descending down a flight of stairs. Before the door closed, Manny smelled the stench of something awful coming from the stairwell.

"Manny, Manny, are you alright Mate? You look as pale as my Green Guitar album," Jansen said, showing Manny the front of the picture.

It wasn't a picture at all but a blouse folded very tightly and pressed behind the glass frame. The garment was folded from the waist up and the sleeves were tucked underneath. Around the neck was an intricately embroidered border, bright purple and blue. The whole blouse looked like it had been soaked in liquid rust because the color of it was almost brown.

Jansen handed the frame to Manny but Manny's mind was still seeing the awful Golgotha scene. The bloodied corpse, bruised and maimed, lying across the lap of His mother. The blood soaked woman, hands and legs steeped in her Son's blood, and the unique embroidering around the neck of her blouse; purple and blue.

Manny held the frame in front of him and stared at the blouse, then he closed his eyes. It was the same blouse!

"Oh, my God, Jansen. This is Mary's blouse! Christ's blood and all."

"I know mate. Isn't it awesome?"

"It certainly is. It's amazing!"

"Anyway," Jansen continued, "The bloke told me the story behind this blouse and said that if I kept it near, the blood would keep me safe from harm, and here I am, alive and well at sixty five!"

"Who was the Arab who gave this to you?" Manny asked.

"He didn't give it to me, mate. I paid a million pounds for it. In 1967 that was a lot of money. It's probably worth a billion dollars today. I bet the Vatican would pay a billion for it right now!" Jansen said, staring at the blouse with Manny.

"I mean, do you remember the guy's name?"

"All I remember is he called himself the Icon Collector."

"The Icon Collector? The Icon Collector wrote me a letter a few months ago and gave me a ton of money!"

"It doesn't surprise me. He seems like a rich fellow. He knows everything that's going on in the world. He speaks several languages and looked about thirty years old at the time. He seemed remarkably fit and tan," Jansen said.

Jansen put his arm around Manny's shoulder and said, "This blouse is yours now, mate. It's a gift! You can keep it with the house. No one knows about this safe and no one knows about the blouse. I built the house in 1968 and the blouse was the first thing I brought in. Mary's lived here ever since."

The house, the money and the celebrity status meant very little to Manny since the world was entering the horrible last days. The enjoyment of such things was only for a moment, but still enjoyable nonetheless. After all, Manny was only human and God put 'things' (and the J. Berry Band) on the planet to enjoy, even for a little while. The instant wealth and fame was a lot to deal with but he thought he had nothing to worry about since Pastor Benson and Joanne would surely keep him in line! One of Joanne's favorite sayings is, "Manny, if you screw up, God will kill you; and if He won't kill you, I will!" Manny wasn't worried about God.

Chapter Seventeen

Manny experienced a new phenomenon in Saudi Arabia: bullets of fire falling from the sky.

The soccer stadium in Riyadh filled to capacity for four nights straight. People from all over the Middle East came to see The Cloud, to be healed, and to see the resurrected Harry. In that order.

Manny and Harry went on stage in the midst of violent protests and creative death threats. A package with a slaughtered dog inside was delivered to his heavily guarded hotel room the first night in Riyadh with a note that said that Manny was a dead dog. You've got to wonder if that was the reason God sent His fire that first night.

At seven-fifteen sharp, only minutes after Manny appeared on the platform, the cloud quickly covered the entire stadium. Bolts of fire shot out of the cloud-like bullets from a machine gun and fell upon the multitudes for several minutes. From Manny's perspective it was raining fire, a fire storm. The once vibrant crowd was suddenly dead in their seats, fire still falling.

"Oh my God," Manny said to Harry, "They're all dead!"

Then as suddenly as the rain started, it quit. Ghostly spirits, as puffs of smoke, appeared above thousands of turbaned heads and vanished with a shriek.

But something else was coming, brewing, bubbling. The multitude resembled an undulating wave, as if a wind were passing over it, stirring up the water. Something horrific formed over the crowd of people and in one violent upheaval it exploded. The terrifying noise of angry demons being exorcised en mass was deafening. Manny put his hands over his ears and crouched down in reflex. The mass of "dead" Arabs was vomiting evil spirits into the air involuntarily and an invisible net was collecting them in bunches throughout the stadium. No horror film could have captured the terror the demons evoked, swirling, struggling, screaming for mercy. The net became bigger and bigger, expanding outward, filling the stadium.

Manny elbowed Harry and pointed at the angels near the ceiling working feverishly to pull the net upwards, while other angels flew around poking their swords into the net, keeping the evil spirits inside. With one strong jerk the angels pulled the net up through the roof and disappeared.

It was quiet again.

As if a hypnotist had clicked his fingers and said, "One, two, three. Wake up," every dead person's eyes opened. At first there was a grogginess in the reorientation while the crowds sat up in their chairs. Then the murmuring began in pockets around the stadium. It got louder and louder before it became a dull roar. Everyone was instantly and amazingly healed but that was not what the chatter was about; as a group, the ninety thousand people went to heaven and stood before the King of Kings and the Lord of Lords. They reported that Jesus rose from His kingly throne and preached His gospel to them. He preached at them like a wild man, similar to those Pentecostal guys on television, pacing back and forth, demanding that a decision be made. They said He resembled a lion that roared, with fire in His eyes and strength in His voice. No one resisted, it was said; they all accepted the Lord right then and there.

Manny had no idea at the time what happened to these people. They were dancing in the aisles and praising Jesus.

Revival broke out in Riyadh, Saudi Arabia and the next three nights of revival were standing room only. Fire came down and the Arabs went up to heaven. Hundreds of thousands of Arabs became believers in Jesus as a result, abandoning their other gods and other religions. These new believers evangelized the whole nation within a week. Even the king and his family was said to have become believers, seeing the mighty miracles the Arab believers were performing.

Manny's team had a week off before entering Turkey and Greece. Instead of returning home, they decided to visit Jerusalem.

In the Tel Aviv airport, Manny received his first report from Saudi Arabia that hundreds of Arab Christians were martyred for their faith; mostly by close family members. The news hit the team hard and was a vivid reminder that evangelization of the world was a very serious and dangerous business.

The Israeli government insisted on transporting Manny's group to Jerusalem by helicopter after warning him that this may not be the best time to visit Israel pending a national security issue. But Manny was an international personality, an open friend of Israel and his presence in Jerusalem at this crucial moment might not be a bad idea.

The borders of Israel were temporarily sealed off to tourism and the citizens were told to remain close to home. Manny wondered if it had something to do with another terrorism threat or if it had wider implications. Nothing in the news indicated that Israel was having a problem that warranted the closure of its borders. Tension filled the air as fighter jets rumbled overhead.

It was late in the afternoon when Manny visited the Temple Mount. The area around the Dome of the Rock was uncharacteristically void of worshippers; only security personnel walked the grounds. Nervous Israeli soldiers were assigned to accompany Manny to the mount but were prohibited from entering the esplanade. Not to be denied, Manny asked the security detail to find a way they could view the temple mount area without causing an incident. At the southern end of the Wailing Wall, in the area of the Jewish Quarter, was a ramp that led to an ancient maintenance door. Inside was a stone stairway leading to the top of the Wailing Wall. Once on the wall, the entourage walked north toward the Dome to view it over the trees.

"Hey, Rock, can I use your binoculars?" Manny asked.

"Sure, what do you see buddy?

"Turn around and look south," Manny said, pointing toward the City of David slightly down the hill. "Just past the Al-Aqsa Mosque, down the hill a bit. I think I see a fire burning."

The military personnel and the bodyguards whipped out their binoculars, straining to see traces of smoke just on the other side of the Mosque. Manny noticed an ancient walled area and almost adjacent to the Al-Aqsa Mosque, a small fire was burning. The soldiers were on their phones pointing down at the fire. Finally someone with authority got on the line and wanted to speak with Manny. In broken English he said the section where the small fire was burning, south of the Temple Mount, was where some believe that Solomon actually built the first temple, just above the City of David where King David built his first palace. It is believed that Solomon's palace butted up against the walls of the first temple and that his palace was built just above his father's palace, cut into the side of the hill. The diplomat further told Manny that many believe that the Wailing Wall is not one of the walls of Herod's temple but is a support wall for buildings that supported the Roman troops called Fort Antonia. They built the Roman fortress on top of the hill so they could look down, directly into the Jewish temple below, since most of Jerusalem's events took place there.

"It's the Holy of Holies," Manny said dropping the phone, putting the binoculars back up to his eyes. "The fire is where the original temple was built. Not over there," he yelled, swinging around, pointing at the Temple Mount and the Dome of the Rock. "Not over there!"

Without warning the Jerusalem air raid sirens began to blare and the soldiers pulled the group down the stairs and into waiting police vans. They quickly sped through the old city and unloaded their passengers at The King David Hotel. Once Manny, Harry, and Rock were safe in their suites and back in the capable hands of the bodyguards, the soldiers ran off to some important task.

Fighter jets roared across the sky, shaking the darkened and bullet proof sliding glass doors. The air raid sirens could be heard through the walls and Manny pulled up a chair to peer out of the curtains, wondering if he would witness World War III with a flash and a plume of smoke. Fear struck him when he realized that he was *really* living in the last days. Believers were being slaughtered in Saudi Arabia, attempts were being made on his life, and now he was in Israel when all hell was breaking loose.

Manny's faith began to drain out for fear until he saw his brother Harry, sitting in front of the hotel TV, smiling, oblivious to the danger around him. That put it all in perspective for Manny just like his Dad said. Yes, on the one hand, these are the last days, judgement of the world and all; but on the other hand, Manny had his brother back and nothing could be better than that! Faith restored.

The roar of jets continued throughout the night and in the morning the news reported that Israel and the United States attacked Iran and North Korea simultaneously, wiping out their nuclear weapons plants. Communist China threatened the United States, as usual, without reprisal; while the Arab nations, supported by Russia, threatened Israel.

And that's all that ever happened in the world in the past; saber rattling and boastful threats by nations too weak to stand up to the power of Israel and the United States. But this time it was different. The time had come. It was the beginning of the end. The birth pangs.

By noon North Korea had flown into Seoul, South Korea, bombing the city into oblivion in retaliation for the United States' attack. Hundreds of thousands of innocent people were killed in a matter of minutes. North Korea's army mercilessly invaded South Korea and was in the process of wiping them out, claiming a swift and decisive victory.

China's aircraft carriers launched an offensive against Japan and wiped out all the American military bases, including the industrial cities of Osaka and Tokyo. China challenged the American resolve, gambling that the United States would not retaliate with nuclear weapons; that America was stretched too thin around the world to deal with the Chinese. They were wrong.

The horror continued as Russia maneuvered their warships into international waters off the eastern coast of the United States, threatening to take out America's nuclear capability. By three pm, fourteen Russian subs and aircraft carriers, practically their whole fleet, were sunk; but not without several nuclear warheads hitting their mark in America. One exploded near Charlotte, North Carolina. Another fell on Baltimore, Maryland, which was meant for Washington, DC. And a third fell outside of Newark, barely missing New York City, its intended target.

Manny watched the carnage from his hotel room in Jerusalem. The feeling of shock and disgust washed over him as he tried to make sense of it all.

Jordan, Syria, and Egypt were mounting an attack on Israel, while leaders of the world were calling for peace. It was all televised globally.

By nine that night, the United States had mobilized their nuclear submarines, fighter jets and long range missiles in an all out attack against Russia and China. Dozens of nuclear bombs were deployed against Russia's military and industrial complexes, utterly destroying their major cities, including Moscow and St. Petersburg. Russia once again became a third world country; a wasteland. Millions dead.

Beijing did not exist anymore. An all out fury was launched against it by the United States and pictures later showed that the thirty mile circumference that once was Beijing became a hole several hundred feet deep. None survived.

North Korea also succumbed to the nuclear bomb. From the north end to the south end, North Korea ceased to exist; a dust cloud and a marshland where a country once was. It would be a hundred years before they could threaten anyone with nuclear weapons again.

Israel didn't fool around either. Cairo, Damascus and Amman were convincingly defeated by short range limited nuclear weapons. The Muslims and Palestinians in Israel were gathered up overnight and thrown into concentration camps. That terrorist threat was eliminated. Israel moved into Jordan and removed the Palestinian homeland forever. Israel was not finished extending her borders.

Within nine hours, at least a billion people had been killed and along with them, dozens of modern cities wiped from the map. The United States maintained its dominance over the world, suffering few casualties compared to Russia, China and North Korea, whose devastation was so complete, they ceased to exist as viable and functioning nations.

Fifty-seven air burst nuclear bombs were calculated to have been unleashed in the world causing countless millions to die instantly, but the fallout over the next few days took the lives of millions more. The Lord only knew how many lives would be lost over the next few months and years. Radioactive clouds carried hot particles throughout the world and the residual effect could only be estimated. Some said that the world would be contaminated for a hundred years, others estimated a seven to eight year period. All agreed that the fallout would cause unprecedented cancer deaths throughout the world. Few realized that this was only the beginning. That soon, a third of the population would perish in like manner and then the end would come.

Almost immediately earthquakes were reported on all the continents, especially the west coasts of the United States and South America.

California's San Andreas fault cracked wide open and San Francisco toppled over like a set of dominos. Los Angeles reported thousands of casualties from mudslides, fires, and the crumbling of large buildings. Film footage from news helicopters showed the ground ripple and buckle like a giant wave, rumbling through the valley.

Tsunamis were destroying islands in the Indian and Pacific oceans. More casualties were reported. The west coasts of Canada, Washington, and Oregon were consumed with tsunami waves, wiping out the inhabitants for miles inland.

Everyone in the world was affected by the devastation. No scientist really knew how an all out, worldwide, nuclear exchange would affect the planet. The explosions released violent energy throughout the earth's crust, dislocating the crust, causing it to bend, break and snap into new positions. The snapping of the earth's crust caused catastrophic seismic waves that were as damaging as the nuclear blast itself, without the radiation fallout. One horrendous event led to another; from a nuclear explosion, creating a devastating earthquake, to the radiation poisoning of the world from the residual fallout. Communication lines were severed in Russia and China and medical facilities were destroyed. Famine and hunger began to spread within days and more deaths resulted. After a week, various diseases began to manifest worldwide, a result of fallout, polluted water and the lack of medicine.

"All these are the beginning of sorrows." Manny turned the page in Matthew, Chapter 24 and read the passages that followed: "'Then they will deliver you up to tribulation and kill you, and you will be hated by all nations for My name's sake. And then many will be offended, betray one another, and will hate one another. Then many false prophets will rise up and deceive many. And because lawlessness will abound, the love of many will grow cold. But he who endures to the end shall be saved.' This is where we are right now," Manny said, a week into the devastation.

Manny gathered Harry, Rock, and the bodyguards together in his suite at the King David Hotel to discuss the situation. The world had been thrown into chaos and it was difficult for Manny to comprehend it all. He became physically ill thinking about how many people were suddenly killed overnight and the families destroyed around the world. It broke his heart to watch on television the millions of people sick and dying from radiation sickness. There was nothing he could do but fall to his knees and pray, clutching the vial of blood.

"Guys, all those years, every year," Manny said, with tears in his eyes, "Dad got up behind his little podium and droned on and on about the last days, how horrible it would be. Worldwide devastation, earthquakes, famine. And all those years I thought he was crazy and the Bible was just a fairy tale book. I was wrong. Dead wrong."

Manny started crying. "And now, the last few days, my old man's sermons are coming back to me. He talked about a Beast and his Prophet taking over the world, establishing one government with locust-like creatures being unleashed from a bottomless pit. All this doesn't seem so far fetched anymore. Dad spoke of the world 'going after' the Beast and worshipping him from right here in Jerusalem; from right next to the Temple Mount." Manny pointed and everyone looked out the window toward the Mount. "I thought at the time, 'how ridiculous, Dad.' I thought 'this is the stupidest thing I have ever heard.' Well, gentlemen, here we are and it's not stupid or ridiculous anymore."

"I thought the same thing," Rock said. "I never thought it would happen in our lifetime."

"Same for me," Harry chimed in. "Whenever Dad talked about the last days, I always thought it was for a time way in the future."

The group, motivated by the current conversation, suggested Manny try and get through to Pastor Benson in Arizona. Communications in and out of Israel was restricted due to security concerns. Once connected, Pastor Benson said that the world calamity had caused the circus tents in Chandler to fill up on Sunday. Over ten thousand people turned out, looking pale and in shock. Pastor reminded Manny of his mission; that this was the greatest opportunity in the history of the world for evangelism.

"And this gospel of the kingdom will be preached in all the world as a witness to all the nations, and then the end will come," Pastor said to the group listening on the intercom. "This is our mission. This is what we have been called to do. The birth pangs have begun and we are not to be alarmed, but to press onward and fulfill our mission." Pastor was animated and talking fast as if time was running out. He reassured Manny and the boys that the nations were still calling and wanting him to visit more than ever. The door was wide open for evangelism. Although much of international travel through the airlines had been halted because of the devastation, private jets were warned not to fly because of the confusion and fallout. But Manny's team decided to fly anyway.

After the team swept through Turkey, they would return home. Arizona was the perfect place to operate the ministry and build Manny's huge stadium because the east coast of the United States was reeling from the nuclear carnage. The rest of America remained untouched except for the flooding in the western coastal cities. Manny wanted to stay close to home, conduct his *Make Straight in the Desert* services from the new stadium, and wait for the end of the world.

The Brethren seized the moment, knowing that the axis of power had suddenly shifted and the world was crying out for a leader. The United States was not to be trusted anymore, insane as she was, to do what she did; wiping out a fourth of the world in less than a day. Justified or not, the unwritten rule was not to use nuclear weapons for any reason. America just could not be trusted anymore. The Western European Union had to step in and take control.

The ten nation Union came forward with a press conference, announcing their solidarity, declaring Europe as one nation; a nation the world could trust and believe in. Democratic elections would be held later in the year and by Christmas, United Europe would have its first president.

The press conference went off without a hitch. The leaders of the Union stood behind the interim president from Spain, Juan Carlos, all cheesing for the camera, as he gave a brief speech.

Then the scene changed to the temple mount, with the Dome of the Rock in the background. The commentator announced to the television audience that the newly formed Western European alliance had negotiated an unprecedented peace between Israel and its neighbors.

"To prove the Union's power in the region and the strength of the negotiated peace agreement," the commentator said, "a temple of peace will be built on the Temple Mount alongside the Muslim shrine." The cameras panned to the trees east of the Dome and then pulled back, giving the viewer a perspective of the temple mount.

"Yes, we have been in intense negotiations for the past six months," Juan Carlos said, "and in light of the current world crisis, a gesture of this nature is needed; no, necessary, to restore faith in the brotherhood of man. As a a goodwill gesture, these Middle Eastern leaders," Carlos opened his arms wide, referring to the kings, presidents and parliamentarians that flanked him on the podium from all the major countries in the world, "these brave men and women have chosen to lay down their swords of animosity and pick up the olive branch of peace, not dedicating themselves to peace only in the Middle East, but throughout the whole world." Carlos held up an olive branch for the viewers. This was Carlos' first appearance on the world stage and he was loving it. Swooping in, a European knight from Spain in shining armor, making peace in a world that had suddenly gone crazy. The world loved this young man instantly. He was just what they needed for a sense of confidence and peace.

Manny and the boys watched the press conference from the airport lounge where they were having breakfast before they left for Turkey. "Turn it up, can ya?" Manny yelled to the bartender. When the volume increased, everyone in the lounge stopped talking, and listened.

"Peace, peace is what this world needs right now. A little common sense and a whole lot of goodwill," Carlos said, acting like he wanted to reach out and hug the camera. On Carlos' right stood the Jewish High Priest decked out in his official ceremonial robes with what looked like the rod of Aaron in his right hand. The Priest's eyes were glazed over as he coldly stared straight ahead. *What was going on in his mind*, Manny thought to himself.

"We have decided to build a World Temple of Peace right here next to the beautiful Dome of the Rock," Carlos said, pointing down to the trees, "and we expect to break ground very soon.

We have invited the other religions, especially the Catholics, to build a church of their own here as a symbol of solidarity if they would like, but they have graciously declined." Which was a lie. No other religious group was contacted concerning participation on the temple mount.

"We so much want the temple mount, indeed, the city of Jerusalem, to be a centerpiece of goodwill to the world; a beacon of light to the nations; to live up to her name as the City of Peace. So please, please put down your weapons and join us in our noble effort to bring peace back into the world. The Bible says to pray for the peace of Jerusalem, but I say to you tonight, let us pray for the peace of the world! Thank you and good night."

Carlos held up a dove in both hands, offering a prayer to the gods, and released it. The camera followed the dove into the sky until the bartender had had enough. After saying something uncomely but funny about politicians, he turned the channel back to the CNN coverage of the world holocaust. Unfortunately for the bar, all sporting events worldwide were postponed. It was a sports bar the bartender kept reiterating, not a war bar. What has the world come to.

"Well, gentlemen," Manny said, throwing his napkin on the table, "Juan Carlos from Spain is quite possibly our coming Antichrist or at least his prophet, and right on schedule! But, as we saw the fire burning down the hill in the City of David the other day, Carlos' new international temple might be built in the wrong place. Oh well, let's just hope we can get our job done before he takes over the world and kills everyone.

Chapter Eighteen

The first shot rang out and hit Manny in the right side of his neck. As he fell to the platform the second shot hit him squarely in the back of the head, spraying blood on the Turkish crowd standing in front of him.

Manny heard a loud ringing noise and felt his body violently surge upward in a blur of red and white light. It happened so quickly Manny had no time to think. The blurry white spots in front of his eyes quickly dissipated and he began to see more clearly.

Is that me down there? Manny thought to himself as he slowly drifted away from the scene and out of his body. The last thing Manny noticed before he disappeared through the rafters of the auditorium was a pool of blood draining away from his body.

Still floating upwards, Manny looked down at the gold dome roof and saw the shooter running with a rifle strapped to his back, heading for the maintenance stairs. He watched the man descend the stairs and disappear down the side of the building.

It was a beautiful day in the city of Ankara nonetheless; the sun glistening off various Turkish rooftops and glass buildings. From this height Manny could almost see the Black Sea to the north.

"Come up here!" a voice commanded and Manny's vision blurred. He was transported up through the sky with blinding speed. When the motion stopped, Manny saw the mountain of God, haloed in a thick, fiery cloud of glory. Thunder, lightning, and voices were coming from the mountain. Everywhere he looked were houses, trees, roads...and people, flying in the sky, thousands of them, coming and going as far as the eye could see.

"It is beautiful," Manny said to himself, "Simply beautiful!" Everything glowed with a golden hue; the trees, the flowers, and the snow-capped mountains off in the distance. And there it was, the mountain of God, not anything he could have imagined in his wildest dreams. It stood out over every other thing there; huge and majestic. It seemed to be the center of the place. A magnificent cloud thundered with lightning and covered the mountain two thirds of the way up; but upon taking a closer look, Manny saw it wasn't a mountain at all! It was a golden city, or at least it resembled a city, built upwards in the sky. Maybe it was a city built on the side of a mountain. Manny couldn't tell from where he stood.

The cloud above the city was spectacular, as it swirled in on itself and then thundered outward; alive, electric, and awesome. Lightning, booming thunder, and a crackling sound filled the air. Otherworldly creatures, thousands of them, flew above and into the cloud, circling and diving like birds in the wind. Their wings were forty feet long, end to end, and some of the creatures had several sets of wings extended in flight.

"Holy, holy, holy" echoed down the canyon. "Holy, holy, holy."

Manny noticed thousands of strange looking houses, as big as mansions, lined along the base of the mountain, sprawling down the hill to where he stood. What caught Manny's eye was the people standing outside looking up at the cloud, watching the creatures' aerial acrobatics like it was a Fourth of July celebration. Often a creature broke from the cloud and swooped down across the valley, revealing how big and awesome he truly was. The sight of the creatures up close was frightening to Manny because they looked part man, part bird, and part animal; with arms, legs, hooves, feathers and beaks. Their heads were a mixed combination of human mouths, bird noses, ears of a deer and hair like a lion; eyes went all the way around their head and each eye blinked independent of the other.

Houses were interspersed up the side of the hill, in amongst thick green trees, bushes, and flowers. On top of the hill, a city of glass and gold extended up through the majestic cloud for miles. The city stretched out for miles and the end of it in any direction could not be seen. Manny recalled the dimensions of the New Jerusalem from the Bible to be fifteen hundred miles high and fifteen hundred miles wide. This certainly fit that description.

Where Manny was standing seemed to be a landing site because people suddenly appeared and began walking toward the city. Some were greeted by family members while others began their journey up the main path alone. Manny watched hundreds of people materialize out of thin air and the usual response was, "Wow, I can't believe it" or "I made it! I made it!" Others bent over and kissed the ground. A steady stream of people beginning their heavenly journey filled the path. Manny wondered how many people came here each day.

Down the winding path to the right was a stream of water lined with tall fir trees. Manny saw people sitting in groups, like a classroom, under the trees. At the front of the group was a teacher reading from a book, explaining the text.

The path to the left wound along the landing sites and disappeared into the trees that covered the hills in the distance. Roof tops poked out of the rolling hills filled with forests.

Directly in front of Manny were trees. Trees went up the hill and trees lined the paths everywhere. It looked a lot like Oregon and Washington because of the trees!

The open areas in front of the landing sites were the size of football fields, made of yellow bricks of gold. Each site had its own path, also made of gold bricks, leading through the trees up the hill to the city. Along the back of the open area where the tree line began, clusters of people gathered, waiting for a friend or a loved one to pop onto the landing site. Occasionally a person of importance waited in the back, usually accompanied by others, and was greeted by certain individuals as they appeared on the site. A Jewish believer was almost always greeted by Abraham and his entourage. A Christian pastor or evangelist was mostly greeted by Apostle Paul or by one of the other Apostles. They would talk intently, huddled together, walking up the path. Then there were the suffering saints, the ones who were called to endure great pain, persecution or sickness; they popped on to the landing site with two or three angels at their side, holding them up. These were the ones Jesus greeted personally, then He disappeared. Evidently, the suffering saint was accorded more favor in heaven than others. Manny made a note of that!

Manny was content to stand at the entrance of heaven and take it all in. He knew his mission on earth was not complete and that he would be going back; so he lingered as long as he could. He wanted to tell everyone back home what heaven was *really* like. *Nothing like it in the world*, Manny thought.

No one greeted Manny to lead him up the hill, at least not initially. He was content to be right where he was. Maybe he wasn't supposed to go up the hill. Maybe it wasn't time to enter heaven. Maybe he wasn't supposed to meet Apostle Paul or the other Apostles yet. Manny just stood there and took it all in.

It gave him time to think, which, on earth he had little time to do. So Manny thought. He thought about his life, his wife and family; and he thought about the last days and the Tribulation. He thought how sorry he was for his sins and he thought about thinking. It dawned upon Manny that he had a perfect memory of his life on earth. He noticed that if he thought about an incident in his life, it came to his mind instantly and he could view it like a movie. The activities of sin in his life, however, could be remembered but not viewed, and that was nice, Manny thought. *Why would I want to review my sin?* he reasoned. Manny remembered wonderful images of his wife, his brother on the football field, and recent events of his worldwide ministry; in living color.

Manny quickly went from one thought to another, one memory to another, enjoying every minute of it, and then it hit him: *I wonder if those in hell will see images of their lives played over and over in vivid color; the lust, the hatred, the bitterness, the murders, the lies and the thefts. That would be horrible*, Manny thought. This mental activity of memory and the reality of it caused Manny to vow that when he got back to earth, he was going to create better memories to take with him to heaven.

Waiting there, it had not occurred to Manny what he was now. *Was he a spirit? Did he have a spirit body?* He recalled the memory of feeling a sharp pain in his head and seeing his dead body on the platform, his blood splattered everywhere. *Was he really dead?*

Manny held up his hand and looked at it closely. "It's my hand," he said out loud, but there was no flesh and bone associated with it. "Why does this seem so natural; I mean, why doesn't it bother me to not have my body on me." People to Manny's left were popping out and landing on the yellow bricks. He turned to see that they were spirits too, without flesh and bone bodies. *But why didn't I notice this before*, he wondered? It seemed so natural, even supernatural, to be free from the body here in heaven.

Manny tried to comprehend, even analyze, what he was now. He thought, *Will the real Manny Benson please stand up?* and laughed. He wished he had a mirror to see himself. All those years, his spirit looking out through his eyes, seeing the world around him from a flesh and blood body. And now, realizing that the earthly body was not who he really was? He was really the spiritual person inside all along? Mind boggling. *Death to the physical body,* Manny thought, *and the spiritual body pops into heaven! That's about the gist of it.*

How can something invisible and spiritual, like Manny's spiritual body, be explained to a physical person on earth, unless he has experienced it for himself? He thought about this for a long time. In the same way a person on earth can see the things around him, in a physical sense, a spiritual person can see the things around him, in a spiritual sense. From a physical body you see the world and physical things only; you cannot see into the spiritual realm as a physical body. But as a spiritual body, freed from the physical body by death, the things of the spiritual realm become visible. That was why Manny could see what he looked like, even though he was invisible to the earthly eye.

Using earthly perspective, Manny held out his spiritual arm and tried to explain it to himself. It was invisible, yet he could see it somehow. The shape was the exact shape of his earthly arm. The same was true for his legs and body. It was as if his spiritual body was poured into a mold of the physical body, and after removing the spiritual body by death, the exact impression of the physical body was imprinted upon the spiritual body. *That was why the spiritual body retained the exact identity of the physical body,*

Manny surmised. That was why Jesus was recognizable after His resurrection. His physical body shaped His spiritual body and that was why Jesus looked the way He did today. Jesus the God, forever, will look like Jesus the Man.

Next, Manny pondered the flight of thousands of spirits, human and angelic, coming and going from the mountainous city when Apostle Paul flew in from the right side and landed.

"You're the teacher I saw by the stream, aren't you," Manny said. "I didn't mean for you to leave your studies and greet me. I'm quite content right here, taking in the scenery."

"You didn't take me away from my students. I was told you were coming and I came as soon as I saw you," Apostle Paul said. "You had been standing here for only a couple of seconds before I came. It seemed longer than that, didn't it?" Manny thought for sure he had been in heaven for more than an hour before Apostle Paul noticed and flew over.

"Yes, time flies," Manny said.

"No, actually, time stops," Paul said without moving his lips.

"You are not using your voice."

"No one uses their voice here when communicating. That was why you could hear any conversation that was being spoken, if you wanted to. It's something you get used to."

"And flying, is that something everyone does here?"

"Yes, pretty much. At first, when people arrive, we walk them up the hill into His presence, at least until they get used to the idea. It took me awhile to get used to it, among other things," Apostle Paul said. "You want to walk or fly?"

"I'd rather fly. Where I'm from, we like to fly."

"You mean like that up there?" Apostle Paul pointed to a huge circular ship, a flying saucer, the size of a jetliner, disappearing between the buildings of the city. Manny wondered what a flying saucer was doing here; where it came from, where it was going.

"Well, not quite like that, but yes, we like to fly in airplanes."

"All you have to do, Manny, is 'think the thought' and off you go," Apostle Paul said, lifting off the ground a few feet.

Manny "thought the thought" and shot straight up into the sky about a mile. Then he "thought the thought" and dropped back down where Apostle Paul was.

"It takes a bit of getting used to but you'll get the idea soon enough."

They both "thought the thought" and began soaring upwards, over the houses and trees, toward the city's entrance. Manny looked out over the horizon and saw hills, mountains, streams, lakes and a forest that went on forever. The golden paths that lead up the hill were filled with thousands of people, making a journey through the front gates and into God's presence.

The closer Manny got to the city, the larger it became. The buildings were not the kind you see in New York City, tall and narrow, lined up next to each other. These buildings were miles wide and miles high, made of glimmering gold. You would expect the sun to reflect off the glassy finish, but it didn't. There was no sun or moon in heaven, Apostle Paul told Manny; nor was there darkness of night. Matter of fact, everything Manny saw in heaven had its own light emanating from itself and these huge buildings were no different. It was as if everything in heaven, including the trees and flowers, glowed; a heavenly golden glow. The place was alive.

From far away the buildings looked like massive walls of solid gold, but up close, there were millions, maybe billions of windows and terraces covering the sides of the walls.

"We have a lot to talk about and not much time to do it in," Apostle Paul said. "Do you mind if we talk while we travel? First of all, in case you did not know, to your right is the City of God, the New Jerusalem. I came here like you, many years ago. I died, came here, and walked that path down below and then through those gates right there," Apostle Paul pointed to the entrance up ahead. "And the beloved disciple Stephen greeted me when I first came in."

Manny stared at the building in front of him as they passed by. Down on the ground, a wall about two hundred feet high ran around the city, also made of large stones of gold. In the wall were designs and patterns of many colors. Precious stones in a myriad of colors were inlaid to create the designs.

The arch on the gate ahead stood about fifty feet above the wall at its height. The doors themselves were two hundred feet high and fifty feet wide, making the entrance at least one hundred feet in width. A giant angel stood at the entrance dressed in a white robe, a purple belt around his waist, a gold band around his forehead, sandals on his feet and hair that fluttered whenever he turned his head to look upon the people passing by. A two-edged sword was in his right hand, held waist high and was never dropped to his side in fatigue. Manny wondered how the angel could hold that sword for so long without getting tired.

"I was so flabbergasted by this place," Apostle Paul said, "I was left speechless on how to describe it to people when I went back. I gave up trying. And Manny, you haven't seen anything yet. Wait until you see the sea of glass where Jesus is."

"Yes, this is pretty overwhelming, even by our modern day standards," Manny offered.

"We are all spirits here," Apostle Paul said. "That means we have yet to receive our glorified bodies. Jesus is the only One who has received the glorified body and He is magnificent; more than you can imagine. In a little while, when Jesus goes to earth for His Bride, all of us here will receive a resurrected body. It is the event we are waiting for, just like the church is waiting for Christ's return. We are patiently waiting for our new bodies."

"I have never understood how a person can go to heaven," Manny said, "live here for thousands of years, and still be considered dead; to be resurrected later. It seemed too much to comprehend."

"There are approximately five hundred million people in heaven right now," Apostle Paul said, "and all of us are dead, so to speak. Yes, we live as spirits in the presence of the Lord, but we are spirits without bodies; bodies that died on earth. We are clothed temporarily by this habitation called heaven. Without this, we would be naked, unclothed, without a place to live. When Jesus, who is our life, the one who clothes us, returns for the church, we will return with Him to be resurrected from the dead and receive a bodily habitation to live in forever. As spirits here in heaven, we are alive to God but dead to everything else. Spirits need bodies to function in. What I mean is, as spirits we cannot go anywhere else except heaven. We cannot go to earth without a body and we cannot travel to the faraway lands without a body. All we can do here in heaven is wait and rest in God's presence until He snatches away the church from earth and clothes us with new and everlasting bodies."

"What about the angels? Scripture says they live here too."

"The angels are an interesting subject and remain a mystery," Apostle Paul said. "Some are a source of great joy and some are a source of great sorrow."

"I have read your writings," Manny said, "and most of them are difficult to comprehend."

"That's because I got it from here! I learned it from heaven. When you go back, you will suddenly understand my writings and be able to explain them to others. The things of the Lord are spiritual and heavenly. These things cannot be understood by the earthly mind."

"I have so many questions."

"Yes, I understand completely, but that's not why you are here. For now, you are to receive just enough revelation to get you through the next few years on earth. I went through the same thing when I first came into heaven. Just coming here opens up a flood of questions. My questions were not all answered either. I received just enough information to fulfill my ministry and nothing more. The fact of the matter is, all your curiosities and wonderings about this place will forever be answered when you finally come to rest here."

"That's good to know," Manny said, "I understand the world is about to enter a great tribulation. Several nations have already destroyed each other. It's frightening and I wish I knew what to do."

"After today, you will come to know more," Apostle Paul said, "thinking the thought" and landing in the midst of a group of men at the front gate. Manny landed too and glided superbly next to the Apostle, alighting like a ballerina with one leg up.

"Nice landing, Manny," Apostle Peter said, laughing out loud in an audible voice. The sound of it rang all the way down the hill. "It's really great to have you here with us." The smile was Peter's distinguishing feature. He beamed with exuberant joy.

"Yes, very glad to finally get to meet you," Matthew said, and the other Apostles chimed in their greetings. They acted like brothers meeting for a Christmas dinner, joking and comfortable with each other.

"Finally get to meet me?" Manny asked, bewildered. "It's you men everyone wants to meet! You are the famous ones. Everyone studies and reads your writings. You're the famous Apostles of Jesus!"

"Yes, I suppose that is true," Paul said, looking at the Apostles and smiling. "But what Matthew is referring to Manny, is that we too have read about *you* in a book!" The Apostle let that sink in.

"You're kidding me, right? Me in a book?"

"Actually, several books. Yes, they are a fascinating read too," Apostle Paul said. "Signs, wonders, miracles, fire, glory. The works. More than we ever did as individuals or as a group put together. You are the famous one to us, Manny!"

"Holy Cow!" Manny said.

"Isn't that a Hindu belief, Manny?" Paul said, looking at the Apostles, and then all of them roared with laughter. The twenty foot angel craned his enormous neck and glared over in their direction. When he saw it was the Apostles, he seemed embarrassed and quickly turned back to his guard duty.

"You are written about because of the end of the age; the time we've all been anticipating," Matthew said. "You've been assigned to bring in the end, Manny; and we are very interested in the end because that's when we will be clothed with our new bodies. We wait for our new bodies like you on earth wait for the Rapture."

"We Apostles are known for being with Jesus during his earthly ministry. You are known as the end times Apostle before the Rapture of the church. Very, very soon," Peter said, "we'll all have brand new glorious bodies!"

"But I am not worthy to be honored in this way. I don't deserve to be written about in a book or to be here with you!" Manny said to the Apostles.

"None of us deserve God's grace, Manny" Andrew added. "Jesus chose us, we didn't choose Him. Most of us didn't have any idea, until we died and went to heaven. None of us were worthy of any honor and we know it. We were chosen, we fulfilled our ministry, and now, here we are, just like you."

"There were points throughout history," Apostle Paul said, obviously the teacher among the group, "where significant events were highlighted, peaks of the mountain poking through the clouds. Some events were so pivotal to the history of mankind in relation to God's plan that there was a need for God to provide additional revelation to the one involved in the event. God has brought you here to provide you with revelation and inspiration so you can fulfill your ministry."

Apostle Paul and Manny said their farewells to Peter and the Apostles. Manny counted them one by one as they flew off into the distance, thinking how strange it was to see them flying. No one back home would believe that he saw the Apostles, let alone that they can fly! Manny counted eleven Apostles taking flight, twelve counting Apostle Paul. Was there an Apostle missing?

"Paul, did Judas Iscariot make it to heaven?" Manny was trying to remember his Sunday school lessons.

"I'm afraid not. We haven't seen him here and the Lord has not mentioned him either."

"Yes, I'm sure. Poor guy. I counted eleven men taking flight. Are you one of the twelve Apostles?"

"Oh, heavens no!" Apostle Paul said, almost embarrassed at the thought. "I am the thirteenth Apostle! Matthias was chosen to succeed Judas."

"Well my father, for one, believed that Peter jumped the gun and cast lots for Matthias prematurely; when you were supposed to be the twelfth Apostle, not Matthias."

"That's not correct. No, I was chosen years later to be an Apostle, as a man born at the wrong time, to be the thirteenth Apostle but I'm not the last Apostle, Manny; I'm only the thirteenth!"

They flew the two miles underneath the archway leading to the city and when Manny was inside, he could not believe his eyes. The hill he thought the city was built upon was not a hill at all, but a gigantic mountain. The buildings were actually built into the side of the mountain and encircled it for miles and miles. The mountain could not be seen from the outside because the gold buildings hid it all the way to the top. Hundreds of roads came from the huge buildings off in the distance in all directions. Manny thought it had to be a land for giants.

It was leveled off where they stood and a hundred miles ahead of them the mountain began to angle upwards. As Manny's eyes tracked the mountain from the base, where a huge metropolis sprawled along the valley floor, another city could be seen in the side of the mountain several miles up. Manny looked up still further and another city was built into the side of the mountain, and another city and another; city after city spiraled up the mountain for miles. The top of the mountain could not be seen because a cloud covered it, the same cloud Manny saw from the landing site.

The sky was completely obscured by the cloud that surrounded the mountain, yet it was sunny outside and a perfect climate. *But where was the light coming from if the cloud covered the whole city?* Another mystery.

Manny tried to get a perspective of the enormity of this place but it was difficult to do; his mind could not grasp it.

"Let me just stand here for a moment," Manny said. "It's more than overwhelming."

"Yes, it is still breathtaking, even after the *two days* I have been here!"Apostle Paul said, looking over at Manny, waiting for him to get the joke and smile. But Manny didn't smile. He didn't get the joke.

"One day as a thousand years and a thousand years as one day, Manny. I've been here two thousand years in earth days but in heaven's time, I've only been here two days! Do you understand my humor now?" Manny did and smiled.

"So how long have I been here already?" Manny asked.

"Oh, about five seconds, give or take," Apostle Paul said, pretending to look at a wrist watch.

"That means my body is still lying there on the platform in a pool of blood and people are running all over the place. My assassin is bolting for the exit right now."

"Is he? Are you sure you are actually dead?" Paul asked quizzically. "When a person comes here for the first time, one can never tell if he is dead or not. Sometimes God gives a vision of a horrible event as a warning. Are you sure that's not happening to you right now?"

"I'm pretty sure. I saw my dead body lying there in a pool of blood. Isn't that pretty sure?"

"I don't know,"Apostle Paul said, turning away with a smile. "One can never tell."

Chapter Nineteen

He woke up in the cozy leather seat and looked out the window. It was pitch black outside. The jet ran into turbulence and the glasses on the table clinked noisily. That was what woke him up. Everyone was asleep, including the bodyguards. Manny got the impression these guys didn't eat or sleep. They were always on duty.

Manny wobbled into the bathroom and after washing his hands he looked in the mirror. His face was glowing. *It was such a vivid dream,* Manny thought, *so real in every detail. Was I really there or was it merely a dream like the Apostle said?*

"Everything alright, sir?" Sam asked.

"I think so," Manny said, jerking toward the door, alarmed that Sam was standing there. Manny must have left the door open. "I just had the most amazing dream and well, it's still on my mind, Sam."

"Do you want to talk about it, sir?"

"Yeah, I do, Sam. Maybe you can help."

Huddled together at the back of the plane Manny told Sam how he was lifted up into the air and saw his own body lying on the platform, the back of his head blown off and blood pooling on the floor. From above the auditorium he saw the assassin running across the roof and down some stairs.

"Did you see any other assassins, Manny?"

"No, I only saw this one guy. I knew he was the assassin because of the rifle. Why do you ask?"

"Normally these shooters work in pairs. If one can't get a shot, the other usually can."

"I saw *this* guy by accident. We practically ran into each other as I floated by. It was so real."

"When we get to the airport I will alert the authorities at the auditorium and I will personally scan the rafters for shooters. Do you want to cancel the event? It would be understandable under the conditions." Sam was referring to the condition of the world.

"A wise old man once told me," Manny said, "'The gospel must be preached at all costs.' The show must go on, Sam! Don't cancel a thing."

Rock woke up and saw Manny sitting alone at the back of the plane.

"Hey, Manny! Want some company?"

"Sure, Rock. Just sitting here contemplating my dream."

"You too? Phew, I had a doozy. I'll tell you mine, if you tell me yours. Want to hear it?"

"Sure thing Rock. Fire away."

"Well, we were in an auditorium and I heard a couple of rifle shots. I knew it was a rifle because it sounded like the kind we use for hunting around the farm. The next thing I know, you are lying on the floor. So I look up where the shot came from and I see a guy running with a rifle toward an open door. I grab Harry and point toward the rafters and off we go to chase down the shooter. The bodyguards grabbed you and hauled you off. Never knew what happened to you. Anyway, Harry and I bolted through the back door and ran toward the fire escape hoping he'd come down that way. Sure 'nuff, there he is, wearing an orange maintenance jump suit. He sees us, stops, and takes a shot. The next thing I know I'm floating in the air like in a hot air balloon, seeing the whole city all around. The last thing I remember is seeing the shooter in orange running across the parking lot with Harry in hot pursuit. Then I woke up. It was as real as can be."

"Did you see what happened to Harry?" He glanced at Harry squirming in his seat.

"Nope. I just remember floating up in the sky. What about your dream, Manny?"

Manny told his dream in vivid detail, including the part where he was standing with Apostle Paul gazing at the flying saucers in the distance. They compared notes, realizing they were in the same dream.

Rock yawned, bored with the conversation and left Manny to find some food. They promised to watch each other's back and stay out of the way of flying bullets.

Back at his seat, Manny couldn't sleep so he settled in to read his Bible, something he hadn't done in a few weeks. The flight to Ankara was still another eight hours long, so this gave him a good time to ponder his dream of heaven. About two hours into Manny's Bible study, Harry rousted himself from sleep and downed a bottle of water.

"Hey, little brother, what are you reading?" Manny held up the Bible so Harry could see the cover. "What has you so absorbed?"

"Oh, just some ideas I got from a dream," Manny said, putting the Bible on his lap. "And talking about dreams, have you had any lately?"

"Matter of fact I have; just now. Want to hear about it?"

"Let me guess. I got shot, then you ran outside with Rock and he got shot. Sound about right?"

"Yeah, that's right. How did you know? I chased the guy in orange down the street and when he stopped to take a shot at me, I tackled him like in the old football days and splattered his head all over the pavement. The little guy didn't know what hit him. I heard a shot and turned to see another guy across the street firing a pistol at me, so I picked up the sniper's rifle and got behind a parked car. It all happened so quickly. Anyway, I aimed the rifle and hit the guy in the chest with my first shot. What a dream! It was so real."

"Did you see what happened to me or Rock?" Manny asked, sitting forward in his chair.

"Yeah, when I was running back to see how Rock was, I saw your bodyguards dragging you out the back door and throwing you in one of the ambulances. I stood over Rock with my hand on his bloody chest to see if he was still breathing. He wasn't. I watched as the ambulance drove over to a waiting helicopter. They stuffed you in and off it went." Harry cracked open another bottled water and gulped it down. "It was so real, Manny! I'm still thirsty from the ordeal."

"Anything else happen that you can remember?"

"It was chaos. People busted out the back door and from around the corner. Police were everywhere. I knelt down and looked at Rock's pale face. He was dead alright. But we've seen a lot of dead people look like that in the crusades and they came back to life. So I knew that Rock would probably be OK. They threw Rock in another ambulance and took him away."

"At what point in the dream did you wake up?"

"Well, let me think."

Harry closed his eyes so he could see. "Yes, as I knelt there with Rock, a Turkish man came over and calmly said some things to me. That's when I woke up."

"What did the Turkish man want, Harry? It may be important."

"He told me to take a good look at the dead assassins, to memorize their faces. So I walked over to the first guy and I took a good look at his face. Then I walked over and looked at the second guy; the one I drilled with the rifle and memorized his face. He spoke to the Turkish policemen and they went through the assassins pockets, searching for identification. There was none. He told me when I got back from my dream, to tell you what happened so this tragedy could be averted.

"Did he tell you his name? Who was this man?"

"I think he said he was a coin collector."

"You mean the Icon Collector?"

"Yeah, that was it. He had a heavy accent when he spoke, but yeah, the Icon Collector."

Manny must have fallen back asleep because when he opened his eyes, he was looking up at the mountain in heaven. Then Manny heard a familiar voice in the distance.

"Manny, I brought a friend." He wheeled around to see Apostle Paul walking down the path with his old buddy Rock.

"Hey Rock, what a shock to see you here. We must have fallen back asleep," Manny said greeting his friend. "Here we are together! We both must be dreaming again."

Of course Rock was wild eyed, looking around everywhere. If his neck was flesh and blood, it would have twisted off by now.

"No, no...I was being chased...I got shot in the chest...I'm not dreaming," Rock said, very distracted by all the cool stuff in heaven. "No, no, I'm not dreaming...I was shot in the chest."

"Of course you're dreaming. We are on the jet. We must have fallen asleep."

Apostle Paul leaned over and said, "Manny, are you sure *he* is dreaming? Look at all these people flying here and there. Can you tell which ones are dead, which ones are dreaming and which ones are in a vision?"

"I didn't know it worked that way," Manny admitted. "I thought you had to die in some manner to get here."

"Yes, you have to die to stay in heaven, but to visit...?"

"But I died in a dream to get here!"

"Did you?" Apostle Paul said. "Anyway, I've got work to do, people to greet and teach, so you boys are on your own. The Spirit will guide your journey from here. Remember, Manny, fulfill your ministry. We're all counting on it." The Apostle "thought the thought" and disappeared.

Turning to Rock, Manny asked, "How are you, buddy? Heaven's pretty cool, huh?"

"Yes, beyond cool," he said, eyes bulging from the overload. "The Apostle wants me to join him later for a Bible class down by the river, isn't that totally cool? He said I need to learn some things, you know, doctrine and stuff."

"He's quite a gentleman, huh Rock?"

Manny became concerned about Rock. Harry spent twenty-five years down by the river when he died. He wondered why Rock was going down there? Wouldn't he have time to learn from the Apostle when he *really* died? This was just a dream, right?

He let Rock enjoy this amazing moment and when he saw Rock's attention finally focus on the flying saucers out in the distance, he leapt at it.

"Hey buddy, let's go check out the space craft behind the mountain. Whatcha think?" Manny said. "Ready for some adventure?"

"Always," Rock replied.

"Did Apostle Paul tell you about 'thinking the thought' to fly yet?"

"No," Rock said. "When we walked up the hill he said you would fill me in on all the details."

Manny told Rock everything he knew about heaven and how to "think the thought" for flight. Rock shot up further than Manny in his first attempt at takeoff. After imitating Superman a few times and accomplishing a roll or two in the air, Rock finally got the hang of flying.

"Takes a bit of getting used to, doesn't it?" Manny said, imitating Apostle Paul's demeanor.

To avoid the traffic, Manny led Rock to their right toward the golden buildings that rose endlessly into the sky. Then they made a slow turn and followed the buildings northward a few hundred miles, keeping their eyes fixed on the flying saucers. The mountain was now to their left as they picked up speed and Manny looked back at the hordes of people and vehicles covering the sky. But up ahead, where the angelic creatures lived, was a different picture.

The fifteen hundred mile area that surrounded the mountain seemed to be divided down the middle; the cities of the humans on one side and the cities of the angels on the other. The human cities resembled those on earth, with meandering roads and different shaped buildings, reflecting the creative nature of the human soul; *much like their Creator*, Manny reasoned. The angelic civilization, on the other hand, was made up of long buildings resembling army barracks, arrayed in a circular fashion around the flying saucers' landing sites. The buildings circled outward for miles until they were met with other barracks that circled in their direction. From high in the sky and as far as the eye could see, it looked like a valley of concentric circles, as if someone had dropped thousands of rocks in a lake of water, creating a circling wave effect. There were no individual buildings, no meandering roads and no sky filled with millions of people going about their business; just thousands of circles and thousands of flying saucers arrayed within the circles.

Manny and Rock stopped in mid air when they saw a group of beings shoot up from the midst of the valley and began moving very quickly toward them like a swarm of bees. Manny noticed his absence of fear, but tried to feel it anyway. *Fear is such a natural reaction on earth*, Manny thought, *but here, there was nothing to fear.*

Instead of running for his life, as would be his normal reaction, Rock simply gawked at the spectacle and said, "Look at that Manny; that's really cool." To Rock, everything was cool in heaven. And it was.

Within seconds the swarm was close enough to become recognizable. Thousands of fierce angelic figures filled the sky, coming to an abrupt halt in front of Manny, hovering in the air. He noticed that many of the creatures had an odd appearance, something like he'd never seen before. A grayish-green color with long snouts and scales on their skin like a snake or an alligator. The back of their heads protruded upward in the shape of a cone and their greenish ears were pointed outward, or they had no ears at all. These reptile looking creatures seemed to have a permanent crazy-like smile fixed on their faces because their mouth and alligator teeth wrapped around their long snouts, jutting upward at the end where the upper lip meets the lower lip. Two human-looking angels with large foreheads and jowls, dressed in white garments and gold bands around their heads, moved forward and greeted Manny and Rock without moving their lips.

"We didn't expect you here, Mr. Benson," the angelic creature said, bowing his head in humility.

"Where did you expect me?" Manny asked.

The angel looked up at Manny in surprise, not having anticipated his question. He acted unsure of himself and fidgeted as he glanced over at the other angel, wondering what to say.

"Yes, um, my name is Gergon, sir, and this is Layster," the other angel said. "You might say we are on holiday, taking a break, sir, while you tour the city. Your one minute on earth can be weeks and months here. So we are on holiday. You don't need our presence here, sir. We serve you exclusively, invisibly, on earth. We take care of your business affairs there, sir." Gergon waved his arms toward the hovering host of angels and they all bowed their heads in unison.

"I guess I don't understand what is going on here," Manny said. "Would someone tell me what's going on? You sure don't look like angels I imagined. What are you?"

Gergon looked over at Layster and shrugged his shoulders. "He's yours, Layster, you've got to answer his questions."

"Normally sir, we don't have conversations with the Eternals; so it is awkward for us to do so," Layster began, clearing his throat. "We mostly deliver messages; not carry on conversations. And, we are not technically angels, sir, as you would expect. Our Master refers to us as Living Creatures. We serve Him and you, sir."

"Eternals? Living Creatures?" Manny said, "What is an Eternal?"

"You are, sir. You are what we call an Eternal." Layster turned to Gergon in embarrassment. Manny almost felt sorry for him, if he wasn't so darned big and mean looking!

"OK," Manny said, "Obviously you are struggling here, so let me set you at ease. All I want to know is why you are here with all these angelic creatures and what is going on."

Gergon thought he knew what to say next, so he said it. "The reason we are uncomfortable, sir, is because we, that is us, I mean the Living Creatures, do not have mutual communications with the Etern...I mean you humans. What I mean to say is, we do not have conversations, interactions, with the Eternals on earth like the angels do. We just take care of your business. That's all we do. The angels do much more. The angels, sir, are more like you in many ways."

"Let me get this straight: you are saying you Creatures don't have relationships with humans on earth, correct? Where you interact and carry on conversations?"

"Yes, that is correct," Layster replied. "Well, you are not supposed to be here in the Living Creature's abode, I do not think...conversing with us," Gergon said. "None of the Eternals come here, nor do they converse with us, ever. The angels converse with you but not us. You Eternals normally, I mean almost always, go directly into his throne room upon arrival; but never come here." Gergon pointed toward the cloud on the mountain and everyone's head turned to see, then turned back.

"Let me ask this once again: Why are you all here, hovering over us in the air; thousands of you, in a threatening manner?" Manny asked strongly, getting a little perturbed.

"Well, sir, we are…" Layster looked over at Gergon who shrugged again, "we are your Living Creatures, sir! We go where you go."

"You are what? But there has to be thousands of you!"

"Yes, exactly, sir. Seven thousand three hundred and forty three, to be precise, sir. And Mr. Simon here has seven thousand two hundred and eighty…creatures with him, sir. We are all here, sir. At your command. Fourteen thousand six hundred and twenty-three to be exact, sir. We were not expecting you, I mean, to meet in this way, to be seen in such a manner, at our abode."

"Are you saying that you guys are our angels? Is that what you are saying?"

"No sir, I mean, yes sir," both Living Creatures said in unison. "We are at your command, sir."

"How long have you been our angels, slash, Living Creatures?" Manny asked.

"Sir, do you mean how long have we been Living Creatures, or how long we have been in charge of your families, or how long we have been in charge of you? What are you asking?"

"Let's start with an easy question: how long have you been Living Creatures?"

"We are all ten thousand, six hundred and fifty nine years old…in earth time. In heaven we are approximately ten and a half days old," Layster said, more confident with exact calculations, rather than trying to formulate and interpret human concepts, which is difficult to know.

"OK. Tell me about your cities and how you came to be our Living Creatures?"

Gergon spoke, confident that he had the hang of human conversation. "In the beginning the Father assigned us these abodes you see below and we have dwelt here until His calling forth to serve the Eternals. Our cities were full in the beginning and as the Eternals filled the earth, we left our abodes to serve them on earth. Over the years, these cities became more and more vacant. Today, only a few billion Living Creatures remain in the cities; for all the lineages on earth have been born and we have emptied the cities to go serve them."

"How many billions of Living Creatures are you talking about?"

Layster chimed in. "Two hundred billion, four hundred million…give or take a few hundred thousand."

"A few billion? Two hundred billion isn't a few?" Manny asked. "There appears to be a lot of you still left in heaven."

"First of all," Gergon said, "compared to the trillions that once occupied these dwellings, a few billion is a mere trifle."

Manny looked over at Rock and said, "Trifle?"

Gergon continued speaking. "There are wicked Eternals throughout history whose Living Creatures go back to the city when they die. Their job is finished. That's a few billion creatures. Then there are the righteous Eternals who are in heaven after they die. Their creatures go back to this city, unless they attach themselves to the righteous Eternal's lineage, if need be; which most do. That's why a Late Eternal can have thousands of angels attending him. Like us here with you, Mr. Benson. We have gathered over the centuries to be your guardians."

"You mean Late Eternals referring to humans who are born later in history, right? So you are saying that many of the Living Creatures that were attending my ancestors, have attached themselves to me and my family?"

"Yes, that is correct. And finally there are Living Creatures that have never left these cities because their host has not been born yet, or their host never was born in the first place."

"So, let me get this straight. You are not angels but Living Creatures? Creatures that act like angels most of the time?"

"That is correct," Layster smiled, he was successfully communicating with a human.

"Ok then, where are the other angels, the others like yourself that are the *real* angels?"

"Well, sir, they are everywhere; just not here in our abode."

"So, why did you come to greet us in the air? Rock and I just wanted to look around and check out your flying saucers," Manny asked.

Layster looked at Gergon quizzically and asked, "Sir, when you say flying saucer are you referring to the Cherubim?"

"Those things," Manny said, pointing to the north. A saucer in the distance alighted from the circular launch pad and slowly ascended, disappearing through the thundering glory cloud.

"Yes, those are Cherubim, for the most part," Layster said. "They are the transport vehicle to other lands for us Living Creatures, is what I mean. They are called Cherubim or chariots of fire." He pointed over at the gold wall where it met with the thunderous cloud. Creatures, with and without wings, flew in and out of the cloud, passing through the wall and disappearing, then reappearing in another location. "Those are the angels, sir. They use the vehicle, also the chariots, to transport into glory. Both the angel and the vehicle is called Cherubim."

"What do you mean? Where is glory?" Manny asked.

"Up there, sir," Layster pointed up the mountain towards the Lord's tabernacle. They watched as a flying Cherubim entered the cloud and vanished. "Above His tabernacle are the portals to glory that lead to universes unimaginable. We've never been there, sir. As far as we know, the Angels are the only ones who go there, in those vehicles."

"Apostle Paul said he went there once," Manny said, still looking at the cloud.

"Unimaginable," Layster said again.

"Yes, unimaginable," Gergon repeated. The host of hovering Creatures nodded in agreement.

"Well, Rock and I wanted to take a ride in one of those Cherubims. Can you arrange it?" Manny motioned toward a cigar shaped Cherubim that was just coming through the cloud.

"It is not my will that can permit such things," Gergon said. "You are being summoned elsewhere and will not be allowed to enter our cities or the Cherubim at the moment. I understand, though, at a later date you will be permitted back and will take a journey into glory. After all, the glory is your destiny and heavenly purpose."

"We are here, sir," Layster added, looking up at the cloud, "because we are *your* helpers; we go where you go. And right now, we are to accompany you into God's glorious presence and then, we are to make sure you get back to your plane before it lands. Our holiday is over."

Chapter Twenty

Mr. Boergenes opened the display case and reached in to touch the rare and priceless manuscript. The memory of those days was vivid, even though it was so long ago. The parchment felt like dried leather, stiff and brittle, yet he turned the page anyway. *The Lamb has opened the first seal*, he thought to himself.

Squinting at the handwritten Greek text, he was embarrassed at the scribbles. *It was granted to the one who sat on it to take peace from the earth and that people should kill one another.* His fingers backtracked across the parchment, but the lettering was faded. *He opened the second seal.*

"It has begun," Mr. Boergenes sighed out loud. "And it will continue until the end!" He spoke in English, to no one in particular, since the twenty or so guards in the foyer spoke only Turkish. *Only a few years before we prophesy in the temple; then we will be with our Lord forever.*

He didn't know if the third seal was opened but in certain regions of the world a quart of wheat cost a day's wages. This was the case in Russia, where atomic bombs wiped out the entire farming industry. Citizens were selling bread and other items at inflated prices.

It was an undeniable fact that over one and a half billion people were killed in the short war and millions were still dying from the fallout. This constituted a fourth of the world's population and was evidence that the Lamb had opened the fourth seal.

Mr. Boergenes placed his forehead on the edge of the display case and closed his eyes. Both hands grasped the faded Revelation manuscript. In a tremble he was there, standing once again before the majesty of God's throne. The area before the throne was immense, miles across, and millions upon millions of souls filled the place. *Many more people than when I was here before.* Just ahead was the cloud of God booming with thunder, alive with energy and electricity. The cloud swooshed in and out, swirling like a controlled tornado; bolts of lightning shooting in all directions. The glory of God covered the arena for miles. If there was a ceiling, it could not be seen.

He buckled at the knees and fell to the ground, bowing his head in reverence and awe. The ground was like a golden mirror and the reflection of his face could not be seen; for when he looked upon his own image in the glass, all he saw was the image of the living Christ looking back at him. *One does not see himself here in this place. Only the image of Jesus.*

"Cousin, it is so good to see you again," the Image within the ground said.

"It is good to see you too, Master!" he replied. "Thank you for letting me come."

Mr. Boergenes slowly picked up his head to see the Father who sat on the majestic throne and the outline of a glorious Man standing next to him. The face of God was unrecognizable because it shone outward like the sun on a hot day. The natural impulse was not to gaze too long on His brightness, for there was something frightening about the image. A slight movement of His head caused rays of light to shoot across the valley and sounds of loud thunder resulted from a twitch from His finger. The Cherubim creatures that encircled the throne, who dove endlessly into the cloud like birds playing in the wind, roared loudly whenever God made any kind of movement at all.

God's throne sat on the inside edge of the cloud, facing the sea of glass where all the souls worshipped. The greatest amount of energy and power emanated from where God the Father sat and pulsated inward and outward in waves. The fearsome cloud began and ended at the throne and the depth of the cloud extended behind the throne forever. It was as if God stepped through a door into heaven from the mysterious place behind the throne.

Jesus stood to the right of the Father, also glowing as the sun. He was lit up like a light bulb, shining outward, so much so that His face was unrecognizable. Mr. Boergenes dared not look further upon God's glory, bowing his head again to see the image of Jesus in the golden glass on the floor beneath him.

"Cousin, I have called you here to meet with Manny and to prepare him for the days to come; to share with him his destiny," Jesus said. "Danger lurks at the door, so take wings to your fortress. Reveal yourself there, in the secret place, under the blood.

"Stand to your feet and come near so that I can see your face," the Lord said. Mr. Boergenes stood and walked toward the platform. Jesus stepped out of His fiery glory and materialized as a Man dressed in a brilliant white robe down to His feet, with a gold sash around His chest. *He looks like the Jesus I once knew, but His hair is white, not brown as I remember.*

Jesus walked down the wide steps of the platform and met Mr. Boergenes beside one of the fires that burned continuously before the throne.

"You look well, cousin!" Jesus said, reaching out to him.

"I am well, Master," Mr. Boergenes said, falling into His arms.

Jesus moved His lips close to Mr. Boergenes' ear and whispered, "You know I love you, son, do you not?"

"Yes, I know You love me, Lord. I have not forgotten."

"Nor have I forgotten. The Father has answered your mother's request and granted for you to sit at My right hand, when this is all over."

"Lord, I am so pleased. It is my only desire."

Mr. Boergenes released the manuscript from his grip and instantly was back in his body. He steadied himself and repositioned it in the display case, making sure the ancient Revelation was open to the correct page. Then he boarded his private helicopter for the ride to the Ankara airport. He wanted to arrive early for Manny's meeting and had a lot to pray about before then.

Manny flew upon the heavenly highway that flowed toward the mountain, with fifteen thousand angelic-like creatures trailing close behind. Now he knew why the highway seemed so crowded; people with their angels were flying up to the tabernacle.

The closer they approached the entrance, the louder the cloud became. Crackling, snapping, booming and swooshing sounds dominated the air.

"Reminds me of the lightning during the monsoon season in the desert, Rock."

"Yes, it's awesome," he replied. "Nothing like it."

The entrance into the cloud narrowed and the souls landed on the ground to walk the rest of the way. Countless angels, twenty feet tall, stood to the right and to the left of the opening, surrounding the mountain, watching every person as they entered. Their huge heads darted in every direction resembling the movements of a bird. Manny and Rock's angels bowed to them slightly as they passed by.

"What are these?" Manny asked Layster. "And why are they here?"

"Sir, these are the Seraphim; but we call them the Watchers and they guard the entrance to the temple."

"Guard the temple from whom?"

"From intruders, sir."

"Are there intruders here?" Manny asked.

"Well, you tell me," Layster said, cowering down as he looked back at them. "Would you try to intrude after seeing these warriors?"

Manny got the point. Any kind of intrusion would indeed be foolish.

They passed through the opening with thousands of other people, everyone conversing with one another. The cloud enveloped the crowds, ushering them into a wide open area, an area so large that the ending of it could not be seen. Scattered over the acreage were millions of people in various stages of worship. Some were standing with both arms in the air, others were on their knees, but most were flat on their faces, prostrate before the Lord.

Miles ahead, on a raised platform formed out of the side of the mountain, sat the glory of God. The booming, crashing electric cloud; cascading upwards like a mushroom cloud. Odd looking Cherubim creatures twirled about, diving into the cloud, roaring like animals. *An awesome sight*, Manny thought.

He noticed that the cloud he just walked through was above, behind, and in front of him. It swarmed in the direction of the platform like a river torrent, swirling around and around, in all directions. The closer he got to the platform, the harder it was to walk. His impulse was to collapse onto the ground right then and there, but he kept moving forward. The atmosphere around him slowed down and he moved in slow motion. But he continued to move forward.

Rock dropped to the ground a mile back and Manny noticed that the angelic creatures hovered all around the outskirts, hundreds of thousands of them.

Only humans are allowed to worship here, a voice said.

Manny finally gave in and fell to the golden floor. He made a futile attempt to crawl but it was fruitless. There was no way Manny was going to make it to the platform where God sat, as much as he wanted to.

At another time you will come here and then we can visit. For now, you have a destiny to fulfill.

Manny opened his eyes to see Jesus' face, like an image on a flat screen TV, looking up at him from the floor. The sound of His voice came from everywhere at once and could be heard perfectly. Manny tried to speak but no words came out. He attempted a thought but his mind went blank. In utter exasperation Manny gave up and clung to the floor. From the recesses of his mind Manny said *I surrender, Lord. I surrender.*

"That's where I want you, Manny. At the end of it all."

In a labored fashion, Manny managed to crank his head up to see a man standing over him, the same man he had seen and conversed with in his visions.

"It is my turn, ghost, to visit and encourage you," the man said. "So many years ago, at the cross, you lifted my faith when I had all but given up. You and my wife held up my faith when I was about to fail the Master. Jesus was dead, slaughtered like an animal, and all hope was gone. The universe was falling apart. My Master was dead, lying in a pool of blood, never to live again. Then, like a ghost from the past, you came to the present and spoke hope into the future. That is why Peter and I ran to the tomb! We had hope in your words, ghost. We wanted to desperately believe you."

"You didn't need to believe me," Manny managed to say, his head plopping back to the ground. "All you needed was Mary's report of His resurrection."

"And we did believe her report, for she was wonderfully hysterical about it. But her report was early on resurrection morning. It was her report that caused us to run to the tomb. It was your words of faith, Manny, that sustained us for the three days prior to His resurrection. And for that I am eternally grateful."

"Who are you exactly, may I ask?" Manny inquired, his face pushed into the floor.

"Yes, you may ask," the man said, helping Manny to his feet. "But first we must go back. I will explain everything later. You and I have a destiny to fulfill."

Manny's soul was so full of the glory of God he could hardly think or move. They walked arm in arm through the crowd, picking Rock up on the way, flying back through the entrance with the Living Creatures falling into formation from behind.

"Manny, when you get to the airport, I want you to meet me in the lounge," the man said. "You need to wake up now!"

"Manny, you need to wake up now," Harry said, poking his brother's chest. "We're about to land."

The bodyguards could hardly keep up with Manny when he bolted out of the jet. He headed straight for the lounge, glancing around like a mad man.

Alarmed, Sam asked, "Manny, who are you looking for?"

"The man in my dream," he replied.

"You mean the guy who shot you?"

"No, another man. He told me to meet him in the lounge. I don't see him."

Manny sat in a chair where he could see his jet. The pilots were removing the bags from underneath the belly and Rock was obviously discussing his dream with Harry on the tarmac, waiting for their luggage. Then the lounge windows began to shake as three helicopters appeared from around the corner and hovered near the helipad. The rotors kicked up a flurry of dust, causing the boys to end their conversation and run into the lounge.

When the dust cleared, a dozen or so men filed out of the helicopters and surrounded the third helicopter in military precision.

"Hey, Sam, do you recognize what that says on the side of the helicopters?" Manny asked.

Sam unfolded his binoculars and took a peek. "It looks like Turkish writing to me."

One of the flight attendants waiting in the lounge spoke up. "I know what it says. Let me have those binoculars." She pronounced the words out loud in Turkish and said, "The Property of the Icon Collector. Antalya, Turkey."

"The Icon Collector?" Manny said. "What's he doing here?"

"I suppose he's here like everyone else," the flight attendant said, "to see the faith healer from America."

"Oh really, do you think so?" Manny said.

"Of course, why else would he be here? The whole country is here, it appears. All the hotel rooms are booked and there are people sleeping on the sidewalks around the auditorium waiting to get in. Ankara is abuzz with excitement. That's why I'm leaving; too many people!"

"So you know about the meeting, huh? What are people saying about this faith healer," Manny asked.

"My Mama loves him; thinks he's a saint," she replied. "Of course she's Catholic and all the Catholics love him. But the Muslims aren't quite sure about him. Some think he is the antichrist and others don't really care, as long as he heals people. They say he'll heal anyone regardless of their religion."

Manny kept his eye on the helicopters. The Icon Collector's bodyguards stood nervously around for the longest time. It usually meant trouble, Manny knew, when there was a delay like this; exposed in the open like that.

"Sam, can you find out what's going on?" Manny asked.

"No sir, I cannot leave your side," the bodyguard said.

So Manny called Rock and Harry over and asked them to find out why the Icon Collector was not coming out of his helicopter.

"And what do you think of this faith healer," Manny asked the woman.

"Oh, I think he is a phony," the flight attendant said, acting put off by the question. "Just full of baloney."

He noticed that the flight attendant was rubbing her swollen knees. A closer look revealed knobby knuckles and an obvious pained expression on her face, a telltale sign of inflammation and arthritis.

"How old are you?" Manny asked.

"I'm almost thirty," she blurted, then blushed, becoming self-conscious. "Do I look older to you?"

"No, no, you look fine. I asked because my wife, Joanne, once had terrible arthritis throughout her body and she used to rub her knees like you are doing."

She pulled back her hands and tried to straighten her tiny skirt, very self-conscious now.

"You say she *used* to have arthritis?"

"A very bad case of it I'm afraid. But the Lord healed her instantly," Manny said. "Do you want to know how?"

"Of course, I'm on the edge of my seat. Tell me."

"The phony faith healer you are talking about touched her and she was instantly cured. Now she can do handstands and cartwheels like in High School and all her pain has disappeared, vanished. Snap, just like that!" Manny snapped his fingers.

"Sorry to interrupt," Rock said, "but airport security said that they are having a difficult time waking him up." Rock pointed out the window at the helicopter.

"Waking him up? Maybe he had a heart attack. Isn't he an old man?" Manny asked.

"They've called the paramedics to the scene," Rock replied, "but the body guards won't let them near him."

The white and red striped ambulance parked just outside the ring of security and the paramedics tried to get through to the helicopter, but were held off by the guards with automatic weapons.

"No, he isn't an old man," the flight attendant said. "They say he is a mystic, a holy man, and he lives in an ancient mansion down by the ocean."

"How do you know these things?" Manny asked, turning his attention back to the woman.

"The Boergenes family is something of a legend around here," she said, rubbing her knees again. "My grandmother used to tell stories of a man who lived by the sea who came to her church and displayed precious religious artifacts to the congregation. She said he was very nice and even let her touch the blouse that mother Mary wore on the day she held her crucified Son. She said it was stained with Christ's blood."

"That is amazing," Manny said, staring out the window again.

"I don't know if I believe it, but after that day, my grandmother didn't have to use crutches. She said the blood on that blouse healed her of arthritis."

"I believe it," Manny said.

"Believe it or not," she said, "I wish I could touch that blouse. I am in such pain."

Suddenly out of nowhere, a storm blew in and a cloud descended over the airport. Manny rose from his chair when he saw the shadow move across the tarmac and stand still over the helicopters.

"Tell me more about that man," Manny said, pointing out the window. "It is a fascinating story."

"They say he is a mysterious man, never showing his face," she said. "His face has rarely been seen because he wears a hood, sunglasses or a hat whenever in public. No one knows what he looks like. I haven't seen any pictures of him. Everyone thinks he is a wealthy recluse and in Turkey there is an unwritten law that the Boergenes family is to be left entirely alone. No paparazzi, no autographs, no news reporters. And I understand from grandmother, that this is the way it has been for hundreds of years.

"The Boergenes family is allowed to maintain their own personal army. And they are the only family in Turkey that is allowed to have an army accompany them wherever they go, weapons and all; except of course for the Turkish royal family. They travel with an army too. And as you can see outside, no one goes near or challenges the bodyguards. They have permission to kill at will. The Boergenes family go and do what they want. They are treated like royalty some say.

"There are hundreds, maybe more, militia on his property at all times. They say his mansion is equipped with military tanks and rocket launchers to protect the family, which no one has ever seen; the family I mean. They are total recluses. No one dares go down to the mansion without permission. Even tourists are steered away from the estate for fear of stiff prosecution and no one wants to risk going to a Turkish prison; they are the worst in the world, you know.

"Does your grandmother know who the Boergenes' are and why they are so special?" Manny asked.

"There is a lot of speculation and local folklore. Some say they are a royal Turkish family from centuries ago. Others say they are simply wealthy business owners who've inherited the family business and want to be left alone. There could be some truth to this because there are many Turkish families who have maintained their businesses for centuries and have become famously rich.

"A popular folk tale is that the Boergenes dynasty is connected to the lineage of Christ somehow. This is what my grandmother believes and most of the local Catholics. This explains why the government leaves them alone. They know the secret of who the Boergenes family really is; a secret national treasure of sorts. And my grandmother believes this explains why the Boergenes family have rare and precious artifacts in their possession."

"Which story do you believe?" Manny asked, reaching into his pocket for the vial of blood.

"I don't know what to believe. Mary's blouse didn't heal my grandmother. The old woman wanted to believe in the fairy tale, so she got better. Until I experience it for myself, I won't believe."

"Well, I believe," Manny said, slowly pulling out the cork. "I came all the way from Arizona to attend the faith healer's meeting. I don't think he's a phony."

"Arizona? Isn't that where the faith healer is from?"

"Yes it is." Manny tipped the vial and a drop of liquid fell on his finger. He immediately felt a surge rush through his being and colorful images flashed into his mind.

"Do you mind if I pray for you right now?" he asked, touching her hand.

"No, not at all," she said, closing her eyes like grandma taught her.

The flight attendant didn't hear a word Manny prayed because she slumped over in her chair and rolled onto the floor. WHAM! The crowded lounge suddenly went strangely quiet and when Manny opened his eyes, he saw everyone at the bar and on the various couches had fallen to the floor. Rock and Harry fell also, including all the bodyguards.

Manny stood alone in the lounge and looked out the window. Mr. Boergenes' guards began to quickly pile back into the helicopters.

"Mr. Benson, Mr. Benson," yelled the Icon Collector's bodyguards running into the lounge. "You must come with us right now. You and your men." Manny pointed at "his men" lying on the floor. "Do not worry. We will retrieve them." More help came from the tunnel and the boys were dragged to the waiting helicopters.

At the same time, military soldiers ran into the lounge from the lobby and dragged as many people out into the hallway as they could. They thought the people in the lounge had been gassed and were wearing masks.

"Where is Mr. Boergenes?" Manny asked, safely on the helicopter, buckling his seat belt.

"In the pilot's seat," the co-pilot said, "fast asleep."

Sure enough, there he was, slumped over against the window, with his helmet on. Manny sat forward to get a glimpse of his face but all he could see was the back of the helmet.

"Does this happen often?"

"He's not actually asleep, he's in a trance. We were halfway here and he went out cold. And no, it doesn't happen often; at least when he's piloting the chopper. It may happen more often when he is alone in his chapel, but we have no way of telling."

"Where are you taking us?"

"Look down to your left," the co-pilot said. "The airport is under attack and we had to get you out. Sir, this would be a good time for you to put your helmet on." Manny obeyed as he watched out the window.

Military jeeps were converging on the small airport and men were fleeing in the direction of Manny's jet. There was gunfire and an explosion.

"Oh my goodness," Manny screamed, "They blew up the lounge."

The helicopter made a sharp turn to the left and Manny caught a glimpse of the lounge windows exploding outward, glass falling all over the tarmac. The Turkish military converged on the bombers and killed most of them before they boarded a helicopter and fled. Manny was concerned that the bomber's chopper would come after them, but instead, they went in the opposite direction. His other concern was for the safety of the woman he prayed for in the lounge. He wondered if she got out alive.

"Don't worry, sir, their chopper is not equipped with fire power," the co-pilot said. "Ours is! We could blow them out of the sky and they know it."

"So where are we going?" Manny asked again.

"We are taking you to the auditorium, where your meeting is being held tonight. It's the safest place in Turkey right now. There are more soldiers at the auditorium than there are people. The place is already packed to capacity. They will know what to do with you there."

"What about him?" Manny nodded toward the Icon Collector.

"Oh, we'll take care of Mister B until he comes out of his trance. Don't you worry about that. We will die before we let anything happen to him. His life is far more precious than ours."

"You know," Manny said, "I believe I was supposed to meet a man in the airport lounge today but he didn't show up. Do you know anything about that?" Manny asked.

The co-pilot glanced over at Mister B and said into the headset, "You say you were supposed to meet a man in the lounge? Did you know who it was?"

"No, he didn't give me his name but... and this may sound strange to you; I met him in a dream."

"A dream you say? Mister B went into a trance at the house and when he came out of it, he was in a hurry to get to the airport," the co-pilot said, scratching his chin. "Could it be him you were to meet?"

"Honestly, I do not know. I'm beginning to be confused about what is real and what is a dream."

"I'm not sure what Mr. B wanted to do at the airport. He didn't say anything about meeting you in the lounge."

Safely on the ground, Manny's team was escorted to the lush waiting room reserved for celebrities. Rock was happy with the abundance of food and private restrooms. Harry was still thirsty and quickly gulped a couple of waters before stuffing an extra in his pocket.

The assistant assigned to Manny's entourage came back with news of the airport bombing. No one in the lounge was killed because they were all lying down. The bomb was set off near the windows and the explosion blew shrapnel four feet above the ground in all directions. If people were sitting in chairs, couches or at the bar, their heads would have been blown off. The only injuries were to the military personnel crouched over, helping those on the floor.

It was unclear who the bomb was intended for: Manny or Mr. Boergenes. Frequent attempts upon Mr. Boergenes' life were common place. If he had not been sleeping in the helicopter, he would have been in the lounge when the bomb exploded. His nap saved both his and Manny's lives; it was the blood that saved everyone else.

The bodyguards found the one shooter from Manny's dream hiding in the auditorium rafters, holding a scoped rifle. When discovered, he ran out the door and was shot several times in the back before he got to the stairs. Manny made sure Rock stayed in the bathroom during the ordeal; no reason to let him get killed again.

When Harry heard the shots, he ran to the rear of the auditorium and before he got to the door, a man in an orange maintenance suit stepped in front of him. *I recognize this man. It's the same man I killed in my dream!* As Harry opened the door for the man to exit, he stuck out his foot and tripped him; then jumped on the assassin's back and slammed his face into the asphalt. There was a muffled gunshot sound and the assassin's body arched briefly and went limp. The impact of the fall caused the shooter's finger to recoil and fire off a round into his own stomach.

Chapter Twenty-One

On the day Manny landed in Ankara, the Turkish army invaded Northern Syria and Iraq, attacking Kurdish terrorists there. For many years the Kurds had used Syria and Iraq as rebel bases and Turkey was hoping the international community would ignore their aggression, in light of the present world condition. Little did Turkey know that the Brethren's Western European Union was looking for an opportunity to establish a foothold in the region. The country of Turkey was a natural land bridge between Europe and the Middle East. European armies had marched through Turkey for centuries conquering empires as far as eastern China and Mongolia. The Brethren's immediate goal was to utilize the conduit of Turkey to rid the Middle East of Israel's hated enemy, Ishmael's family, the Arabs and the Muslims; ending the age long wars against Jacob's family, the Jews.

If the Union could seize control of Turkey now and place an international peace-keeping force in the region, made up of the armies of the ten Western European Nations, the Brethren would be on their way to controlling the Middle East. Once the Muslim nations were defeated, Israel and the Brethren would bring the world to their knees through the exploitation of their vast oil resources, causing Israel to become the wealthiest nation on earth. And Juan Carlos,

Israel's up and coming savior, would become the richest and the most powerful man on earth.

Juan Carlos II of Spain was put in charge of the international peace keeping force that invaded Turkey. He choppered into Istanbul with the first wave of attacks. Carlos watched from the air as fighter jets from Bulgaria bombed Istanbul and outlying areas into submission, softening the battle field. Then he sent troops from Greece and the Aegean Sea to sweep Turkey southward in a massive military campaign.

The roar of fighter jets on the outskirts of Ankara could be heard from inside the auditorium. It was eight o'clock and fire from the cloud rained down upon the crowds. The walls and the platform vibrated from the shock waves of distant bombs, but Manny thought it was a manifestation of God's presence in the building. Soldiers and security personnel scattered for the exits and Manny wondered what was happening. An army of men ran toward the stage, led by someone Manny had seen before, a familiar face; the man from his dream.

"We've got to go Manny. Follow me," the Icon Collector said, running out the exit. "We'll be safe on my compound."

They instinctually ducked beneath the rotor blades and entered the helicopter, the same helicopter Manny rode in from the airport. The Collector buckled himself into the pilot's seat and put on his helmet. Manny looked over at the co-pilot he rode with earlier and the co-pilot leaned back and grinned.

"Have a nice nap, Mr. B?" Manny said.

"No one but Lenny here calls me that. So I gather you two have met?" The Icon Collector said. He was on the microphone to the other helicopters while flipping switches and pushing buttons. He told Lenny to confirm that the weapons were hot and to watch for incoming.

"Gentlemen, we have a destiny to fulfill! So let's get Mr. Benson to Antalya safely."

"We met at the airport. Didn't he tell you?" Manny said.

"Actually no. I came back to earth when the cloud descended on your meeting and watched the fire fall upon the people," Mr. B said. "I will never get used to seeing demons leave people like that, Manny."

"So you're the man I've been seeing in my visions," Manny said. "And you're the one who spoke to me in heaven!"

The helicopter lifted off the ground and within seconds it propelled into the sky, pulling Manny back into the seat. Off in the distance the sky was lit up with fire and explosions. Behind, two helicopters followed, carrying Rock, Harry, and the bodyguards.

"That is correct," the Collector said. "I first saw your ghostly image at The Baptism, nearly two thousand years ago. Many years before you were born."

"You what? If I went back to the past two thousand years and saw you in a vision, how could you come forward two thousand years from the past, unless you were a ghost in a vision like I was?" Manny said, dumbfounded. "I mean, are you really here right now, or are you talking to me from a vision?"

"I am really here right now," the Icon Collector said. "Touch me if you don't believe it. Go ahead touch me."

Manny reached out to touch the Icon Collector when the helicopter swerved violently. A missile screamed by the window, veering away from the chopper.

"We are under attack, Manny. Hold on to your seat," the Collector said. "Evasive maneuvers. Fire at will."

"Who's attacking us?" Manny asked, literally holding his seat.

"I am not sure at the moment but our intel says that Europe has invaded Turkey. We are trying to communicate with the attackers to inform them that we are not with the government."

"They want us to land, sir," Lenny said.

"How many are there?" Mr. B asked.

"Just one chopper, fully loaded. I am sure more are on the way," Lenny replied.

"Inform them that we are not landing and give them warning of our capability."

"All of our capability?"

"No. Just sufficient cause to think twice."

"Manny, you visited me two thousand years ago. You were transported backward in a vision to where I was; to the time of Christ. But I have not done the same. I have not come forward two thousand years, transported by a vision, to visit you," the Icon Collector said. "I lived in the time of Christ and I currently live in the time of Manny Benson. Think about how that could be."

"Sir, they don't believe in our capability," Lenny said.

"Make them believe. Show them the Wrath of God," the Collector said. "The Wrath of God" was a code phrase for a deadly maneuver the pilots drilled on every day for years. It was so named because it brought a gruesome end to any intruder foolish enough to challenge Mr. Boergenes' authority.

Suddenly the three helicopters stopped on a dime, pivoted in midair and fired upon the lone chopper. They didn't have a chance. The attackers exploded into a ball of fire and the Icon Collector said into his headset, "May God bless them, in the same way they were to bless us." Several voices echoed, "Amen." Manny said Amen too.

Juan Carlos was on the ground and his troops surrounded the auditorium. He was surprised that Manny was gone so quickly. The plan was to kill Manny Benson per the Polycarp Directive and blame it on the international peace keeping force as an "unfortunate accident of war". The speech was already written.

Carlos watched as the Union's surveillance helicopter was blown out of the sky by the Icon Collector. *Those must be military helicopters,* Carlos thought, *and Manny Benson is most likely on one of them, being transported by the President and the Prime Minister to a safe location. I will kill all of them at the same time. This may be my lucky day.*

"Track their movements. I want whoever is in those choppers!" Carlos commanded. "And I want them all killed!"

"We're lit up, sir. They are tracking us," the co-pilot said. "It looks like their whole army is following."

"It is OK Lenny, the Lord told us to 'take wings to the fortress' and I intend to obey his word," the Collector said. "Inform the boys at the compound that this is the day they've been training for and they must be ready for anything. Those anti-aircraft missiles might finally come in handy. God will deliver us until the end."

"Twenty minutes, sir, and we will be at our location," Lenny said.

"Who are you, Mr. Boergenes?" Manny asked. "How could you have lived and known Christ so long ago, and yet, be alive today? Did you get resurrected by the blood of Christ like my brother, Harry? Even the Apostle Paul and I joked about bringing him back after so many years."

"No, I was not resurrected," he said. "That's funny about the old Apostle, because he and I had the same conversation just a few hours ago when I was in a trance. He asked if I had any relics of his, like old bones or one of his garments, in order to bring him back to life. He really wants to be here for the Rapture."

"Is that possible?" Manny asked.

"All things are possible with God."

"Especially for the anointing that is in that blood, isn't that correct?" Manny said.

"Yes, that is correct. You figured out the secret of the blood, did you?"

"Actually no. I can't take credit for anything. The Lord told me about it."

"We have a few minutes before we land, so let me tell you about the precious blood of Christ. A few days before Jesus' death, Mary of Bethany anointed Jesus' feet with spikenard. This ointment is found only in India and is made out of the dried roots of an herb called nard. The ointment has a wonderful odor and was used as a perfume in Bible times. Because it was so expensive, few used it for its original purpose of preparing a body for burial. The oil adheres to the skin for a long period of time and is a strong preservative, preventing the skin on a dead body from deteriorating quickly. Preserving Jesus' skin for burial was not the reason He allowed the women to anoint Him with the ointment."

"Women?" Manny said. "I thought only one woman, Lazarus' sister, anointed Jesus."

"No, two women anointed Jesus, both named Mary, both anointed Him in Bethany, but two different women," the Collector said. "The first woman was Mary of Bethany. She anointed Jesus' feet. Her brother was Lazarus. The second woman was my wife, Mary of Magdala, who anointed Jesus from head to toe at the home of Simon the leper. I know because I was there!

"When Jesus was crucified, most of the blood in His body went to His feet and poured for several hours onto the ground. The blood from the thorns on His head and from the nails in His hands, streamed down His oily body and dripped off His feet onto the ground in front of me." The Icon Collector started to weep and flipped off the switch to his headset. All three helicopters were listening to his story and choking up. One by one the headsets clicked off for a few seconds. Manny took the opportunity to blow his nose.

"The spikenard ointment," the Collector continued, the headsets clicking back on, "preserved the precious blood of Jesus to this day. That's why Mary of Bethany anointed His feet six days before His death; so it would have time to soak in to His skin. Jesus knew that most of the blood would pour from His feet. That's why Mary of Magdala anointed His whole body, including His feet again, two days before His death. Jesus wanted to preserve His own blood for us. He knew the anointing would remain in the blood and that the spikenard would preserve the blood for all these years."

"That explains why the blood you gave me is oily and gritty to the touch," Manny said.

"Yes, the oil is the spikenard and the grit is from the dirt, where the blood hit the ground."

"Tell me more about the anointing and why it adhered to Christ's blood. How does that work?" Manny asked.

"The anointing of the Holy Spirit is the most important aspect of the Believer's life," the Icon Collector said.

"And the least understood," Manny replied.

"Yes, that's true, Manny. It's just as important as the words He spoke and the works He accomplished, but Christianity today has lost the true meaning of the anointing. That's one of the reasons Jesus preserved His blood for us; so we can know what the anointing actually is in these last days.

"The anointing came upon Jesus at His baptism. You were there, Manny. You know what I mean. The anointing is simply when the Holy Spirit comes upon a person and fills him with power. Jesus was so filled with the Spirit, that the power of God exuded from His body.

"Throughout the centuries, Bible scholars have tried to explain Jesus' popularity. Some have said that Jesus spoke words of truth and that's what made Him popular. Others say that Jesus was a real nice man, that his Godly personality attracted people to Him. Still others have said that crowds followed Him because of the miracles. The truth is, the anointing of the Holy Spirit so filled Jesus, that power continually flowed from His person and touched people. That was Jesus' secret; the power of the Holy Spirit. He was the Power of God on earth.

"Why does the anointing stay in the blood? Jesus' blood was symbolized by the blood sacrifice in the temple. When a sacrifice was made, the people experienced the power of the Holy Spirit, because where the blood is, the power of the Holy Spirit is. Simple as that.

"The blood I gave to your friend to give to you contains the anointing of the Holy Spirit, the Power of God. It is Christ's blood perfectly anointed with the Holy Spirit of power. When you use the blood, it is the anointing of Christ that performs the miracle.

"Manny, ever wonder why the cloud of glory accompanies your meetings? It is because of Christ's blood. God's glory and power is in that blood.

"Sir, the landing site is just ahead," Lenny said. "Do you want me to take it in?"

"Yes, you take over," the Collector said."Your hand is steadier when it comes to flying into trees. How far back is the enemy?"

"They are right behind us, sir."

"You know what to do."

For over a thousand years it has been the responsibility of the attendants to protect the Icon Collector at all costs. Initially, in the sixth century, the attendants consisted of unmarried Catholic monks who joined him in his destiny. His destiny became their destiny. But it didn't take long before the monks grew old and died. Before the monks became extinct, Mr. Boergenes convinced many of the younger ones to marry and build homes on the mansion's property. For six hundred years their children took over the responsibility of caring for him, until the Knights Templar arrived, marrying the women on the estate and turning the property into a military compound. When the Knight's destiny changed from searching for ancient relics in Israel to protecting One in Turkey, they changed their name to the Knights of the Beloved, to reflect their new calling.

There was one time in history when the Icon Collector's life and precious artifacts were severely threatened by an outside army; in the late twelfth century when the Ottoman Turks plundered Antalya and invaded the mansion. The Knights of the Beloved converted the Boergenes mansion from a quiet monk retreat to a noisy compound of warfare seventy- five years before the Ottomans attacked. Without the Knights' rigorous battle training, the Ottoman would have conquered the estate and added the ancient artifacts found there to their booty.

Ignoring the local folklore and legend concerning the Icon Collector, the Ottoman Turks stormed the property with a hundred men, searching for gold and treasure. Once past the gate, killing twenty men, the Turks proceeded down the hill toward the mansion. Coming upon the servants' quarters, they found them abandoned. After torching the buildings, the Turks headed for the mansion and were surprised that the huge wooden doors to the foyer were wide open. The soldiers fanned out and searched the lower level of the mansion. When they discovered that the doors to the downstairs rooms were locked and the second floor was blocked off, it dawned on them that they might be trapped. Panic seized the Turks as the doors to the entrance were slammed shut. From their secret tunnels underneath the mansion, the attendants entered the mansion and slaughtered the invaders, pulling their bodies into the tunnels, never to be seen again. From then on, the locals believed that the mansion was supernaturally protected by God and because of this, subsequent superstitious invaders avoided disturbing the estate for fear of being cursed.

Lenny flew to the secondary landing pad down by the water's edge. The other two helicopters touched down near the mansion with six enemy choppers on their tail, led by Juan Carlos. It was pitch black outside and the attendants positioned themselves throughout the compound, ready for hand-to-hand combat. Several missiles narrowly missed Harry and Rock's helicopter as they were running for cover, exploding into the side of the mansion. Rock grabbed at the pain in his chest, thinking it was a side ache from the hard sprint to the house.

The second helicopter was hit as it landed, spinning sideways down the hill, smashing into trees. None of Manny's bodyguards were in the burning helicopter. They were in the other chopper, running behind Rock and Harry with their weapons drawn.

Enemy soldiers wearing night vision goggles rappelled down from their choppers, but were shot before their feet hit the ground. Expert snipers on the roof picked the enemy off with single shots to the head, even in the dark.

Two enemy choppers further up the hill unloaded their soldiers, who made their way toward the mansion from different directions. One platoon approached from the west and the other approached from the east. The thick forest of trees slowed their progress and the platoons became isolated from one another. Using the trees as a natural defense and knowing the terrain like the back of their hand, the attendants swiftly eliminated the enemy to the west, using their knives and neck wire. The enemy was quietly dispatched.

The platoon to the east made it to the rear of the mansion by moving slowly and staying together. In communication with Carlos, they knew that the other platoons were neutralized. It was their mission to search for and kill Manny Benson and the Turkish leadership, if they could be found.

Through a cellar window, the platoon entered the mansion and reconned their way to the first floor, blowing open one of the doors with explosives. Searching the vast foyer area, the dozens of heavy oak doors leading into the mansion were locked and difficult to break into with only the butt of a rifle. The platoon leader didn't know where he was or which way to turn. He felt trapped. Being a young man, he panicked. "We're trapped," the platoon leader said. "Retreat back down to the cellar!"

Similar to what happened to the Ottoman Turks in the twelfth century, the present day attendants came out of nowhere, in every direction, with lightning speed, and quickly killed the whole platoon. To avoid spilling blood on the marble floor, each soldier was choked and dragged into the tunnels. They were confirmed dead there.

Harry and Rock were led into the dark mansion, through winding hallways and down narrow stairs. Doors from behind were slammed shut and the scraping of metal sliding across the wall to bolt the doors shut was heard from behind, echoing down the hall.

Rock felt faint but what could he do? It was dark and they were running for their lives. He fell to his knees but a bodyguard from behind reached under his arms and carried him into the room. The final sliding bolt was slammed shut and a light was turned on. Blood was gushing out from a wound in Rock's chest. The front of his shirt and pants were soaked in blood. Rock's face grew pale and his eyes fixed in a gaze. He was slowly dying.

The co-pilot, Manny, and the Icon Collector just finished covering the helicopter with camouflage when Carlos' chopper flew over. They watched it fly in circles from a small overhang in the hill; a beam of light searched frantically trying to locate them.

Twenty foot trees went all the way down the rocky hill from the mansion and lined the beach to Antalya Bay. An opening was carved out at the bottom of two large trees, big enough for the helicopter to fly underneath and land undetected. It was impossible for Carlos to see them under all the trees, especially at night.

The three crawled on their knees underneath the overhang through a circular concrete opening. It was the size of a large sewer pipe and Manny supposed it was meant to appear that way from the cliff. *Who would want to crawl into a sewer pipe if they were out exploring and happened upon this hole in the cliff?*

At the end of their fifteen yard crawl Manny heard scratching noises and it smelled like wet dirt. "Don't worry," said the Collector, "I am scratching off the mud and dirt so I can open the hatch." Manny heard the Collector grunting, turning the round creaky door handle. Once he opened the hatch, he crawled in, stood up and turned on a light.

"This is the hatch from a World War Two submarine," the Icon Collector said proudly, turning the handle and locking it. "Safe and sound, I might say, even from nuclear attack."

"Where does the hallway lead?" Manny asked, admiring the perfectly squared walls.

"It winds for about a mile inside this hill and ends directly under my house! There are dozens of interconnecting tunnels and stairways burrowed for miles throughout this rocky hillside but none of them connect with this tunnel. There are only two entrances, and you went through one of them. The other entrance is found in my chapel."

Juan Carlos was furious. *How many times will Manny Benson escape my grasp?* He thought with a curse. *The gods will slip up one day and then I will have him.*

Carlos' army caught the President and the Prime Minister of Turkey hiding in Istanbul, so Juan Carlos became disinterested in chasing Manny. But he wondered whose army whisked Manny away from the auditorium and where he went. Carlos immediately left for Istanbul to demand that Turkey withdraw its troops from Syria and Iraq, or else. He quickly forgot about his unsuccessful manhunt in Antalya, but the

image of Manny Benson was always eating at his
thoughts.

Chapter Twenty-Two

There was barely room for one person to stand up. Manny was six foot four inches tall, his head touched the ceiling, and his broad football shoulders grazed the walls. Lenny scrunched his way between Manny and the Icon Collector and went ahead to the security room to check on the progress of the attack. The tunnel was a little bit larger a few yards in and Manny could almost stand up without banging his head. Recessed fluorescent lights lit the tunnel path and imbedded in the stone walls were sewer pipes and electrical cables.

"We have about a thirty minute walk before we reach the security room," the Icon Collector said. "Down here we'll have plenty of time to talk."

"I hope so," Manny said, "I have a lot of questions."

"I know you do, Manny," the Collector said, running his hands across the beautiful wooden slats on the ceiling. "Do you know how old this tunnel is? It was begun in the late 400s right after the mansion was built, and it took thirty-five years to dig out. That included all the rooms that were built down here too. I helped with the construction. I have spent a lot of time down here."

"Wait a minute. What do you mean you helped? Are you telling me you knew Jesus Christ in the first century and now you are telling me that you lived here in the fifth century? Who are you anyway?"

"Manny, I understand it is hard to believe, but I think you know who I am," the Icon Collector said, turning and looking up at his face.

"I suspected who you were when I saw you at the cross," Manny said, looking at the same man from his visions. "But it really dawned on me when you spoke to me in heaven. I don't know the Bible like I should, so when you told me that you and Peter ran to the tomb, I wasn't sure which one you were."

"Yes," the Icon Collector sighed, turning and walking again,"if you read the gospels, it doesn't say who I am, does it?"

The Icon Collector continued walking and when he came to the first set of steps, he climbed up and was eye level with Manny.

"And I don't recall the Bible talking about the marriage of Mary Magdalene to anyone either," Manny said.

"There are many things the gospels left out. They were not important details to the story of Jesus," he replied. "The gospels are about the life of Jesus, not anything or anyone else, really. The stories around His life are what should be remembered and recorded. For instance, we know about Peter's marriage from the gospels only because Jesus healed his mother-in-law. Other disciples were married too, you know."

"No, I didn't know that."

"Unnecessary details to the story. I was married to Mary Magdalene; the one that Jesus cast out seven demons from. She was a wonderful wife and mother, but the church sees her in the wrong way. They assume she was a prostitute because she had seven demons and that is totally false."

"And the Da Vinci Code people say that Mary Magdalene was secretly married to Jesus," Manny said.

"That she was the Holy Grail; that her womb was the chalice that carried the blood of Jesus by bearing Him a child. I knew Leonardo and he didn't believe this drivel in the least," the Collector said. "If anything, his paintings diverted grail hunters from discovering the truth."

The tunnel became steep and Manny had to bend over, putting his hands on his knees to walk. He'd be sore in the morning.

"Do you know the truth of the Holy Grail?" Manny asked, breathing hard.

"I've walked this tunnel for fifteen hundred years, back and forth every day," the Collector said, slowing down and stopping. "That's how I exercise. It's also a way to rid the tunnel of mice and rats I find along the way. They like to chew on my artifacts, and that's not good; not good at all!

"To answer your question, yes. I know what and who the Holy Grail is. In the first century there circulated a rumor that one of Jesus' disciples, the *holy vessel*, possessed the blood of Christ and because he had this blood, he would not die until Christ returned. They said this blood held the secret to long life, the fountain of youth. As time went on, the rumor changed and the vessel was not one of the disciples, but the holy cup Jesus used at the last supper. Their assumption was logical because the wine in the cup was symbolic of Christ's blood. The myth grew to the point that the sacred cup magically filled with wine whenever someone drank out of it. The Catholics adopted that idea in their Eucharist.

"The myth turned into a legend during the life and ministry of Polycarp, who lived in Ephesus in the early 100s. He became my disciple. His ministry was marked by extraordinary miracles, signs, and wonders until the day he mysteriously died. He attributed his power and longevity to the blood of Christ in a small clay vessel, the vessel I gave him as a gift."

"I suspected you were the one who gave Rock that clay pot," Manny said sadly. "I dropped the pot and it smashed into tiny pieces."

"How did you recover the blood, if it was broken into pieces?"

Manny reached into his pocket and showed the Icon Collector the tiny vial. "I scooped up the blood and put it into this vial. I take it with me everywhere."

"How did you figure out how to use it?" the Collector asked.

"I found out by accident. After the pot broke I put some of the oily substance on my forehead and the cuts instantly disappeared. Then I put it on my wife's forehead and she was healed of arthritis. So I rubbed the substance all over my body, and here I am!"

"That's amazing, Manny. Polycarp discovered its power by accident too. Yet, I had the blood in my possession for a hundred years and had no idea it was anointed like that. I found out when Polycarp told me just before his death."

"Have you used it to work miracles?" Manny asked.

"No, I never have," the Icon Collector said. "Christ Himself breathed on me and said, 'Receive the Holy Spirit.' His anointing was transferred to me in that way. I did not need to use the blood from the clay pots."

"So, after Polycarp, the Grail hunters were convinced that the magical cup of Christ existed?"

"Yes they were; they searched for it with a vengeance. The word 'Holy' means 'sacred' and 'grail' is Latin for 'cup' or 'vessel,'" he said, taking a turn in the tunnel and pausing before climbing a second set of steps. "It was not called the Grail until after the turn of the century, when the British Knights began looking for it. The Roman Catholics used Latin words for everything.

"The Grail hunters did not know exactly what they were looking for; a magical last supper wine cup, or some other sacred vessel that *actually* contained the blood of Christ. They were not really sure. The rumor became a myth and eventually turned into a legend. The truth was lost in the growing legend, thank goodness.

"Then the Gnostics added to the legend and came up with the nonsense that Mary Magdalene was the Holy Grail. Da Vinci perpetrated the rumor to divert the Grail hunters from discovering the real truth. The Grail hunters were dangerous characters, fierce warriors, and would stop at nothing to acquire the Holy Grail for their king."

"Did Da Vinci know the truth of the Grail?"

"He did and protected the secret with his life," the Icon Collector said. "And I am so grateful to him for that."

They came to an iron door that appeared to have been built during the Roman times, with large brass hinges and a rusty keyhole. The door was inset to the right about two feet into the clay hallway wall. Manny looked ahead, down the long dirt hallway, and wondered how far it went. It angled upward and seemed to narrow much further down. The Icon Collector swept his hand across the top of the door frame and found a long iron key.

"That's original," Manny said sarcastically.

"What do you mean?" he said with a quizzical look on his face.

"That key on top of the door frame. It's the first place an intruder would look."

"Do you know how many people have been down here over a thousand year period? Maybe sixty, including Leonardo and a few kings."

The key clanked into the hole and the Collector pulled the handle. The door creaked a little and then the seal around it made a shushing sound when the Collector pushed it open.

"Don't let the old door fool you, this room is state of the art!" The lights went on automatically. Inside it looked like a sterile laboratory, a library, and a museum; all in one. The room was the size of a basketball court and to the left were rows and rows of glass display cases of different sizes. Along the right wall were enclosed bookcases with glass fronts. A third of the way down the right wall, between the book cases, was a reading desk with a green covered attorney's lamp. On the desk was a wooden stand to hold a book upright for easier reading. All along the back wall was an archeological laboratory of long glass tables, magnifying glasses, lights, and tools of every kind. On the back wall were dozens of world maps from different time periods, spread out from left to right. Drawings, paintings, and Byzantine icons were interspersed on the wall.

"Nice in here, huh, Mr.Benson?" the Collector said, referring to the climate.

"Sure is Mr. Boergenes," Manny replied, taking a deep breath.

The air in the room was considerably cooler and drier than in the tunnel. The air purifier, conditioner, and heating system were set to mimic the dry winter conditions in Israel, where most of the treasures came from. The dry heat helps in preservation.

The Collector tossed Manny a pair of latex gloves and a surgical mask and said, "Sorry, but you have to put these on. Some of the artifacts are thousands of years old and quite fragile. If I had known about germs, bacteria, and oily fingers fifteen hundred years ago, these relics would look a lot better than they do."

Mr. Boergenes led Manny toward the back of the room and paused in front of the first display case. The walls behind the cases and the ceiling were paneled with polished cedar wood from the ancient forests of Lebanon.

"Looks like oak," Manny said, looking up at the ceiling.

"Actually it is cedar. The mason who built my mansion in the fifth century found it in one of the underground vaults near the temple on the mount. He believed it to be wood from Solomon's temple that was never used. He dug it out from the rubble and paid the priests to help him haul it away."

"This case here," Mr. Boergenes said, "holds my oldest artifacts." He carefully opened the door and delicately brought out an unrecognizable piece of charred metal.

"Here, take this," the Collector said, "and tell me what it is. By the way, it is priceless, so do not drop it."

It was heavy to the touch, the size of a softball and slightly rounded, with crude rivets on one side. To Manny it looked like a piece of junk, but he didn't dare say so.

"I have no idea what this is."

"It is the bronze serpent Moses held up on a stick in the wilderness. Now do you recognize it?"

"Nope," he said, handing it back.

"The rest of it is on the shelf, broken in pieces."

Then the Collector reached in and pulled out an old piece of fur the size of a small dog and handed it to Manny. "Guess what this is? Isn't it amazingly preserved?"

Manny looked at it and shook his head. "Nope. I'm drawing a blank."

"This is the badger skin that covered Moses' tabernacle in the wilderness."

Then he reached in with both hands and brought out a large chunk of rock. The smooth face was burned where the Hebrew letters were carved into the stone. Manny held the jagged rock and said, "I know this one. This is a piece of the Ten Commandments. Am I right?'

"You sure are, but which one?"

"What do you mean which one? Wasn't there only one Ten Commandments tablet?"   Manny saw the movie.

"No sir, there were two tablets inscribed by God's hand and this is a fragment of the first one. I have most of it. Remember Moses broke the first one? This is the one he broke!"

Manny put his latexed finger into the grooves where God wrote the words. He imagined Moses holding this same stone tablet and a chill went through him.

The Collector moved to another shelf after putting the Commandments away. He reached in and brought out a shiny wooden box with leather hinges. Opening the lid, he said, "This box alone is priceless because it is three thousand years old, but look at what's inside!"

Manny bent over and looked. From this perspective it looked like a folded patched blanket, the kind grandma used to make. The patches were twelve inches square and sewn together by hand with thin leather thread. The colors were terribly faded and washed out. When the Collector slowly brought it out of the box, it was a garment of some kind; but it was ripped and stained.

"Can you guess who's this is?" the Collector said. "I'll give you one clue: his brothers sold him into slavery!"

"Joseph?" Manny answered.

"Yes. You do know your Bible after all. I made the man rich who sold this to me in Capernaum. He said it was in his family for years and he didn't mind selling it to me. I believe Jacob made the box as a memorial to his son."

Once the garment was placed into the box and scooted back on the shelf, he said, "I have artifacts from Abraham, Isaac and Jacob too, but I am sure you will appreciate the contents of this next display case: the artifacts of King David and Solomon," the Collector said with excitement, moving in front of the next case. "Most of these items were given to me by the Knights Templar, soon after they rescued them from the temple vaults."

He opened the two thick wooden doors and stood back so Manny could see all the items in the nine foot high cabinet: knives, swords, gold drinking cups, crowns, wooden and metal boxes, and a dark brown leather bag three times the size of a bowling ball, pulled together at the top and tied with a leather string.

"Let me show you what is in this bag," the Collector said. "You won't believe it." The bag had two thick leather handles on the sides and since the bag was on the bottom shelf, all he had to do was carefully move it onto the floor. "I acquired this from a family in Northern Israel who said they had it since Ahimelech the priest. At that time the family had possessed it for thirteen hundred years!" Mr. Boergenes scratched his head, looked up at the ceiling and said, "I have had it for eighteen hundred years on top of that. So it must be three thousand, one hundred years old!" He separated the handles and loosened the strings at the top of the bag. With both latex gloved hands, he reached in and slowly picked it up. The hair appeared first, then the protruding forehead and finally the whole head came out of the bag. Manny stepped back in shock and stared at the face, as the Collector rotated it.

"Manny, meet Goliath!"

Amazingly his reddish beard and hair were still intact, but the eyeballs were dried out in their sockets, still open. The skin seemed mummified and shiny. His head was huge and the nostrils flared, as if his nose had been broken. Probably a result of his fall after David hit him with a very smooth rock that could still be seen embedded in Goliath's forehead, slightly to the left of center. Manny leaned in to look more closely. Half of the rock was deep in the skull, the other half sticking out through the skin. His burley and wrinkled neck had several chop marks on it signifying that David hacked at it several times before dislodging the head. Manny recalled his Sunday School lessons about how David killed Goliath, who could have been thirteen feet tall or taller, with a hand leather sling. He imagined young David with one foot on Goliath's huge head and the other foot on his chest, hacking away to remove the head from his body. *It must have been like cutting down a tree with a sword.*

"Unbelievable," Manny said. "Almost as amazing as being in heaven."

After the head was safely back in its bag, Goliath's sword was unsheathed and given to Manny. He'd never seen such a large sword, and heavy, probably weighed forty pounds.

"David used Goliath's own sword to cut off his head. Feel how heavy it is, Manny." The sword was so heavy, Manny could hardly hold it up with two hands.

"Before David was king, he retrieved Goliath's sword from Ahimelech the priest," the Collector said. "David used that sword to kill thousands of men. Over the years it has made me wonder about his physique. He must have been muscle bound to wield such an instrument. He killed over a thousand men at one time with it. The man was a killing machine."

"So, talking about David, do you have any of his Psalms written by his hand?" Manny asked.

"Yes. Over there." The Collector pointed across the room at the bookshelves. "And Solomon's Proverbs, part of the Book of Isaiah, all of the original Gospels and much, much more. All originals, of course."

Of course, Manny thought.

The Icon Collector moved down the row of cabinets, skipping several, and stopped in front of one in the middle. He placed his hands on the glass, closed his eyes and sighed.

"This case is full of my wife's mementos. I have not opened it in years. She was a wonderful woman. I loved her very much; still do. Next to her is Mary's cabinet, the mother of Jesus. My mother Salome, who was Mary's sister, her mementos are in with Mary's. Both very wonderful women."

"Wait! Your mother and Jesus' mother were sisters?" Manny exclaimed.

"Yes. That means you were Jesus' cousin, correct?"

"That is correct."

"That means you knew Jesus before you knew he was the Messiah?"

"Yes. He was my cousin, but he grew up in Nazareth and I grew up in Capernaum, on the Galilean sea. I saw Him once, maybe twice a year, my whole life. Our families traveled together every year to Passover and we played together as children."

"I thought John the Baptist was Jesus' cousin. Isn't that true?"

"Yes. We were all cousins. Mary, Salome and Elizabeth were sisters. John was a year older than Jesus and I was a year younger!"

Lenny the co-pilot poked his head in the door and said something in Turkish. Mr. Boergenes excused himself, stripping off his gloves. They spoke for a moment and Lenny left, saying he was sorry for interrupting, in English. The Icon Collector's shoulders slumped and for a moment he paused to gather his thoughts. Slapping on new gloves, he joined Manny in front of the display cases.

"Is everything alright?" Manny asked.

"Lenny just received a report that your friend, Rock, has been hurt in the fighting."

"We must go to him," Manny said.

"We cannot just yet, it is not safe. There is a concern that the EU army will counter attack the compound, so we just have to wait. We have a capable doctor who is caring for him at the present and they are safely locked down in one of our shelters."

"I have the blood," Manny raised his voice. "I must go and heal him."

The Collector took Manny by the shoulders and said, "The Lord spoke to me about your friend and said *if* he should pass away, you are not to save him with the blood. Do you understand me, Manny? It is not the Lord's will."

"I understand," Manny said, dropping his head. "I wondered why Apostle Paul invited Rock to join him down by the river. Now I know. It is sad to see a good friend go, isn't it?"

"Yes. I know exactly how it feels," the Collector said, reaching out and touching the glass on his wife's cabinet. "We felt the same way when we watched Jesus die. A horrible feeling indeed."

A good five minutes passed as the two men stared at the floor in deep reflection. The full impact of being human in a sinful world weighed on both of them, especially Mr. Boergenes, who had been human longer than any person in the world.

Manny fought back the intense feelings of anger and disbelief, the same emotions that overtook his life when his brother Harry died. Then he recalled the ecstatic joy after Harry was raised from the dead. *I'm sad now,* Manny thought, *but I will rejoice again soon, when I see my friend down by the river, sitting under the trees, with the great Apostle.*

Mr. Boergenes patted Manny on the back and slowly turned to face the cabinet, opening the double glass doors. At eye level, several clay pots sat on the shelf.

"These look like the same type of pots you gave me!" Manny said, taking one from the shelf. He noticed the wax seal was broken around the lid and the letters in the wax were lost.

"Manny, we've talked about the legend of the Holy Grail, but are you familiar with any of the other ancient legends?"

"Only what you've just told me so far."

"Let me tell you more then. Joseph of Arimathea collected Christ's blood from Golgotha and gave it to the disciples in these clay pots." The Icon Collector pulled a pot from the shelf and held it in his hands. "Within a few years I collected all eleven of these pots.

"I come from a family of wealth and was an astute collector at an early age. I bought and sold items all over Israel while working in my father's business. Then Jesus came along and asked me to follow him. He told Simon Peter that he would become a fisher of men and he told me that I would become a collector of images. The word 'image' in Greek means 'icon' in English and I have been called the Icon Collector ever since.

"Not to surprise you, but I am the Holy Grail!" the Collector said, "And always have been. I am the sacred vessel who has possessed Christ's image, which is in His blood, for two thousand years. I am the cup the Grail hunters have been looking for and are still looking for. They just don't realize what and who the Holy Grail is!"

"Let me try and understand. Why are you the Grail," Manny said, holding up the pot, "and not what's in this clay vessel?"

"Because, in order to find the cup of Christ's blood, you have to find the disciple who possessed it in the first place. I am that disciple and the key to finding the blood. Like I said earlier, I have been alive for two thousand years.

"After the Apostles were dead and gone, there was an assumption that I, the Holy Grail, died too. After all, how can a person live longer than a hundred years? No one found my body, even though they looked everywhere for it. After a hundred years, the Grail hunters ceased looking for me. They stopped believing that I was the Holy Grail. They assumed I was dead.

"The legend evolved to say that I hid the blood before I died and that is what the Knights Templar were searching for when they stumbled upon my compound here in Antalya. Some of them have lived here ever since, or at least their heirs have. Lenny is an heir of the Knights and I am very blessed to have him here."

"What you are saying is," Manny reiterated, as if he didn't hear it the first time, "that I am in the presence of the Holy Grail? You are the Holy Grail?"

"That is correct, Manny. And more amazing than that, is the destiny you and I have to accomplish before the Lord returns. It's already written in the Book."

The Icon Collector walked to the door, stripped off his gloves and mask again, and tossed them into a garbage can. Manny still had his on when they stepped out into the tunnel. He was in shock. He didn't think he could take anymore.

"You have not seen anything yet, Manny." the Icon Collector said. "Up at the end of this hall is my favorite room, and it will unsettle you. Believe me." Manny believed him, his mind was already blown!

Chapter Twenty-Three

At the end of the tunnel was a double metal door. The Icon Collector searched for the key on the door frame again. Finding it, he said, "There it is, right where I left it."

Manny heard a humming sound coming from a door to his right. He put his hand on the gray painted door and it vibrated slightly. He was told the room housed the air conditioners, generators, air purifiers, and motors for the humidifiers. The electrical boxes, sprinkler system controls, cable boxes, and the alarm systems were also in that room.

Once the metal doors were open they entered a ten foot hallway and walked into an open area. This room was the same size as the previous but seemed smaller because of the seven offices across one wall and a long wooden display table on the other. To the right were glass enclosed displays that ran up to the ceiling and extended the length of the room, about sixty feet. It reminded Manny of the local pioneer museum, where the stuffed polar bear was reaching into the fake waterfall trying to grab a salmon jumping in the air. The pioneer in a coonskin cap stood off to the side holding a musket. That display case, like these, was full sized and had glass fronts ten feet high. The light in the displays was dimmed, so the contents were not clearly seen. Direct lighting was harmful to the ancient relics.

Three well-worn leather couches and ottomans sat on a beautiful Turkish rug in front of the glass displays in a semi-circle. At the end of the couches were tables with lamps. In the middle was a large ornate coffee table, obviously well used. On the table were old Bibles and a manuscript five inches thick.

The Icon Collector scurried off to his office to check on the progress of Rock's injuries and the possible war. His office was equipped with the latest intelligence equipment and he monitored every inch of the globe from there. The Collector kept up with the latest technology in each new era, but the twentieth century by far had been the most exciting for new technological innovations. He purchased each new invention throughout history, if possible; and if not possible, Mr. Boergenes travelled to the inventor's country and attempted to glean from his genius. He would bring the ideas here to the mansion and work on his own experiments. When the world was slow in developing inventions and ideas, as in the first ten centuries after Christ, the Collector spent his days studying the prevailing religious thought and doctrines; such as monasticism, gnosticism, and the Catholic movements.

Boergenes also monitored various planets and stars deep in space. The Vatican's scientists kept him regularly informed about a star called Wormwood, but Mr. Boergenes was especially concerned about the large planet called Planet Nine.

"Hey Manny, come in here please," the Icon Collector called. He was on the global phone and looking at the 50 inch TV screen mounted on the wall over his messy desk. "I want to show you something that is *really* interesting."

Manny walked through the door and saw nothing but snow on the big screen TV. "This can't possibly be more interesting than being eye to eye with Goliath's head, could it?"

"Well, if the scientists can zoom in and hold the images, you will be the first outsider to witness Goliath's ancestors," Boergenes said as he rolled back his black leather chair and sat down.

The most powerful and advanced binocular telescope in the world was just outside of Tucson on Mount Graham, owned by the Vatican and operated by Jesuit scientists. The telescope was called the Vatican Advanced Technology Telescope or VATT. There are three telescopes grouped together on the mountain to form the Vatican Observatory. Attached to one of the telescopes was a mirrored device that the Jesuits named LUCIFER, an acronym for Large Binocular Telescope Near-Infrared Spectroscopic Utility with Camera and Integral Field Unit for Extragalactic Research. The scientists called the mirror Lucy. Although the Vatican told the public that they were searching for extrasolar planets, what they didn't say was that they found one and were obsessed with monitoring it day and night. Matter of fact, the Vatican spent multiple millions of dollars building their observatory on Mt. Graham in order to study this one planet.

"Manny, we are waiting for the telescopic imager to travel through deep space and focus,"

Mr. Boergenes said, still holding the phone to his ear.

To get the world's most powerful telescope to track the sky was no small feat. The giant instrument slid on a ring of pressurized oil. The pumps had to be activated, all the gauges checked and then the computers had to be rebooted. The telescope's electronic sensors must be cooled with liquid nitrogen to keep the megapixels from buzzing with quantum noise.

"It may take a few minutes to get an image, Manny, so let me tell you why we are looking at this screen." The Icon Collector sat back and hit the speaker button on the phone and laid the phone on his lap. Then he clasped his hands behind his head, not taking his eyes off the monitor.

"Many thousands of years ago, fallen angelic creatures invaded our planet, mated with human women, and produced giant hybrid children called Nephilim, the Titans of mythology. The mating of the fallen creatures with human women, and the evil it ultimately produced, was the main reason God destroyed the earth with a great flood." The Collector looked over at Manny and said, "And that's the short version."

"1,500 years before the flood, though, and this is the long version, the fallen creatures from the heavenly realm brought with them knowledge of advanced technology. They built elaborate cities and temples everywhere on the earth. These fallen ones, with the help of their Nephilim offspring, constructed vast pyramids and cities, utilizing levitation technology, and harnessing the energy grid that surrounds the earth. The flat topped pyramids were constructed to accommodate the landing and the launching of their large interstellar flying craft. They built these flying machines to explore the deep regions of space. With their advanced technological knowledge they developed vehicles that transported thousands of Nephilim into outer space.

"The Nephilim first traveled to the moon in their giant transport ships and set up a base of operations, building an outpost of structures to support travel to nearby planets. It took 3 days to travel to the moon from earth. From the moon they traveled to Mars, 48 million miles away, and it took nearly 300 days to get there. But Mars' air was too thin for the Nephilim. The atmospheric pressure on Mars was a hundred times less than earth's, which made it barely habitable. So they built large underground cities, equipped with elaborate air conditioning systems, but they continually needed supplies from earth. There were few renewable resources on Mars and none on the moon. Their search for a habitable, livable planet continued."

"Why did the Nephilim feel the need to go into space?" Manny interrupted, as he found a comfortable chair, sat down, and listened intently.

"Twelve billion giants had virtually used up all the earth's resources before the flood. So, being the 'gods' that they were, the Nephilim-Titans created human butcher farms for food. Humans lived in concentration camps worldwide. Then they were systematically and ritually sacrificed to the 'gods' and eaten. Near the end, before the destructive rains came, the different giant tribes were warring against each other, creating utter chaos on earth. That's why they were looking for another planet to populate," the Collector said, looking back at the screen, "they had completely destroyed the earth and her resources. They were looking for another planet to exploit.

"The Nephilim ended up traveling far into outer space, past the Milky Way galaxy until they found the planet they could comfortably live on. Planet Nine was about ten times the size of earth and so large that today it is estimated there are over fifty billion Nephilim living there." Mr. Boergenes said. He was now intently staring at the TV screen and obviously distracted by what he was seeing. The spiraling image on the screen slowed down, the sharp digital lines came into focus.

"It has been 5,500 years since the giants settled on Planet Nine," the Collector said, suddenly standing, shoving his leather chair out of the way.

"The last few hundred years Planet Nine had become overpopulated and extremely violent," he said, looking over at Manny, whose eyes were open wide. "These beasts could not stop fighting with each other and exploiting everything around them."

Large brown objects appeared on the screen but were blurry. The telescope was focusing on only one thing, Planet Nine. Clouds, blue water, and the rounded right edge of the planet came into view. Hundreds upon hundreds of flying discs of all sizes hovered in the upper atmosphere. Squadrons shaped in a V moved quickly in and out of view of the telescope, temporarily blocking sight of Planet Nine's atmosphere. Then in a split second, clouds parted just as a squadron passed by, and the criss-cross of city streets appeared in a squared cluster. It was a large city with pyramids and spired buildings.

Manny stood to his feet and gasped. "Oh my goodness!" he said. "Unbelievable!"

"We are going to pull back in a minute," the scientist said over Mr. Boergenes' speakerphone, loud enough for Manny to hear. "And capture the incoming. Then we're done!"

The rotation of the earth and the oblong orbit of Planet Nine allowed the scientists at the observatory a short window to view the planet each week. Most times images were very blurry. The fuzziness was understandable, since the planet was 88 million light years from our Milky Way Galaxy and seven billion light years from earth. Today, though, the high powered telescope was seeing perfectly and everyone at Mt. Graham was excited about it. They wanted to make sure they captured the large spacecraft on video so they could accurately calculate how far they were from earth.

The screen image shook for a second, then blurred. The scientist on the phone said, "Hold please, for a brief moment. Coming into view."

"Normally," the Icon Collector said, looking at the phone in his hand, "it would take about 20 years to reach earth from Nine." He gestured toward the TV screen. "But every 10,000 years Planet Nine makes a full orbital rotation and brings it close to earth." The Collector looked up at the cedar wood ceiling in his office and imagined where the planet was in space right now. "That's why we can see everything so clearly. The planet is very close!"

The blurry image on the screen slowly stopped moving backward and attempted to focus. Garbled brown digital pixels appeared, as the telescopic lens was struggling to sharpen the image. Then, there it was.

"Is that what I think it is?" Manny asked.

The side was rusty brown. Scrapes and long dents marred the hull from years of meteors hitting it. The appearance of the spaceship ran chills up Manny's spine because it looked very ancient. Oval windows lined the length and it resembled a long blimp gliding through space, ever so slowly. Toward the middle of the TV screen was a multitude of smaller spacecraft that looked like the flying saucers that are seen in science fiction movies. And to the right, further back, were hundreds of cigar shaped flying vessels, like the one to the left, moving slowly in the direction of earth.

"Sir," the voice said through the speaker phone. "We are now calculating how far away they are."

"Father Sergio, can you give us an estimate on how many years and months it will be until you anticipate their arrival?" Mr. Boergenes asked the Jesuit scientist.

"Yes we can. Give us a few more minutes please."

"Arrival?" Manny exclaimed. "Are you kidding me?"

"Manny," the Icon Collector said, "the Vatican Observatory in Italy found Planet Nine in the 1980s and these spacecraft and transport ships were moving around the upper atmosphere of the planet. Seven years ago the observatory on Mt. Graham saw the armada of spacecraft begin moving away from their planet, in earth's direction."

"Sir, we estimate their arrival in approximately three years," Father Sergio said loudly into the speaker phone. "And the Vatican has just given us a blessing to baptize them into the church..." The Collector said "Thank you very much," and they suddenly cut him off and hung up.

"What? Baptize them into the church?" Manny put his hands up to his forehead in utter amazement and looked over at the Collector.

"These creatures' ancestors *were* 'baptized' with God's wrath in Noah's flood," the Collector said, pointing at the screen. "And I assume now, in about three years, they are coming to earth again to return the favor!"

Chapter Twenty-Four

Lenny came in holding a satellite phone and offered it to Manny. He walked out of Mr. Boergenes' office, plopped down on one of the couches shaking his head, and quickly dialed home. *Joanne's probably beside herself,* he thought. *She's probably heard about the war in Turkey and is biting her nails waiting for my call. But what should I tell her about Rock? Amy, I'm sure, is upset too. What do I tell her about the aliens coming in a couple of years?* He was beside himself.

After a few minutes of phone conversation, the Icon Collector came out of his office and sat down. Manny got off the phone and didn't have time to tell Joanne about Rock, thankfully. God had a plan, Manny knew, and maybe it wasn't Rock's time to go.   Hopefully he would have good news to share about him soon.

"How's Rock," Manny asked.

"Not well, I'm afraid. They are going to take him to the hospital. We will know more later."

"How's the war upstairs progressing?"

"The helicopters left the compound and may be back in the morning. We killed a lot of their men. They may retaliate, but my men are ready for an all-out war. We are safe down here for now."

But another situation was brewing. Three Middle Eastern countries were ready to invade Israel but the Pope's emissaries intervened. Israel's government finally gave the go-ahead to build Jerusalem's third temple down the hill from the Temple Mount in the old city of David. The news was leaked and the Muslim world went berserk. The Apostle smiled to himself knowing that the plans he offered to the Jewish High Priest were merely King David's rough drafts of his possible temple sites, but the plans were tossed aside by the king. The western Wailing Wall that borders one end of the Temple Mount is not a wall of the original temple at all but merely a remnant of the Roman barracks that was constructed on top of the hill. The Romans placed their huge military barracks above the temple to keep an eye on all the temple's activities.

In 70 AD the Romans destroyed the Jerusalem temple in order to quash another Jewish uprising. Jerusalem and the surrounding areas were left desolate for hundreds of years, being sparsely occupied by the neighboring non-Jews or as they liked to call themselves, Palestinians. The location of major Jewish and Christian sites was lost and destroyed after the Roman destruction. So, Emperor Constantine's mother, Helena, made a journey to the Holy Land to locate and restore the Biblical sites of the Christians and the destroyed holy temple. Instead of using accurate Biblical and archeological data to identify holy sites, she had visions and dreams of where she thought they were. This was how the Roman foundation wall became the famous Wailing Wall on the Temple Mount. Constantine's mom saw it in a vision. For 1,700 years the Jewish people have been bowing and worshipping at the wall of a Roman military installation.

"Are you hungry Manny? It's been awhile since we've eaten."

The leather couch was comfortable, so Manny put his feet on the ottoman and leaned back. Yes, he was hungry and food arrived within five minutes and was placed on the coffee table in front of them. Manny observed that these men, servants, attendants of the Collector, were extremely polite and liked to bow to Mr. Boergenes often, treating him like royalty.

"This is my favorite sandwich from Cesme," the Collector said. He leaned over and carefully picked up half a sandwich and placed it on his lap into a handkerchief he took from his back pocket. "Cesme is a small town down by the beach," he said taking a bite. "This is kumru bread and can't be found anywhere else in the world." He placed the half sandwich back on the blue plate on the table, leaned back, still chewing his one bite and crossed his legs. "That kasseri cheese is from our own goats and we grow the tomatoes, make our own sausage and pickle our own cucumbers." With that the Collector leaned forward again and took the slice of pickle that had squeezed out of the top of his sandwich and tossed it deliciously into his mouth.

Manny consumed his kumru sandwich from Cesme within minutes and turned to observe this amazing Icon sitting next to him on the couch. His hair was dark brown with a contemporary hair style, not too short but not too long either. Maybe a hint of gray sneaking out around his temples. Nothing to suggest this man was two thousand years old. He must have a hair stylist, Manny imagined. The Collector's profile was of a typical middle eastern man with an olive complexion and a nose that was somewhat large but fit his face. Manny reached up with his right hand and touched his own nose and traced it with his fingers, then looked over at Mr. Boergenes' nose. Manny's nose had a sway in it like a ski ramp at the Winter Olympics, but the Collector's nose didn't have a slope in the middle like Manny's. His went straight down to the end with a slight bump in the middle. The Collector wore a finely cropped beard that was almost black. It was perfectly shaved above his cheeks but not down his neck. He seemed thirty years old by the way he looked, but had a slight slump in his shoulders that betrayed his real age.

The Icon Collector took the Bible that was on the coffee table and placed it on his lap, thumbing through the pages.

"I have so many questions; too many to have answers for," Manny said tiredly, shifting his weight on the couch. "I don't know where to start."

"I realize it is a lot to take in, so let us continue with these artifacts in front of you and go from there." Mr. Boergenes clicked the remote and the first display lit up. "You can ask questions as we go along and see where it takes us. We'll take our time. We are both very tired but we have much to accomplish after this."

The display to the far left of the room in front of them showed a thin well-worn bed mattress on the floor with a blanket folded on it. The pillow was faded and small. The wooden chair to the left had an old yellowish garment slung over it. On top of that was a purple rope belt. A woven mat was on the floor and a pair of leather sandals sat on the mat. There was a nice maple colored table to the right of the mat with a candle on it. Also on the table was a wooden box propped open. On the wall at the back of the display were drawings and writings framed in glass to protect them.

"This is how I found Jesus' room when I went to Mary's home to collect her things," the Collector said. "Mary never went back to her home after her Son died. She was covered in blood from holding Him in her lap after Joseph of Arimathea took Him down from the cross. She was in shock and so was my wife and my mother, Salome. We all stumbled back to my home and the blood on Mary's blouse was dry by the time we got there. We were all bloody from the ordeal."

"I have seen that blouse. Matter of fact I own it now," Manny said, sitting up. "You sold it to Jansen Berry in the 1960s. Do you remember that?"

"Yes I do remember. He was very famous then. He seemed so nice and sincere, I let him steal the blouse from me!"

"Steal? He paid a million bucks for it."

"But the Vatican was offering fifty million. It is priceless. I think he stole it!" Mr. Boergenes looked down at the remote in his hand and fingered the buttons.

"Do you want it back? I would love for you to have it," Manny sat up to face Mr. Boergenes.

"Maybe you can give it back to Mary yourself one day. I'm sure she would appreciate the gift," the Collector said, glancing over at Manny.

"That's what I will do. I'll give it to Mary as a gift during the Millennium," Manny said, pleased with himself for thinking of it. The Collector smiled because it was his apocalyptic revelation preserved in the last book of the New Testament that told of the thousand year reign of Christ, the Millennium. That thousand year period will occur sometime after the Great Tribulation has destroyed the earth and mankind, the other impending event the Collector wrote about in detail.

Jesus' family was somewhat poor," the Collector continued, "and the children did not have bedrooms. So they slept on bed rolls. In the morning the beds were rolled up and set to the side.

"See that table? Jesus made it, and the chair. And that garment on the chair? He wore it at the Last Supper. I know because I was there, sitting right next to him. Whenever I could I sat embracing the Savior." The Collector leaned back again and looked up at the ceiling, reminiscing about his past for a moment. "We loved each other very much," he said. "Those are his walking sandals," the Collector said, pointing to them with the remote control in his hand. "The ones he wore when hiking through the hills. Better ankle support Jesus said.

351

"Mary did not have a lot of possessions, but I arrived at her house with a horse, a cart and a couple of servants. Since I was a collector by nature, I carefully gathered all of her things and stored them at my house. She did not need anything after she moved in with my family because we provided her with everything. A couple of Mary's daughters also came to live with us. And at the time, the possessions of Jesus were not a big deal to anyone. He did not have much to speak of and what He did have was of pretty poor quality. What I mean is, His garments, shoes and bags were old and well worn. He was a simple man. But I took it all, wrapped everything very carefully, and stored it at my home.

"I say all that to say this: When I put His pillow into a bag I noticed there was hair on it. Hair from His head. Back then it was considered worthless but now it is priceless. So I carefully took the hair off the pillow and set it aside. When I began to roll up His mat on the floor, I noticed toe nails sprinkled on it. Can you imagine Jesus cutting his toenails with a knife and leaving it on the mat? It didn't mean much then, but it is priceless now.

"Since we are on the subject, I want to say that Jesus was a man, like any other man; except He was divine. We went to the bathroom together, we bathed together, and ate together. I cut His hair. He cut mine. We wrestled on the ground and played games together. Once we skipped rocks across the water. He was an extraordinary man, indeed. But He was an ordinary man, a human being, who did ordinary things.

"Those drawings on the wall back there, were drawn by Jesus. He was a teenager when He drew that one." Mr. Boergenes pointed to the picture of the horse and chariot. "I believe he was drawing King David in his chariot. And that one looks like David and Goliath." It depicted a beastly character screaming from pain as the rock hit him in the forehead.

"Over there to the right is a sample of His writing from school. And there, is a letter He was writing to a friend but did not finish.

"And over here," Mr. Boergenes turned in his seat and pointed to the long display table, "is where I keep Jesus' other letters, notes, and drawings of the furniture He designed and built. Leonardo found those things especially exciting to see."

"What? Leonardo Da Vinci came here?" Manny practically jumped out of his seat.

"Yes, he sat where you are sitting. Of course we didn't have the display case or the technology then, but he saw the same things you are seeing."

"Who else has been here?"

"I am afraid you will not recognize the names, but many of the famous monks throughout history have come here. For example: Mark Aiden visited in the early 650s. He was a missionary to the English people when they were called Angleish; Monk Bede visited somewhere in 700. He was the first English historian; Saint Francis of Assisi visited in the 1200s and he came here looking like a pauper, with a raggedy monk's habit. I traded his old one for a new one. I still have his habit in storage. Saint Francis convinced me to live as a monk, believe it or not! That's why I dress the way I do.

"You might recognize the name John Wycliffe, he visited in the 1350s; or Martin Luther. He spent a year here in the early 1500s, just before he nailed his famous '95 Theses' to the door of the Wittenberg Cathedral.

"Then there is Tyndale in 1500, Brother Lawrence in 1640, who wrote the best book ever written about the presence of God; Judson Taylor, and many more I cannot remember.

"Oh yes, King Arthur came and visited for about a year. Did you know that Arthur was a very tall man? He had to be at least eight feet tall, maybe taller," the Collector said in reflection. "And then a few Popes and kings came, after the Crusades were finished, of course.

Mr. Boergenes clicked the remote and the next display lit up. It was spectacular. Three rough crosses came into view. The bottom of the wood posts sat in round holes in the cement and the crosses stood upright. A dark wooden cross stood in front of the other two. It was obvious what they were. Nothing had to be said about that! Manny jumped to his feet and put his hands and face against the glass. He couldn't believe it. It was another unbelievable day!

"Don't push too hard against the glass or the alarm will go off," the Icon Collector warned. "On second thought, let me turn the alarm off!" He clicked the remote on the table in front of him and the little red lights stopped flashing.

"The cross of Jesus!" Manny sighed, staring at the detail. It was simply a rough couple of posts shaped like railroad ties, and about the same size. He was surprised how much smaller it was than what he had imagined. Like when he visited the Alamo and discovered it was just a tiny little building, or when he visited Jerusalem and how disappointed he was at the size; so much hoopla over so little.

"I've always wondered what happened to it. I imagined it was thrown in the trash, lost forever," Manny said, nose pressed against the thick glass.

"It was trash, but Joseph gathered it into his cart anyway, along with many other items of garbage from that day. One person will see trash but a collector will see treasure."

"You even got the sign Pilate wrote and nailed to the cross. He really did write what he said in three languages. Amazing is all I can say!" Manny said. "Are those the actual nails in the cross?" Manny was beside himself.

"Of all the items I have collected over the years, these pieces of wood were the easiest to collect; and the cheapest," the Collector said. "The day before the Resurrection, I asked Joseph if I could come by and go through the trash from the Crucifixion. He told me to take the whole mess, if I wanted; it was just taking up room in his barn. To him it was just rubbish, caked with mud and blood. To me it was potential collector's items, especially if Jesus was who He said He was. It was a good thing I went over there too because he was going to have the crosses burned after the sabbath, because of the blood. Actually he was already in violation of the Jewish law for having the bloody items in his possession in the first place. So I gladly took them off his hands. Jesus taught us to not worry about the law. Believing in Him, He said, fulfilled the law. That teaching right there put Him on this cross. And that teaching today has separated a lot of churches!" Mr. Boergenes reached down and turned a latch at the bottom of the glass front.

"It is funny but for several years after the Crucifixion, my friends thought I was crazy for keeping the crosses, the whips, the old wine skins and other Crucifixion rubbish. They said I was being foolish and morbid because Jesus was coming back soon; that I didn't have time for this old garbage. Jesus was coming, they said, all we have time for is the gospel, and I believed that too! But I collected and stored Jesus' mementos anyway. You were the one who told me to continue collecting these relics."

"I'm glad you kept these amazing things," Manny said. "They are wonderful!"

The Collector tugged on a handle and the front of the display opened like a door. It made a low hissing noise and the regulated air inside the display escaped.

But, you know, Jesus did not come back like we all thought and this collection of rubbish could now be sold for billions of dollars. I know five people right now who would pay their life's fortune to have these things. There are three countries that would pay billions right now! But money is not the point. The point is to obey and follow. If I had not done that, you would not be seeing this. Jesus told me to follow my heart. Then you came to me and confirmed it."

Manny couldn't believe what he was hearing. Standing before him was the sacred vessel, the Holy Grail and one of the Disciples (he just wasn't sure which one) talking about money like he was in a flea market. Historians and church theologians have glorified the early Disciples and have made them seem holier than they were. This great man standing in front of Manny was talking like an ordinary man, like he would talk with any friend. This "holy" man didn't require Manny to "get down and pray" and didn't offer any "great" words of wisdom. He seemed like an ordinary fellow, just like Manny himself.

"You know, I like you, Mr. B!" Manny said. "You're a lot like me. Just a regular guy for the most part. OK, so you're two thousand years old; that definitely sets you apart. And you knew Jesus, heck, He was your cousin. Of course, that makes you very different from me. But beyond that you seem like a regular guy. That gives me hope because the church has made me feel that I have to be perfect and have a holier-than-thou attitude, when I'm just a simple guy trying to get by in the world. Do you know what I mean?"

"Yes I do," Mr. Boergenes said. "I know exactly. I have read many things over the years about the Apostles and the further along in history we go, the more holier we become. They have painted Jesus the same way. But He was a regular guy Himself, except He was God. Have you ever thought that God might be a regular guy, or at the very least, wants to be? He, of course, is God, but He is also a man and touched with how weak we are. I know this because I knew Jesus when He was a man in the flesh. He was ordinary in an extraordinary way."

The Collector swung the display glass door wide open and said, "My ambition as a young man was to be a collector. Yes, my father owned a fishing business and I was required to work for him, but by nature I was a collector. I was an icon collector when I discipled with John the Baptist. I was an icon collector when I was discipled by Jesus of Nazareth. What I am saying is, in the same way Simon Peter by nature was a fisherman, and a good one I might add, I was an icon collector. I was an icon collector all these years, even when I was traveling and preaching the Gospel for my Master. I have picked up things from around the world, in just about every country, in just about every decade. I am a man-collector by calling, but I am an icon collector by trade. I won't apologize for that. And I realize if the religious people of the world knew what I really was -- a collector of icons -- and not a religious fellow who prays all day on my baggy knees, dreaming dreams and seeing visions, they might hang me on this cross right here, for being normal and ordinary! That's all I am is normal and ordinary."

Manny leaned in and looked at the cross of Jesus without the glare from the glass. It was different than he ever imagined. What made the wood dark, almost black, was the age old blood stains. The wood was not smooth either. Large splinters covered the beams and Manny could not imagine the pain Jesus must have endured.

"I have read that my knees bulged from praying so much in my old age. Do my knees look bulgy? I have read that the statue of the goddess Diana tumbled to the ground when I bound the devil in her presence. I do not "bind" the devil. Never have. It is amazing, but I have read many erroneous things about my life and the life of the Apostles from very reputable men of the church, and most of it is fairy tales. People want to believe that there is some kind of magic to the Christian walk, but there is not. They want to believe that we Disciples are different or special. We are not. There's no special Christian or holy man. Only Jesus. We are merely men following Him the best we can; me included. The most I am is a follower, and the least I am is an icon collector."

They were both staring intently at the cross now. Their heads almost bumped seeing the same thing.

"That's very encouraging to hear," Manny said, "because I don't feel worthy to be so blessed and honored in this way. I'm not a holy guy like my dad or people I know in the church. I don't even measure up to my buddy Rock, bless his heart; yet I'm so blessed."

"That is the way the Lord does it though, Manny," the Icon Collector said. "He did not call you because you were good or holy. He called you because *He called you.* That's the same for me and my brother, James. We were not worthy or holy. The Lord called us and all we did was respond to Him. I do not know why He called me. Of all people. All I wanted to be is a collector but God has done so much more."

Manny saw pieces of black leather on the upper section of the cross and noticed that Mr. Boergenes was looking at it too.

"Do you know what that is, Manny?" The Collector touched it with his bare finger and said, "Go ahead touch it, Manny! Go ahead!" Manny reached in and touched it, then jerked his hand back.

"You touched the skin of Jesus Christ. Out of seven billion people on the planet today, we are the only two who have touched the actual skin of Jesus," the Icon Collector said. "Point of fact, we are the only people who have touched Jesus' skin in nearly two thousand years except for one other person 350 years ago. This is the only skin sample of our Lord Jesus in all the world. It scraped off His back as He struggled on the cross."

"It is unbelievable. How did you preserve it?"

"First off, it was the ointment that soaked into His skin that has preserved it. Second, after the blood dried, I wrapped the cross in burial cloth per your instructions, and then durable packing material so it could be transported. It was not until the early 500s, after the tunnel and the rooms were built, that I unwrapped it for the first time. I discovered it then and realized that I had the only remnant of Jesus' skin."

"Who else has touched it?"

"Only one other person. A woman named Madame Guyon of France in 1681."

"I have not heard the name," Manny said.

"I do not imagine you have. She was thirty-four years old when I invited her to my home, and when she saw the cross, she rushed and embraced it. I about had a heart attack. When she opened her eyes, she saw the skin and kissed it. Of course it happened so quickly I didn't know what to do. It was not my cross, I told myself. It was the Lord's cross and He could do whatever He pleased with it, and He did. She kissed it. Well, something extraordinary happened to her when she went back to Paris; miracles broke out around her and demons were exorcised. Similar to your ministry now. She was imprisoned several times for practicing witchcraft and eventually she died in prison. But this cross changed her life completely. After Madam Guyon's kiss, I decided to limit access to it."

Mr. Boergenes stepped over the lower barrier and stood beside the cross, inviting Manny to do the same. The Collector put his forehead where the blood stained the wood and closed his eyes. Manny followed his lead and gently laid his forehead on the middle cross too.

"I have not done this in fifteen hundred years," Mr. Boergenes said. "Not since I first unwrapped it in this room. The Lord and I loved each other immensely."

Manny glanced over and saw the Icon Collector embracing the cross like a lover. Then it hit him. *I know who this man is!*

Manny closed his eyes with the new revelation fresh in his mind and immediately felt a jolt, as if the Icon Collector fell against the cross and moved it. When he opened his eyes to see what happened, Manny was at the beach. It was a beautiful day too, the coastal breeze gently blowing the trees. And then Manny saw Jesus walking along the sandy seashore. *Here we go again*, he said to himself. *I wonder where we're going this time!*

A scruffy bearded man walked with Jesus in the sand and the Icon Collector was following behind.

"Greetings Ghost," he said. "What brings you here?"

"Well," Manny replied, walking in the sand next to him, "I'm not sure. I was just with you, I mean, a later version of you, at your mansion. Now, here I am."

"You were at my house in Jerusalem or Capernaum?"

"Neither. You have a house in Antalya, Turkey. I am in that house right now."

"Where?"

"You have a hundred acres in Turkey, I mean, it's not called Turkey yet but it will be and is near Ephesus, on the coast. You will have a church there one day."

"Ephesus? I am going to Ephesus? And then to Antalya?"

"Yes. You go to Ephesus with your wife and Mary, the mother of Jesus, around 68 AD, just before Jerusalem falls."

"Falls? The Romans I bet! That's thirty-six years from now. Are you sure?"

"I was right before, wasn't I?" Manny said, motioning toward the Lord. "He rose from the dead like I said, didn't He?"

"Yes He did and I am so glad you bolstered my faith during that time."

"Let me give you some more advice: keep collecting everything you can and don't stop. You will be glad you did. Especially the wooden crosses you received from Joseph. Wrap them in burial cloths to preserve them and don't unwrap them until you get to Antalya. You will understand later. It may seem like rubbish now, but it will be priceless later. Anyway, this is what you just told me from your house in Antalya."

"But the Lord will be back very shortly and will reign over Israel forever. I am told that it is foolish to hold on to such worldly possessions in the light of His return. The gospel must be preached above all else."

"Well, I don't know if I should be the one to tell you this, but Jesus doesn't come back real soon. Matter of fact, you will live a very long time, believe me on that one."

The scruffy bearded man turned around and pointed at the Icon Collector. The Lord also turned and looked in his direction.

"Who is that man?" Manny asked.

"Oh, that's Peter. The Lord is telling him about his future and it does not sound too good." The Collector went into deep thought and said, "Do you know what happens to Peter? Is it written in your book?"

"The Book doesn't say, but there is a tradition that Peter is crucified upside down in Rome many years from now."

"Are you sure?" The Collector said, looking shocked. "That sounds horrible."

"But just recently," Manny explains, "in my time there is evidence that Peter actually died in Jerusalem and not Italy. One day you will understand. *Where* Peter dies is a very big deal. And wait until you find out what happens to you, John! You won't believe it."

A shocked look came over the Apostle's face. "How do you know my name? Who are you?"

Peter glanced back at the Collector and asked, "But Lord, what is going to happen to this man?"

Jesus stopped walking and paused for a moment. He looked over in John's direction again and said, "If it is my will that he remain till I come, what is that to you, Peter?"

"There He goes again," John said, "inferring that I am not going to die until He returns. I am not sure why the Master keeps saying this about me."

"Jesus has said it to you before?"

"No, not directly. When He was preaching to the crowds near Caesarea Philippi a couple of years ago, Jesus looked right into my eyes and said, 'Some are standing here who will not die till they see the Son of Man coming in His glory.' That's when the rumor started that I would not die. Some of the other Disciples thought that Jesus was speaking about His transfiguration on the mount, you know; when we saw His glory. But I personally do not know what to think. Jesus has always said many things that I do not understand."

"Do you like to read books?" Manny asked.

"Yes, I have read a few."

"Do you like to read the book from the beginning, or do you thumb through the manuscript to the end and read the last chapter first?"

"Sometimes, if I do not have the time to read the book all the way through I will go to the end to see what concludes, is that what you mean?"

"Yes. That's what I mean. So let me ask, do you want to know the final chapter for your life, or not?"

"If it means I am going to die a horrible death, I do not want to know," the Apostle said. "But if it is something that would be beneficial to me and my loved ones, then I would like to know. Yes, I think I would like to know! Can you tell me?"

"Yes I can. At least most of the final chapter. Where I am from, it is the last days, the end times, the final hour before Jesus returns."

"Are you saying that Jesus doesn't return soon in my time?"

"Yes. In fact, where I am from, Jesus still *has not* returned."

"And you are saying that I am still alive in your time in the future?"

"Yes, you live a very long time into the future. I am actually in the same room with you right now, in the future. And you won't believe what I am doing at this very moment, other than speaking with you."

"Tell me please."

"I am standing with you, underground in a room, holding on to the cross of Christ. The one you have in storage at your home. It has become very valuable. Priceless."

"Priceless? But it is just a piece of wood and rubbish."

"Yes, a piece of wood soaked in the blood of Jesus, with the skin from His back on it.

Probably the most valuable icon in the world, worth a fortune if you wanted to sell it."

"If I am in the room, what am I doing? What do I look like? How old am I?"

"You are embracing the cross with your eyes closed," Manny said. "You look exactly like you do now. You have not aged one day in over two thousand years."

The Apostle was speechless. Two thousand years? He looked at the Master at the same moment Jesus looked back at him, still walking and talking with Peter. Jesus smiled at the Apostle, nodded his head and turned toward the ocean. The warm breeze was blowing the Master's hair and He raised His face, looking off into the distance. When Jesus saw the fishing boats casting their nets into the water, He smiled, nudged Peter with His elbow and pointed out toward the water. *They were both fishermen of sorts*, Manny thought.

"What is your name," the Apostle asked, "in case I want to find you later?"

"My name is Manny Benson. Look for me in the 1960s. I was born in 1966."

At that moment the Apostle John's wife appeared and jumped on him, knocking him to the ground. Jesus and Peter swiveled from their positions to see Mary Magdalene screeching for joy, sitting on her husband in the sand. Jesus smiled and put His arm around Peter. Peter smiled too.

"We are pregnant, John, we are going to have a baby," she said hysterically.

"We are? I mean, WE ARE?" The Apostle grabbed her around the waist and rolled with her in the sand. "Master did you hear that?" John yelled to the Lord. "We are going to have a baby!"

"Yes, Cousin, I heard," Jesus shouted back at him. "That is truly wonderful!"

Suddenly Manny came back to himself and the Icon Collector Apostle was sitting on the couch, watching him.

"I was just with you on the beach," Manny said, still holding on to the cross.

"I have wondered all these years at what point in our lives you visited me there," the Apostle said. "Now I know. Interesting timing, I should say. That was the last time you visited me and I wondered what happened to you."

"And I know who you are finally!" Manny retorted.

"Honestly Manny, you would have known who I was from the beginning if you paid attention to your lessons in Sunday School and read your Bible once in a while," he chided.

"Your wife, Mary, was pretty excited about the news of her pregnancy, wasn't she?"

"Oh yes. We were not able to have children for a couple of years but then the Master prayed for us and we got pregnant."

"Was it a boy or a girl?"

"It was a boy and we named him Emanuel. We called him Manny for short."

"You're kidding me," Manny said, stepping away from the cross and sitting down next to the Icon Collector on the leather couch.

"Manny grew up in Capernaum, got married and had one child. He took over the fishing business when I moved to Ephesus. When the

Romans came in 70, he and his family escaped to Greece and he eventually came to Ephesus. Manny took over my ministry in Ephesus when I moved to Antalya. Then his son took over the ministry from him when he passed away. All the way down Manny's line of heirs, for two thousand years, each child only had one child; just like you and Joanne, Manny!"

"Did you and Mary have other children?" Manny asked.

"No, we never did. But I tracked my son Manny's genealogy over the years, right up to modern times. Do you want to know who else is in his lineage?"

"Well, of course I want to know. Who?" Manny asked.

"You are!"